Janet Haslam was born and bred in Derbyshire, in the same village on the edge of the Pennines where her ancestors have lived for generations. She now lives in a nearby village with her husband and three children. Her first two novels, *Rachel's Daughter* and *Proud Harvest* were also published by Corgi.

Rosy Smith

Janet Haslam

CORGI BOOKS

ROSY SMITH
A CORGI BOOK : 0 552 14297 2

First publication in Great Britain

PRINTING HISTORY
Corgi edition published 1996

Set in 10/11pt Monotype Plantin by Kestrel Data, Exeter.

Corgi Books are published by Transworld Publishers Ltd,
61– 63 Uxbridge Road, Ealing, London W5 5SA,
in Australia by Transworld Publishers (Australia) Pty Ltd,
15– 25 Helles Avenue, Moorebank, NSW 2170,
and in New Zealand by Transworld Publishers (NZ) Ltd,
3 William Pickering Drive, Albany, Auckland.

Printed and bound in Great Britain by
Cox & Wyman Ltd, Reading, Berkshire.

Rosy Smith

PROLOGUE

I

1956

'Come on! Come on!' Nanny insisted, glaring down her long nose at Rosy. 'I haven't got all day to wait for your dilly-dallying.'

'I'm coming.' Rosy's voice was stiff, but did not contain the annoyance she would have liked to put there. Jane Richardson had been Nanny to the Hardaker twins since they were born and she jealously guarded that position, with a sharp tongue and an even sharper impatience. And Rosy, at the moment, was getting more than her fair share.

Fortunately, it would not be for much longer. She had recently left school and was only doing odd jobs at the house until she could get herself a proper job. She had not asked for the work and did not really want it. Mr Hardaker, the owner of Derwent House, had told her that until she found what she wanted she could come over to the house with her mother, who was housekeeper there. She had felt it would be rude to throw his kindness back in his face so, for the time being, she was the odd job girl. Unfortunately, that meant most of the time she was Nanny's assistant: a situation Nanny made plain she had no desire for either.

The only thing that kept Rosy coming over to the house with her mother was the ten shilling note Mr Hardaker put into her hand every Friday afternoon, which was very welcome.

Rosy shoved her arms into the sleeves of her old navy

blue gaberdine coat, then pulled the heavy front door open. She hurried outside, fastening the coat buttons as she went.

Despite Nanny's loud tuttings, Rosy did not stop until she was down the path and had reached the top of the two steps leading to the long tarmac driveway. She only stopped then because she knew if she did not stand ready to help Nanny lift the large, twin pushchair over the steps, she would never hear the end of it. Rosy thought it was all rather silly. She could have got the pushchair down without any trouble; or she would have gone out of the back door, like everybody else. But it was one of the woman's silly rules. And one of the first things Rosy had learned was that no matter how stupid or ridiculous she felt they were, Nanny's decisions were never to be questioned and her rules were always obeyed.

So, as always, Rosy waited beneath the lilac tree at the top of the steps. In summer its thick foliage turned the steps into a shady seat, but now the branches were bare and stark, and dripping with the rain that had so recently stopped falling. She gave a shiver and pulled the hood of her raincoat up over her head and tied it tightly beneath her chin. She stuck her hands into her pockets and glanced round at the dark stone walls of the large house, as it loomed over her. The front door was still open but there was no sign of Nanny or the twins. They could have been in the middle of a blizzard, but Nanny would always make her wait the obligatory couple of minutes. It was her way of showing who was boss.

Hoping that the previous day's interview for a sales assistant at the Midland Drapery would go her way, Rosy turned her gaze to the swollen river, rushing past the bottom of the garden. She gave another shiver. After January's heavy snow and over a month of almost constant rain, the water was several feet above its normal level. There was no fence, no wall to hold it back, just the length of the lawn on the far side of the drive between her and the waters that tumbled by with frightening speed. Its thundering din echoed in her ears and she gave another shiver. Fortunately, the lawn was steep enough to ensure the river never reached the drive and Derwent House was always safe from flooding.

Nevertheless, Rosy found it difficult to understand why the Hardakers had bought that house. Mrs Hardaker had once told her it was such a beautiful view, looking out on the river and the meadow across the other side to the village. To the back also lay fields, going up the steep hill, or bank, that was topped with the wood. But Rosy could not help but wonder if the view had lost some of its magic, now they had two small children.

The pushchair came up by Rosy's side then. 'Look . . . water.' Guy, the elder of the identical twins by twelve minutes, pointed a tiny finger at the swollen river, his eyes widening on the sight.

'Yes, water,' Nanny repeated drily. Then added a sharp, 'Front!' to Rosy.

Rosy gave a sigh and obediently took the front of the pushchair.

As they lifted it down the two stone steps, Nanny muttered, 'That must be the understatement of the day.' She glanced briefly at the girl's long, thin, pale face and blond hair scraped back into a severe ponytail, then she turned the pushchair and set off down the drive at a brisk pace. Not for the first time she wondered how anyone could have given the mousy child such an unsuitable name. Rosetta Smith! Rosy! Just because her father wanted to fancy up the plainness of Smith. The man had a lot to answer for, she thought irritably.

'Water! Water! Water!' Now Nicholas joined his brother and the two pointed and bounced excitedly in their seats.

Rosy smiled, but the older woman's face remained bland. It was very rare to see a smile lift her thin lips. It annoyed Rosy, having to watch the two little boys being brought up by such a sobersides. The woman's features were usually as gloomy as the long black coat she wore, summer and winter alike. But John and Dorothy Hardaker were content to leave the care and upbringing of their children to the woman. So it was nothing to do with her.

With a resigned sigh she began to follow, and repeated her hope that the Midland Drapery would be her first place of work – real work.

'That was the second heavy sigh in the space of the same minute,' Nanny snapped. 'What's wrong with you now?'

'There's nothing wrong with me!' *Not that I'm about to tell you, anyway*, thought Rosy. She gave another, mutinous, sigh and walked on. 'It's the twins you're supposed to be looking after . . . not me,' she muttered belligerently.

Nanny gave a snort. It could have been irritation. But Rosy guessed it was more likely to be disgust. Then the woman fell silent and did not speak again until Guy stood up and tried to climb over the T-strap that stopped him falling out of the pushchair.

'Sit down!' Nanny's voice was insistent, but held none of the sharpness that had been directed at Rosy. She laid a restraining hand on the two-year-old's shoulder and pressed him back into the seat. Nicholas took his brother's lead and also attempted to stand up on the footrest. Then he leaned so far forward he almost toppled out of the pushchair.

'Walk!' he protested, when Nanny shoved him back into the seat, none too gently.

'You can walk on the way back. Walk now and we'll never get to the village until the shops are closed.'

The two curly brown heads in the pushchair turned to each other, both muttering in the gobbledegook that

Rosy had noticed they seemed to understand perfectly well. She smiled to herself, but did not bother looking to see if the older woman was sharing the joke. She knew there was little chance of finding any responding amusement on the woman's pinched face. She was not disappointed. With head erect and shoulders and spine straight and stiff, Nanny marched down the drive with her long black coat flapping round her legs like the wings of an angry crow.

They were at the gatehouse standing at the end of the drive, before Nanny slowed the pace. Phoebe Slater lived in the tiny, two-up, two-down stone cottage. She had been the housekeeper at Derwent House before Rosy's mother and it was usual to stop and check that the old lady was all right and if she wanted anything getting from the village shops.

'Stay here!' Nanny barked at Rosy, as she parked the pushchair outside the cottage gate. There was a sharpness in her voice that would not have been out of place on a parade ground and her dark, pebble-like eyes momentarily sliced through Rosy, as if daring her to disobey.

Where would I be going? Rosy thought sarcastically. She grimaced to herself, as she watched the tall, skinny woman march through the pocket handkerchief garden and rap loudly on the door.

Phoebe had seen them coming and opened the door immediately. 'I've got a list and money on the table,' she said, inviting Nanny to come in and get it, the way she always did. But, as Nanny was about to step inside, she suddenly remembered the jar of marmalade she had for the old lady. It was in the shopping bag hanging on the pushchair handle and she called to Rosy to bring it in.

Aye, aye, Captain! Rosy thought, but kept silent as she reached into the bag and pulled the marmalade out. Her eyebrows lifted in surprise as she looked at the jar. It was one her mother had given Nanny to pass

11

on to Phoebe several days ago. It wasn't like the super-efficient Jane Richardson to be forgetful. She kept the thought to herself and carried the marmalade into Phoebe's tiny, cluttered kitchen. 'Here you are,' she said.

'That'll be grand with a bit of toast.' Phoebe's round face crinkled in a smile beneath her mop of erratic silver hair. 'Tell your mam, thank you.'

'I will, Mrs Slater.' Just as Rosy spoke one of the twins began to cry, very noisily.

Nanny gave a sigh. 'Duty calls,' she said, and grabbed Rosy roughly by the arm and hurried her out of the cottage and back to the fractious children.

In all, Rosy could not have been away from the twins for more than one minute – too short a time for anything to happen – or so she would have thought. But as her gaze fell on the pushchair her breath stilled in her lungs and something cold crept over her skin, and she knew she had been wrong . . . very, very wrong!

It was Nicholas who was crying. His small body stretched and jerked in fitful spasms and he wailed as if his heart was breaking. But it was not the sight of Nicholas's distress that brought Rosy up short and lifted Nanny's hand to catch the horrified gasp that flew from her lips. It was the sight of the left-hand side of the pushchair – empty!

Guy was nowhere to be seen.

II

'It can't be!' Dorothy Hardaker wailed, then sank back into the chair, her thin body shaking as if in a fit, a moan rumbling in her throat that sounded more animal than human.

The large policeman, whose dark presence seemed to fill the room, turned compassionately to the distraught woman. 'I'm afraid everything points to it.' His voice was gentle and he looked to John Hardaker, as if seeking help. But he found none. The loss of his son had wiped away John Hardaker's voice. He had gone deathly pale and he looked to be closer to the point of collapse than his near-hysterical wife. Nanny was like a statue, cold and lifeless, spine stiff, perched on the edge of the chair the way she had been since walking into the house and first sitting down; as if to crumple and fall against its support would unleash an emotion that would sweep her away.

'Are you really sure of what you saw?' The policeman turned to the young blonde girl whose legs and coat were covered in mud. Despite her dishevelled appearance she was the only person who still had the power of speech.

Rosy's head wagged from side to side, full of uncertainty. But then she said, 'I think so . . . I don't know. I saw something blue . . . and red. The same colours as Guy's coat,' she added flatly. She closed her eyes, trying to recall the image, trying to prove she had been wrong. She did not want to believe she had seen Guy's little body being washed down the river, but the tighter she squeezed her eyes the clearer it became. It was all there in her mind, as if she was still standing on the river-bank. She could not see Guy, only his coat, only his coat, she kept telling herself. Suddenly the emotion she had been holding back in the horror of it all surged upwards. With a choking gasp tears rushed from her eyes. Guy must be dead. They had left him for only seconds. Yet in that short space of time he had, somehow, got himself out of the pushchair and run away.

'Perhaps he took his coat off,' she said, looking up through her tears at the large policeman. 'He could have done. He was able to,' she added, more in hope than certainty. She felt she shared the blame for letting Guy out of her sight and inside she was begging to be told she had been wrong and it had only been a coat she had seen sucked beneath the filthy, churning river.

But the policeman's shoulders lifted in a shrug that told her he did not believe himself, when he replied, 'He might have done.' And Rosy could only fall silent and blame herself for not being quicker in those first terrible moments. If she had been she might have found Guy before he had reached the river. But no, she had panicked, running first one way then the other like a headless chicken, falling to her knees and crawling through dead leaves and mud beneath the bushes, supposedly searching but going nowhere she could not have seen by merely turning round with open eyes. She should have thought of the river first and gone immediately through the bushes behind Phoebe Slater's cottage and begun to search the bank. She should have! She had not.

By the time her thoughts had collected enough to take her to the most dangerous point, it was too late. As she reached the bank she saw the red and blue of Guy's coat being swept under the bridge. Then it was gone. Sucked beneath the swirling surface and carried away too fast for anyone to do anything but stand helplessly and watch. Because she had not acted fast enough. Neither had Nanny – but the last thought did not occur to Rosy in her troubled state.

'We'll make a search of the banks.' The policeman returned his attention to John Hardaker – this time he looked up. 'But it does seem that your son might have fallen into the river. We'll get the frogmen out – but I'm afraid that won't be until the water has settled down a bit. It's running far too fast for us to do anything at the moment.'

John Hardaker nodded slowly. Then he looked round at the three women in the room: at his trembling, moaning wife; at the frozenly insensible Nanny; at the sobbing Rosy. And it was in that moment that his senses seemed to return. 'Where is Nicholas?' he suddenly asked.

'Mum's got him,' Rosy quickly assured, lifting her head and calling a halt to her own emotion. What she was feeling could be nothing compared to what he and his wife must be going through. 'He's all right. He's quite safe.' Wiping her tears away she offered him a tight, watery smile of reassurance. It came out more like a grimace, but he seemed to understand and gave a little nod in acknowledgement of her concern. Then he pulled his sturdy body out of the chair with an effort that made it appear he was dragging a lead weight, and turned to the policeman. 'Is there really nothing can be done?' he asked. 'Not knowing is . . .' His voice trailed away and his chest lifted on a heavy sigh.

Rosy had never considered John Hardaker to be short before; against her own five-feet-seven-inches his square, solid build seemed that of a very big man. But the policeman dwarfed him, and even standing apart as they were, John Hardaker had to bend his neck in order to look up into the uniformed man's face.

The policeman gave a nod. 'I understand, sir,' he replied, politely and with great concern. 'As I said, we will search the river-bank for any clues and we'll take a look around the fields. But I don't want to give you false hope . . . it doesn't look good.'

John Hardaker nodded, it was all he could do. His body crumpled and his sturdy frame seemed to diminish right before Rosy's eyes.

'Mr Hardaker!' she cried worriedly, leaping to her feet and grabbing his arm and helping him to the nearest chair. He had always been kind to her and, though she would blush to admit it, she had a soft spot for him herself, and seeing him brought so low made her forget what her mother would call 'stepping out of her place'.

'I should be letting the others know what's what,' the policeman said. 'Will you be able to manage, miss?' He picked up his tall hat from the sideboard and his gaze travelled anxiously round the room's three other occupants, before settling on Rosy.

'Yes,' she replied. Her voice was uncertain and the officer remained unconvinced.

'I really should be going and helping them take a look around before the light goes.' His voice was flat. From what the girl had seen it appeared the lad had tumbled into the water. But, even though he felt it was a fool's errand, he still had the need to go out there and lend a hand to his colleagues already searching. He hated the job when children were involved. Under normal conditions the poor mite wouldn't have stood a chance, but with the present spate his little body could already have reached Trent Lock.

Rosy gave a nod and led the policeman out of the room and across the polished wood floor of the hall to the front door. In the hall they found her mother, Nell, anxiously pacing the floor with Nicholas in her arms. The boy was no longer crying, but he was red-eyed and clung tightly to Nell's neck.

'It might be a good idea to take the little one in there.' The officer jerked his head back towards the drawing-room. 'It might . . .' His voice trailed away and his huge shoulders lifted on a shrug. 'Well . . . it might help a bit,' he finally concluded, with resignation.

'Yes, it might do a bit of good,' Nell Smith agreed, although her voice was flat and her feet dragged as she moved slowly towards the drawing-room door. Before she went through it she stopped and glanced back at him. 'You'll let us know the minute you find . . . anything?'

Anything! Rosy thought, feeling something tighten in her chest as, with a departing nod, the policeman put his hat on his head and walked out.

The appearance of Nicholas did have some effect. Dorothy Hardaker stopped moaning and shaking. She did not speak, but held her arms open to take her son and Nell uncoiled his small arms from around her neck and placed him down on his mother's lap.

Dorothy Hardaker's arms immediately fastened round her son and she sank back into the large red armchair, and held him so close and with such force that the boy gave a whimper and Nell hesitated, not sure if she should take the child back. But then she began a gentle rocking to and fro that seemed to be comforting herself as much as the boy, and he settled down and rested his head against her shoulder and Nell moved away.

For several minutes John Hardaker watched his wife and child. Then he gathered himself enough to once more stand up. Going, a little unsteadily, to his wife's side, he laid his hand on the top of the boy's curly head and looked down on him with a rawness of expression spilling from his eyes that put a lump in Rosy's throat.

'I think a good strong cup of tea wouldn't go amiss,' Nell said, taking charge and brushing her hands down the white, lace-edged apron she always wore in the late afternoons. For most of the working day her short, round form was encased in the big, wraparound pinafores which were more suitable for the constant round of work needed to keep such a large house in order. But once all the heavy and dirty work was attended to and the only job left was the cooking and serving of the evening dinner – which she always prepared earlier – Nell liked to play the part, and look as if she really was the head of a household with several staff beneath her.

'Don't bother with a cup for me.' Everyone'e eyes spun round in surprise and Dorothy Hardaker stopped rocking. The still and silent form of Nanny suddenly returned to life and she stood up, her long, thin frame snapping upright like an arrow shot from a bow. She straightened her black skirt and ran a hand over her smooth cap of short black hair with an air of nervousness in her actions. But when she turned her head slowly to John and Dorothy Hardaker there was no sign of any uncertainty in her grave face. 'I shall go and pack my bags right away,' she announced.

Rosy had the feeling the woman's breast would have quivered as she spoke, had she had a breast to quiver. As it was, her flat chest affected what could have been called a heave beneath her baggy fawn twin-set.

'I realize exactly where the blame lies,' Jane Richardson continued stiffly, when no-one else spoke. 'I know you will not want me to stay here now. You will no longer consider me fit to care for Nicholas. I shall not embarrass you by staying. I shall go immediately.'

No-one moved, and for several seconds the atmosphere could have been cut with a knife. The tension in Rosy's body was so great she held her breath, but was not aware of doing so. She could not believe what she was hearing: Nanny was actually taking responsibility. She had felt sure the woman would push all the blame onto her, making out she was the one who had left the twins alone.

It was John Hardaker who finally broke the spell. 'Yes,' he replied tersely, his hand remaining firmly on his son's head as his wife returned to rocking backwards and forwards. 'I think that would be for the best.'

Something flashed momentarily in Nanny's eyes. Her lips moved as if she was about to speak, but changed her mind. Then she turned abruptly and marched out of the room without uttering another word.

As if she had been expecting him to object, Rosy thought incredulously. As if she had been expecting him to tell her to stop being silly and beg her to stay and continue to care for his remaining son. She bit her lip and stared at the burgundy red carpet, and waited. She was sure she would be the next. She had been with the boys, along with Nanny, she must share some of the blame for leaving them unattended. She gave a sigh. He would tell her she also had to go.

Would he make her mother go with her, she suddenly, and very anxiously wondered? If he did they would be homeless, because the cottage they lived in at the back of the house went with her mother's job. She felt a whimper rise in her throat and bit down harder on her lip. Her mother had worked her fingers to the bone to give her and her sister Maggie a good home since their father died. Now she had repaid her by getting them put out on the streets.

'I'm sorry, Mr Hardaker,' she whispered, not daring to look up and see the censure in his eyes – or in her mother's. 'I'll go, as well. Only let my mum stay on. She had nothing to do with it.'

Nell gave a gasp and rushed to her daughter, pulling her into her arms. Rosy's face fell against her mother's shoulder and she began to cry once more, very noisily. 'I . . . didn't . . . I . . . wouldn't have . . .'

'Hush, Rosy. It wasn't your fault. I don't hold you responsible for anything that has happened.'

It was several seconds before Rosy realized it was John Hardaker's voice, not her mother's. She looked round. He was standing right by her side, his hand resting on her shoulder. 'Do you mean that, Mr Hardaker?' she asked, through her tears.

His smile had a certain tightness and did not reach his eyes, but his voice was sincere. 'Yes, Rosy, I do mean that!'

'Oh thank you, Mr Hardaker.' She pushed herself free of her mother's arms and almost dipped him a curtsy. So great was her relief that if he had asked her to kiss his feet she felt she would have done so. 'I'll . . .' She had been about to say: 'I'll make it up to you.' But she realized that would have been a stupid thing to say in the circumstances: how could you ever replace a lost child? Feeling her tears returning, she dropped her head and tried to blink them back.

'Go and get yourself cleaned up,' John Hardaker gently instructed.

She did not need telling twice. She was only too willing to get out of that room and leave behind the sorrow that emanated from the people and clung to the walls, the floor and the furniture like a tangible substance. It even tainted the air that filled the spaces in between and put a funny taste on your tongue and a heaviness in your lungs. She spun quickly away and was out of the door before she heard John Hardaker say, 'I think we'll have that cup of tea now, Nell.'

*　　*　　*

It was exactly one week later when Rosy was summoned to John Hardaker's study.

It was morning and breakfast was only just over. Rosy had begun on the washing-up while her mother was clearing the table in the dining-room. Up until a week ago the Hardaker's had always eaten the first meal of the day in the conservatory that had been built on the end of the house. But that gave them a splendid view of the surrounding countryside, all the way to the village – including the river. So now their meals were taken in the large dining-room which, to Rosy, was far too grand for everyday use, but was at the back of the house and looked out on the scattered houses that dotted the hillside, before the wood hid the brow from view.

It had been a depressing week. They had been inundated with callers giving their sympathy and bringing flowers for Dorothy Hardaker. There were flowers everywhere, in the hall, in the dining-room, and the drawing-room was full of them. In fact the house was beginning to look like a funeral parlour and, where at first a knock at the door had lifted Rosy's hopes and had her begging that this was it, that they had found Guy, the sound of anyone now arriving at the front door set her teeth on edge and added to her depression.

The river was still rolling past with more speed than was normal, but it had shrunk back to the confines of its own boundaries. Despite the police making a diligent search of the banks and the surrounding countryside, nothing had been found to suggest Rosy could have been wrong; that in her panic she had mistaken a piece of flotsam for the boy's coat. Little Guy Hardaker had vanished without trace. Even the most optimistic now had to concede that he had stumbled into the water and been washed away.

Naturally, Dorothy Hardaker was finding it all difficult to bear. There were times when she became so possessive of Nicholas that Rosy feared the tightness of her arms around his small body would crush him and break his delicate bones. At other times she rejected the child completely, as if the very sight of him was abhorrent to her. Then there were the times when she locked herself in her bedroom and would not see even her husband.

'It's the shock,' Nell assured, when Rosy voiced her inability to understand the woman's actions. 'If they could find Guy's body and lay the poor little mite to rest, then that would put an end to it and she'd get some rest, as well.'

Despite nodding her head in agreement, Rosy was still confused. She knew Dorothy Hardaker was mourning for Guy but, even so, she could not understand how the woman could turn her back on her remaining son, as she had done so often in the past week.

'That's the lot!' Nell bustled through the door and plonked the silver tray and tea service down on the kitchen table. 'Mr Hardaker wants to see you in his study,' she said, turning to her daughter very seriously.

Rosy gave a grimace. 'What about?'

'How should I know!'

Rosy did not miss the censure in her mother's voice and she frowned. 'Is he angry?' she asked warily. The morning had started badly with the postman bringing the much awaited letter from the Midland Drapery: the job had been given to someone with experience.

Nell rested her work-worn hands on her well-padded hips and gave her daughter a telling stare. 'Should he be?' she questioned pointedly. 'Have you been up to anything?'

'*No Mum!*' Rosy was quick to reply, but then she hesitated, rubbed her hands nervously down her red tartan skirt and began to wonder if she *had* done something to upset her employer. She had been, more or less, in constant charge of Nicholas since Nanny walked out. It hadn't been easy. Little as he was, he was missing his brother and could not understand why suddenly he wasn't there. There had been times when he had gone into black depressions that matched his mother's and he had seemed inconsolable. But she had managed to work him out of his moods and put a smile back on his face, and she could not think of anything she might have done to the boy that could have upset him enough for his father to reprimand her.

'Well, you'd better get off and find out what it is.'

Nell jerked her head at the door. 'But you mind your manners. Don't you be rude. And that means don't go answering back – whatever the question. Just nod your head and say yes and no.'

'Yes, Mum.' Rosy did not point out that if she was asked a question that needed a proper answer, Mr Hardaker would think she was a halfwit if she merely nodded her head and replied yes to everything. But she knew her mother had not fully accepted that the Hardakers did not hold her in any way responsible for Guy's death. She was still worrying they might change their minds and make her go the way of Nanny. 'Don't worry, I'll be very, very polite,' she promised, laying her cheek next to her mother's and giving her a quick hug.

'Get off with you!' Nell slapped at her arm, although she had to smile. But the smile slipped from her face as she watched Rosy go through the door and her mind turned back to wondering what reason John Hardaker could have for sending for her. He had never done so before. He was always pleasant to Rosy when he came across her in the house, but any orders and instructions were always given to herself, to be relayed to her daughter.

By the time Rosy had reached the study door her mother's uncertainty had rubbed off and she felt her stomach turning to jelly. It had to be this morning, she thought, convinced that after the rejection from the Midland Drapery her confidence was about to get the second slap of the day. The strongest desire was to turn and run and it took all her strength to clench her fist into a tight ball and tap lightly on the door.

John Hardaker immediately summoned her to enter.

Gulping back the lump in her throat, she tugged her red jumper straight, ran her hands once more down her kilt, and walked into the oak-panelled room. He was standing by the window, staring through one of the small square panes of glass. He did not speak but, half-turning, waved his hand to invite her to sit on the green leather-backed chair positioned purposely in front of the desk.

Her voice had left her, her mouth had gone as dry as sandpaper. She sank slowly onto the chair and clenched her hands tightly in her lap. It all seemed so formal. Perhaps her mother was right, she thought, and worried anxiously at her bottom lip.

'Don't look so frightened.' He smiled at her and, for a moment, seemed to be back to his old self: all the grief of the past week forgotten.

She returned the smile. He had a pleasant, attractive face, more so when he appeared happy. 'I'm not frightened,' she lied, forcing her voice to false bravado. Then she bit her lip, reminding herself of her mother's warning not to answer back.

He did not speak again, but moved away from the window and, crossing the room to the desk, stopped and stared, very seriously, at the ink-stained top.

Rosy's tension increased. Her hands began to tremble and she clasped them tighter and racked her brain for some reason for him wanting to see her, some misdemeanour or small transgression. She could not think of anything and she wished he would speak and put her out of her misery. But the silence continued and she glanced nervously round the austere room where he spent long hours conducting his property business. Had it done him any good, she wondered? All the work had bought him this grand house but, even before Guy went missing, she would not have described him and his wife as happy. There was not the closeness there that she would have expected of a married couple.

'You have looked after Nicholas this past week,' he suddenly said, startling Rosy's attention back to him, just as his pale eyes pivoted up to meet hers with a swiftness that physically jolted her body.

It was a couple of seconds before she could reply

with a guarded, 'Yes'. Then she had to take the length of time needed to nervously lick her lips and swallow, before being able to ask, 'Have I done something to . . . ?'

'You haven't *done* anything, Rosy,' he quickly put in, cutting her off mid-sentence. 'Except look after Nicholas very well.'

Her eyebrows lifted and her eyes widened. 'Oh!' was all she could utter. She had imagined many reasons for him wanting to see her, but to compliment her had not been one of them.

He smiled again. 'You look as if you don't believe me.'

'Oh, I believe you, Mr Hardaker,' she quickly assured.

'Good.' His smile warmed on her face and she felt an embarrassed blush rush up her cheeks, and she dropped her gaze quickly to the blue and gold carpet on the floor. His smile deepened and he pulled out the desk chair and sat down. 'We need to get a new nanny for Nicholas. He needs someone to look after him full-time – especially while my wife is not well,' he added flatly.

Rosy nodded her head, although she could not understand why he was telling her this. She was well aware they would get another nanny. Right from the twins first being born Dorothy Hardaker had had someone to look after them for her. She had never done things like change nappies and feed them herself. Even if she was in peak condition she would not have known how to go about tending to all Nicholas's needs.

'How do you feel about taking the job?'

'What . . . !' Her hand flew to her mouth. 'Sorry, I mean, pardon?' Her neck shrank into her shoulders, as if she expected her mother to have appeared behind her to give her a sharp clip round the ear. 'But . . . well . . . !'

John Hardaker sucked on his bottom lip in an effort

to stop himself breaking into a broad smile and insulting her. He wondered, not for the first time, how she could have come from the same parents as her sister, the flighty Maggie. 'Don't you want the job, Rosy?' he asked carefully.

'Oh yes!' There was no hesitation in her reply. 'It's just . . . well . . . I never . . .'

'Thought I would consider you,' he completed for her. 'I know you're only fifteen. But Nicholas likes you. And, well, getting a fully trained nanny in has not done us much good. I think you could do the job . . .' He hesitated and grimaced. 'I was going to say just as well. But I hope not. I would not be offering you the position if I didn't think you could do it better. We do not want a repeat of what has gone.'

'No, Mr Hardaker. I won't let that happen. I'll keep Nicholas safe for you. I'll never leave him again, not for anybody.'

He smiled again, although his eyes were shadowed with the sadness of his loss. 'Does that mean you will take the job, Rosy?'

'Oh yes, Mr Hardaker. I'll take it – with pleasure.'

'Well, then . . .' he spread his hands out on the desk, '. . . you know where everything is so there is nothing I have to tell you. You can go and get on with it.'

'Yes, Mr Hardaker.' She leaped out of the chair, eager to get back to the kitchen and tell her mother the good news. She was at the door, before a sudden thought stopped her in her tracks. She spun back to him, her mother's warning about politeness spinning inside her head. 'Thank you, Mr Hardaker,' she rushed out, her voice bubbling with excitement. 'Thank you so much!'

Then she hurried out of his study with her head held high, experiencing only the mildest guilt that she was feeling so happy abaut something that had come out of such sad circumstances. For beneath the childish excitement was something else, some strange feeling she had never experienced before. She suddenly saw herself to be leaving childhood behind and changing into a woman. Who needed the Midland Drapery? She had a proper job now, one with responsibilities. She was no longer the odd job girl. She was the nanny!

CHAPTER ONE

1960

Rosy smiled as she saw him coming down the yard at the little village school. His tie was twisted halfway round his neck and his wrinkled grey socks, shoes and knees were covered in mud. The pocket of his shirt was ripped, his curly hair was standing on end and one cheek was glowing red. He had been in a fight – again!

As he came towards her she held her hand out to him, the way she always did. There was never a day when she was not there waiting for him. Her promise to his father to keep him safe and never leave him again had not been forgotten once in the four years she had cared for him.

'Now what have you been up to?' she enquired, her resigned gaze taking in his dishevelled appearance.

He grinned and stuck his grubby hand into hers. 'Terry Williams picked on me.'

Her head shaking in disbelief she steered him towards the corner of the playground, out of the main stream of parents and pupils leaving the school. When they had reached a quiet spot, where she could try and do something to restore his appearance to one of respectability, she stopped and pulled him round to face her. 'And I don't suppose you did anything to goad him!' she said pointedly, and crouched down and straightened his tie and did the best she could to brush the mud from his legs and clothes.

He shook his head and grinned again.

'Oh Nicky!' It was spoken with affectionate despair, as she smoothed the soft brown curls down flat on his head. 'Mr Brownlow will be sending for me again. And

29

you know how furious he was last time.' Mr Brownlow was the headmaster and Rosy had been summoned to his office more times than she cared to remember. Always for the same reason – Nicky and his fighting. Hissing the air through her teeth she stood up. 'Why do you do it?'

'They pick on me.' His grin vanished and, head slumping forward, he stared at the ground and kicked at the toe of his shoe.

He made such a sorrowful sight: full of remorse and, despite Rosy's ministrations, still very dishevelled and woebegone. He looked lost and alone and she felt the all too familiar tug at her heart and pulled him into her arms. 'What am I going to do with you?' she asked, shaking her head and lifting his chin to look down into his face with all the affection she felt for him. His grin returned. 'Shake me up.'

A smile broke on her lips. It was their little joke. If he was being only mildly naughty, she would affect a threatening air, say she was going to 'shake him up', then tickle him until he laughed so much tears ran from his eyes and, on occasions, he almost wet himself.

'Just wait till I get you home, monkey.' She took hold of his hand and they walked out of the playground and down the lane.

She knew she should have been more angry with him. But she never could be as firm as she told herself she ought to be. She was soft with him, but only because she loved him so much. She could not have loved him more had he been her own son.

In a way he *was* hers. She was the one who did everything for him, who was always there for him. She did think his father had some affection for him, but John Hardaker was a man who found it difficult to show his emotions, so she could not be sure what he was or was not feeling. But his mother could go days without setting eyes on the boy.

Rosy could not remember when Dorothy Hardaker

had last held her son in her arms. Or even touched him. The woman kept herself locked away in her bedroom most of the time now. If she came downstairs it was to go out, and where she went was a mystery; unless she came back loaded with shopping bags full of clothes to add to her already overflowing wardrobe.

'Gillian Land wet her knickers today,' Nicky related very importantly. 'Right in the middle of sums.'

'Well, I hope you didn't laugh at her.' Rosy's voice took on a sternness that belied the amusement bubbling inside her.

Nicky shook his head, not very convincingly. Then he changed the subject and chatted furiously, going through all that had happened during the day.

In the village they stopped at the newsagent's and got ice-creams to eat as they walked. It was a warm day, the clouds fluffy and high in the sky, and they were in no hurry. At a leisurely pace they took the path across the meadow to the road which crossed first the railway, then the river. Nicky did not fall silent until they had almost reached the bridge over the river.

'What did you have for dinner?' Rosy knew what was going through his mind and she wanted to steer him to other things. But she could not take his mind from his fears and when they reached the bridge she felt the familiar tightening of his hand on hers, and she tightened her own grip in reassurance.

It always happened. He walked over the railway bridge without even noticing, but as they approached the river bridge she would feel his small body beginning to tense. Then, as they stepped onto the bridge, his grip increased and he clung to her as if she was his very life. It was as if, in his eyes, the solid stone structure, strong enough to take cars and lorries, was nothing more than rotting wood and about to crumble. She had tried talking to him about Guy and the terrible day he had died. She had explained how the river had been very high and fast, and that Guy had been too young

31

to swim. But their conversations on the matter never got anywhere, because his thoughts on the matter were very contrary. While one part of him feared the river another part of him would not believe Guy was gone forever. It was because they were twins, she told herself, wishing she had a better understanding of how it felt to be one of a pair, so that she could properly understand Nicky.

But his fear of the river had made it one of Rosy's first priorities to teach him to swim. It wouldn't help if the river was in full spate as on the day Guy died, but it would mean he had some chance if he happened to fall in when the flow was not so fast. She had also wanted to get him used to water before he was old enough to fully comprehend how his brother had died, and then not be able to go anywhere near it.

She turned her head to look over the bridge wall and up the river towards the solid stone structure of Derwent House. In truth, she could not understand how his parents could stay there. If it had been anything to do with her she would have moved to somewhere where there was no river, and no danger to Nicholas. But she knew that would not happen. John Hardaker was too proud of the building his hard work had got him.

She had to admit it was a lovely house, with its sprawling grounds and old coach house and assortment of outbuildings surrounding a courtyard that spoke of another age. It had seven bedrooms in all, but only four rooms and a conservatory downstairs, because the drawing-room and dining-room were both big enough for two rooms each. And there was the beautiful view across the meadow to the village. If the river had not been between the house and the meadow it would have been perfect. But at least John Hardaker had made a concession to his remaining son's safety, by having a swimming-pool installed at the back of the house when Rosy said she wanted to teach Nicky to swim.

Only a few yards past the bridge they turned up the drive to Derwent House, through the large stone gateposts and past Phoebe Slater's old cottage. The small stone cottage now stood empty. The shock of Guy's disappearance had been too much for the old lady and she had died a few weeks after.

As they began the long walk up the drive, Nicky performed the ritual of changing sides with Rosy: so that he was on the side furthest from the river. But he did begin his incessant chatter once more and his steps were much lighter as he half-walked, half-skipped by her side. 'Are you going to show me some more diving?'

'If you like.' She smiled at his eagerness, pleased her swimming lessons had been successful: it was only the river that put fear into him. The river that had taken his brother's young body and never given it up. Guy had never been found. The swollen waters had carried him off to heaven only knew where.

'Very good!' Rosy called, as she sat on the side of the pool, her legs dangling in the water.

'Well done!' A certain pride filled John Hardaker's voice. Nicky had just done six lengths of very strong crawl, from a diving start.

Rosy smiled. It was not usual for John Hardaker to come to the pool and watch his son's achievements. Neither was it usual for him to let his feelings be known, and there had been signs of some real emotion in him for a moment or two there.

'Why don't you come for a swim?' she invited. He often had a swim later on in the evenings, when Nicky was in bed and he could have the pool to himself.

'Yes, Dad. Come on! I'll race you.' Nicky was more than eager and quickly swam to where his father was standing.

John Hardaker looked down at his son for several

seconds. Rosy had the feeling he was searching for an excuse, but could not find one.

'Come on, Dad.' Nicky persisted. 'We can all have a race. Or you can race Rosy – If you think I'm too fast for you!' he added proudly.

'Perhaps your dad is busy,' Rosy said, offering his father a way out, as she slid into the pool and glided up to Nicky's side.

John Hardaker watched her easy movements and the way her body shimmered beneath the surface. Her swimsuit was the colour of pale harebells and with her long blond hair and slender white limbs she appeared to have turned to silver. She blended in with the pale marble pool and put him in mind of a mermaid. He knew he would like nothing more than to be in the water with her, and he broke into one of his very rare smiles. 'How could I refuse such an offer,' he said, and spun round and hurried to the changing-room at the end of the long pool, where the towels and swimsuits were all kept.

He was back within seconds. Rosy and Nicky were floating on their backs, pretending to be tree trunks and the sudden splash, as he dived in very close by Rosy's side, was so unexpected that it startled her. With arms flailing, she sank and took in a great gulp of water.

'Oh . . . !' she gasped, spluttering and coughing as she burst to the surface and wallowed unsteadily as she fought to regain her breath and right herself.

John Hardaker quickly reached out to steady her. 'Are you all right?' He looked embarrassed more than concerned, as if he now regretted his playful outburst.

'Yes. Yes.' Rosy was quick with her reassurance, eager not to condemn him for trying to enjoy himself. But before the amusement bubbling up inside her chest could reach her face and turn to laughter, Nicky had set about his father.

'Get off her,' he demanded, his thin arms flailing

wildly at his father's broad, solid chest. 'Why did you do that?' he cried. 'Why did you do that?'

'Whoa there!' John Hardaker grabbed his son's wrists and held his hands at bay.

'It's all right,' Rosy insisted, taking Nicky in her arms and pulling him away from his father. 'It was only a joke. I wasn't hurt.'

But Nicky was not placated. 'You tried to drown her.' The accusation was flung hotly at his bewildered father. 'I saw you. She was choking. You made her.'

'No, no, Nicky!' Rosy held him tighter, as he tried to wriggle free and get at his father once more. 'Stop it! Don't be silly! You'll hurt yourself.' It was taking all her strength to keep hold of him and she glanced hopelessly at John Hardaker. 'Perhaps you'd better go,' she suggested, hoping he would not take offence at her ordering him about.

He hesitated, his features forming in anger. 'I was only playing a trick, Nicky. I wasn't trying to hurt Rosy . . . or you.' His voice was stiff. Rosy could see he was having great difficulty controlling himself and she was grateful when, his voice softening, he added, 'Come on, let's have that race now.'

But Nicky would not be cajoled. 'No!' he refused, his voice rising to a scream. 'I don't want you in my pool. Get out! Get out!'

'Please!' Rosy mouthed, looking beseechingly at John Hardaker, as she clung frantically to the squirming boy.

He hesitated for only a moment. Then he turned away and his arms cut fiercely through the water, his temper revealed by a show of silver spray on each side of him. When he reached the side he hauled himself up and threw himself out, and strode quickly to the changing-room.

Rosy usually managed to avoid being furious with Nicky, no matter how badly behaved he had been. But his reaction had been so uncalled for and had plainly hurt his father so much, that when John Hardaker had finally vanished into the changing-room, she found it impossible to hold her anger in check.

'That was very naughty!' She felt responsible and embarrassment increased her guilt and she swept him out of the water and plonked him down roughly on the side of the pool, making his wet legs slap noisily against the tiles. She was sure John Hardaker would be furious with her later, and she could not blame him. 'Your dad was only playing. You owe him an apology and I suggest you go after him and give it.' At that moment her fury matched his father's.

'Won't!' He folded his arms tightly and his bottom lip extended in a mulish pout.

'Oh Nicky!' She scraped her hands through her wet hair in exasperation. 'Why did you do that? You splash me and I splash you and you don't mind it!'

'You nearly drowned. I heard you choking.'

'Coughing and spluttering is not choking!' she snapped, frustration growing in the face of his stubbornness. 'I'd swallowed a bit of water, but nowhere near enough to drown in.'

He did not reply, but sat like a belligerent statue, staring at the water. He looked so hopeless. It seemed as if the weight of the whole world was suddenly pressing down on his young shoulders, and Rosy found her anger wilting and her more usual compassion and love taking its place.

'Nicky . . . what is it?' she asked. Wrapping her arms around him she pressed her cheek against his damp shoulder. Despite his continual fights with the boys at school he was never aggressive at other times. He didn't even argue much at home, especially not with his father.

She gave an inward sigh. His father was never around for him to argue with. Today had only been the third time John Hardaker had come into the pool while they were there, and it was the first time he had actually come into the water and joined his son. In fact it was the first time he had ever made the effort to get involved in anything the boy was doing. She gave another sigh. The first time and the last, she thought. After the reception he'd received he would not be rushing to repeat the performance.

She looked up into Nicky's face. The pout was gone and now he appeared to be totally downcast and on the verge of tears. 'Oh Nicky!' she brushed the shiny mat of wet brown hair away from his forehead and peered deep into his sorrowful brown eyes. 'What is it? Why did you get so upset over nothing? Tell me?'

Coiling his thin arms around her neck his body fell against her and she felt the first gentle sobs shivering against her shoulder. 'Guy choked,' he finally said, in little more than a whisper.

'What?' She held him away and frowned into his eyes. He had never said anything like this. 'What do you mean?' she questioned carefully.

'Guy choked. When he drowned. I heard him.'

'Oh, love!' She pulled him into her arms again and held him tighter. It wasn't possible. The pushchair had been too far away from the river for him to have heard anything. Besides, he had been too young to remember. He only remembered what people had told him about the events of his brother's death and his immature mind had obviously added bits of its own.

'Perhaps you only dreamed it,' she said gently. She could not lie and say Guy didn't choke, because she knew he must have done, and just the thoughts of that thick grey water filling his tiny lungs made her own chest ache. It was a feeling she did not want Nicky to share. 'No-one saw or heard anything of Guy going into the water. We were all too far away.'

Lifting his head to look into her face, he said, 'Perhaps he didn't drown. We might find him one day.'

She smiled thinly at the spark of hope lighting the big brown eyes. 'If he hadn't drowned I think we would

37

have found him by now.' She did not point out that, as usual, he was contradicting himself: one moment thinking he had heard Guy choking; the next suggesting he might not have drowned after all. It was just too much for his young mind to cope with. Death was something you should not encounter at close quarters until much later in life. Certainly not while you were still in your pushchair.

'The river was too high and fast for even the strongest man to get himself out.' She spoke plainly, but kept her voice gentle. Guy had not been just his brother, but his twin. They had shared the womb, been born together and spent the first two years of life together. Even if he could not remember all the details of Guy's disappearance, there must have been some feeling of loss which his young mind found difficult to understand.

'Guy must have died, Nicky.' She held him away and looked deep into his troubled eyes. It was four years since his disappearance. It was no longer possible to hope for a miracle. 'You mustn't go thinking there is a chance he will turn up someday. He won't, love.' It hurt her to be so blunt but she could see it was needed. If he was allowed to continue thinking his brother would come back one day he was only causing himself more pain. 'We can remember him and love him, but we can't bring him back.'

He fell against her, his thin arms coiling tightly round her neck again. She felt the wetness of his tears running onto her already damp skin but she did not speak any words of comfort. She held on to him and let him have his time of grieving, and hoped that, when he was ready, he would continue the conversation.

But when he finally looked up it seemed Guy had been forgotten. 'I love you, Rosy,' he said, as he screwed his fists into tight balls and scrubbed away the remaining tears from his eyes. 'I'm glad I've got you.'

'And I love you and I'm glad I've got you,' she

echoed with feeling, even though a heaviness sank in her chest that the love he gave to her should really have been going to his parents. 'But you've also got your dad, and he loves you, as well,' she added, her smile both fond and sad.

She did not say he had got his mum and dad, because she could not have said truthfully that his mother still loved him. The woman had become so strange since his brother's death that she did not think she could remember how to love anyone. If she did she certainly did not show it, either to her son, or her husband.

'And what you did earlier must have hurt your dad,' she continued. 'And we never want to hurt people we love. So I really do think you should go and apologize to him.'

For a long moment he stared at her bleakly and she had the feeling he was about to refuse. Then his head began to nod in slow agreement. 'I'll do it after dinner,' he said, his voice so low she only just caught the words.

She shook her head.

'What's wrong with doing it now?' she asked, gently but firmly. 'He's still in the changing-room. Why don't you go in there to him?'

He hesitated. Finally gave a nod. Then without speaking a word, stood up and walked slowly across the pale blue tiles to the changing-room door, with a desolation that put a thin smile on Rosy's lips. He could have been going to see a tyrannical headmaster, she thought sadly.

'It's a long time since I've seen that.' Nell was at the sink in the large oak furnished kitchen, washing the dinner pots. She inclined her head towards the window, where John Hardaker and Nicky could be seen walking through the orchard hand in hand. She turned a puzzled gaze on her daughter. 'Has something gone off?'

'No.' Rosy's reply was matter-of-fact. What had

happened in the swimming-pool was nothing to do with anyone else, and she had no intention of telling even her mother. 'Why should anything have gone off? It's quite normal to see a father and son together.'

'Not that father and son!' Nell replied bluntly, turning away from the censure in her daughter's blue eyes.

Rosy had to admit to herself that her mother was speaking the truth. It was a rare occasion to see Nicky and John Hardaker together – being normal!

It pleased her. John Hardaker was always so content to leave the responsibility for Nicky in her hands and he had so little to do with his son. She had worried he would not know how to accept the olive branch the boy was offering. It had been a brave decision, but she had felt it was better for Nicky to go to his father alone and she stayed out of it, letting them come to terms for themselves. It could have gone wrong, but it hadn't. It had worked and now they seemed to be closer than they had ever been. 'Where's our Maggie gone?' she asked, changing the subject before her mother began to probe.

'Nowhere. She's broke so she's spending a night titivatin'.'

Rosy blew a sigh. Maggie was a herding animal. She could never be alone for very long, so sooner or later the emptiness of the cottage would get at her and she would come over to the house, seeking company – or rather someone to irritate.

It happened sooner rather than later. Rosy was putting the last of the clean pots away on the shelves of the tall oak dresser, when she saw her sister coming out of the cottage that had been converted from the old coach house. But, instead of coming directly across the courtyard to the house, she went the other way and out through the gap that lead onto the orchard and stopped the courtyard being completely closed in on all four sides.

'Where's she bouncing off to?' she asked. Bouncing was the least rude way Rosy could describe the manner in which her sister moved. The way Maggie swung her rounded hips from side to side and thrust out her ample breasts defied any description of modesty. 'The titivatin' must have been concluded successfully,' she added drily, hoping her sister was not going to bother Nicky and his father, who could still be seen at the far end of the orchard.

Nell peered through the window at her elder daughter. 'So it seems,' she said, shaking her head in despair. Maggie might not be going dancing or pubbing it tonight, which were her usual nightly entertainments, but she had certainly gone to town on the titivatin'. Her long black curly hair was backcombed and held up in a high, stiff beehive which wobbled when she walked. Her red trousers were so tight that, although Nell could not see from that distance, she knew they would show the bump of the large mole on her backside. And a skimpy black crossover top clung to her amply filled circle-stitched bra in a way that made it appear she had a couple of clown's pointed hats stuck on her chest. Not for the first time Nell asked the Almighty how she could have been landed with two such different children. Then she quickly thanked Him for Rosy, just to make sure He realized she wasn't complaining about both her offspring.

'Why does she have to come over here?' Rosy plonked the last cups on the shelf and closed the cupboard door with more force than was necessary. 'I wish Mr Hardaker would tell her not to.' She always found Maggie an embarrassment.

Since becoming Nicky's nanny Rosy had moved out of the cottage and into the house, to sleep in the room next to his so she was close if he should need her during the night. She had thought that being away from the cottage and not having to share the intimacy of a bedroom with Maggie, might make her become a little

41

less conscious of her sister's flightiness. But it had made no difference. There was no getting away from the fact that Maggie was common. She had the looks to be a beauty but she wasted it by being tarty. 'I dread to think what he thinks of her when she comes flouncing round the house as if she owns the place.'

Nell glanced at her younger daughter, then turned back to the window to see Maggie go right up to John Hardaker and Nicky without any consideration that they might not want to be interrupted. She gave an inward sigh and hoped Rosy's innocence would never leave her. Unfortunately, *she* was not so innocent and she knew exactly why Maggie made frequent visits to the house. She also had the uncomfortable feeling she knew why John Hardaker would never put a stop to her visits. And who could blame the man if he was taking advantage. It was being offered to him on a plate and he certainly wasn't getting it from that wife of his.

Smoothing down her starched white apron, Nell turned away from the window and the cause of her distress. 'I'd better go and see to her.' Her voice was flat, which was her usual manner when they were alone and she was referring to the lady of the house, who was becoming stranger and more troubled with every passing day.

Dorothy Hardaker's attendances at the dinner table were getting fewer and fewer. Not that Rosy had any complaint. Since Nicky had been old enough to sit at the table and dine with his parents, she had been expected to also dine with them. Having Dorothy Hardaker there had never been a pleasure.

Rosy never felt comfortable in the grand room with the long table and crystal chandelier, and Dorothy Hardaker's presence only increased her unease. When she was there it was only to cause trouble: sniping at Mr Hardaker; speaking to Rosy as if she was a dog who should be grovelling at her feet. So it was always a relief for Rosy when her mother was instructed to get a tray ready to be taken up to the woman's room.

It was the tray that needed fetching down now. They never went to get it before washing-up because Dorothy Hardaker complained she was being rushed if they went up too early.

'I'll go,' Rosy offered.

Nell smiled with gratitude, then with affection as she watched Rosy go through the door. Her long, straight blond hair was lovely and her eyes were a vivid blue. Her face was just a little on the long side, as was her nose, but she could never have been called plain now, not like when she was a child. Nell gave a sigh. If people didn't compare her to Maggie she would have been looked on as a beauty in her own right. But nobody could miss Maggie and so Rosy's quiet reservation paled into insignificance beside her.

When she reached Dorothy Hardaker's bedroom Rosy tapped lightly on the door, then waited to hear the key turn in the lock before going in. There was never any call to enter, just the click as the door was unlocked.

Neither did Dorothy Hardaker speak when you went in. So, in her usual manner, Rosy walked silently across the thickly carpeted floor, picked up one dirty plate from the dressing-table, another from the bedside table, cup and saucer from the window-sill, and the milk jug and sugar basin from the dressing-table stool that, for some reason, was standing in the middle of the floor.

The only time Dorothy Hardaker opened her mouth was to complain or bark orders, so the silence was gratefully received and Rosy went about her business without looking at the tiny, dark-haired figure hovering by the bed.

When the silence lasted until she was on her way out, Rosy thought tonight was going to be a lucky one and she was going to get away without being lambasted by the woman's vicious tongue. It was not until her hand closed round the large, ornate, brass doorknob that she was proved wrong.

'Tell my husband I will be needing the car.'

Rosy paused and turned round. 'I think Mr Hardaker is going out himself,' she said without thinking.

Dorothy Hardaker's brown eyes narrowed and glittered with anger. 'Then tell him he will have to walk. *I* shall be needing the car!'

The dirty pots on the tray balanced on Rosy's arm rattled, as she took a moment to compose herself and think what to say. 'I'll tell him to come and see you,' she said, regretting she had not kept her mouth shut and just passed on the message and let him sort it out.

'You will tell him I shall be having the car!' Dorothy Hardaker flung back.

'I don't . . . I don't think it is part of my duties to relay such messages to Mr Hardaker,' Rosy replied, calling on all her strength to keep her voice even. She was determined not to become a go-between for an argument between husband and wife.

Angry spots of colour flared in Dorothy Hardaker's cheeks. 'I don't think it is part of your duties to disobey me!' she retorted, the hiss of her voice reminding Rosy of a snake. 'I am the mistress in this house,' she continued, her lip curling as if a nasty smell had passed under her nose and her hand flapping dismissively towards the door. 'Now go away. And do as you are told!'

Rosy turned and hurried out without giving a reply.

Not until she was pushing backwards through the kitchen door, the tray still shaking in her hands, did she speak, muttering, 'That woman! If I didn't know why she was like it I'd chuck something at her.' If little Guy's body could have been found and put to rest she was sure Dorothy Hardaker would be better. But they'd never found hide nor hair of him and so there was no real end to it for his mother. Time was doing nothing to heal her, she got worse by the day.

'What's wrong with her now?' Nell looked up from the table, where she was polishing the silver cutlery on a clean tea towel before putting it away in the drawer.

Rosy plonked the tray down on the draining-board, sending the rosebud china clattering about and milk slurping from the jug. 'She only wants the car tonight! And I am supposed to tell Mr Hardaker *he* can't have it!'

'Tell him she wants the car and let him go and sort it out himself,' Nell said, a note of weariness entering her voice. There were times when she wished she could tell the Hardakers just where they could put their job, and take herself and her daughters right away from this miserable house. But there was no chance of that. There was no way she could afford to get them out of the tied cottage. Besides, she had grave doubts that Rosy would ever have consented to go and leave Nicky behind.

Maggie chose that moment to come through the back door. 'Got any tea in the pot?' She went right up to the large willow pattern teapot, lifted the lid and peered inside.

'Leave that be!' Nell slapped her hand away. 'We're all cleared up now. If you wanted a cup of tea you should have stayed at home and brewed up.'

'Why use your own stuff when you can get it for free?' Taking a large green apple from a dish on the dresser, Maggie sat down at the table and began munching on it noisily.

Nell heaved a sigh, but kept quiet, knowing she would only have been wasting her breath.

'What you doing?' Maggie peered at Rosy over the top of the apple as she took another bite, and spoke with her mouth full. 'Do you want to come down to The Derwent for one?'

'No she doesn't!' Nell returned sharply, before Rosy had the chance. 'Going into a pub without a man to escort you. I'd die of shame! Besides, I thought you'd got no money.'

'I haven't,' Maggie replied without concern. 'I was going to ask for a sub.' She turned to Rosy. 'Take no notice of her, she still thinks we're in the dark ages. Are you coming?'

Rosy shook her head. 'I can't. You know I've got Nicky to put to bed.' Had she been free she would not have gone. She had never been able to understand how Maggie could find enjoyment by spending an entire evening drinking and smoking.

'They've got to let you have some time off, you know. It can't be legal the hours you put in.'

'I'm happy with the situation. So I don't see it should matter to anybody else,' Rosy countered pointedly. Mr Hardaker was always reminding her that she was allowed to have time off and she knew she only had to ask. But there was nothing she wanted to do and she was content to be there with Nicky. She always felt needed when she was with Nicky.

Maggie stood up and tossed the half-eaten apple into the coal bucket. 'Have you got five bob I can borrow?' she asked her mother.

'Of course Mum hasn't got five bob you can borrow!' Rosy put in angrily, scowling at her sister. 'And if she had she wouldn't be giving it to you to throw away.'

Maggie's sherbet pink lips pouted with disdain, then parted on a breathy sigh. 'You really should let yourself go, our Rosy. You act like an old woman – and a miserable one at that. It's this place. Working here, living here, you're never free of it. It'd be enough to turn a saint to drink.'

'Well it hasn't turned me to drink. So if you want one I suggest you go and find one by yourself.' Deliberately turning her back on her sister, Rosy put Dorothy Hardaker's dirty pots into the washing-up bowl. Then she wiped the spilled milk from the tray and put it away. It was almost Nicky's bedtime so John

Hardaker would not keep him outside much longer and she was desperate for Maggie to be gone before they came in.

Maggie seemed to get the message. With a shrug she turned for the door. 'I'll see you later,' she tossed at her mother.

'And don't make it too much later!' Nell returned pointedly.

When the door had closed and her sister was out of hearing, Rosy glanced at her mother. 'I thought she hadn't got any money,' she said drily.

Nell gave a snort. 'She'll find some . . . somewhere!'

And Rosy knew where – propping the bar up at The Derwent. Being penniless was not a condition that affected Maggie for very long. She knew the ways, and had the means, to get exactly what she wanted out of a man. Fortunately, Nicky and his father coming through the door stopped Rosy upsetting her mother further by putting that opinion into words.

'Mrs Hardaker asked if she could have the car tonight,' Rosy said, immediately turning her thoughts away from Maggie. She glanced at John Hardaker as she spoke, but did not look at him for too long for fear he gave her the reply, which she had no wish to pass on. Now the message had been relayed she wanted nothing more to do with it.

His lips thinned and it was a moment before he said, 'She knows I want it.' He spoke as if to himself, so no-one answered. 'Will you tell her . . .' he began. Then to Rosy's relief changed his mind. 'It doesn't matter . . . I'll tell her myself.'

As he went out of the door Rosy grimaced at her mother. Nell's reply was to tilt her eyebrows in a manner that said, here we go again!

CHAPTER TWO

'*Out!*' Dorothy Hardaker's voice echoed through the house.

Rosy stood at the stove heating some milk for Nicky's bedtime drink, and hoped the argument would be a short one. She guessed, correctly, that the single word had not been an order to John Hardaker to get out of his wife's bedroom, but that he had enquired where she was going. The answer had been the very brief, to the point reply.

There was what sounded like a pause, but Rosy knew it was where John Hardaker was speaking. Dorothy Hardaker's voice could not be missed, even over the distance between bedroom and kitchen, but her husband's voice was never heard to rise. Their arguments consisted of hearing Dorothy Hardaker's shrew-like screeching, punctuated by the silent spaces, which you could only guess were his replies.

'I'll go where I damned well please!' the woman persisted. 'And I don't ask *you* or anybody else for permission.'

Rosy was so busy listening in that she almost let the milk boil over. 'Oh . . . !' she gasped, sweeping the saucepan away from the gas only a moment before the expanding liquid erupted over the sides. As it was, milk went all over the draining-board and down the side of the mug as she tipped the remains quickly into it. 'Oh . . . oh . . . botheration!'

Nicky laughed and Nell's eyebrows rose knowingly. 'Curiosity killed the cat,' she said, standing up from bending over the grey tiled hearth to brush up the remains of a fallen coal. Putting the brush and dustpan

48

down she picked up the dishcloth and went to her daughter's aid. 'Here, let me.' She shoved Rosy out of the way. 'Have you got enough left?'

'Not really.' Rosy grimaced into the Mickey Mouse mug, which was only three-quarters full. She glanced at Nicky. 'Will you have an extra biscuit instead of a full mug of chocolate?'

'Two,' he replied cheekily, as she handed the mug of chocolate to him.

'One,' she repeated, taking the lid off the biscuit tin but holding it back. 'Three biscuits is enough for anyone to go to bed on.'

'I could stay up later,' he suggested.

The look of innocent hope on his face put a smile on Rosy's. His parents' argument was continuing in the background. His mother's voice was still, intermittently, screeching through the house. Yet he seemed not to care. In fact he was far more concerned with whether he was going to get one, or two extra biscuits. 'Go on then . . . take two.' Her heart melting she offered the tin to him and he dived in and came out with two digestives and two custard creams. 'And don't go being sick on me,' she warned pointedly.

He grinned, his mouth already too full of crumbs to reply.

Just then a mighty crash came from upstairs. Rosy's startled gaze pivoted to her mother. 'What the . . . ?' she began. But her words were cut short by the sound of shattering glass, followed by a volley of lesser bumps and crashes. In the next moment a frightened little gasp turned her attention back to Nicky. The mug of chocolate was suspended drunkenly in his hands. His mouth had dropped open and biscuit crumbs were pouring over his chin and onto the table, and his eyes were wide with fear.

'It's all right.' She was quickly by his side and took the mug from his grasp and put it down on the table, before its contents also spilled. Then she pulled his chair out and lifted him from it and hoisted him up in her arms. He buried his face against her shoulder and clung to her and she could feel his small body trembling. 'Someone must have knocked something over,' she said, offering what she hoped would be an acceptable explanation to him, at the same time as praying for peace to return to the house.

'Yes . . .' Nell began, but was brought to a halt by the noisy slamming of a door upstairs. Then the light running footsteps of Dorothy Hardaker were heard coming down the stairs and going straight out of the front door. Within seconds the car engine burst into life and it leaped off down the drive at a rapid pace.

For several heartbeats Rosy could only stare at her mother and Nell could only return the stunned gaze.

'Do you think . . . ?' Rosy began, jerking her head at the door leading into the hall and up the stairs. There was no sound to indicate John Hardaker was still in the house and she could not speak fully what was on her mind, not with Nicky there to hear.

Fortunately, Nell was on the same wavelength. She gave a nod. 'I think I'd better go and . . . er . . . see what wants clearing up.'

As her mother went out, Rosy sat down at the table and shuffled Nicky round to sitting on her knee. Wondering what was going to be found up there, she stared apprehensively at the door her mother had gone through, as if it might provide some answer. There was no sound, nothing from John Hardaker and her arms tightened protectively round Nicky. She couldn't have . . . ! But even as she thought the words, Rosy knew there were times when Dorothy Hardaker was capable of anything; times when she was afraid herself of the tiny woman's uncontrollable outbursts; times when she made sure Nicky never went anywhere near his mother's room.

'Finish your supper,' she said, gathering the

scattered biscuits and mug of chocolate and putting them in front of him.

'Where's my dad?' Despite his terror he had not cried, but now tears brimmed in his big brown eyes.

Feeling the same doubts and despair, Rosy cuddled him closer. He hadn't asked, where's my mum and dad, just my dad. 'He's upstairs,' she said. 'He'll be helping my mum to clear up whatever got broken.' The confidence of her voice belied the uncertainty she was feeling. 'Now come on.' She picked up the mug and put it into his hand. 'Get that down you. Or you're going to be late and you know what late means.' She affected a scowl. 'Grumpy in the morning!' she added meaningfully.

It was a weak smile that touched his lips, but it was a smile. She responded in kind, just as the door opened and a pale, slightly unsteady John Hardaker walked into the kitchen.

Rosy let out an audible breath of relief. She did not care if he heard, or what he thought. She really had imagined his wife had done something terrible to him and her relief was so potent it just had to come out.

'Are you all right?' she asked.

'I'll live.' He touched the far side of his head, then grimaced as he held bloodstained fingers up. 'Your mother said you would show me where the first aid box is.'

She did not have to put Nicky down. In an instant his mug of chocolate was plonked on the table, splashing chocolate raindrops on the cloth, and he was squirming off her knee and was across the room before she was on her feet. His top half vanished into the bottom of the ceiling-high oak cupboard standing by the back door and he came out with a small brown leather case.

'Sit down.' Rosy pressed John Hardaker into a chair and studied the wound on his head. His fingers had been covered in blood and she had expected something

51

much worse than the small, but deep cut half-concealed by the hair at his temple.

'It just needs a plaster to stop it bleeding,' he said, lifting his hand to once more touch the damp area.

'Stop it!' She pushed his hand away.

'Yes, Dad,' Nicky put in importantly, as he put the case on the table, clicked the twin fasteners and lifted the lid. He turned very seriously to his father. 'If you touch it with dirty fingers you'll get it infected. Rosy says so.'

John Hardaker glanced knowingly at Rosy and she bit her lip, not sure if he found his son amusing or annoying. But then he turned back to Nicky. 'So, Doctor Hardaker, who do you think has the cleanest fingers to deal with it?' he asked, duly serious, but with a suggestion of playfulness that brought relief to Rosy.

Nicky studied his own hands at great length, turning them first one way then the other. It was several seconds before he finally looked up. 'Rosy had better do it,' he said, equally seriously, making it impossible for her to conceal her amusement any longer.

There was a responding smile on John Hardaker's face when he looked up at her. 'So, Rosy Smith,' he said, with a strange intentness about him. 'Are you to be my angel of mercy?'

She was not sure why she blushed. It could have been the intimate way he had spoken her name; it could have been the unusually affectionate timbre of his voice; it could have been the way his eyes softened on her own. It was all so unlike him. Then the way he was acting with his son was unusual, she told herself, and, flustered with embarrassment, dived into the case and sorted out antiseptic, cotton wool and plasters.

Perhaps the bump on the head had affected him, she thought, as she went to the sink to wash her hands. But as she bathed and cleaned the wound, she reminded herself he had been acting differently with Nicky before the argument with his wife.

'You might have a scar,' she said, as she dabbed gently at the damaged area and tried to flatten a protruding piece of flesh. Whatever had hit him had had a sharp point which had forced the skin downwards and left it puckered. 'But it will be mostly hidden in your hair.'

'Aren't you going to stitch it up?' Nicky enquired.

Rosy shook her head. 'I can't do that. A doctor has to do stitches.' She paused and studied the wound. 'Perhaps you should go and get it looked at properly,' she said, uncertainty clouding her voice. No matter what she did the puckered flesh would not lie flat. Part of it was still standing proud and, if it healed that way, he was going to have a permanent lump on the side of his head. A small lump, but nevertheless a lump, which would not all be hidden by his hair.

'It will be all right,' he insisted brusquely.

Rosy smiled thinly. Getting back to normal, she thought. The gravelly hardness had returned to his voice and, when she said, 'Perhaps you should have an X-ray,' the scowl that came to his face did not belong to the man who had been sitting in front of her these last few minutes. She gave a resigned sigh. 'Well, it was only a suggestion,' she said.

'I am perfectly all right,' he assured in an insistent growl. 'I have no need of further treatment, and no intention of going anywhere where I should have to answer a hundred and one questions before I even got through the door.'

Rosy gave another sigh. It was more a matter of it having to be all right, she realized. If his ear had been hanging off he would not have got professional help. His wife had done it and he wasn't going to go admitting that to anyone. She did not suggest he could have lied, but finished cleaning the cut and straightened it out best she could. Then she pressed a plaster tightly over the top, hoping it would provide a little pressure to hold the flesh flat while it healed.

'There . . . all done.' She collected all the bits of dirty cotton wool and dropped them in the bin. She made him a cup of tea and while she was waiting for the kettle to boil warmed up another saucepan of milk to make Nicky a fresh hot chocolate. Then she left father and son together with their drinks and went upstairs to help her mother.

'Good grief!' She stopped short, framed in the bedroom doorway, shock freezing on her face as she looked around the usually elegant crimson and cream room. 'What the devil was she doing?'

Straightening up from her dustpan and brush, Nell placed her hands on her rounded hips and gave a breathy sigh. 'God knows,' she said, looking round the shattered room in despair. Everything was upside down. The covers had been torn from the bed and the bedside cabinet was lying on its side, all its contents spilled over the floor. One of the wardrobe's double doors had been torn off its top hinge and was hanging precariously by the bottom one alone. Everything had been swept off the top of the dressing-table and perfume, make-up and a cloud of talcum powder were spread over the blood red carpet. And the dressing-table mirror was now reduced to one jagged, angry looking corner sticking up like a solitary stalagmite; the rest appeared to be scattered everywhere in lethal splinters. 'But I do know she needs help.'

She isn't the only one, Rosy thought, as she stepped forward, only to come to a grinding halt again, not knowing where to begin. 'What on earth made her do this?' Dorothy Hardaker had had many fits of shouting, but she had never resorted to this wanton destruction before. Now it was her mother's job to clean it up, she thought with annoyance. 'I'll go and get the vacuum.'

Nell gave a nod. 'We'll have to get the big bits up by hand first.' She bent down and returned to scraping bits of glass and pottery carefully onto the dustpan.

With the two of them working together the job was soon done and it was not much above half an hour later, when Rosy said, 'I can't see any more bits.' Switching off the vacuum cleaner she turned two full circles, first to study the carpet, then the whole room. The mess had all gone and the carpet was now clean. The bed had been re-made with fresh sheets and blankets – the others had been taken downstairs to be given a good shake to clear them of glass before being washed. The single dagger of glass had been removed from the dressing-table mirror and all that remained was the bare wooden back. The wardrobe door was still at a funny angle, there was nothing they could do about that, but the rest of the furniture had been put straight. The red and cream room had been returned to a certain normality.

'I hope it was a one off,' she said. But as she hooked a wayward strand of long blonde hair behind her ear she felt it was a vain hope. She could not believe that anyone who was fully aware of what they were doing would have committed this mayhem. 'I suppose this is going to be the order of things from now on,' she added bleakly.

'She's more to be pitied than blamed,' Nell said.

'I know.' Rosy fixed a meaningful gaze on her mother. 'But he can't expect you to be cleaning up messes like this on a regular basis. If it carries on something will have to be done.'

'Rosy . . . !' There was warning in Nell's voice. 'It's none of your business. I'm paid to do it, so I'll do it without complaint.'

'Yes, Mum.' Rosy forced herself to sound contrite, knowing it was what her mother wanted to hear. But, for all her sympathy for Dorothy Hardaker, she did not want to see her mother constantly clearing up after a mad woman. And, like it or not, what had been done in this room had been done by somebody not right in the head – no matter what reasons there were for the cause of it, she thought, as she pulled the plug from the socket on the wall and coiled the flex around the vacuum cleaner's stout, cylindrical body. She picked it up and put it away in the store cupboard under the stairs.

'How are you feeling?' she asked, when she returned to the kitchen.

John Hardaker looked up from the table, where he had been staring pensively into his empty cup. 'I'm fine. It's nothing to worry about,' he replied shortly, his manner making it obvious he wanted the matter to be forgotten.

Rosy took the hint. Without speaking she went to the table to take the dirty cup away from him, using the action to give the wound on his head a surreptitious inspection. The plaster was still holding it firmly in place and it didn't look so bad. The colour had come back to his face and he did appear to be none the worse for the events of the evening.

He looked up then. 'Everything's back to normal,' she said, speaking quickly to hide her embarrassment at being caught staring at him. 'Except the wardrobe.' She whisked the dirty cup and saucer from under his nose and hurriedly carried it over to the sink. 'I'll get Ivan or Joey to fix it.' Ivan Fletcher was the gardener-cum-handyman. Joey was his younger brother, and his assistant.

'I'll take a look at it myself.'

Rosy's eyebrows lifted in surprise and she turned from the sink to stare at him in amazement, she was unable to stop herself. But . . . ! John Hardaker considering doing it himself! It was on her mind to ask if he knew which end of a screwdriver was which, but she thought better of it.

He smiled. 'I think I should be able to put a couple of screws in without much trouble,' he said, as if he had read her mind.

Rosy blushed so furiously that she had the feeling

the blood rushed up her face so fast it actually collided with her hair. 'I wasn't . . .' she began, then closed her mouth, realizing that what he was really saying was he preferred to do it himself rather than have everyone knowing what had gone off. 'Yes,' she agreed simply, and turned her attention back to Nicky.

His second mug of chocolate was empty, but he was still eating his biscuits. Or rather *a* biscuit, she corrected, seeing he now had a half-eaten fig biscuit in his hand, which he had not had before. 'How many of those have you had?' she demanded.

He looked sheepish, but Rosy got no further.

'I hope that's got it all out.' Nell came struggling through the back door with all Dorothy Hardaker's bedding clutched in her arms and dropped it on the table. She had taken it out the back to give it a good shake and her face was red and her mousy hair escaped in all directions from her bun. 'I've given it a good do.' Her work-roughened hands prodded and squeezed the bundle. 'I can't feel anything sharp.'

'I shouldn't worry about it.' John Hardaker stood up and thrust his hands deep inside his trouser pockets. His expression darkening, he added, 'It will serve her right if there is still glass stuck in there. Just make sure they only go back on *her* bed.'

He spoke with such feeling that Rosy's mouth dropped open and she stared at him in surprise. For all their arguments she had never before heard him utter one word against his wife.

'They'll be clean as a whistle when they go back on the bed,' Nell retorted, unable to conceal her indignation at the way he had spoken, her hands continuing to prod the sheets, now with more zeal than was necessary.

Rosy was too stunned to say anything. It was not like her mother to make her feelings known to John Hardaker, no matter how much she disagreed with what he had done. But at that moment she was angry with him and she was letting him know it, even though it was also obvious she was not easy with the situation. Whenever Nell was uneasy she bustled round like a bear with its tail on fire. And she was bustling now. The sheets had been prodded and turned and turned and prodded, her pinny straightened and her hair smoothed down several times, before John Hardaker spoke again.

'I'm going out,' he announced, turning for the door. But then he paused and hovered uncertainly, for a moment studied his toes. 'Thank you.' He looked first at Nell, then to Rosy.

Nell gave a shrug. 'There's nothing to go thanking me for. It's my job. You pay me to do it.'

He shook his head, a thin smile stretching his lips but not reaching his eyes. 'It isn't your job to have to clear up messes like that. I'll have a word with her when she gets back.' He hesitated. 'I hope you won't have anything like it to do again.'

'It doesn't matter, Mr Hardaker,' Nell was quick to reply. 'It's a shame so much got broken but the clearing up was no trouble to us. You haven't got anything to apologize for.'

His smile stretched a bit further but still did not touch his eyes. He gave her a nod, then glanced briefly at the table. 'Good night, Nicky,' he said, and turned away and was gone almost before the boy had time to reply.

Rosy looked at her mother and tilted her eyebrows. *Nothing to apologize for!* she thought. Her mother was soft, but there was no changing her. Of course they had to clean up all the messes, no matter what the Hardakers decided to do. But they weren't slaves and didn't have to do it with total compliance. They had voices and they could make themselves heard. Not that her mother would ever have opened her mouth to complain.

'Come on, you!' She suddenly leapt on Nicky and swept him off the chair, where he had been silently observing it all. 'You're already forty minutes late for bed. Get up those stairs.' She began to tickle him and he collapsed in giggles. 'It's very strange how you can go quiet at eight-thirty every night. It never happens at any other time of day.' He was still giggling as she dragged him out of the door and up the stairs.

After Nicky had been bathed and put to bed, Rosy returned to the kitchen to find her mother sitting at the table reading John Hardaker's newspaper. 'You still here?' she questioned with surprise. After the evening meal was over and cleared up, Nell usually retired to the cottage until the following morning.

'I thought I'd hang on until he gets back. Just in case she arrives home before him.' She glanced pointedly at her daughter and folded the newspaper up and put it down.

Rosy's smile filled with affection. She went to her mother and wrapped her arms around her neck and pressed her cheek to hers. 'There's no need to hang on,' she said. She knew she was only staying because she did not want to leave her daughter alone in case Dorothy Hardaker came back first and was funny with her. 'I'm not afraid of her.'

'I know that!' Nell replied drily. 'Well, maybe you should be a bit frightened of her. Whatever happens between the two of them, she is still mistress of this house and, as such, has the power to hire or fire you at will.'

'You're worrying over nothing, Mum.' Rosy let go of her mother and walked to the window and gazed out. The sun had dipped below the horizon and was out of sight, but its final fingers stretched a ruddy hue over the western sky. The river ambled past in an elegant glide, the surface blinking silver white and pewter grey as it rippled gently beneath the darkening sky. The cows in the meadow on the far bank grazed with a laziness that seemed to be unaffected by the coming night and was almost hypnotic. Everything looked so peaceful. There was nothing to show that earlier the house had been a battle ground. Rosy shook her head in disbelief. 'She's got all this and she can't see how well off she is!'

'Losing a child has a terrible affect on a mother,' Nell said, moving to her daughter's side. 'Some manage to hide it, some don't. But however they handle it, whatever they show to the world, it's something they never get over.'

'What about Nicky?' Rosy asked. 'She hasn't lost him. She's thrown him away. It was her who turned her back on him. She doesn't care if *he's* alive or dead. And she acts that way because she lost Guy?' she added, unable to conceal her incredulity.

'No, I'm not saying that. What I'm saying is don't judge her too harshly. They'll not find him now.' Nell paused sadly. 'That poor woman's got to live the rest of her life wondering what happened to the poor little mite.'

'I know.' Rosy's voice was flat with resignation. 'What worries me is where she will end up. Because I think it is too late – that even if they found anything of little Guy she couldn't change now. She's gone too far. But I can never forgive her for the way she treats Nicky.'

Nell nodded her head and gave her daughter's arm several affectionate little pats. 'But don't be too hard on the woman. What goes round comes round. And being hard on others only gets the same back.'

'Nell Smith you're soft. But I love you!' Rosy shook her head in despair, but there was a smile on her face and she flung her arms around her mother and held her tight.

'You daft lump, get off me!' Nell flapped her arms

and tried to shove Rosy away. 'Get off! You're suffocating me.'

Rosy laughed and let her mother go, and wished all children could have a mother who cared as much as her's did.

CHAPTER THREE

After that evening Dorothy Hardaker's wrecking sprees became a regular occurrence. Before the week was out her bedroom was clear of breakable ornaments. They had all been thrown at the wall or used as missiles against her husband. The only thing she now had to throw was the crockery on the tray that was delivered to her every mealtime. Nell had soon stopped sending her the best china and gone out and got a stack of cheap pots, which didn't suit Dorothy Hardaker at all. But her husband told her in no uncertain terms it was all she was getting.

She was also put straight about the dressing-table mirror, which was replaced once only to be immediately broken again. The second time it was repaired John Hardaker warned her it would not be done again.

Rosy thought he was being a bit hard on Dorothy because, when in a rage, his wife was incapable of knowing what she was doing. But she was proved wrong. The dressing-table mirror was needed for all the preening and prancing she did before going out in the evening. So during further outbursts Dorothy Hardaker had been very careful to aim all her missiles in the opposite direction and keep her mirror safe.

'I don't understand,' she said, to her mother. 'She knows exactly what she's doing and could stop herself if she wanted to.' It was a disturbing realization.

The evenings out also became more frequent and now every night Dorothy Hardaker would insist on having the car. No-one knew where she was going. But she never returned until at least midnight, or, more often, the early hours.

She also began to spend money as if it was going out of fashion. New dresses, suits, shoes and underwear all appeared. Some to be worn only once, then handed to Nell to consign to the dustbin.

'Look at this!' Nell help up a black taffeta cocktail dress with a matching jacket.

'It's beautiful!' Rosy was gazing admiringly at the dress, just as John Hardaker came through the door.

He hesitated, taking in the open longing in her eyes. 'Have it if you want it,' he said.

She looked up in surprise. 'Oh no,' she said, shaking her head. 'I couldn't. I really couldn't.'

'Why not?'

It was such a simple question, yet one she found difficult to answer. 'Well . . .' she began, with an embarrassed shrug. 'It's . . . well . . . I wouldn't have anywhere to wear it.' It wasn't that she didn't want the dress: it was beautiful and far beyond her own pocket and she would have loved to own it – even if it was only to see it hanging in the wardrobe. But she wasn't sure how Dorothy Hardaker would react to having her clothes given away without her knowledge.

She turned to her mother for help, but realized she was wasting her time if she expected to find a reason for not having the dress there. Nell was already busy holding it up in front of her, measuring it up against her body. She either did not see, or chose not to see the uncertainty on her daughter's face.

'It would fit you,' she said, the pleasure of the statement oozing from her voice.

'Yes . . . Mum . . . but . . . ! It would be a waste to just stick it away in a cupboard and never let it see the light of day.'

'It'd be a bigger waste to chuck it in the dustbin!' Nell exclaimed with feeling.

'Well . . . yes . . .' Rosy was still reluctant.

63

'You should keep it,' John Hardaker said. 'It would go well with the colour of your hair. And you might have a reason to wear it, in the future.'

It wasn't what he said, so much as the way his gaze lingered on her waterfall-straight blond hair that made her feel uncomfortable. She felt heat creeping up her cheeks and wanted to get away before her embarrassment was noticed. 'I'll try it on before I make my mind up,' she said, quickly taking the dress from her mother and hurrying from the room.

Dorothy Hardaker was several inches shorter than Rosy and the skirt was on the short side. But in every other way dress and jacket fitted like a glove.

It could have been made for me, she told herself, as she inspected her reflection in the small dressing-table mirror. She opened the wardrobe to get a better view in the full length mirror on the inside of the door. 'Oh dear!' she murmured, running her hands down the luxurious fabric of the pencil slim skirt, fingering the tiny pearl buttons that secured the short, waist-clinching jacket. She had to have it, whether Dorothy Hardaker objected or not. It was like nothing she had ever owned before. It was a woman's dress and just putting it on made her feel like a woman.

She stood on tiptoe and turned a full circle, just as there was a tap on the door.

'Mr Hardaker!' she gasped, unable to conceal her surprise when she half-opened the door to find him standing there. She had not dared to open it completely for fear it was his wife who would see what she was wearing.

'Does it fit?' he asked. He made no move to enter, but his eyes ran up and down the length of the dress that was visible to him. Rosy felt heat creeping into her cheeks.

Keeping her hand firmly on the half-open door, she gave an embarrassed little nod. 'It's a bit short. I don't think it will turn down, so maybe I shouldn't keep it.'

'Let me see.' Putting one finger against the door he pushed it fully open. He was not exerting any real strength but, although she felt uncomfortable with the situation, she also felt rather silly, and she stood back and let the door swing wide, not knowing what else to do.

'Nonsense!' he exclaimed, looking her up and down once more, before bringing his gaze to rest on her wide, uncertain blue eyes. He broke into a smile. 'It looks wonderful,' he assured, and let his eyes return to linger on her slender legs and the short hemline that showed all of her shapely knees. 'When you are seen in that you will start a new fashion. One I will very much approve of,' he added, his gaze again lifting to her's and his smile broadening.

The colour in her cheeks increased rapidly and she clutched at the door again and held it ready to close on him, if he should make a move to step over the threshold. Which, at that moment, she had the distinct impression he might do.

'Well, if there was nothing else . . .' She glanced pointedly at her watch. 'I'd better be getting ready to fetch Nicky.' It was another hour before Nicky would be coming out of school, but it was the best excuse she could come up with on the spur of the moment.

He gave a nod and sucked on his bottom lip for a moment. 'You will keep the dress?' he finally said.

She wasn't sure if it was a question or an instruction. All the same she gave a quick nod and began to swing the door to. 'So I'd better get out of it before I mess it up,' she said, a moment before the door closed with him still standing there. With a sigh she fell back against it and pressed her ear to the wood, listening for the gentle pad of his footsteps walking away over the carpet. There was nothing, not even the smallest sound to indicate he had gone. She looked down at the shiny brass knob and half-expected to see it turn before her eyes. It remained still and she lifted her hand and, careful not to make too much noise, slowly turned the key in the lock.

There was a slight click, which must have carried to him, for a moment later she did hear his footsteps walking along the landing and down the stairs. With another sigh she pushed herself upright. She wondered just exactly what he had had in mind. Or had he had anything in mind? Had she overreacted? He hadn't actually done anything. He'd only looked at her, for heaven's sake!

Pulling the wardrobe door fully open she stared at her reflection, and grimaced. The dress made her look like a woman and, to begin with, wearing it had made her feel like a woman. But she certainly hadn't acted like one.

'Oh damnation!' she muttered with feeling. What had she done? All he had been doing was coming to make sure she was keeping the dress, because in the kitchen she had made it clear she was in two minds. She scraped her fingers through her hair and gave a groan of self-derision. The dress had been paid for by his hard earned money and wanting her to keep it had only been protecting that. His reaction had been nothing more than a desire not to see his cash wasted by being thrown in the dustbin. And she had acted like an idiot. What must he be thinking?

'You're nineteen years old, girl,' she reminded herself firmly, and took the dress off and hung it carefully in the back of the wardrobe. She pulled on a more suitable outfit of blue dirndl skirt and white sleeveless blouse and felt more at ease in her ordinary clothes. But not so much at ease that she did not sneak down the stairs and out of the front door like a thief. Being especially quiet as she passed the door to the study, where John Hardaker conducted the property deals that provided him with his comfortable lifestyle.

*   *   *

66

The weather had not been particularly good that year but the day was one of the rare warm ones, with high clouds like fluffy white sheep skipping across a blue sky. It was the type of day that put a smile on everyone's face and made the main topic of conversation their hope that it would stay until the end of the month and the annual summer holidays.

'Hi there,' Sue Wheeldon called, as Rosy and Nicky walked through the door of the newsagent's and sweet-shop her father owned. 'I was hoping to see you.' Her rosy cheeks puckered in a broad smile. 'Me and Jean and Annie have booked a caravan at Southport for the first week of the hols. It sleeps four. Do you want to come with us?'

'The first week of the holidays?' Rosy replied in-terestedly, as she lifted the lid of the ice-cream cabinet for Nicky to make his choice. 'I'll have a choc-ice,' she told him. It would be nice to get away, she thought, as he scrambled to reach to the bottom of the cabinet. The four girls had been friendly since schooldays and, though not so often now she had the responsibility of Nicky, she still enjoyed the occasional night out with them.

'It'll be great,' Sue assured, then leaned over the counter to peer up at Rosy from beneath her thick brown fringe, and say confidently, 'I've got myself a new swimsuit . . . a bright red bikini.'

Rosy laughed. 'I'd like to come. If I can stand the competition,' she added jokingly, as she handed Nicky's ice lolly and her own choc-ice across to Sue. 'But I'll have to check with Mr Hardaker first.' The local annual holidays were the last week of July and the first in August. She could not think of any reason John Hardaker would stop her going, but she had to ask him first, before making any definite arrangement.

'Righty oh,' Sue replied, as she took the money and tipped it into the till.

Enjoying the sun, and their ice-creams, Rosy and

Nicky took their time and walked slowly across the meadow filled with grazing black and white cows.

'Gordon Gregory's going to Skegness for his holidays,' Nicky suddenly announced. 'Can we go there?'

The weather had even affected the children, Rosy thought, smiling fondly into the big eyes looking up at her with such pleading. But she had to say, 'I don't think so, love.' With the situation between his parents being as fraught as it was, the last thing they would be thinking about were summer holidays. It was no good allowing his hopes to rise, only to have to squash them later. 'I don't think your mum would like Skegness,' she added, seeing his face instantly crumple. Dorothy Hardaker was more the French Riviera type, but they wouldn't be going there either, at least not together.

'I don't want *her* to come,' he said with feeling.

Rosy frowned at him. 'You know that's not a very nice thing to say about your mum.' Her voice was stiff with warning, even though she understood why he felt that way.

Taking no notice of the reprimand, he said, 'We could go with dad. Dad would like Skegness. Gordon's dad does.'

'Oh no!' The words flew from her lips. The earlier events of the afternoon suddenly returned to her mind and she could see Nicky's innocence creating a very embarrassing situation for her.

'Why not?' he asked, looking at her oddly.

'Well . . .' She hesitated, feeling heat warming her cheeks that was nothing to do with the sun. 'I don't really think your dad would like Skegness, either,' she put in hurriedly, attempting to cover her embarrassment and not succeeding.

Nicky scowled. 'It's you,' he insisted darkly. 'You don't like Skegness and you don't want to go.'

'No it isn't, love.' She crouched down and pulled him into her arms. 'It isn't anything like that,' she said, and stroked a consoling hand over his mop of brown curls. 'People don't just go off on holiday together. It wouldn't look right if I went with you and your dad, and your mum didn't come. You'll understand better when you're older,' she added, even though she hated speaking the words. It had always infuriated her when her mother had pushed off some question with: 'You're not old enough to know,' or 'you're too young to understand.' But Nicky *was* too young to understand the full implications of what he was saying, and she was worried if she said too much to him he might repeat it to his father.

'Besides, your dad is very busy at the moment. So I don't want you going asking him and pestering him!' She fixed him with a pointed gaze, hoping the message had got across. After the way John Hardaker had looked at her earlier, the last thing she wanted was Nicky going to him and putting ideas into his head. 'So will you promise me you won't do that?' she asked.

He gave a nod. 'Yes,' he said, looking totally crestfallen. 'I promise.'

'Good boy.' She gave him an affectionate squeeze, before standing up again and continuing on their way.

As they reached the steps at the far end of the path, which took them up to the higher level of the road, they bumped into the short, plump form of Frances Hallsworth coming bouncing in the opposite direction. Frances, or Franny to her regulars, was the landlady of The Derwent. Franny always bounced, whatever she was doing. She seemed to have an endless supply of energy just bursting from her. ' 'lo Rosy. Hi there, young man,' she called.

Nicky realized he was in for a long wait and skipped down the bank to the fence of the railway line, so he could get a better view of any passing trains.

'Hello, Franny.' Rosy leaned on the steps' wooden railing, also knowing what was to come and making herself comfortable for it. You could never get past Franny without having to go through a third degree to find out if you knew anything she didn't – which was almost impossible. When it came to the village Franny's head was like an encyclopedia. She knew everything that was going off, everybody, and everything about them. If she didn't she made it her business to find out. In fact, when she was standing behind the bar, she had become a mother confessor to her customers, always ready to listen with a sympathetic ear, or give a bit of advice if it was needed.

'What's a matter with Dorothy?' she asked, rowing right in and pulling no punches.

Rosy gave a shrug. 'I wasn't aware there was anything the matter with her,' she replied. She had no intention of relating the secrets of Derwent House to anyone, but least of all to a gossip like Franny.

'She's taken to coming in for a drink most nights.' Franny's ruddy face dimpled with unaccustomed indignation. 'Don't like to see a woman drinking on her own. It's not right. An' she can't half knock it back!'

'In The Derwent!' Rosy was stunned. She knew Dorothy Hardaker's evening excursions took her drinking, you could smell it on her when she came back. But she hadn't thought she would be doing it on her own doorstep.

She wondered if Mr Hardaker knew. 'Does she come in every night?' Despite not wanting to get into a personal conversation, she had to ask.

Franny nodded, and a strand of silver-blond hair fell out of the bun piled high on top of her head to add inches to her shortness. 'Not every night, but she appears more often than not.'

Rosy gave a grimace. 'And she comes in the car,' she said, as if speaking to herself. All the rows and fights they had gone through because she insisted on having the car . . . to go no further than the bottom of the drive and across the road!

'I don't know about that.' Franny took on an expression of great shock. 'But if she does I'll tell you this

. . . she isn't fit to drive by the time she leaves. And I'll tell you another thing, she doesn't always leave on her own!'

'Oh damn!' Rosy scraped frustratedly at her long hair. 'Have you told Mr Hardaker this?'

'Nay, lass, I'd never tell him a thing like that!' Franny's back and shoulders stiffened with indignation.

A crooked smile pulled at Rosy's lips. 'No,' she replied, even though she was not convinced. Franny would say anything, if it was of benefit to her. She blew a breathy sigh. If Dorothy Hardaker was putting her life in danger by driving after drinking too much, then her husband should be told. There would be no point trying to talk to her. She wouldn't listen to her – just tell her to keep her nose out and mind her own business. John Hardaker was the one, but even he didn't have much hold on his wife now. Besides, before he could do anything someone had to tell him, and she did not want to be that someone.

'Are you sure John hasn't seen anything for himself?' Franny asked, staring into Rosy's eyes with an intense compassion that made her appear like a mother hen and would, in other circumstances, have made Rosy smile.

As it was, she only shook her head. 'I don't know,' she replied honestly. She paused, considering the likelihood of John Hardaker already knowing the truth. 'He can't know.' If he did, surely he would have stopped her, she thought, as she watched Nicky waving frantically to the guardsman of a train that had just passed by.

Franny reached out and laid a hand on her arm. 'Well somebody should put their spoke in, or she'll end up killing herself.'

Rosy wasn't so sure, but she did not say so. She gave a nod and, eager to end the conversation, called Nicky back and said goodbye to Franny.

What a day, she thought, as they walked down the

71

lane towards home. First the dress and Mr Hardaker coming to her room like that. Now this.

'*Can we go for a walk after tea?*' Nicky tugged impatiently on Rosy's arm and she realized, from his frown and the tone of his voice, that she had been ignoring him.

'Yes, if you like.' She smiled down at him.

But he was not placated. His frown deepened to a glower. 'You weren't listening to me!' His bottom lip protruded in a petulant curl. 'I had to ask you three times!'

Rosy's smile expanded, but only with affection. There were times when he was so tough, and times when he was so sensitive the least little thing cut him to the core. 'I'm sorry.' She gave his hand a loving squeeze. 'I was deep in thought. I won't do it again. Where do you want to go for a walk?'

'Through the woods,' he replied without hesitation, and, his moodiness forgotten, began chattering ten to the dozen.

But despite her assurance that she would not do it again they hadn't gone far before Rosy was only half-listening. Her mind was taken up with worrying about Dorothy Hardaker and what she was doing to herself, and to her husband and son.

'We can have a swim before tea, as well,' Nicky suggested eagerly.

'That sounds like a good idea to me,' she agreed, and he began chattering again. She heard how Philip Fletcher had tripped up and tipped a jar of dirty paint water all over Susan Bartram's skirt; how Carol Turner had jabbed a pencil into her brother's hand and the lead had broken off and Peter had had to be taken down to the doctor's to have it taken out; all about the horrible dinner he had been made to eat; she was even aware enough to praise him when he said he got a red star for a picture he had drawn of a boat.

But then Dorothy Hardaker and her problems got

the better of her again and she did not hear about the game of football at dinner time, or the biscuits Mrs Tomlinson, his class teacher, had brought for everyone because it was her birthday. Neither was she aware of the tightening of his grip as they crossed the bridge, or the way he changed from her left to her right when they turned down the drive, so he was on the opposite side to the river. Not until Joey Fletcher's voice broke into her troubled thoughts did she wake up to the moment.

'Want to see what I've got?' Joey called from the gatehouse cottage, as they passed by.

'Yes please!' Nicky replied excitedly.

Rosy was too concerned at seeing Joey coming out of the tiny grey stone cottage door, bold as brass, to find any enthusiasm about anything he might have. 'What are you doing in there?' she gasped, holding Nicky back as his eagerness transported to his feet and he tried to drag her forcefully to the gate. 'How did you get in?' She looked at Joey sternly. The cottage had stood empty since Phoebe's death. 'You haven't broken a window – have you?'

'I wouldn't do that, Rosy.' Despite his reassurance his face looked rather sheepish below his mop of black hair and she had the awful feeling he was up to something he shouldn't be. Although Joey was twenty-two, and built like a battleship, he had a mental age of twelve and you had to watch him. Not that there was any harm in him, the watching was for his own safety, rather than anyone else's. Joey might be a giant but he was a gentle one.

'Did you climb through a window?' she asked, and suddenly thought it might be wise for her to take a look inside the cottage and find out what he was up to. With that thought in mind she finally allowed Nicky to pull her across to the gate.

'No!' Joey insisted, his healthily tanned face crumpling in a frown. 'I got through the door,' he said, and fished deep inside the pocket of the navy blue boiler suit he always wore for work. A moment later he proudly announced, 'I've got the key,' and his frown changed to a grin of pleasure as he held up a large, multicoloured woollen pompon with the key dangling from it.

'Where did you get that?' Rosy could not believe her eyes. 'You'll have to give it back.'

'No!' It was almost a wail and Joey quickly shoved the key and pompon back in his pocket, as if he thought she was going to snatch it off him. 'Mr Hardaker, he gave it to me,' he said plaintively. 'Said I could have the cottage for my den.'

'What?' First her eyes, now her ears were deceiving her.

'Are you coming in to see what I've got?' Turning his attention away from Rosy he directed the question at Nicky.

'Yes.' Nicky looked pleadingly at Rosy. 'Come on!' he urged. 'I want to see!'

'All right,' she finally agreed. John Hardaker had obviously said something that had totally confused Joey. So she had better find out exactly what he was doing there, then go and find Ivan and get him to come and sort things out. She wasn't going to get any sense out of his daft brother.

But it was not many moments after stepping through the door into Phoebe's old kitchen, before Rosy was taking back the last, unchivalrous thought. Joey was not daft. He might be a bit backward, but that was all it was. The cottage had not been touched since Phoebe's death, yet he had cleaned it all up and there was not one cobweb left to see. In the middle of the floor was Phoebe's old kitchen table and on it was a selection of boxes, tins and jars, all neatly arrayed as if they had been put in their specific places.

Rosy looked more closely. From the largest box was coming a persistent squeaking noise. But she did not mention it. Joey was grinning like the Cheshire cat and she did not want to spoil his moment of revelation. Another box was filled with grass and moss and a third contained leaves and twigs. A jamjar was home to an assorted family of gnats and bugs, and a tobacco tin without a lid was squirming with worms. Her nose curled with distaste when she saw the last.

'Agh . . . ! Joey!' she gasped. 'What are you doing with those?'

'They're for my babies,' he said proudly, and lifted the lid of the large box to reveal a bird's nest, complete with five chicks. 'They're blackies,' he said. Then added, 'Blackbirds,' just in case they had not understood the first description.

All the tiny birds had the beginnings of darkish, shiny feathers, but they were not very obvious and Rosy wondered how he could be so sure what they would look like when they had grown. The most prominent view was the pink tongues inside the wide open mouths that were begging for food at the same time as making the continual demanding noises.

'Where did you get them?' Nicky enquired, his eyes widening with glee.

'Oh Joey!' Rosy bit her lip and scraped her fingers through her hair. She did not want to spoil his pleasure, but . . . ! 'You can't . . . you shouldn't have taken them from their mother,' she said worriedly.

'I wouldn't do that, Rosy.' Joey's pale eyes filled with intense hurt. 'Their mother was dead. If I'd left them they'd have died. That's why I brought them here. I know you don't have to touch them otherwise. Our Ivan's told me that.' He lifted one of the tiny birds, holding it in his work-roughened palm with a gentleness Rosy would not have thought possible for such big, paw-like hands. Then he picked up a small wriggling worm and dropped it into the gaping mouth.

The worm was gone in a second and he glanced up sheepishly. 'I don't like doing that,' he said, with a concern that tugged at Rosy's heart. 'It's not very nice for the worms, but the babies need live food. They'll die without it.'

'Oh Joey!' Rosy uttered emotionally, all her previous irritation and impatience now gone. 'How do you know that?'

'I know all about birds,' he said, putting the chick back in the nest and taking another one out. 'And animals,' he added, as he sent a second worm to its doom. 'I like them so I read all about them. Our Ivan tells me a lot, as well.'

Rosy shook her head, not knowing what to say. She didn't know if he really had been given permission to use the gatehouse cottage for his aviary, but she would speak to John Hardaker and find out the truth before she upset Joey by telling him he had to move himself, and his flock.

After giving Nicky a few more minutes to look at the baby blackbirds, she dragged him away. But not before he had made her promise to let him come down and see them at regular intervals.

The kitchen was empty when they got back to the house. Coal lay ready in the grate, but a fire was not needed during the day in the present heat, so Nell never lit it until early evening.

'Go and get out of your school clothes,' Rosy instructed, giving Nicky a gentle shove towards the hall door. 'I'll have a drink ready for you when you come down.'

He went without complaint, and Rosy was pouring orange squash into his mug, when she heard the office door opening. A moment later John Hardaker came into the kitchen.

'I was looking for your mother,' he said, standing right behind her so she had to turn round to see him properly. 'Where is she?'

Rosy gave a shrug. 'I don't know. We only just came in.' She looked him up and down. He was wearing a

76

dark grey suit, which looked much too warm for the present climate. 'I found Joey in the gatehouse,' she went on without thought. 'Did you know he's moved in? He said you'd given him the key but I told him he must have got it wrong, that you would have said something else.'

'I did give him the key,' he replied, his tone making it obvious he saw nothing odd in doing so.

'But he's moved in. He thinks you've let him have it for his den.'

He gave a dismissive shrug. 'He's got his words mixed up. I said he could have it for his shed.'

She rubbed at her forehead, trying to find some sense in what he was saying. 'Do you think that is wise?' she finally asked.

He gave another shrug. 'He can't do any harm to it. It pleased him to be given a place of his own; like Ivan's shed.'

'Then why didn't you give him one of the old stores?', she asked pointedly.

On the far side of the yard was a row of buildings that had been a stable block and store-rooms. The stables had been turned into a garage. Ivan's shed for his gardening and handyman tools was next to that. Then there were two other rooms, both used for the storage of odds and ends, which could all have gone into one, leaving the other free for Joey's shed.

'He would be a lot safer up here,' she added seriously. 'Where we could see what he was doing and keep an eye on him.'

'He was happy to have the gatehouse!' John Hardaker replied, in a manner that showed he did not expect to have his decisions questioned. 'I was happy to give him the gatehouse. I really don't think it concerns anyone else!' He laid particular emphasis on the last, causing her cheeks to flood with heat.

'I just thought . . .' her voice trailed away. It was not really any of her business. She was, what Nell would have called, overstepping the mark. Turning away from him she replaced the bottle top and put the bottle down on the table. Then she picked up Nicky's mug and went to the tap to fill it with water.

She had expected John Hardaker to have gone when she turned round, but he was still there, standing with head bent, looking down at the morning's newspaper that lay on the corner of the table. 'Will it be all right if I have the last week in July off?' she asked. It was as good a change of subject as any, she thought. And she did want to let Sue know quickly.

His head lifted sharply. 'Holiday?' he questioned, a frown forming on his brow.

'Yes,' she replied, a little uncertainly. It was the first time she had asked for more than a day off at a time, but she was entitled to holidays and she found his strange reaction disconcerting. 'To Southport,' she rushed out, as if she had to justify herself. 'With Sue and Jean and Annie . . . in a caravan.'

His features darkened. 'You mean it's all arranged? Without asking me first!'

'No. I haven't said I'll definitely go. I'm asking you first . . . now!' she added pointedly.

'Oh . . . I see,' he said. But as he turned from her and fixed his gaze on the black hole of the fire grate, she doubted he could see anything.

'I know it's short notice. But they've only just asked me.'

He rubbed thoughtfully at his chin and it was a moment before he looked round at her. 'So it isn't actually booked yet?'

'The caravan is booked. Sue asked me to go along to make it a foursome.' She was hoping that bit of information might twist his arm into saying yes. She could not understand why he was dragging his feet.

But he did not reply. His gaze returned to the dormant grate and his hand returned to rubbing his chin.

The silence seemed interminable and, unable to wait any longer, she said, 'I didn't think you'd mind when I had any holiday. It isn't as if you've got anything booked yourself.'

It at least prodded a response from him, but not the one Rosy wanted.

'I'm afraid you're wrong about that.' Taking his hand from his chin he rested it in the only space on the cluttered mantel, between the matching walnut clock and letter rack. 'I shall be away myself that week.'

'*You're* going on holiday!' She could not conceal her surprise.

'No,' he replied simply. 'It's business.'

'All week!' She had never known him be away for more than one or two nights. His business was all local and did not call for him travelling very far. 'Where to?' she asked suspiciously.

'A conference,' he replied bluntly, not explaining where the conference was taking place. 'I shall be away all week and I don't want you being away at the same time. It would be too much to expect your mother to look after Nicky, and do everything else,' he added, turning from the fire and striding out of the room, making it very obvious he considered the conversation at an end.

Rosy's anger was so great it did not occur to her that, with him away, her mother would only have had Mrs Hardaker and Nicky to see to.

CHAPTER FOUR

Rosy did not get her holiday. John Hardaker refused to give way and, though it annoyed Rosy to have to do so, she finally told Sue she would not be going along with them.

But Nicky had managed to get himself invited along with his friend Gordon. He had gone off yesterday with his bag clasped tightly in his hands, a huge smile on his face and so much excitement bursting from him he could have been going to the moon, instead of a week in a caravan at Skegness.

Rosy missed him desperately, but she was pleased the Gregorys had been kind enough to take him along. Life at Derwent House had not been exactly pleasant over the summer and she felt Nicky deserved a respite from all the tension.

Things had taken a definite turn for the worse over the past week. Dorothy Hardaker had started making regular visits to the pub at dinner time, as well as in the evenings. John Hardaker was furious but Dorothy would not listen to anything he had to say and their animosity increased, their arguments becoming louder and more volatile.

Whether it was the evening or the middle of the day, she never came home until they threw her out and she was so drunk she was a danger to herself and everyone else.

The car would be heard careering unsteadily up the drive and Rosy and Nell would give each other a telling glance, knowing she was back. Although they never spoke it, they both sent up a silent prayer that John Hardaker would keep a low profile and stay in his office.

Some days he did keep out of the way. Other days his anger got the better of him and he would be in the hall, waiting for his wife to step through the door. Then all hell was let loose.

Just the sight of him was a goad to Dorothy and the moment she saw him standing there she would begin spitting and hissing like an enraged cat. At the beginning she also picked up the nearest object and hurled it at him. But after the second occasion Nell made sure the hall was clear of all the ornaments and anything small enough to be thrown. So now they only had themselves to hurl at each other, which they managed to do with alarming ferocity.

It was not a happy atmosphere for anyone to live in and Rosy dreaded to think what affect it was having on Nicky. He didn't say much about it, but she had noticed he seemed to have unusually quiet, withdrawn moments, which she had to work very hard to make him snap out of.

A few days in Skegness with a boy of his own age would do him the world of good, she thought, as she reached the top of the hill and turned to look back through the trees towards the house. Having nothing to do, she had taken herself off up the fields and through the wood at the top of the bank behind the house.

It seemed strange to be on her own, not to have Nicky bounding about and leaping round, not to have his incessant chatter ringing in her ears.

When she reached the old cottage at the edge of the wood, she stopped. After finding a safe part, she sat down on the crumbling stone wall that surrounded what had been the front garden. It was now overflowing with brambles, and weeds and grass stood taller than the wall had originally been.

From there she had a good view of the whole village. Down to the left was the pub, standing by the stone bridge crossing the river which gave it its name, the

Derwent. On the opposite side of the river, the tall grey steeple of the church. Straight in front of her the meadow stretched across to the girls' school. To the right the cluster of the village, with its handful of shops and unconforming selection of tall houses and short grey stone cottages stretched along either side of the road to Derby.

It was all so peaceful. The sun was high and warmed her skin and she had the feeling she could have stayed there all day: dreaming; missing Nicky; hoping the weather was just as nice in Skegness. She lost count of time, but she judged she must have been sitting there for ten to fifteen minutes when she heard the first noise.

She turned her head and looked around, wondering what it could be. The bank was overrun by rabbits and it was not unusual to see a squirrel running up a tree. But it had sounded more like the grunt or snort of a badger, and badgers were night creatures and didn't often come out during the day.

She had turned to the other side and was peering into the wood's gloomy undergrowth, when she heard it again. This time it was more muffled and she strained her ears to catch it. But . . . ! She looked round in surprise. It was coming from the empty cottage.

With a deepening frown, she climbed off the wall and stood staring undecidedly at the remains of the peeling brown paintwork on the old door. She looked around. There was no-one to be seen and a sudden feeling of unease crept over her. For a moment she wondered if Joey had moved in up here, as well. But surely he was happily installed in Phoebe's old gate-house cottage. Whatever was inside had got there by its own devices and had not been put there by Joey.

It was best to go, she told herself. It was only an animal and, if it had got into the cottage without her help, it could get out again. The window panes had been smashed and the windows boarded over long before now. But the boarding did not completely cover the holes and there were plenty of places where an animal could have climbed through without any trouble.

It could get out again with the same lack of trouble, she assured herself, and turned to walk away, just as the sound came again – louder this time.

She stopped short and peered back over her shoulder. The cottage's state of dilapidation seemed to have grown since she had first arrived there. Its emptiness now shouted at her and increased her feeling of isolation. The sun suddenly lost all its warmth and her flesh felt cold, the tiny hairs standing on end as a shiver ran over her skin. She wanted to run and get away from that spot which suddenly seemed to be a million miles away from civilization. But a tiny voice at the back of her mind asked, 'Is it something in trouble?' and the question turned her feet to lead. The last sound had had a very distinct ring of pain about it.

She deliberated for only a second. Then she knew she had to take a look. If she walked away she would never know what she had left behind and she would for ever wonder if it had been something in pain, something she could have helped.

Closing her mind to the possible danger she was putting herself in, she crept quietly up to the nearest window. The wooden boarding had been nailed at a slant across the window frame and there was a reasonably sized opening to peep through at the bottom corner.

There was a large bramble beneath the window and she wrapped the full folds of her blue cotton skirt tightly round her legs so it would not get tangled in the thorns. Then, treading down the bramble so she had a flat spot to stand on, she placed her hands on the broad stone windowsill to steady herself on the uneven ground, and stretched up on tiptoe and peered inside.

The light inside was dismal and it took a few seconds before her eyes adjusted and she could make out what she was looking at. The walls were filthy and covered in cobwebs which made her shudder, thinking of the size of the spiders that had made them. On one wall was a small fireplace, filled with pieces of stone and soot that had fallen down the chimney. By the side of the fireplace was propped a broom and on the floor was a pile of dirt to indicate it had been put to use. Her eyes wandered across the floor. It was mucky, but it *had* been swept. She could see the streaks and lines left by the coarse broom.

Her eyes widened. She wondered who was silly enough to waste their time sweeping the floor, when the rest of the place was in such a state. She was halfway to thinking Joey must have moved in up here, as well, when her gaze reached the far side of the room and she had to push up further on her toes to peer round and see into the corner. In the next moment her eyes nearly popped out of her head.

On the floor was a large red tartan blanket. On the blanket lay a man, naked. At least what she could see of him was naked, which only amounted to his extremely hairy legs and a pair of very white feet. She assumed the rest of him was naked, because the woman straddled over him and hiding his top part from view was completely undressed.

Rosy's hand flew to her mouth to shut off the gasp that rushed from her throat. Her gaze froze on the man's hands as they clenched the woman's fleshy buttocks while she moved up and down on top of him. Up and down in a slow rhythmical pattern that caused him to groan and his fingers to dig deeper into her flesh.

A deep laugh rumbled low in the woman's throat and she curved her spine back and lifted her arms and stretched them up and over her head. The man gave another groan and his hands left her bottom and reached up in front of her to her breasts. She gave a little squeal, lifted her hair and tossed it over her shoulders, and squirmed with pleasure.

Rosy's head moved from side to side in slow, frozen disbelief. She could not pull her astonished gaze away from the long black hair that had obviously been ruffled by the hands now fondling her breasts. She did not have to see the oval mark of the large brown mole on her bottom, to know who it was.

Oh, our Maggie! she gasped in silent disbelief, as her senses returned with a jolt and finally gave her the strength to swing away from the window and stop looking. She had not wanted to see and could not understand why she had allowed herself to stand and watch like that. She wasn't daft and she knew well enough what their Maggie was, but she would have preferred not to have had it thrust under her nose in quite such a blatant manner.

In her rush to get away she almost lost her balance. Her feet got caught up in the bramble she was standing on, which suddenly leapt to life and sprang out in all directions. A sharp thorn tore painfully down her leg and she bit her lip to stop herself calling out and giving her presence away. The last thing she wanted was to be found out and to have them know she had seen them.

'Oh damn!' she muttered in a panicky whisper, as she tried desperately to extricate herself from the bramble's clutches and it kept fighting back. As fast as she loosened herself from one bit, another took hold. In reality it was only a few seconds before she was free, but it seemed like an eternity as the thorns clawed at her flesh like grasping fingers.

It was with a great sigh of relief that she finally stepped free. Then she crept quickly, but quietly down the overgrown path and out of the garden and vanished into the wood. Her legs were so sore she had the feeling they had been torn apart and must be dripping with blood. But she did not dare stop to look until she was well into the trees and the cottage was hidden from sight.

Not until she reached the gates to Derwent House and turned up the long drive did she suddenly stop and ask herself what she was doing? *She* had done nothing wrong. *She* had nothing to feel ashamed or guilty about. Yet she did feel guilty. In fact her body was crawling with a feeling of complicity, as if she had been a part of it, as if she was as much to blame as her sister and the man, whoever he might have been.

She hadn't been able to see enough of him to know who he was, but she knew she would not be on to a loser to bet he was married. Why else would they have been there, in the dirty cottage – doing that! Maggie, she thought sadly, wondering how her sister could allow herself to get into such depraved circumstances.

She was nearing the house when she heard the sound of an erratically revving engine. She turned around to see Dorothy Hardaker and the Rover come hurtling into the drive, its left side scraping noisily against the stone gatepost.

'Oh, no!' she gasped, watching in disbelief as the car swung from side to side of the tarmac drive, brushing the higher grass bank to the right and almost going over the edge of the lower one on the left. Rosy held her breath, fearing at any moment the car would veer off down the opposite bank and straight into the river.

She was so busy considering the safety of the car and its driver that she did not consider her own safety, until it was almost too late. As the unsteady vehicle approached her it suddenly swung right up onto the bank where she was standing.

Fortunately her reaction was instant. She leapt away, lost her footing on the slippery grass and landed on her back. But in all her panic she somehow found the sense to draw her knees up to her chest so she was in a ball, and her legs were safe when the car careered past, missing her by inches.

The terror of almost being mown down put strength in her limbs. Before the car had found its way back onto the drive she was on her feet and giving an angry shout, but Dorothy Hardaker was too busy fighting with the steering wheel to hear, as the car bumped and bounced along the bank before finally finding its way back to the terra firma of tarmac.

'I could have reached out and touched her and she never saw me!' Rosy spoke to herself, shock taking over from the momentary fury and trembling through her limbs. She could have been dead now, she realized, as she clutched her arms round herself and watched the car, by some miracle, get through the narrow courtyard entrance without hitting the solid stone wall on either side.

At other times Rosy wanted John Hardaker to be out when his wife arrived home, but today she hoped he was going to be there. What had just happened could not go on. It could have been Nicky on the drive. The thought of what could have happened increased the trembling in her limbs. Someone had to stop her, she told herself, and stepped carefully down the grassy bank and onto the drive. 'And John Hardaker is the only one who could do it,' she said, speaking out loud and tightening her arms around herself as she began walking up the drive.

'Just when you want him to be in.' Rosy dragged a chair from beneath the table and dropped onto it, a heavy sigh shuddering from her chest. Her mother had just informed her that John Hardaker had gone out some time before. 'Well, I'm not having that and I'm going to tell her myself.' By the time she had reached the house her fear had turned back into anger.

Nell turned worriedly from the sink and the potatoes

she was peeling. 'You can't,' she gasped. 'It's not your place.'

'Someone has got to do something,' Rosy insisted. 'She needs help. And all we're doing is standing back and watching her get worse and worse.'

'I know.' Leaving the half-peeled potatoes, Nell picked up a tea towel and wiped her hands. 'If she carries on like this much longer she'll kill herself one day.'

Rosy's expression darkened. 'What bothers me is that she'll kill someone else first. Probably more than one. Why does he let her do it?'

'It isn't for us to wonder why.' Nell set her hands on the table and gazed pointedly into her daughter's troubled blue eyes. 'She wouldn't listen to either you or me, so keep your nose out of it. It's up to him to stop her. If he wants to.'

'What do you mean?' Rosy eyed her mother suspiciously. 'Do you think he's hoping she'll kill herself?'

'No, I do not!' Nell snapped, her well padded frame stiffening in offence. 'And you'll do well to keep thoughts like that to yourself. What I was meaning was he lets her have her own way so he can have a quiet life.'

Rosy gave a snort of disbelief. 'A quiet life!' she scoffed. 'It's only the fact that he isn't in the house at this moment that is saving us from having to listen to yet another of their blazing rows!'

'Yes, well . . . there could be a lot more.' Nell went to the oven and peeped inside. 'And two wrongs don't make a right!' she added drily, and pulled out a bakewell pudding and a large egg and bacon flan.

The rich warm smell of fresh baking floated round the kitchen and filled Rosy's nostrils, and it was a moment before she asked, 'What do you mean by that?'

'I mean a paddy doesn't cure anything.'

'I am not throwing a paddy!' Rosy was greatly affronted by the accusation.

'In that case you can help me by fetching that vase of dahlias out of the drawing-room. I noticed this morning they were past their best. But I forgot to bring them out.'

Rosy opened her mouth to speak, then closed it again. The flowers had only been cut two days before and were perfectly fresh. She had checked their water herself that morning before dinner so she knew it was all right. She also knew it was just her mother's way of bringing the conversation to a close. Which meant she considered the matter finished and was not prepared to listen to one more word about it.

'Right!' she said, and spun round and hurried out. If she wanted the blessed flowers, she could have the blessed flowers, she thought mutinously. She swept into the drawing-room, grabbed up the large red and gold glazed Chinese vase in a manner that showed no consideration for its age or worth, and was on her way out again.

'Whatever do *you* think you're doing?'

Rosy came up short. She turned to find Dorothy Hardaker slumped in a very ungainly fashion in one of the high-backed leather chairs by the fire. It was a surprise. She usually never ventured into any room except her bedroom. It would be a surprise to her mother, as well. She would not have sent her in there if she had known the room was occupied.

'I said what do you think you're doing?' Dorothy Hardaker repeated impatiently.

For a moment Rosy could only stare at her, not knowing what to say. Even had Rosy not witnessed her driving home, it was obvious she was very drunk. Her voice was slurred and her eyes seemed to have a will of their own, she was having great difficulty keeping them focused on Rosy's face. She was also having a struggle to aim the cigarette in her hand at her mouth.

'I said . . . what do you think you're doing?'

she repeated yet again, the preciseness of her voice indicating great irritation.

'I'm taking the flowers to change their water!' Rosy forced her voice to a calmness she was far from feeling. Here was the chance to give Dorothy Hardaker a few home truths, but her mother's warning to not meddle was ringing loud in her ears, and she could only stand and look at the pathetic woman.

A bitter smile curled Dorothy Hardaker's lips and she tried once more to find her mouth with the cigarete. She managed it – after two attempts. Taking a long noisy draw, she screwed her eyes into bitter little slits, and spat out, 'Who do you think you are to look at me in that manner?'

Rosy shook her head in bewilderment. Go on and tell her, a little voice urged. But all she said was, 'I wasn't aware I was looking at you in any particular way.'

'Don't be so impudent!' She tried to get up, but failed and sat down heavily again. The cigarette fell from her hand and scattered ash over the carpet and she almost fell out of the chair and flat on her face as she leaned forward to retrieve it.

Rosy's stomach curled, partly with compassion, but also with a certain amount of disgust, as she looked at the sight the woman made. There was nothing that gave any indication of authority. At that moment Dorothy Hardaker lost all credibility in Rosy's eyes. All she could see was a pathetic drunk. Dorothy Hardaker! A drunk!

It was the first time Rosy had ever considered her to be an alcoholic, but she suddenly knew that was what she had turned into. It was a stunning realization.

'Are you waiting for something?' Dorothy Hardaker slurred nastily.

A tight smile pulled at Rosy's lips and she shook her head in disbelief. John Hardaker must have known before now what his wife was, but had done nothing about it. 'You nearly killed me when you came up the drive,' she said, realizing that if she did not speak up this could go on for ever. 'I managed to jump out of the way. But I'm not so sure my mum would have moved so quickly . . . or Nicky!' she added meaningfully.

Beneath the ruddy alcoholic flush Dorothy Hardaker's face blanched. 'Why you . . . !' she spat. 'How . . . how dare you speak to me in that way?'

'I dare because if I hadn't told you you nearly mowed me down you wouldn't know about it,' Rosy replied. She would not back down now she had begun and she plonked the Chinese vase down heavily on the china cabinet, the nearest thing to hand. The display of Crown Derby inside the cabinet rattled and shook from the force, but she did not notice. She turned squarely to Dorothy Hardaker. 'You can't go on like this.' Pulling herself under control and keeping her voice calm and even, she walked slowly towards the woman in the chair. 'You're killing yourself,' she said. If she didn't drive the car into the river, the amount of alcohol she continually drank would eventually poison her.

When she was standing in front of the chair she leaned forward and placed a hand on each arm, bringing her face closer to Dorothy Hardaker's. She hoped the position might give an aura of confidentiality, as if this was just between the two of them – woman to woman. She had to grit her teeth to stop her nose screwing up in disgust at the undesirable stench of second-hand gin. 'It was me standing there,' she said gently. 'And I had the sense to get out of the way when I saw you coming. But it could have been Nicky standing there. *It could have been your son!* And you still wouldn't have seen him!'

'Yes, I would!' Finding the strength of co-ordination from somewhere, Dorothy Hardaker straightened her spine and glared hatefully into Rosy's eyes. 'I would have known Nicky. I would have seen him.'

'What with?' Rosy enquired drily, having the feeling she was wasting her time. 'Don't try and tell me you can see anything properly at the moment.' She no longer cared if she was overstepping the mark, and she said, 'Even when you're sober you look straight through Nicky the way you look straight through everybody else.' She shook her head in disgust.

Dorothy Hardaker screwed her mouth into a bitter line that was so tight her lips became almost invisible. For several seconds her eyes fixed Rosy's with a cool mutiny. Then they suddenly lit with a spark of malicious glee and, with lightning speed, she crushed the glowing end of the lighted cigarette against the back of Rosy's hand as it lay on the chair.

A painful scream tore from Rosy's mouth and she tugged her hand free. She was so angry she was beyond conscious thought and her other hand came up and back automatically, ready to strike the smirking smile from Dorothy Hardaker's face. But before she could swing her hand forward her wrist was grasped and she was brought to a standstill. The next moment her arm was forced down and her body pulled backwards until the curve in her spine was so great she feared it might snap.

'Let me go!' she screamed, straining to get free from her unknown captor, who had entered the room so silently she had not known they were there. 'She had no right to do that. Let me get at her!'

'No!' That it was her mother's voice increased Rosy's anger and she fought harder to get free. But Nell held her fast and Rosy was stunned by her mother's strength. No matter how she pulled or twisted her arm, her wrist remained imprisoned in Nell's grasp, and the burning in her right hand was becoming so intense she could not use it to help get away.

'Let me go, Mum. Please!' she begged, tears of pain and frustration prickling at her eyes.

'No!' Nell insisted, just as another voice joined in.

'What the devil . . . ?' John Hardaker demanded, as he came rushing through the door.

'It's nothing, Mr Hardaker,' Nell attempted to assure.

'Nothing!' Rosy blazed, finally wrenching her arm free of her mother's grip and standing up straight once more. She held out her arm, sticking the angry red burn right under his nose. 'She did that!' she said, jerking her head at the silent figure in the chair, who had already lit up another cigarette.

Getting weapons ready for the next attack, Rosy thought bitterly, as Dorohy Hardaker puffed away with a lack of concern that refuelled her desire to hit her all over again. 'She almost ran me over and didn't know anything about it.' She lowered her hand then. The pain was becoming unbearable and bitterness filled her voice, as she said, 'And when I pointed out that she was so drunk had Nicky been standing there she would have mowed him down, she put her cigarette out on me!'

'What!' John Hardaker took Rosy's hand in his and stared in disbelief at the circular burn. She winced in pain. He gave a noisily indrawn breath and looked up into her eyes with concern and anger filling his own. 'Go and put it in cold water,' he instructed.

Rosy frowned uncertainly.

'I thought butter was the best thing,' Nell put in.

'No,' he insisted. 'Water will cool it down and help ease the pain. Go on and do it,' he ordered, with a determination that brooked no refusal.

Rosy was still hesitant. She glanced round at Dorothy Hardaker. She had no intention of going anywhere and letting the woman get away with it. She would rather have suffered a month of pain than back down now as if nothing had happened.

As if he had read her mind, John Hardaker said, 'I'll deal with that.'

'It really isn't anything, Mr Hardaker,' Nell

protested, not exactly wringing her hands, but clutching them nervously in front of her.

He did not listen. Releasing Rosy's injured hand he took hold of her arm and steered her to the door. 'Go with her, Nell,' he said, and beckoned her across.

Nell hesitated. 'Rosy can manage on her own,' she said, not wanting to leave him alone with his wife. Their rows were volatile enough when Dorothy Hardaker had done no more than come home from the pub. She was frightened what might happen if they were left alone at the moment.

Whether John Hardaker knew what was in her mind of not, he was not giving her the chance to interfere. 'Rosy needs you!' he insisted. 'She needs to get that hand in water!' he added pointedly, when Nell continued to hold back.

His manner prodded her with guilt for her hesitancy. She crossed the room without another moment wasted and he handed Rosy to her and pushed them both through the door and closed it behind them.

'Oh dear!' Nell breathed with feeling. 'Now look what you've gone and done.'

'*What I've done!*' Rosy turned to her mother in amazement. 'It was her! She did this to me!' She stuck her burnt hand under her mother's nose. The movement caused the searing pain to expand, as if her skin had shrunk too small for her flesh and was now being torn apart. She grimaced and sank her teeth into her bottom lip.

'Come on and sit down.' Nell pulled a chair from under the kitchen table and pushed Rosy gently onto it. 'I'll get a bowl of water,' she said, concern for her daughter suddenly overshadowing any worries about their livelihood.

'Thanks, Mum.' Rosy looked up and attempted a smile which looked more like a grimace. At least it was taking her mind off her scratched legs, she thought, and nursed her painful hand, not letting go until Nell put the washing-up bowl on the table in front of her.

'Oh . . . !' she gasped. The relief was instant, as she lowered her hand carefully into the water. 'It works.' She couldn't believe it, but the pain had almost instantly disappeared. 'It's like magic.'

'Well I never.' Nell's wagging head mirrored her disbelief. 'And I always thought it was butter you had to put on burns.'

Rosy smiled, this time for real. But it was only a moment before it was wiped from her face. The sound of shattering china suddenly crashed through the air, coming from the drawing-room. It was followed by Dorothy Hardaker's voice exclaiming, 'No I will not!' in a screech so loud Rosy feared for John Hardaker's eardrums, him being in the same room and having no muffling effect of the walls to help him bear it. There was a thud, then a second crash of splintering pottery.

Rosy's shocked gaze pivoted to her mother's. The china cabinet!' she gasped in alarm.

Nell's head moved slowly from side to side. 'It wasn't loud enough,' she replied, but there was no reassurance in her voice, either for Rosy or herself. Dorothy Hardaker's avoidance of the drawing-room had made her think it not necessary to remove all the breakable valuables from the room. In fact, she had put many of those removed from the hall into the drawing-room, thinking they would be safer there.

There was a third crash. Dorothy Hardaker screamed. Then a heavy thud, followed by silence.

Rosy's mouth dropped open and she stared bewilderedly at her mother. For several moments neither of them could move.

'What . . . ?' Rosy managed to utter, before her briefly returned voice vanished again. Her gaze swung from her mother to the kitchen door, then back to her mother.

Nell shook her head, knowing the question her daughter's tongue was finding difficult to put into words. 'I . . .' she began, trying to help but finding her own voice equally elusive.

The silence stretched on. Rosy and Nell strained their ears for any further noise coming from the drawing-room. But there was nothing. No cry, moan, footstep or shuffle to indicate there was anyone still in there.

'Whatever's happened?' Rosy finally brought the words they were both thinking out into the open.

Nell shook her head again. 'Heaven only knows,' she said. 'But we'd better go and find out.'

'Yes,' Rosy agreed, but reluctantly and, as her mother would have moved to the door, she reached out and grasped her arm and held her back. 'Perhaps we should wait,' she suggested.

Nell opened her mouth, but the sound of the drawing-room door opening and urgent footsteps coming down the hall put an end to her reply.

The next moment the kitchen door flew open and John Hardaker burst in. His shirt sleeve was torn completely away from the shoulder and hung loose on his arm, revealing a deep jagged cut below his shoulder. He had one black eye and blood running from his nose and also down his cheek from two vivid gashes. 'I need help!' he gasped, for a moment supporting himself heavily against the table and taking several long, noisy breaths, as if they were enough to bring himself under control.

'Sit yourself down,' Nell said, full of concern. 'I'll get the bandages.'

He shook his head. 'Not me . . . In . . .' He suddenly spun away from the table and turned back to the door. 'In the drawing-room,' he called, and raced from the room with the same speed he had used to get into it.

'Oh my God!' Nell's hand covered her mouth and her anxious gaze flew to Rosy. 'You stay there,' she instructed, before hurrying after him.

'Not on your life!' Rosy's hand was out of the bowl

of water and laying a trail of drips across the floor as she quickly followed her mother. At that moment she could only think the worst had happened, and she would not leave her mother to deal with it alone.

At the drawing-room door she stopped short, grasping the frame for support while she studied the sight before her. Now it was out of water her hand was beginning to hurt again, but the scene before her eyes made her own pain of very little consequence. The red and gold Chinese vase lay in pieces at her feet, the dahlias spread all over the carpet. One shelf of the bookcase had been cleared and the books tossed all about as if by a whirlwind. The mantelpiece had been wiped clean, the two silver goblets were lying in the hearth, surrounded by the broken remains of the three Minton dishes that had also stood above the large marble fireplace.

Standing in the middle of all the mess was John Hardaker, staring down at the floor in a stunned stupor. Rosy's gaze slowly followed his and, as it settled on Dorothy Hardaker's lifeless body lying there, she lifted her hand to her mouth. But she was not sure if she actually gasped or if the sound got stuck somewhere in her throat.

The woman looked as if she was nothing more than a boneless rag doll. A dark bruise covered the left side of her chin and appeared to be growing and stretching up her cheek right before Rosy's eyes. But it was the way her head lolled crookedly over the corner of the metal fender that was the most frightening sight.

It was not until Rosy stepped cautiously forward, that she saw the dark halo of blood seeping from beneath the woman's hair and spreading across the cream marble hearth.

CHAPTER FIVE

Acting on instinct Rosy raced out of the drawing-room and grabbed up the telephone. Her finger was dialling the last digit of Doctor Hampson's number, when John Hardaker's hand slammed down on the telephone, cutting her off.

'What . . . ! What are you doing?' she gasped, her startled eyes pivoting to his face. 'We've got to . . .' But she could not finish saying they had got to get help, for her voice trailed away as the icy glare of his gaze filled her with fear.

'No! You can't! Wait! Let me think!' His voice was clipped and breathless and, keeping his hand firmly on the telephone, he stared at Rosy with unseeing eyes.

It was several seconds before she could summon up the courage to object. 'We can't wait.' Her voice displayed her bewilderment. 'Your wife needs help and we must get it straight away. We've got to!' she insisted, taking hold of his hand to pull it away from the telephone. 'You've got to let me call the doctor. It might be too late if we wait.'

His hand refused to move. 'It's already too late,' he ground hopelessly.

'*No it isn't!*'

His head spun round and so did Rosy's, to see Nell standing framed in the drawing-room doorway. 'It isn't too late,' she repeated. 'Get the doctor, Rosy!'

'She . . . she isn't . . . dead?' he asked, uncertainty vibrating his voice.

'No . . . she isn't dead,' Nell assured, and he let go of the telephone and, with an animal groan, his body crumpled, until he was down on his knees and his

98

forehead was pressed against the polished wood floor.

For a moment Rosy could only stand and stare at him, wondering if he had gone mad. Because she could not believe the actions of the last few minutes had been those of a sane person.

It was Nell prompting, 'The doctor!' that brought her back to the moment and the fact that she could now make the call without hindrance.

'He won't be long,' she called out, speaking to her mother who had gone back to Dorothy Hardaker. She considered John Hardaker to be beyond hearing, but he proved her wrong and looked up.

'Larry?' he questioned, and the bleakness in his eyes tore at something deep within her.

'Yes,' she replied. 'It's Larry Hampson who is coming.' Reaching down she tugged at his arm. 'Get up. Please get up.' She could not bear to see him this way, broken and bowed. It took several attempts and when finally she got him upright the floor was smeared with blood from his face. 'You should get cleaned up,' she suggested.

But he did not move. For a long moment he stared into her eyes with an expression she could not comprehend. Then suddenly he threw his arms around her neck and fell against her. 'Rosy! Rosy! What am I going to do? Help me! Please help me!'

He had her pinned against the telephone table, or she had the feeling they might both have landed on the floor. His weight was so great against her that she was powerless to move him and could only press her hands against the table to give herself added support, her pleadings either went unheard, or were being ignored.

Neither did the sound of the doctor's car coming up the drive and pulling into the courtyard stir him. Not until the large, red haired figure of Larry Hampson came striding hurriedly through the door did he finally move.

'What have we here then?' Larry asked, peering from

beneath his shock of bright hair at first John, then Rosy, who was now covered in almost as much of John's blood as he was himself. 'Who needs my attention first?'

John shook his head then and lifted himself slowly away from Rosy. 'In there,' he said, turning to Larry and giving a nod towards the drawing-room.

Rosy remained silent, not sure if her overwhelming relief was for being released from John Hardaker's intimate embrace; or if it was merely a reaction to knowing Dorothy Hardaker's much needed help had finally arrived.

Dorothy Hardaker's injury turned out to have looked far worse than it was. There were no broken bones and she suffered only a mild case of concussion, a stiff neck and three stitches in the wound on the back of her head. The hospital kept her under observation for two days, then they sent her home.

At first the sense of relief running through the house was almost tangible. But as the days wore on Rosy began to think the fortunate might not be so fortunate after all. Dorothy Hardaker made it quite clear she had a score to settle with both her husband and Rosy, and that she was going to make them pay for it.

'I'll take a bath after lunch,' she said, not looking up from the magazine she was reading.

Rosy did not reply. She put the lunch tray down on the table and took a pink satin dressing-gown from the hook on the door. The woman's return home from hospital had turned Rosy into a lady's maid. She was at her constant beck and call. Except for going into the bathroom Dorothy had not once left the bedroom in the four weeks since coming out of hospital. Meals, magazines, anything and everything had to be brought to her on demand. The table and chair had been ordered on the very first day; so she could eat in comfort. The second day's order had been for a radio, then the demands had been reduced to the daily newspapers, a certain magazine or a box of chocolates. Until the end of the week when she had decided she simply could not live without a television.

Rosy could not remember the last time Dorothy Hardaker had watched a television programme and she hoped it was a sign that things were definitely changing. The hospital had told her she was drinking too much and had got to stop. Rosy had thought the warning a waste of time but, so far, she had been proved wrong. Dorothy Hardaker had not touched a drop of gin, or any other alcohol. They had made sure there was none in her room before she came home and she hadn't been anywhere to get her hands on any; and Rosy was very happy to have to swallow her words and be proved wrong.

'And I need some more shampoo and you can get me a bottle of Amami at the same time.' Dorothy Hardaker's gaze remained glued to the magazine as she spoke.

Rosy gave the woman a sideways glance. Setting lotion! she thought. It was another good sign. If she felt like doing herself up she must be feeling better.

'Did you hear me?' The magazine rustled with annoyance, before being slapped down on the bed. A hard glare hit Rosy in the face. 'If you don't reply I don't know if you've heard me or not!' she spat nastily.

'Sorry,' Rosy quickly apologized, only too eager to do anything to keep the peace. 'I was miles away. But I did hear you. I'll get them when I go and pick Nicky up from school.'

'That's no good. I want them after lunch. When I have my bath. You'll have to go and fetch them while I'm eating.'

And when do I eat? Rosy held her tongue. If she did not do all the running around then her mother would have to do it, so she complied with the string of demands and orders, keeping her grumblings and complaints to the minimum.

'You'll need this,' she said, changing the subject before she said something she regretted. She held the dressing-gown for Dorothy Hardaker to slip her arms into as she climbed out of bed, even though she was already wearing a quilted bedjacket. It was only October but the weather had turned cold enough for January, with biting winds and relentless rain.

Dorothy Hardaker shrugged into the dressing-gown. 'What culinary delights do we have today?' she asked, her nose wrinkling with distaste as she peered over the tray.

'Chicken soup and a pork chop,' Rosy said, allowing her annoyance to show in her voice. Her mother prided herself on her cooking and it was never less than perfect, but Dorothy Hardaker usually found something to gripe about.

Today was to be no exception. The little snub nose wrinkled further. 'Didn't we have chicken soup on Tuesday?' she enquired tartly.

'Probably,' Rosy replied, then fell silent again as she pulled the chair out and set the meal on the table, then leaned the tray up against the wall for when she came back to fetch the dirty pots.

Dorothy Hardaker's mouth tightened and her dark eyes narrowed. 'Then tell your mother to get a bit more variety into the meals. It shouldn't be too difficult for her to come up with something different every day!'

Rosy's nostrils flared on a noisily indrawn breath and she wheeled away and hurried from the room. A dozen sharp retorts circled inside her head – all rude. When she slammed the door behind her, her teeth were sinking so hard into her bottom lip that she expected to taste blood at any moment.

'I'll swing for her one day,' she declared with feeling, as she stormed into the kitchen. Her anger had not been lessened by the walk down the stairs and she could still feel the tremble of fury in her limbs. What made matters worse was John Hardaker had been growing more and more strange since the fight that put his wife in hospital. He was out more than he was in, and when he was in he was stuck in his office and not to be disturbed.

Nell glanced round from the stove, lifting her eyebrows in a manner that said, *not again*! Then she turned back to the plate on which she was setting John Hardaker's dinner, and gave a sigh. As usual, the meal was to be put in the oven to keep warm until he came home. Which could be any time. Since his wife had come out of hospital Nell had wasted more and more meals, having to throw them away when he didn't turn up.

'You'd do better to control your temper and button your lip,' she said, not looking at Rosy but with more than a touch of warning in her voice. It wasn't very often that she wished her younger daughter could be more like her elder. Maggie could handle any situation with a few well chosen, if not exactly ladylike words. Rosy's apparently more placid and easy-going nature appeared to allow the sarcasm and barbs to be discarded as easily as water off a duck's back. But the outward appearance was very misleading. Although she did not always show it, the smallest slight would cut into Rosy's kind nature far more deeply than into Maggie's thick skin, causing far more pain. When Rosy was hurt she nurtured that hurt, letting it grow inside her until it all came out in a mighty explosion. If such an explosion should happen with Dorothy Hardaker at the moment, they could all end up regretting it.

'I think we've had enough trouble with uncontrolled tempers for a good while yet,' she said pointedly. A good long while, she thought.

It was the final straw. Rosy had expected a bit of sympathy, needed a bit of sympathy and all her mother could do was have another go at her. 'I haven't said a word to her,' she snapped angrily, letting her frustration out on the wrong person. 'I could have done!' She folded her arms tightly, her head nodding backwards and forwards with determination. 'Oh yes, I could have done!' she repeated with feeling. 'But I'm not daft!' She flashed her mother a meaningful glance. 'I know life is easier if you just nod and agree to everything she says. Well I have just nodded and agreed and what does it get me! *I* have got to run round to the village while *she* is eating her lunch. I've got to get her some shampoo and – would you believe – setting lotion!'

'What's she got to have that for in such a hurry?' Nell asked, as she spooned the last of the apple sauce onto John Hardaker's plate, then put the saucepan beneath the tap to fill up with water. As she was turning the tap off again she suddenly stopped. 'She isn't thinking of going out?' She turned to face Rosy, her expression filled with the anxiety that was in her voice.

Rosy gave a shrug. 'She hasn't said so. I imagine it's just a sign she's feeling more like her old self again.' She added the last for her mother's benefit. She was herself beginning to wonder just why they were needed in such a hurry.

'She's up to something. Let's only hope it doesn't involve a pub.'

Rosy grimaced and went to her mother. 'You know what you say to me: keep your nose out of it. Well, if she has decided she is going to get up and go out again, there isn't much we can do about it.' She gave the well padded shoulders an affectionate squeeze and felt guilty for not keeping her anger in check. If she had not let it out her mother would not now be fretting about something that might not happen.

'I'd better get off,' she said, changing the subject back to the errand she had to run. She glanced at the clock and gave another grimace. Both the Co-op and the chemist closed for lunch in fifteen minutes. If she ran all the way she would only just make it. 'Keep it warm for me,' she said, and grabbed some money from the red oxo tin on the dresser and raced out of the door, snatching her coat and putting it on as she ran through the, thankfully, not too heavy rain.

She made it to the chemist, hot and breathless, with five minutes to spare. She was walking back through the village, the shampoo and setting lotion in her pocket, when she saw Franny Hallsworth coming in the opposite direction on the other side of the road.

'Coo . . . ee!' Franny's short dumpy form bounced across the road, waving frantically.

Rosy gave an inward sigh of despair, knowing the conversation would turn personal. She was not disappointed.

'How's Dorothy?' Franny enquired without preamble.

'Coming along fine,' she replied, determined she was not going to feed the woman's thirst for gossip.

'What was it she did – fall over?'

'Yes,' Rosy agreed easily. 'She tripped up and fell and banged her head. She had a nasty cut but it wasn't anything serious.'

Franny pursed her lips knowingly. Then she leaned forward, putting her face close to Rosy's and, in a confidential manner, said, 'Drunk, I suppose!'

Rosy's expression did not waver. 'She had had a drink,' she said, knowing there was no point in denying the fact. Dorothy Hardaker had been constantly under the influence, and it had usually been purchased from Franny's pub. 'But she wasn't incapable. It was just an unfortunate accident.'

Franny's spine stiffened and, thankfully for Rosy, straightened up and put the close proximity of her face at a safer distance. The plump shoulders went back and her rosy cheeks swelled out as her lips tightened in disbelief. 'You can say what you like,' she said, affecting great offence. 'Everyone knows she would have been blind drunk.'

Well, if you know why are you asking me? Rosy wondered, and, irritation getting the better of her, snapped, 'I really don't think it is anyone else's business.'

Franny smiled knowingly. Then, as if Rosy had not spoken, she said, 'It looks like the other one is going the same way.'

Taken by surprise Rosy was unable to keep a flicker of doubt from showing on her face. She did not know what Franny was talking about, but she had not wanted Franny to know that.

Seeing she had scored a point, Franny's smile broadened. 'He's in the pub . . . John,' she added, just in case Rosy had not understood. She inclined her head towards the White Horse public house which she had just passed. 'Where he is every dinner time.' A gleam of victory entered her eyes that told Rosy she was well aware she was telling her something new.

'Yes,' Rosy replied, forcing herself to lie with a confidence she was not feeling, and enjoying the obvious displeasure that entered the older woman's eyes. 'He still hasn't come back to The Derwent!' She had not known he had become a regular at the White Horse, but pointing out that Franny had still not got him back in her own pub was scoring at least one point.

The pink in Franny's cheeks turned to florid magenta and her mouth tightened so much that her lips disappeared from view.

Rosy looked up at the sky. The rain had stopped and she wished it would start again, and give her a reason to hurry away. Then a sudden thought brought her gaze down to the empty shopping bag in Franny's hand. 'If you're going in the Co-op I should hurry up. They close in a minute,' she said, glancing at her watch.

'Oh glory be!' Franny gasped, her momentary fury forgotten. 'You're right. I haven't got time to stand gobblin'.'

'No you haven't,' Rosy readily agreed, happy to have

found a release from the prying. She smiled as she watched Franny's dumpy form hurtle towards the Co-op door – back in the direction she had come from – which made it obvious she had purposely come up the road to meet her.

But Rosy's happiness was very brief. As she passed the White Horse she could not help but look in the car park. Sure enough the black Rover was standing there. She carried on walking and wondered if what Franny had said was true: was he really a regular customer there? Or had she seen his car on passing and thought to make something of it?

He was regularly away from home, she knew that. But she had thought he was going to the offices he had in Derby, where he employed Bill Cowlishaw and a couple of secretaries. It had never previously been his habit to visit the office very often. He had always been happy to leave the collection of the rents and the upkeep of his houses and cottages to Bill, leaving himself free to deal with buying or building more of them.

When she crossed the road and passed the Co-op she could see Franny through the window, carefully watching the scales to make sure Bob Randal didn't give her short measure. But the smile that came to her lips was soon gone, and she could not help wondering how, after seeing the pathetic state his wife had got herself into, John Hardaker could turn to drink in search of a solution to *his* problems. She could not understand it. Then she could not understand anything about him of late and could only think his strange behaviour was guilt for what he had done to his wife.

She crossed the main road, intending to go through the stile and take the path across the meadow. But as she placed her hands on the wall to ease herself through, she glanced back up the road and saw the black Rover turn out of the White Horse car park and come towards her.

Immediately he saw her he stopped the car and leaned across and pushed open the passenger door. 'Want a lift?' he called.

Her mind had been filled with the vision of him having to hold onto the bar to keep himself upright. To see him there in full command of his senses was a great relief and she quickly ran across the grass verge and only replied with a laughing, 'Yes,' as she flopped into the seat.

Not until the car was moving off again, did he say, 'I want to go and take a look at a plot of land before going home. It shouldn't take too long.'

'Oh!' She turned to him with a grimace. 'I've been to get Mrs Hardaker some shampoo. She wants it as soon as she's finished her lunch. You'll have to drop me at the end and I'll walk down the lane.' Her disappointment was evident. The lane being the same length as the meadow her short car journey wasn't even saving her any time.

But John Hardaker was not in any mood to give consideration to his wife. 'She can wait,' he replied bluntly.

'But . . . but . . .' she stammered uncertainly. Dorothy Hardaker was going to be furious with her. 'She'll be waiting for me to run her bath.' *And it will be me who gets it in the neck for not going straight back to her,* she thought.

'If she wants a bath badly enough she'll run it herself,' he insisted, making no attempt to slow down and driving straight past the end of the lane.

'Besides, Mum has lunch waiting for you,' she said, making one final attempt at protest, albeit feeble. She could see he was not going to listen.

Well, it wasn't her fault, she told herself, and settled back in the seat to enjoy the unexpected drive. She had done as she was told. She had run to the shops and got the shampoo and setting lotion. It was not her fault if John Hardaker had picked her up and taken her off to look at some bit of land before going home. He was her boss and she was hardly in a position to refuse him any more than she could have refused to run the errand in the first place.

'We could get a dozen houses on there,' John Hardaker said, as he climbed back into the car with an expression of self-satisfaction planted on his face.

Rosy had to smile. All she could see was a patch of rough wasteground. There was a mound of earth stuck in one corner with a selection of rubble sticking out of it that defied description. An old iron bedstead and grubby mattress had been dumped in another corner and right down at the far end was what appeared to be the local childrens' den, built of old tyres, broken planks and cardboard boxes. There was nothing what-soever to put her in mind of a row of spanking new houses.

'Your imagination is obviously better than mine,' she said, giving him a wry grimace.

He threw back his head and laughed loudly. It was something he had not done for a long time and the sound filled Rosy with pleasure. Without thinking what she was doing she reached out and laid her hand on his arm.

'That's better,' she said. 'It's time you let yourself get over . . .' Her voice diminished on the last as she realized she was speaking out of turn. Colour crept into her cheeks and she withdrew her hand slowly, hoping the action would be less noticeable than if she had snatched it back as if burnt, which was what she felt she wanted to do. 'I'm sorry. I didn't mean . . .' Dropping her gaze she stared at her fingers as they toyed nervously in her lap.

He turned in his seat and smiled, and laid his arm along the back of her seat. He gazed at her face, causing the heat in her skin to increase. 'There's nothing to be embarrassed about,' he said.

'I'm not embarrassed,' she replied far too quickly. A

lie which immediately increased the very emotion she was adamantly denying. Warmth raced through her body and her cheeks felt as if they were about to burst into flame. She hurriedly covered them with her hands and gave him a sheepish, sideways glance. 'Well, I suppose I am. I shouldn't have said . . . well . . . what I said.' She dropped her hands again and her shoulders lifted on a shrug that echoed her uncertainty.

His smile deepened, then slowly diminished, his expression becoming strangely intense. He lifted the blond hair that was lying on her shoulder and let it run through his fingers. 'You can say what you like, Rosy. I shall not be offended.'

He made her name sound like a caress and her heart began to hammer against her chest as a mixture of fear and excitement thumped through her veins. Some-where inside her head a voice was telling her to get out of the car and get away from him. Yet she remained where she was, frozen, as if some great hand was holding her down.

'I was speaking of you and your wife and it's none of my business,' she began, her voice coming faster and faster as his hand moved further up her hair and she could feel the warmth of his fingers against her neck. 'I . . . well, I know you've been worried and I . . . we . . . mum and me have been worried about you. It's nice to see you getting back to normal.' She wondered what she was talking about. He had shown about thirty seconds worth of normality and she was talking about everything being fine. 'But it isn't really any of my business and I shouldn't have opened my mouth.' The words rushed from her lips without one pause to draw breath. 'My mum would be furious,' she added, on a more restrained note, as the rain returned and the patter of raindrops began to bounce on the car's roof.

At mention of Nell his smile reappeared. 'Well she has nothing to be furious about,' he assured, bringing his face down closer to hers so that she felt the warm waft of his breath with every word he spoke. There was a faint smell of alcohol on him. Nothing excessive, but it did remind her of Franny's words.

His hand tightened round the back of her neck, the thumb and finger administering a slow, circular caress beneath her ears, and she forgot all about Franny Hallsworth. Her skin began to tingle and she was not sure if the little gasp she gave was from anxiety or pleasure. She had never been touched in such an intimate way before and, although one part of her was telling her it was wrong and she should push him away, another part was quite liking it. 'I . . .' she began, then could not think of anything to say.

His smile deepened and he pulled her forward and before she had time to protest his lips were on hers. They were warm and soft and any thoughts of objection soon fled her mind and she responded to him freely.

When finally he pulled his head back, she found her arms wound tightly round his neck and his brown curly hair in an untidy disorder where her fingers had run through it. 'Oh . . . I . . .' Heat rushed to her face and she knew her cheeks had turned to magenta. 'Mr Hardaker . . . I . . . I'm sorry.' Her embarrassed whisper was almost lost in the sound of the rain now battering loudly on the car's metal body. She loosened her arms but he did not let her go and so she had to leave them round his neck, because she did not know what else to do with them. But she did drop her gaze, unable to look him in the eye.

'Don't ever apologize for being warm and loving, Rosy.' He lifted her chin and made her look at him. 'It is a gift and nothing to be ashamed of.' He smiled fondly. 'But please stop calling me *Mr* Hardaker. You know my name is John, so use it.'

'Oh I couldn't!' she burst out, her mind filling with thoughts of her mother's reaction if she heard her being so familiar.

He shook his head, knowing the reasons for her forthright objection. Nell was one of the old school, who firmly believed in not stepping out of one's place. 'Maggie always calls me John and your mother has managed to live with it so far,' he pointed out.

It was not him speaking of her mother that drained the blood from her face, it was the mention of her sister. Maggie! She was acting just like Maggie! She had not thought it would ever be possible, but she could not run away from the way she had responded to him. Warm and loving he had called her. Wantonly, she would call it. Not only was he a married man, he was also her boss!

'Oh no!' She brought her arms from around his neck then, forcing them down the meagre space between their bodies and pushing him away. 'I shouldn't have done that. It was wrong. I don't know what came over me. No! No!' she insisted, shoving harder at his chest when he refused to let her go.

'You've done nothing wrong!' he countered with equal force. 'For heaven's sake, Rosy,' he ground, as she pushed so hard on his chest he feared for the safety of his ribs. 'We only kissed! And you were willing. I didn't force you.' He moved back in the seat of his own accord, before she did him permanent damage.

'No!' It was little more than a whisper and she turned in her seat and stared numbly at her lap. 'I never said you forced me.' Her voice heavy. 'I . . .' About to admit she had liked it she brought herself up short. 'I didn't object because I wasn't thinking what I was doing.' She glanced up, meeting his gaze with great embarrassment. 'Well, I'm thinking now, and I know I shouldn't have done it.'

He shook his head. 'Don't let my so-called marriage stand in the way. Dorothy hasn't been a wife to me for several years. Our marriage is one in name only.'

'But you *are* married all the same!' she said, without looking round at him. 'You have a wife and I shouldn't have let you lay a finger on me, never mind kiss me.'

There followed a silence, in which she felt his eyes studying her carefully and her embarrassment increasing.

'It means nothing.'

'No! Don't say any more.' She wrapped her arms around herself in protection and pressed back into the seat. One of the bottles in her coat pocket dug into her hip and she was reminded of her real reason for being out. 'Please take me home,' she said. She glanced at her watch and realized Dorothy Hardaker would be tearing her hair out at not yet having got the shampoo or setting lotion. She wouldn't need them then, she thought drily.

It was a great relief when, without further argument, he turned in his seat and started the engine.

They did not speak until the car came to a standstill in the courtyard and they were home. Then he turned to her. 'Getting married does not make it impossible for you to have feelings for someone else,' he said.

She shook her head very determinedly, trying to physically push away the meaning of what he was saying. 'No!' she insisted fiercely. The word hung heavy inside the car, as the rain sounded like a hail of bullets battering on the roof. 'You have no right to even suggest it. You are far too old for me!'

'Rubbish!' he countered fiercely. 'What has age got to do with it?'

She didn't know the answer to that one, or even if there was an answer. Perhaps age didn't matter. But there were other factors to take into account besides their differing years: not least of all his wife. 'You are a married man and I won't be anyone's mistress!' she stated bluntly. Visions of a naked Maggie in the dirty old cottage filled her mind and she leapt out of the car and raced across the yard, not waiting to hear his reply.

The rain was pelting down so hard that it hit the stone slabs and bounced up again. Her feet and legs were soon drenched as they caught the spray going in both directions. By the time she reached the back door her coat was covered in dark, damp streaks and her hair hung round her face in wet rat's tails. But she had no concern for her condition. Had the day been a bright sunny one her race from the car would have appeared odd and raised the suspicions of her mother, who she knew would have heard their arrival and be standing at the window watching. The rain at least gave a reason to her haste and at that moment she could only feel gratitude towards the drips running down her neck and staining her clothing.

John Hardaker followed her with equal speed and as her hand closed on the door latch he was right behind. She had the feeling he was wanting to say something. She also had the feeling she did not want to hear what it was. So she pushed the door open and stepped hurriedly inside, wanting to get to the safety of the kitchen and her mother.

As expected, Nell was at the window. As Rosy burst through the door she turned around, her cheeks were red with the anger that bristled from her.

'Where the devil have you been!' she demanded, glaring at Rosy in a way that made it obvious she was the errant party.

'It is my fault,' John Hardaker intervened, as he brushed the rain from his hair and made Rosy's cheeks warm with the recollection of how her fingers had messed up that same hair.

'It doesn't matter whose fault it is!' Nell snapped.

Rosy's mouth dropped open. She had never heard her mother speak to John Hardaker, the lord and master, in such a fierce manner before. He also found it odd. For as she turned her shocked expression on him he suddenly forgot his hair and looked up at Nell in surprise.

'She's gone!' she declared bluntly, her angry gaze swinging from John Hardaker to her daughter and back again. 'Your wife!' she stressed meaningfully, just in case he had not got the message. 'Her room is empty and she's gone!'

CHAPTER SIX

Rosy glanced at the rain lashing against the window. 'She can't have gone far. Not in this.' Dorothy Hardaker was not one to walk anywhere at the best of times. In weather such as this she would not have poked her nose out of the door without knowing the car was waiting for her.

'Rosy is right,' John Hardaker agreed, going to the window and standing staring out at the deluge. 'She must be in the house somewhere.'

Nell's shoulders lifted on a shrug. 'If she is I can't find her. I've looked everywhere.'

'We'll all look,' Rosy suggested. She did not doubt her mother's credibility but Dorothy Hardaker was not beyond any trick to get her own way. Besides, she had the need to do something to find the woman.

'You'll not find her,' Nell grumbled, making obvious her displeasure at being doubted. 'I've told you she isn't here. The house is empty.'

John Hardaker shook his head and turned to Rosy. 'I don't think there is much point. If she has gone out she'll come back when she's ready. If she's hiding somewhere then let her stay hidden. I'm not getting involved in silly games.' His chest lifted on a great sigh and he raked frustrated fingers through his hair, leaving it all dishevelled and reminding her once more of what had happened between them in the car.

His lack of concern for his wife was lost in her moment's embarrassment. 'Well I'm going to look,' she insisted, and was so eager to get away from him and the discomfort he was causing her she was out of the door and running up the stairs before anyone could stop her.

Was this what life was going to be like from now on, she asked herself, as she looked round Dorothy Hardaker's empty bedroom? Would she never again feel easy in his presence, never be able to speak to him as she had before? All for a few stupid minutes of insanity!

The bathroom was also empty. The bath was full of water, but its cleanness and clarity proved it was unused. The other upstairs rooms were also empty and her search of the downstairs ones proved equally fruitless.

'She isn't here,' she said, her voice as heavy as her heart when she returned to the kitchen to find her mother up to her elbows in flour, alone.

'I told you that before.' Nell cast her a withering glance.

'I know. I just felt I had to do something.' Rosy did not explain why she felt she had to do something. She did not really understand the reasons herself. But she did know she felt even more guilty now, for allowing John Hardaker to kiss her, than she had before knowing his wife had disappeared. With a sigh she went to the oven and opened the door and peered inside. 'Which one is mine?' she asked, forcing her nose not to turn up at the sight of the two dried up dinners.

'The bottom one – if it's fit to eat!' Nell's tone made it obvious she was of the opinion anything left in the oven would now be past redemption.

'It'll be all right,' Rosy assured. But as she pulled the bottom plate out and looked at the congealed gravy-coated food, she had a change of heart. She glanced at her mother, but seeing her tight-lipped expression thought better than to speak her mind. 'Where's he gone?' she asked, as she went to the table and sat down.

'To look round outside.'

'Outside!' Rosy could not conceal her amazement. Her gaze pivoted to the window. The car was standing outside the closed garage door, its black shape only just discernible through the grey sheet of rain. 'He must be mad!'

'Perhaps he felt he had to do something . . . as well!' Nell replied pointedly.

Rosy gave a grimace. 'Point taken, Mother,' she said, acknowledging that she had been out of order to question his reasons. She dropped her head and began sawing at the dried up pork chop, but she could not stop herself wondering if he had gone out because, like herself, he was now regretting what had happened between them. Was he now too embarrassed to be around her for long and, if so, where did that leave her?

He might want her to leave! It was a stunning thought. But she could not deny that he might no longer want her around and insist she leave, not wanting her in his house, with his son! 'Oh Nicky!' The words slipped out before she could catch them.

'What about Nicky?' Nell stopped working the pastry and looked up with a frown, floury hands poised above the bowl.

'Oh . . . oh nothing,' Rosy stammered, covering her embarrassment by struggling to chew the piece of dried up pork that was in her mouth. After a suitable time she gave a big swallow. 'I was just thinking I was going to get drowned when I go and fetch him from school,' she said. 'If this lot doesn't ease off.' She nodded bleakly at the unrelenting torrent through the window.

'She isn't outside,' a very wet John Hardaker announced, as he came through the door and, thankfully, relieved Rosy of her mother's intense scrutiny.

Did you really expect her to be, she thought? 'Well she isn't in the house, either,' she said.

'I'd already told you that!' Nell put in, yet again.

Rosy flashed her mother a glance that asked her to

stop repeating herself. Then she looked at John Hardaker. He had the appearance of having had several buckets of water poured over him. He was dripping all over the floor but he seemed to be unaware of his state and just stood there by the door, his expression as bleak as the weather.

'She'll be all right,' Rosy said, even though she knew the words were empty and useless. Until they knew for certain where Dorothy Hardaker had gone they had no way of knowing how she was.

His head inclined in a manner that could have been either agreement or disagreement. Rosy did not know but she did not comment and fortunately her mother took charge and began fussing round him like a mother hen.

'Come and get dry and get something warm inside you,' she said, dusting her hands free of flour and grabbing a clean towel from the drawer and rushing across to him. 'Here, let me take this.' Pushing the towel into his hand she helped him out of his sodden coat and draped it over a chair in front of the fire. 'Now get yourself upstairs and out of those wet trousers. And this shirt is damp.' She patted the back of his shoulders, where a darker patch showed the rain had seeped through his coat.

He gave a nod of agreement, then went silently from the room.

'It looks like we're going back to the old ways.' Rosy gave a telling grimace. Having Dorothy Hardaker playing the invalid in bed had been a nuisance and caused a lot more work, but at least they had known where she was and that she was safe. Now it seemed they were to return to the long absences and worrying and wondering when, and how, she would arrive home.

'At least my trip to the village wasn't wasted,' she said drily, her head jerking towards the bottle of shampoo and setting lotion sitting on the dresser. 'She'll be needing those when she gets back!'

She turned back to her half-eaten meal. It didn't look any more appetizing now than it had to begin with and she laid the knife and fork down and pushed the plate away. Resting her chin on her clasped hands she stared into the orange flames of the fire. Steam was rising freely from John Hardaker's coat and the smell of warm damp wool was lingering on the air.

She began to wonder if they should be getting worried about Dorothy Hardaker. With her past history it didn't seem unreasonable to assume she had nipped off to the pub. But no-one had actually seen her go. Perhaps she had got desperate . . . Or perhaps not, she amended, suddenly seeing the demanded order for shampoo in another light.

'She did it on purpose,' she said. 'She didn't want any shampoo. It was just to get rid of me, getting me out of the house so she knew she only had you to get past.'

Nell stopped crimping the top of a pie crust and looked up. Once more her floury hands were suspended in front of her. 'Do you really think she's at the pub then?'

Rosy gave a shrug, wishing she could have convinced herself as much as her mother, just as John Hardaker came back through the door, dressed in dry grey flannels and a clean white shirt. He crossed the kitchen and dropped the wet trousers and shirt on top of the steaming coat, then sat down at the table.

Nell tutted under her breath as she wiped her hands clean ready to get the remains of his lunch out of the oven. Not because he had dropped one lot of wet clothes over another in a way in which they would take all week to dry, but because he had done it himself. She didn't like it when he did things which she was paid to do. To her way of thinking it wasn't right. 'Go on through and I'll bring your dinner,' she instructed. 'It won't last much longer.'

He wiped his hand tiredly over his face and did

not move to get up. 'I'll eat it here,' he said.

Once more Nell tutted under her breath. She didn't like him sitting at the kitchen table, never mind eating at it. He should go into the dining-room like he always did. But it wasn't her place to comment and so she glanced at her daughter, giving a nod of the head that was so slight it would have been missed by anyone other than Rosy, who was expecting it and looking for it.

Obeying the unspoken command, she got up from the table and pulled another chair up to the fire and arranged the wet trousers over the back. The shirt she took through to the laundry room and stuffed in the basket with all the other dirty washing.

'Do you want us to get Ivan and Joey to look for her?' Nell asked. She had his plate in her hands and was about to put it down in front of him, but she hesitated, glancing down at it with a grimace. 'This is no better than a burnt offering,' she said. 'I'll have to get you something else.'

'No,' he put his hand on her arm and stopped her turning away. 'It will be fine. I'm not that hungry.'

That's a blessing, Rosy thought, remembering her own fight to get her teeth through the dried up pork and rubbery beans.

'And no, I don't want you to get anyone to look for her. I know where she will be.' His gaze swung to Rosy then back to her mother. 'We all know where she will be.' His voice echoed with the heaviness that dulled his eyes and furrowed his brow.

The bleakness in him touched Rosy's heart. 'She might not be,' she said, attempting to offer some comfort. 'She might have gone for a walk,' she added, ignoring the raised eyebrows her mother was poking at her.

But John Hardaker's expression was also filled with disbelief. So was his voice, as he questioned, 'In this weather?' And she turned away, knowing it had been a stupid thing to say.

The back of his coat was almost dry and, pleased to have found an occupation, she turned it so the front was to the fire. Then she fiddled unnecessarily with his trousers, and despite trying to shove the thought away found herself reliving her wanton eagerness in the car.

What would he think of her? She had been far too willing. She recalled her unresisting response to his kisses, and a warmth came to her cheeks which was nothing to do with the close proximity of the fire. She glanced round, taking a furtive peek at him as he sat at the table. His hair was damp and fluffier than usual and, despite the lines of trouble etched on his features, it made him look younger and much more like Nicky.

He really was a very attractive man, she thought. For his age! That was the problem. He was more than twice her own age. But she had quite liked kissing him.

Stop it, she ordered herself, pulling her eyes quickly away and giving his damp trousers more unnecessary attention. He *was* married.

It was later in the afternoon before the missing lady returned, or rather *was* returned.

Rosy had been to school to collect Nicky and they had been given a lift back in Terry Williams' bread van. By the time Terry dropped them at the gate, to walk up the drive, the rain had thankfully ceased but the ground was very wet and there were plenty of puddles for Nicky to splash in. And the sky was full of dismal grey clouds that threatened to evacuate their contents at any moment.

'We talked about having brothers and sisters at school today,' Nicky suddenly said, as he splashed in a particularly large puddle.

'Did you?' Rosy stopped walking and turned to him, concerned that the subject might have upset him. 'And did you tell them you had had a brother?'

'I said I'd got a brother called Guy and that we were twins.'

She smiled tightly, and her voice was gentle, as she said, 'But did you tell them he had gone to live with Jesus in heaven?'

He looked up then, a frown crinkling his childish features into a perplexity that she would, at another time, have found amusing. With the present subject she only found it increased her concern.

'But if someone is living with Jesus, does it feel as if they're still here?' he asked.

'They still belong to us,' she said gently, wrapping her arm around his shoulders and steering him out of the puddle and on up the drive. 'Guy is still your brother. It's just that you can't see him and be with him any more.'

'But I can feel him!' he insisted.

Rosy's chest lifted on a deep, but silent sigh. 'Yes . . . perhaps you can,' she said, unwilling to hurt him by telling him it was impossible. They had been twins, she reminded herself. They had shared something she, as a single birth, could never understand.

They had reached the house and were about to turn into the courtyard, when the sound of a car's engine made Rosy look back down the drive to the gate.

A large black Mercedes had pulled up at the gates. It was not one she knew. Who is that, she was asking herself, as the passenger door opened and a pair of female legs swung out and planted red stiletto heeled shoes on the ground.

Oh no! Feeling as if her heart had stopped beating, Rosy stood transfixed. Even at that distance it was clearly Dorothy Hardaker getting out of the car. When she was standing up she closed the door and tottered drunkenly round to the driver's side, stuck her head through the open window and appeared to be giving the driver a long, lingering kiss. Then she stood back, laughing, as the tyres squealed and the car made a lot of noise as it sped away.

She must be very drunk, Rosy thought, unable to

believe she would really have wanted her son to see that. She glanced down at him. Fortunately, they had stopped right by the side of another puddle and his attention was taken up with seeing how far he could walk into it, before the water came over the top of his shoes. In the next moment she had hold of him by the arm and was dragging him across the courtyard and into the house, before the puddle lost its interest and he saw his mother walking unsteadily up the drive.

'Go and change out of your school things,' she instructed him, the moment they were through the door. Then, taking no notice of the surprised expression her mother was giving her, pushed him straight across the kitchen and into the hall and up the first two stairs, wanting him out of the way before his mother came through the front door. 'I'll have your drink and biscuits waiting when you come down,' she promised.

He grumbled and his bottom lip protruded in a mutinous scowl, but he went up the stairs, leaving her free to return alone to answer the questions she knew were at that moment forming on her mother's lips.

'Where is he?' she asked.

'In the office,' Nell replied, having no need to enquire who 'he' might be. She was doing a pile of ironing and she carefully laid the hot iron aside and gave her daughter her full attention.

'Well let's hope he has his head down and was not standing at the window a few minutes ago.' Shrugging out of her coat Rosy dropped it on the table in a manner that echoed her weariness with it all, then fixed her mother with a bleak gaze. 'Because if he was, we're in for a hell of a night.'

'What's happened now?' Nell asked, her hand reaching for her throat.

'Mrs Hardaker is back.' There was no joy in the statement. 'She is at the moment coming up the drive.' She folded her arms and pressed them hard against her chest, attempting to still the angry heaving of her lungs, as she thought about Nicky being there to witness it all. 'She has just been given a lift home! By some man in a Mercedes. And I'm sure she gave him a goodbye kiss.'

'What do you mean? A peck on the cheek?'

'No . . . I do not mean a peck on the cheek!'

The sound of the front door opening made them both fall silent and listen as it closed with an un-necessarily loud bang. Dorothy Hardaker's metal tipped heels clip-clopped slowly across the polished wooden floor of the hall. Then, with the same lack of speed, padded softly up the plush carpeting of the stairs.

'She's going to her room,' Nell said, needlessly.

'Thank goodness for that.' Rosy heaved a sigh of relief. John Hardaker had not been in the hall to greet his wife, so he must have missed the little scene at the gate.

It was only a few minutes after his mother had gone up the stairs, that Nicky came down them. Rosy held her breath, for fear he made any comment about her. But he remained silent, and while he dived into his biscuits and glass of Tizer, Nell took a cup of tea through to his father in the office.

Rosy was busy putting the biscuit tin back into the pantry and sending up a grateful thank you that Dorothy Hardaker's return had not caused the ex-pected commotion, when Nell returned.

'He wants to see you,' she said.

'What for?' Rosy questioned, holding back from rushing straight through to him. All she could think was that he had witnessed his wife's arrival, and that he had also seen her, as well. He thought she had got a better view than he had and he wanted to question her, she told herself, her stomach beginning to churn with anxiety.

Nell gave a shrug that said, Don't ask me. 'But he did say he wanted to see you *immediately*,' she stressed.

Rosy gave a nod and turned bleakly for the door, wondering what he was going to say to her.

He was standing at the window, his hands stuffed deep into his trouser pockets, a far away gaze fixed on the fast flowing river. An air of dejection hung around him and, although he had answered her tap on the door, he did not speak when she entered the office.

She could not decide if his silence showed he had seen the Mercedes bring his wife home, or if it was nothing more than a coolness towards herself, after letting him kiss her then turning him down. There was only one way to find out she told herself, but it was still several seconds before she plucked up the courage to speak out. 'Mrs Hardaker is back,' she said, with a confidence she was not feeling.

He did not reply. The silence of the room expanded, like a vice that was opening out and pushing them apart. It was as if he was unwilling to accept she was standing there, she thought. Or perhaps the subject he wanted to broach was too painful. 'You asked to see me,' she pointed out, trying to drag some response from him.

'Yes,' he replied shortly, and glanced round at her with a coldness in his gaze that seemed to reach across the room and run icy fingers down her spine. 'I know my wife has returned.'

Relief washed over her, but only for a moment. 'You saw her coming up the drive?' she questioned, still hoping he was going to say no, that he had only heard her footsteps in the hall.

He nodded his head and replied, 'Yes,' in such a quiet, certain manner that she knew he had seen it all and her heart went out to him.

If it had been yesterday, or even this morning, she would have gone to him and put her hand on his arm and offered him comfort. But now she dare not approach him, fearing to make any contact that might be misconstrued as something more than it really was. 'Then you must have seen Nicky and myself coming up the drive, as well?' she said, just for something to say.

She had expected to receive an intense questioning and, along with it, be subjected to some of the anger meant for his wife. But nothing could have prepared her for the way he suddenly spun round and came for her, as if he was going to physically attack her.

'Yes,' he growled, coming up in front of her and glaring down at her. 'I saw my wife being brought home, but that doesn't matter half so much as seeing *you* brought home in a bread van!'

'What!' she gasped, stumbling backwards in an attempt to get out of the way of the angrily blasted breath that was hitting her right in the face. 'Terry gave us a lift. So we wouldn't get wet.'

'It wasn't raining!' he blazed.

'But it looked as if it might start at any moment,' she countered feebly, stinging from what she considered to be a great injustice. He had no real reason to object to them taking a lift. He was just letting his frustration out on the wrong person. Straightening her spine and lifting her chin, she returned his glare. 'If it had begun to rain as heavily as it had done earlier we would have been drenched. I was trying to protect Nicky from that! Was that so wrong?'

For a moment he looked cornered. Then he spun away and returned to the window, fastening his gaze on the grey outside once more, before he said, 'I don't want to see *you* in that van again! I don't want you having anything to do with Terry Williams.'

The force of his words widened her eyes and made her jaw drop open. He was making it sound as if he was speaking just about her, she realized, shocked and annoyed that he should consider himself in a position to tell her what to do. 'I really don't think it's any of your business who I have anything to do with!' she retaliated, the words clipped as they were forced through her clenched jaw.

Settling his hands on his hips he turned to face her squarely. His movements were slow and controlled, as if to let go would be releasing a force he had no control over. For a time he only glared at her, his eyes filled with an hostility she had never seen in him before, not even during the most violent arguments with his wife. When finally he spoke his words were as clipped and forced as her own had been.

'My son was with you!' he pointed out. 'And where he is and what he is doing is very much my business. I will not have him driving around in bread vans with the likes of Terry Williams!'

Rosy's head slumped forward and she stared at the carpet. 'I'm sorry. I'm sorry.' She had got the wrong impression. It was Nicky he had been concerned for. 'But I think you're worrying for nothing.' Lifting her head she looked him in the eyes. 'I've known Terry since school and don't find anything wrong with him. But I won't let Nicky anywhere near him again.' Terry had a reputation as a bit of a rogue. But he had never done her any harm and, as far as she was concerned, his cheeky personality and ever smiling face was like a breath of fresh air, especially on dismal days like today.

But John Hardaker was not convinced. He stared at her for yet another, prolonged silence. Then he proved she had been wrong to change her opinion, when he said, very emphatically, 'I don't want to see you near him, either. He drives like a maniac. I don't want you getting hurt.'

The protest that came to her mind was brought up short. He turned his back on her and returned to staring out of the window, making it obvious the colourless day was far more interesting than she was. Biting her lip to stop herself saying anything that would cause an all out war between them, she walked to the door. He had made it obvious she was not going to win and she could only conclude his attitude was more to do with seeing his wife, and not wanting to admit it, than from anything to do with her taking a lift in Terry Williams' bread van.

CHAPTER SEVEN

'Somethin's got to be done!' Bill Cowlishaw finished his tea before crossing the kitchen to Nell, who was washing up after doing a pile of baking. Fresh scones, jam tarts and chocolate buns covered the table. 'Thanks,' he said distractedly, as he handed her the empty cup and saucer. He looked worried and, as he turned back to Rosy, he removed his tortoiseshell glasses and pulled a clean white handkerchief from his pocket. He gave the lenses a very thorough polish, using the time for a few moments of deep contemplation. 'Can't you speak to 'im?' he finally asked, and returned the glasses to their proper place on his nose.

Rosy gave a resigned sigh. Every Friday Bill had taken to bringing the rent money he collected to the house. Previously John Hardaker would have picked it up from the office himself, but he had not been to the office in months and so it was left to Bill to do the rounds of the rented properties, bringing the money to Rosy to cash up and bank.

But for the last three weeks he had been four payments short, from the only properties owned in the nearby village of Holbrook. They were terraced grey stone cottages and the roof of one was leaking badly and a second had one small leak. But after several complaints, and no action, all four tenants had banded together, insisting the entire roof was past repair and that they wanted a new one before they paid another penny.

'I can have a try.' She gave a little shrug. 'But I can't promise he'll listen.'

' 'e's got to listen.' Bill tugged at the bottom of the

maroon waistcoat which, along with his trilby, Rosy had the feeling he had been born in. Although the hat would be taken off when he came inside, she had never seen him part company with the waistcoat.

'Them roofs are real bad an' I've got nothin' but sympathy for 'em,' Bill continued, picking up the trilby from the corner of the dresser. 'I shan't be knockin' on any of their doors 'til he's done somethin'. An' you can tell 'im that, an' all!' he added with feeling, and slapped the hat down on his head, while Rosy watched, fascinated. It always fell in exactly the right position: at a cocky angle slightly to the back and to the side. It never failed to amaze her. It was as if he had a magnet in his head that drew it to the spot.

'I'll try,' she promised, not very hopefully. It was six months since the day Dorothy Hardaker had come home in the Mercedes and returned to her old ways. It was also six months since the day she had let John Hardaker kiss her. She did not know for certain which event had affected him most: his wife; or her own rejection. But she did know it was from that day that he had lost all enthusiasm for everything – including his work.

He spent more and more time away from the house. No-one knew where he went. He often came home with the smell of whisky on him so they guessed The White Horse was still one of his main ports of call. And the occasions when he ventured inside his office were getting rarer and rarer.

Bill gave a nod. 'See you next week.' He touched the brim of his hat and turned briefly to Nell, to include her, as he said, 'Bye.' Then he was gone.

Nell turned from the sink and wiped her hands on a tea towel. 'They've been complaining about them roofs for weeks. What with that snow at Easter. It's no wonder they are up in arms. You'd have thought he'd have got round to doing something by now!'

'I know,' Rosy replied bleakly. On the first occasion

she had cashed up for Bill she had expected John Hardaker to complain when he found she had been meddling with his accounting. But he had said nothing, and neither had he mentioned the subsequent weeks' entries into the cash book. So, as he never made himself available for Bill's visits, she could only assume he was happy with the arrangement and now expected her to be there to do it for him. But repairs to the property were another matter. Bill, himself, was better qualified in that department than she was.

'He's got to get back in the driving seat before long. He's businessman enough to know it can't all run itself.' At least he used to be, she thought, realizing she was trying to convince herself as much as her mother.

Picking up one of the freshly made chocolate buns she nibbled at it thoughtfully, and wished she was cleverer and wiser to the ways of business. She knew too little about it to know if he had any legal responsibility to his tenants. But surely he had a moral obligation to them.

'I'm going to get Nicky,' she suddenly said, and popped the last of the bun into her mouth.

'You'll be far too early!' Nell protested.

'I'm going the long way,' she called over her shoulder, as she went out of the door. One half of her was telling her it was none of her concern if John Hardaker wanted to let his business run into the ground. But the other would not let her rest and the more she thought about what he was, or rather was not doing, the more angry she became.

On top of worrying about John Hardaker and the business, she arrived at school to find Nicky had got involved in another fight. A chair and an aquarium full of snails had been broken and the moment she walked through the gate she was summoned before a very irate Mr Brownlow.

'What on earth were you doing?' she demanded, the moment she got Nicky out of the school gate and far enough down the lane not to be heard by the small group of parents watching the netball game in the playground.

His bottom lip protruded and all she received was a scowl. It took several promptings from her, before he finally said, 'Brian Simpson said I didn't have a brother. That I was making it up.'

'Oh love!' She stopped walking and pulled him into her arms. 'It doesn't matter what Brian Simpson says. We know Guy was real.'

'He is real!' he insisted, stamping his foot and pushing away from her and racing off down the lane.

He ran so fast she only caught up with him when he reached the busy main road and had to wait for the traffic before crossing.

'Nicky!' she gasped, in a mixture of relief and alarm. She grabbed his arm before he could race off again. 'You mustn't do that! You might have fallen over and hurt yourself.' Her real fear had been that he would race straight across the road without looking. Fortunately, he had not been too upset to remember to stop, and he did not resist her as she led him across. 'Now . . . let's walk properly,' she said, releasing her grip on his arm and taking hold of his hand as they began to walk along the pavement at the other side.

He fell silent, not even asking to stop at the shop for an ice-cream, and they had walked through the village and were crossing the meadow, before Rosy said, 'I can understand what you think and feel because I know about you and I know about Guy. But other people don't know and when you talk about him as if he's alive they find it odd.'

She paused to let him speak, but he remained silent, and so she said, 'Guy is your brother, whether he is alive or dead. No-one can change that.'

'You think he's dead!' he cried accusingly. 'You're like all the others. You think he's dead!'

'No love! No!' He would have raced off again but

she pulled him back, turned him round and wrapped her arms tightly round him. 'I don't . . .' she began, then fell silent, her mind's eye filling with the image of a glimpse of the blue and red of Guy's coat being swept away by the swollen river. She closed her eyes and took a deep breath. Then she looked down at him, lifting his chin so that he was looking back at her. His eyes were moist and filled with a pain he was too young to cope with, and her heart curled for him. 'I don't know for sure if Guy is alive or dead,' she said. It was a lie, she was convinced in her own mind of what she had seen on that terrible day. But at that moment Nicky did not want to hear cold facts. 'I only know I want you to not go talking about him at school again. If you want to talk about him wait until you're at home with me. Because I understand. People at school don't.'

He gave a nod. Then he pushed away from her again, though this time not in anger, and they walked along the path hand in hand, only deviating from it once and having to go into the soft grass when they came upon a cluster of five cows who were standing in their way.

By the time they had reached the lane and were crossing the railway bridge, he was telling her about the papier-mâché head he had made for a glove puppet. They were making the bodies the following week and he had to take some material for that.

'Have we got some red?' he asked. 'I want mine to be red,' he said, as they turned up the drive to Derwent House and passed the gatehouse cottage. Fortunately Joey was not there to delay them.

'If we haven't we'll go and buy some,' she promised, and stared at the river and wondered why Guy's body had never been found. That was all it would take to answer so many questions, solve so many problems. Nicky, his mother, and even his father. John Hardaker might not show it in the same way, but the loss of his son had left its mark on him, as well. If nothing else, his temper was far shorter since Guy's disappearance.

*　　*　　*

The dining-room was never used now. Nicky and Rosy ate their meals in the kitchen and John Hardaker had his on the desk in his office, where he would hide himself the moment he got home. Tonight was to be no different. Had they not heard the car coming up the drive and pull into the courtyard they would not have known he had come home.

'I'll take that.' Rosy stopped her mother as she was about to pick the tray up. 'I want a word with your dad,' she said, turning to Nicky as she lifted the tray from the table. 'So you stay here.'

'Can we swim afterwards?' he asked, lifting his third chocolate bun to his mouth – before deciding the buns were best he had tried the jam tarts and the scones.

She hesitated, gazing down on him with exaggerated sternness. 'I'll think about it. I'm not sure you deserve any treats after today. Besides . . .' she added, her voice lightening as she found it impossible to be angry with him for long, '. . . after eating that lot you're likely to sink.'

He grinned as she walked out.

When she got to the office door she paused, collecting herself and making sure there was no evidence of a smile still lingering on her face. When she felt her expression was suitable to the occasion, she knocked and walked in.

He was sitting on the window seat. At first glance he appeared to be watching the river, but there was a vacancy about his expression that made her doubt he was seeing anything.

She placed the tray down on the desk, then turned to him. 'Can I have a word?'

He looked up then. 'Yes,' he replied, a tremor of uncertainty in his voice. She thought he was finding it odd that she should request to speak to him. On the rare occasions when they did find themselves together now, she usually spoke only when spoken to. But then she saw his eyes go to the tray.

'It's chicken salad. It won't go cold,' she said, altering her opinion that he was showing concern. It was for his dinner, which he thought was going to spoil if she delayed him eating. 'But if you want to eat while we talk I don't mind.'

He shook his head. 'What did you want?'

'The Holbrook Cottages need new roofs,' she said, without preamble. Out of nowhere suddenly came the recollection of a time before when she had stood in that office: when he had given her the job of nanny; when she had walked out of the door feeling like a woman for the very first time. Well, a lot of water had gone under the bridge since that day. It was no shrinking violet who now stood before him. That he was the chief reason for the maturity he was about to get the full blast of, almost brought a smile to her face.

'What . . . ?' He frowned uncomprehendingly, as if this was the first time he had heard of it.

She did smile then, but rather grimly. 'Don't pretend you don't know.' Her head shook in disbelief. 'I told you weeks ago, when we got the first complaint. And I've been reminding you ever since. You also knew they hadn't been paying their rents. Well they haven't paid this week either and Bill refuses to go and ask them again until you've done something about it. He thinks they have every right to complain.'

'If he wants his wages he'll do as he's bloody well told!' he snarled, jumping to his feet, pulling his shoulders back and straightening his spine with a determination that also filled his voice.

Rosy cocked her eyebrows in surprise. It was months since she had seen this much life in him. 'And who is going to tell him that bit of information?' she enquired pointedly. 'Will you be here next week to see him? Or will you be giving everybody a shock by showing your face at the office for a change?'

His shoulders slumped and he turned from her.

'That's no good,' she insisted. 'Turning your back on me won't make the problem go away.' She lifted her hands in the air and gave a groan of despair. 'I don't know what's the matter with you. Why are you acting this way? You know the business can't run itself, so why don't you get back to it properly?'

His head lifted and he looked up at the ceiling as if seeking divine assistance. Then he turned and settled a bleak gaze on her face. 'Get back to it,' he growled, his voice filled with a bitterness that almost made her flinch. 'What for? So I can make more money for my wife to get soused on!' His arm flew through the air as if he was throwing something nasty away.

'I think there is more than one person in this house who is trying to drown their sorrows,' she countered meaningfully. She was being unfair because he was not an alcoholic like his wife. But she had the feeling if he was allowed to carry on much longer he might get there.

'Damn you!' he grated. His jaw vibrated and he balled his fists and moved slowly forward. For a moment she thought he was going to hit her and her first thought was to turn and run from him. It took all her strength to keep her standing there.

'I don't have to ask your permission if I want to go for a drink.' He pushed his face so close to hers she could feel the force of his angry breath. 'It's none of your business what I do!' he spat.

'True,' she agreed with feeling, fixing her gaze challengingly to his and concealing the shiver of revulsion that ran down her spine, as whisky fumes invaded her nostrils. 'But I would have thought you were intelligent enough to recognize friendly advice when it's offered.'

'Friendly advice!' he scoffed. 'You're just poking your nose in!'

'I am not!' She took greater offence because she

knew it was true. She was poking her nose in, but only out of concern. 'I'm trying to make you see what should be obvious to you. You need to get back behind your desk. You need to get back to running the business.'

'Why?' he enquired, with a lack of emotion that made her want to scream. Then his voice rose, as he demanded, 'Give me one good reason!'

Her hands dropped to her sides as if she was defeated. But then her chin jutted out and a defiant gleam lit her eyes. 'Nicky,' she said simply.

His eyes flickered with a pain she had not intended to render. But she would not back down, and she said, 'In case you had forgotten, you do have a son . . .' She was not given time to finish speaking.

'You don't have to remind me of anything!' He pushed past her and almost knocked her flying as he rushed for the door.

She grabbed for the support of the desk and, incensed by his roughness, yelled after him, 'And what about the Holbrook roofs?'

'See to it yourself if it bothers you so much!' he countered hatefully, before slamming the door on her.

'I'm out,' Rosy called, grabbing the side of the swimming-pool and catching her breath. Although she could usually manage eight to ten lengths at a leisurely pace, this evening six had finished her off, and that had been with a struggle. She was still smarting from John Hardaker's anger and the first few lengths had been attacked with aggressive speed and worn her out.

Nicky did not stop. His small arms sliced through the water in a very able crawl and he completed ten lengths, seemingly without any affect.

'I'm going to dive now,' he said, and displayed his superior energy by hauling himself up the side and racing full pelt to the diving-board at the deep end.

'Off the side please!' Rosy called out in warning. She

had taught him to dive off the side of the pool but he had never used the board before.

Ignoring the order he climbed the four steps and ran along the board.

'Nicky!' In panic she struck out across the pool, trying to get to the board before he jumped. But her anxiety was without cause, her assistance not needed. Raising his arms above his head he did a light spring and leapt into the air. Like a pair of scissors his body doubled up, stretched out, and entered the water with his legs straight behind him, if not in an exactly perpendicular and splash free manner.

'When did you learn to do that?' she asked, full of admiration when he popped up like a cork.

He broke into a wide grin. 'At school. Mr Tomes said I was good at it.'

A smile flooded her own face. 'You are,' she agreed with feeling. Then she threw her head back and laughed and thanked the heavens at the same time. She had long been confident that he was an assured enough swimmer to have some feeling of mastery over water. But she had never expected him to gain so much confidence he would be able to do this – at only seven years old – and still with a great fear of the river inside him.

'You are very clever and I am very proud of you,' she said, and lifted him high in the air and held him there, as they both laughed with pleasure.

'And what do we have to be proud of?'

In unison their heads spun round at the unexpected voice. Dorothy Hardaker was standing dangerously close to the side of the pool. She had gone out that morning and, although she usually appeared in the late afternoon to do herself up before going out again in the evening, today she had not returned.

Until now! Rosy thought drily, as she slowly lowered Nicky back into the water. If her appearance was anything to go by she had only just walked through the door. She was still wearing the same sky-blue suit she had gone out in and her navy blue bag was still hanging over her shoulder. Her face was flushed and bore a silly smile, and she was having great difficulty in standing still in the high stiletto heels she had on her feet.

'Nicky can dive from the board now,' Rosy said, just as one of Dorothy Hardaker's feet went completely over on its slender heel. The woman tottered and almost fell into the water.

'I should move back,' Rosy suggested, fearing for her safety. 'The tiles can be very slippery when you have shoes on,' she added, even though she felt getting wet might sober her up. But she would be the one who had to drag her out.

Dorothy Hardaker tossed her head on a harsh laugh, threw her bag down and kicked her shoes off. One went scuttling along the tiles, the other fell into the water and sank. 'He must take after me then,' she said. 'I was very good at diving.' She set off walking round the pool to the diving-board, holding her spine stiff and appearing not to be in full control of her legs.

Rosy's mouth dropped open as she watched her. 'What . . . what are you doing?' she called. Her voice was full of anxiety for she could see exactly what was on her mind. 'You can't! Not in your state.'

Dorothy Hardaker flapped a disparaging hand at her. 'I am in no *state*, girl. And I can do what I damned well please in my own house!'

Rosy could only watch in growing horror as Dorothy Hardaker reached the diving-board steps and tripped up the first one. As she grasped the rail and hauled herself unsteadily up the remaining three steps, Rosy knew nothing she could say was going to stop her.

In panic she turned to Nicky. 'Quick! Get out! Run and get your dad.' She had him to the side of the pool and had pushed him out before she stopped to wonder if John Hardaker was still at home, or if he had rushed off to the pub after their argument. 'Get somebody! Anybody, Nicky!' she called, as he raced dripping across the tiles and out of the door.

In the same moment as Rosy's frantic gaze swung back to the diving-board, Dorothy Hardaker reached the end.

'No!' she called, too paralysed with fear to move as she watched the drunken woman tug her straight skirt up above her thighs and reveal lacy black pants and matching suspender belt.

They were like some their Maggie owned, Rosy thought stupidly, as Dorothy Hardaker lifted her hands above her head, swung them round in the air three times, gave a scream of glee, and fell off.

As she surfaced Rosy was by her side. She grabbed one of her flailing arms, but with another whoop of glee Dorothy Hardaker shoved her off.

'Stop being stupid!' Rosy shouted, and grabbed the first thing available: the woman's hair.

Dorothy Hardaker gave a screech and lashed out, hitting Rosy across the face. Taken by surprise Rosy let her go and floundered unsteadily. In the next moment she was underwater. She did not panic, not to begin with. That came after a few moments, when she realized she could not get herself back up again because something was pressing on her head. It was another moment before her panic striken mind knew what it was: two hands.

Dorothy Hardaker was holding her down! Trying to drown her! The next moments were a blur. All she knew was that her arms and legs flailed madly as she tried to grab, pull and shove at the woman to get her away. But the hands on her head only exerted more force. She was at the point where she felt her lungs were going to burst, when suddenly she was grabbed by the neck and hauled from the water like a drowning pup.

'You bloody bitch!' Rosy heard John Hardaker curse, somewhere between all her coughing and spluttering and gasping for breath. He let go of her neck and she experienced a moment of terror, thinking she was going to sink again. But then his arms came round her and she was being lifted up and carried to the side. Laying her on the tiles he hauled himself out, knelt by her side and supported her shoulders. 'Are you all right?' he asked, his voice full of concern, his gaze fixed anxiously on her face.

'Yes . . . yes . . . I think so,' she gasped, pressing her hand to her chest. It felt bruised from the inside and every breath she took was painful, but she was breathing.

'Where . . . where's Nicky?' she asked. She was suddenly filled with the new horror that he might have witnessed it all – and what that might have done to him.

'He's with your mother. I told her to keep him in the kitchen.'

She smiled her appreciation, thankful he had had the sense to understand.

As if reading her mind, he said, 'I didn't know what was happening, but I thought it best to keep him away.' His tone deepened, became ironic. 'Even though I thought it was his mother who was in danger.' He looked round and Rosy followed his gaze. 'I should have known the only drowning she'll do will be in gin,' he added drily, as they watched her haul herself up the steps and out of the pool.

Her suit was sodden and impeded her movements. Rosy shook her head, wondering how the woman had been able to master her so easily in the water. One was drunk, the other stone cold sober! One fully clothed in a suit which must have weighed her down, the other in a swimming costume! It didn't seem possible, but it had happened. If John Hardaker had not come to her aid she dreaded to think what the outcome might have been.

She looked up at him, at his dripping hair and the

shirt and trousers clinging wetly to him, and she forced a thin smile of gratitude to her lips. 'Thank you,' she said, as imagination of how things could have turned out sent a shiver rippling over her skin, which he felt and saw.

'Do you feel all right?' His brow furrowed in a frown beneath the wet spikes of his hair. He pulled his arm more tightly round her and peered into her eyes, as if expecting to find some answer there that she would not speak.

'Very moving!' Dorothy Hardaker's sarcastic voice sliced between them like a knife.

Her husband's gaze instantly hardened, then pivoted to her mocking smile. Rosy shifted nervously, attempting to remove his arm from her shoulder. Dorothy Hardaker did not want him, but Rosy was sure she would make good use of any little thing she thought might point to some indiscretion on his part. And she preferred her name not to be bandied about the local bars.

'I'm all right now,' she said, pushing his arm away. 'It was nothing, really.' Her breathing was easier, her chest less painful.

Dorothy Hardaker gave a cackle of a laugh. 'Oh dear!' she scoffed. 'I don't think she appreciates your touch!'

Like a spring uncoiling, his legs straightened out and he was standing up and spinning round on her all at the same time. 'If you don't get out of here *now*!' he blazed, thrusting his finger out and jabbing the air between them as if with a knife. 'You'll be back in there and *you'll* be the one fighting for breath!'

'Threats, my darling?' Her eyes widened and she shook her head in mocking disbelief. 'Not exactly the thing to do. Not when you've already put me in hospital once before. I think the police would find it very interesting!' Her finely arched eyebrows lifted expressively.

Balling his fists he moved towards her. 'Do you think anything could be worse than having to live with you?'

Thankfully, Rosy found some strength from somewhere and managed to get to her feet and hold him back. 'Don't!' she cried. 'She's deliberately goading you. Can't you see?'

'Better do as she says.' Dorothy Hardaker's voice hardened spitefully. 'After all . . . she is the little mother of your son! You wouldn't want to go upsetting her!' With that she turned and marched round the edge of the pool and swept out of the door without once stumbling or hesitating.

'She . . . she wasn't drunk!' Rosy gasped, the truth shocking her to her very core.

The angry clenching of his jaw relaxed and he looked down at her with an uncomprehending frown.

'She *was* drunk,' she said, trying to persuade herself. 'That's why I sent Nicky for you. She was stumbling all over the place and I knew if she fell in I wouldn't be able to get her out myself.' Only then realizing she was still holding on to him, she let him go and wrapped her arms around herself.

'Why?' she asked, looking bleakly round the surface of the pool as if she expected the answer might suddenly leap out of the water at her. There was nothing except the gentle rippling of the filtration system. She shook her head, unable to take it in. It had all been a sham. For some reason Dorothy Hardaker had fooled her into believing she was drunk and incapable. Then she had deliberately tried to kill her!

Knowing exactly what she was doing the woman had attempted to drown her. And she had almost succeeded!

CHAPTER EIGHT

'Why does she have to live with us?' Nicky asked, as they turned along the lane leading to the school. He had been quiet since leaving the house and the sudden, unexpected question startled Rosy.

'She is your mother!' she replied, affecting a gentle sternness. 'Where else would you expect her to live?' He did not know all that had happened in the swimming-pool the previous evening and she had no intention of telling him. 'Mummies usually live with you,' she added, as they crossed the road to the school gate.

'Carol Linthwaite's doesn't,' he replied bluntly.

Rosy stopped abruptly and pulled him round to face her. 'Only because she died,' she said, very seriously. 'And I'm sure Carol would prefer to have her mum still living with her. So don't you go saying anything that will upset her.'

He dropped his head and scuffed the toe of his shoe on a patch of gravel by the side of the school's large stone gatepost. 'Well, I wish mine was dead,' he said with feeling, and lifted his head and brought a very determined gaze up to hers.

'Oh Nicky!' She crouched down to be level with him. For a time she gazed worriedly into his face, then she pulled him into her arms. 'Don't say that!' she insisted. 'Don't wish her dead.' She held him tighter as fear rose inside her, fear of what such bitter thoughts could do to one so young.

In response his arms fastened with equal tightness around her neck. 'I wish you were my mum. I do . . . I do!'

Her smile filled with emotion and she held him away and looked deep into the big, troubled brown eyes. 'I'm as good as any mum to you,' she assured. 'Because I love you as much as a real mum ever could. And I'll never leave you. I'll always be here for you.'

In the next moment his smile had turned sheepish and he was pushing her away. It took a moment for her to realize why. Then she saw his friend Gordon coming up the road with his mother and she knew he was embarrassed to be caught having a cuddle. She stood up, giving him the space he needed. 'Go on,' she said, jerking her head towards the school gate. 'Get yourself off and I'll see you this afternoon.'

He grinned up at her in a way that said thank you for understanding. Then he dashed off into the playground with Gordon and they dived straight into a game of football.

She did not go straight back home. The sun was bright and pleasantly warm and instead of going back into the village she continued past the school and down the hill and took the wooden footbridge over the railway into the big meadow.

As she walked through the grass, still damp with early morning dew, she pondered over why she had the need for solitude. Despite what had happened yesterday, Dorothy Hardaker did not frighten her and she was not staying away from the house in a deliberate attempt at avoiding her. She had no reason to avoid her. Forewarned is forearmed, and now that it had happened once she would make sure she never got into a situation where a similar thing could happen again.

After crossing the river by a makeshift bridge, which was nothing more than a hefty plank the farmer had thrown across at the narrowest point, she walked up the fields and into the wood at the top of the bank behind the house.

Since discovering Maggie used the old cottage at the edge of the wood for her assignations, Rosy had kept right away from it. But, for some reason she had never been able to understand, she had always felt a peace when she was close to the empty building, and now she turned towards it, feeling its isolation was just what she needed.

Dorothy Hardaker might not pose a problem for her, she told herself, as she sat on the crumbling garden wall and looked across the fields to the village. But the woman was obviously a far greater problem to Nicky than she had previously believed. She shivered, recalling the cold determination on his face when he had wished his mother dead. He usually said so little about her that she had foolishly imagined he had the ability to close himself off from her. But this morning had shown how wrong she had been and that he did have very strong, and very powerful feelings where his mother was concerned.

'Hey up, Rosy! You look as if you've lost a pound and found a penny.'

Dragged from her pensive thoughts, Rosy looked up to see Ivan Fletcher, the Hardaker's gardener, coming through the woods. 'Hello, Ivan. What are you doing up here?'

'Lookin' for bean sticks.' He tossed three, long straight branches down on the ground, ledged his bottom on the wall by her side, lifted his green-checked cap and ran his hand over his bald head, as if smoothing down the hair he seemed to have forgtten he had lost. Then he pulled out a packet of cigarettes. After he had lit up, he gave a sigh. 'You can't get 'em like you used to.'

Rosy smiled. 'Bean sticks or cigarettes?' she joked.

'Bean sticks,' he replied, not seeing anything amusing in what he considered to be a very serious subject. 'You used to be able to come up here and lay your hands on a couple of dozen without any bother. Now they're all bent. You can pass twenty trees and find none with as much as one straight branch. It's coming to somethin' I can tell you.' He took a noisy draw on the cigarette and fell silent. 'I've had to send our Joey right over the top to see if they're any better on the other side.'

'Perhaps the trees remember you from previous years,' she replied drily. 'They see you coming and twist their branches so you'll leave them alone.'

He gave a half-smile and sucked at the cigarette once more. 'What's up with everybody today? Your Mam's bitten me head off for not plantin' any spring cabbage, and it was her that told me not to. And them two's havin' a right go at each other.' He craned his neck round to look into her face. 'And you aren't exactly full of the joys of spring.'

'Why are they having a go at each other?' she asked, having no need to enquire who 'them two' were. It must still be about last night, she thought. She couldn't think what else it could be. John and Dorothy Hardaker were not in the habit of seeing each other in the morning, or at any other time of day for that matter. Unless they had something specific to say to each other.

Ivan gave a shrug. 'Somethin' and nothin'. Same as usual.'

As usual! Rosy thought, and jumped down from the wall into the grass, making her red and orange floral skirt billow out like a parachute. 'I'll leave you to get on finding your bean sticks,' she said. If the Hardakers were at each other her mother would be wanting her support, so she had better get back.

Ivan's reply was an unintelligible grumble and Rosy walked away wondering how Joey was getting on in his den. She had to admit she had been wrong about him. In all the months he had been allowed to use the gatehouse cottage he had not once done anything to cause any alarm. After rearing his 'blackies' he had tended a thrush which he found out in the lane, having been hit by a car, and at present he was foster parent to two orphaned squirrels he had found after following a couple of men with shotguns, who killed the mother.

The argument was over and all was quiet when Rosy reached home. At least it was until she stepped into the kitchen to meet her mother's angry scowl.

'Where have you been?' she demanded, before Rosy had time to get through the door. She was mopping the floor and she stopped abruptly and turned on her daughter. 'It doesn't usually take you this long to get to school and back again.'

'I wasn't aware there was any reason I had to hurry back.' Rosy pulled her damp shoes off her feet and put them on the hearth to dry.

Nell gave a humph. Putting the mop in the bucket she leant it up against the wall. Then she placed her hands on her hips and fixed Rosy with a telling glare. 'I thought there was going to be murder done and I'd have appreciated you being here! I'd have had no chance of separating them on my own.'

'Well, I'm back now.'

'It's all over now. She's gone!'

'Gone!' Rosy exclaimed in disbelief. 'You mean for good?'

'No I do not,' Nell replied irritably. 'She's gone off on holiday. That's what the row was about. She said she was taking the car. He said she wasn't.'

'So has she gone in the car?'

' 'Course she has. But only after she went for him with the poker.'

'Oh good grief!' Rosy could not understand why she should feel so shocked. She knew the Hardakers were not beyond a physical attack on each other. 'Where is he now?' she asked.

Nell gave a shrug. 'Outside somewhere. He stormed off when she drove off.'

Rosy's chest lifted on a sigh. 'Do you think I should go and look for him?' She did not think he was in any danger. But she could see her mother was worried and would feel easier if something was being done.

Proving her correct, Nell gave a nod. 'It might be wise. He was really wound up.'

'He wouldn't hurt himself,' she said, with the confidence of someone who knows they are right. All the same she went to the door.

But she was saved the trouble of searching for him. As she reached for the latch she was almost knocked flying, as the door swung open and John Hardaker burst through it.

'What the . . . !' she gasped, leaping out of the way as the door cracked against her shoulder before she caught hold of it.

He did not apologize. He went to the table, pressed his hands into the top of it and leaned on his arms, as if a great weight was lying on his shoulders. After a few moments his gaze lifted slowly to Rosy's face. 'Why were you in the wood with Ivan?' he demanded.

She was so taken aback that her mouth dropped open and she could not immediately respond.

'Don't try to deny it!' The tightness of his voice indicated the great tension within him. 'I saw you both. Coming out of the cottage.'

Rosy found her voice then. 'You saw no such thing!' she retaliated, her anger spurred that he could think her capable of such a thing. 'You might have seen me talking to Ivan . . . *at the cottage*! But you did not see either Ivan, or me, coming out of the cottage. For heaven's sake! I was only talking to him. Whatever's the matter with you?' Closing the door she stepped forward, only to be brought up sharp by his next words.

'I don't want you going in the wood with Ivan. Or Joey. Joey is not to be trusted. He acts like a boy but he's got a man's body. He's too big. You wouldn't stand a chance.'

Rosy's head moved slowly from side to side, in a mixture of bewilderment and disbelief. She had never seen John Hardaker this way before and he frightened her. There was an intensity about him that appeared

150

to be verging on insanity. She glanced at her mother, but all she received was a stiff shake of the head, telling her to shut up, not to make any further waves. But she would not lie down and take his abuse.

'Stop it!' she demanded, rounding the table and stopping directly opposite to him. 'Your insinuations are insulting and I'll have no more of them.' She matched his stance, resting her hands on the top and leaning forward, thrusting her face into his and speaking in a manner that brooked no argument. 'Just because you saw me speaking to Ivan. Ivan! If you can think that of either him, or me, you don't hold either of us in very high esteem.'

While she spoke his gaze had remained steely, his lips tightly compressed. But on the last something flickered in his eyes and the determination in him was lost, to be replaced by an emptiness she found confusing.

'I . . . I didn't mean.' His gaze swept bleakly from Rosy to Nell and back again. 'It's just . . .' He sank onto a chair and cradled his head. 'Dorothy. She makes me so mad I'll swing for her one day. I will! I will!'

'You don't mean that. So don't say it.' Rosy hurried round the table to him and laid a hand on his shoulder. 'You don't mean it,' she repeated, fear putting strength in her voice. 'You know, as well as anybody, that she needs help.'

He looked up at her, his lips contorted in a crooked grimace. 'She refuses to be helped. Without her assistance there is nothing can be done. She isn't mad. They can't certify her.'

His voice rose on the last and Rosy's hand tightened on his shoulder. 'I'm sorry,' she said, stabbed with guilt for bringing the subject up. Dorothy Hardaker would not agree to anything, if she thought it was her husband's idea.

He did not speak and she took her hand from his shoulder and dropped it to her side in a manner of defeat. 'Why won't you turn your mind back to work,' she said, and moved to the other side of him and turned her back on her mother, so she could not see the warning glances being flashed her way. 'It would help you.' If he would only get himself back into the working pattern of life he would find himself too busy to brood about his wife.

'How can I do my work without my car?' He sounded like a child who had had his favourite toy taken from him and Rosy had an overwhelming urge to slap him.

She refrained from resorting to a physical assault, she refrained from pointing out that there was plenty of work in his office to keep him going for the time being. But when he turned to her, and cried, 'She's in my car! What am I supposed to do without transport for a week?' she could hold back no longer.

She tossed her head and gave a snort. 'You'll have to walk,' she stated bluntly. She did not point out that he had been without his car enough times in the past, when his wife had it parked permanently in some pub car park. Instead, she said, 'You could always spend a bit of your money and buy yourself another.'

A shocked gasp came from over by the sink.

'Oh stop it, Mum!' she snapped. 'He could afford to buy a garage full of cars. So don't expect me to feel sorry because he's lost one for a *whole* week!' She lifted her chin in defiance and thrust it forward at him. 'Go on!' she insisted. 'Tell me I'm wrong. Tell me I don't know what I'm talking about!'

His lips compressed into a mutinous line. But she had got her message across, for he said, 'I suppose next you'll be throwing the Holbrook cottages at me again? Telling me how stupid and tight-fisted I am not to have dealt with them.'

She shook her head. 'The thought hadn't entered my mind,' she replied honestly. 'But, since you mention it, it would give you something to think about.'

'I have plenty to think about,' he countered fiercely.

'And if the blessed Holbrook cottages are still causing you so much concern, I told you before . . . do it yourself!'

She did not point out it had been he who brought the subject up. 'Right!' she replied icily, her chin taking on a defiant tilt. 'I will! You just see if I don't!'

'Good!' he spat, and not waiting to hear if she had more to say, rushed for the door and out of the room.

That afternoon Rosy did as she had promised. Helping her mother with the daily housework had done nothing to calm her anger and the more time passed by, the more determined she became to prove she could do it. She knew he had not really expected her to pick up the gauntlet, because he did not think she was capable. Well, she would show him!

As soon as lunch was over she went into the office, took the files of old invoices from the shelf and searched through them. There were several from builders who had previously done remedial work and she took them out and spread them on the desk in front of her.

Ten minutes later she had organized three builders to take a look at the cottages and send her a quote, and she was feeling very pleased with herself.

But her few moments of enthusiasm soon wilted and she began to wonder if she had done the wrong thing. She had acted out of anger, determined to show John Hardaker that if he wasn't prepared to do his job, she was more than capable. But now she was seeing another side to what she had done. A side that told her he might be more than willing to let her take the work off his hands. It would give him more time to spend in the pub, and doing it for him wasn't exactly giving him any incentive to get back to normal in order to keep the business going.

Her head slowly shaking with the sadness of it all, she stood up and went to the door. The wheels were now in motion but she could not do anything more until the builders' prices came in.

As she closed the door behind her and walked down the hall towards the kitchen, she wondered where John Hardaker had gone to: if he had walked right round to the village and the White Horse; or if, having no car to take him and knowing his wife would not be there, he had finally gone back to The Derwent at the bottom of the drive. She knew for certain he would be at one or other of the two pubs. What she could still not work out was how he could go drinking the way he did – when he had seen what it had done to his wife.

Heaven forbid lightning doesn't strike the same spot twice, she prayed inwardly.

It was evening before she realized her prayer had been almost prophetic. John Hardaker had stumbled up the drive and fallen flat on his face in the hall.

Unfortunately, Nicky had been coming down the stairs and had seen it all. 'Is he dead?' he asked worriedly, staring down at his father's inert body with wide, frightened eyes.

'Dead drunk!' Nell stated bluntly.

Rosy had been almost too furious to speak. She had managed to reassure Nicky, then tell him to go and wait for them in the kitchen. Then her lips had remained clamped tightly shut as she helped her mother lift him off the floor and heave him up the stairs. She had taken great pleasure in dropping him none too gently onto the bed.

'Serves you right!' she snapped, when he complained of a splitting headache the following morning.

It was a full week before her anger had subsided enough to make it possible for her to speak to him in a civil manner.

'Rosy,' he implored, holding his hands out in supplication. 'How many more times do I have to apologize before you will accept it.'

She was sitting at his desk when he walked into the office. She made no move to get up. Over the week she had spent more and more time at that desk, sorting first one thing out and then another.

She had deliberately ordered a complete new roof along the entire length of the Holbrook cottages, even though the man she had employed to do the job said it wasn't that bad and could have been patched up to give several more years of service. She had hoped that if he saw her throwing his money around without just cause, he would throw her out of his chair and be only too ready to jump back in and keep a tight hold on the purse strings.

Unfortunately, that was not the case. He was more concerned with getting her to accept his apology than getting her away from his desk.

She glanced at him, her gaze cool and filled with disbelief. 'What you did was unforgiveable. So how can you expect me to accept any apology? Besides, it's Nicky you should be begging forgiveness from.'

Whenever she thought of that evening her anger seethed, and it did so now, to such a point that she had to stand up and walk round the desk and across to the window.

'As if that boy, *your son* . . . !' she ground, swinging round and jabbing a finger at him, '. . . has not seen enough of drunks with his mother! How could you?' Her disgust was so great she did not care if she was speaking out of turn. If someone had had the sense to do the same to Dorothy Hardaker before it had been too late, she might never have got into the state she was now in. 'How could you?' She turned back to the window, unable to look at him. 'How could you?' Her head shook from side to side. 'You're as bad as she is. You don't have any real feeling for Nicky. You can't have.'

'That's not true!' he countered fiercely. 'And you know it isn't!'

She craned her neck round and looked at him over her shoulder. 'No,' she said, with great bitterness. 'I don't know anything about you. I thought I did. I was under the impression you cared for your son. I was also under the impression you were a good business-man.' She gave a shrug and turned from him again. Her gaze was fastened on the grey river, when she said, 'But I was wrong about the second so why should I believe I was right about the first?'

'I *am* a good businessman!' he retaliated.

Her eyes did not move from the river, but her mouth twisted in a grim smile. The slur against his compe-tence to do his job had meant more than the suggestion of any lack of ability as a father. She turned on him abruptly, her gaze pivoting to his with the force of a winging dagger. 'You *were* a good businessman . . . *once!*' she stressed pointedly, her voice brittle as ice. 'You had to be to make all the money you've made. But not now. Whatever you had in that department you've lost.'

'That is not true!' His clenched fists hung impotently by his sides. 'What do you know about it? You've only been doing it for a few days and you think you know it all.'

'I know more than I should know,' she replied meaningfully. 'And that only because the person who should be doing it is too wrapped up in feeling sorry for himself.'

His finger shot out and stabbed at her nose. 'You've gone too far. You have no right to speak to me that way and I won't have it.'

'You can please yourself,' she retorted, her chin thrusting out defiantly. 'It's time someone put you straight and I don't care if you like it or not. You have become pathetic, really pathetic since your wife came out of hospital. I know it was you who put her there and that you feel guilty about that, but you have Nicky to consider and his welfare should be uppermost in all you do.' She lifted her own finger then and jabbed it into his chest, trying to prod some reaction from him. '*You* are his father,' she ground. 'If you'd only start acting like one!'

But he did not respond. He just stood there, staring at her with his mouth half-open. Frustration burned inside her and she wanted to scream at him, to shake him until some sense dropped into his silly head. 'Oh . . . !' she gasped. There really were times when she felt she had had enough. She glanced at the pile of invoices lying on the desk. 'I hope you are not expecting me to carry on with this . . . ' her hand swept across the desk, '. . . look after Nicky and do all the running about for your wife?' She fixed him with a mutinous glare. 'I can't do it all. I *won't* do it all!'

'You don't have to run around after Dorothy.'

She gave a groan. He had the unfailing knack of making the wrong choice. He had not told her to leave the invoices, that he would take the pressure off her by taking over the running of the business again. He had told her she did not have to attend his wife!

'And if I don't run up and down stairs, and out to the shops at the click of a finger, my mother would have to do it!' Her gaze hardened pointedly on his. 'And if you think I would allow that, you are greatly mistaken.' Folding her arms tightly across her chest, she turned away from him. 'My mother does enough running around now. She is not going to become a skivvy for your wife!'

'I'm not asking her to. Neither am I asking you to. Rosy . . . ' he spoke her name gently, and came to her side and laid his hand on her shoulder. 'There is a way that we could be happier.'

Her eyes widened and she stared at him in disbelief.

'I could be happy here if you would only get yourself back together.' She could see he was about to make a pass at her and as she pushed his hand from her shoulder she stepped away from him, and pretended she had not understood. 'We've all got used to your wife and can put up with her shindigs. It's you that is the problem now. Can't you see what we can see? More importantly what Nicky can see! You owe it to him, as well as to yourself, to get back to normal.' She dropped her head and stared at the carpet so hard the blue and gold diamond pattern had blurred and seemed to be going round in circles, before she looked up at him and said, 'I don't understand you. Getting stuck into work would take your mind off things much better than getting stuck into a bottomless glass.'

His head drooped and his neck appeared to shrink into his shoulders. He gave a sigh of remorse. 'I've tried to apologize,' he said. 'It was only one day. I learnt my lesson and I haven't done it since. Now have I?'

'No,' she agreed. 'But that one day was one too many.'

He gave a nod. 'I know. But there are days when it doesn't seem worth going on. When I look at my life and all I see is an empty void. You could change all that, Rosy. You could give me something to live for.'

She stared at him in amazement.

'Oh don't say Nicky!' he put in forcefully, before she had the chance. 'He is my son and I love him, but he's happier with you than with anyone else. He wouldn't miss me if I wasn't here.'

'That is utter rubbish! He needs you – as a father – as someone to look up to – as someone to model himself on.'

He gave a bark of ironic laughter. 'I'm sure you would be over the moon if he turned out like me.'

'If he turned out like the man who is standing before me now, the answer is no!' she replied bluntly. She looked at his solid, well-built frame. The body of a man. But at the moment it covered a little boy! The second thought made her hesitate. It was not easy for her to knowingly hurt anyone. But now she had got this far it would be lunacy to turn back before reaching her goal. She was only hoping that giving him the full facts might spur him to see the light.

Summoning all her reserves of courage, she lifted her chin and fixed him with a gaze of such confidence she even began to believe it herself. 'If he turned out like the man you used to be, then I would have no objections.' That was not exactly true. She would not wish Nicky to ever possess the coldness that his father at times displayed. 'But if he turned into a drunk it would break my heart. And, like it or not, a drunk is what you will turn into, if you don't get a hold on yourself.'

He moved to object but she did not give him a chance.

'What I say is true!' she insisted. 'You might have gone over the top on only one occasion, but you go drinking every day, without fail. It is only a matter of time before you reach the depths of your wife. Unless you have the sense to stop it now – while you still can!' She stepped forward and placed a hand on his arm. 'You said yourself that Mrs Hardaker refuses to be helped. You must not refuse. You have to do it, for yourself you have to do it. But before you can give up you have to recognize the habit for what it is.'

He made her jump when his hand suddenly came up and clasped hers as it lay on his arm, and she covered her embarrassment with an uncertain smile. 'I have recognized it, Rosy. I know what I am and what I'm turning into.'

'Then you should also know you have to put a stop to it.'

He gave a nod. 'But there doesn't seem any point.' He eyed her hopefully.

She gave a sigh. He was trying to make her feel responsible. That she could give him the reason to stop drinking, a reason to live, a reason to go on. She refrained from pointing out, yet again, that he had a son who should be reason enough, and she turned him towards the desk. 'There is work to be done. If you'd let yourself get into it you'd find your mind so occupied it wouldn't have time to think of anything else, and you wouldn't have any spare time to fill by propping up a bar!'

For a long moment he stared bleakly at the desk and its clutter of papers. Then he turned his head to look into her eyes. 'Help me,' he said.

'You did it all yourself before, so you don't need my help. If I did, it would give you too much spare time to go off and get into trouble.'

He shook his head. 'I didn't mean with the work. I meant . . . be there for me. The way you are always there for Nicky.'

She hesitated uncertainly. She had the feeling whatever answer she gave was going to make or break him. If she said no he would turn away from the desk and drown his sorrows in Scotch. But if she said yes . . . what was she agreeing to? She had to take a deep swallow to unclog her throat before she could speak. Then she said, 'You know I am always here if you need me . . .' she gave a small, nervous shrug, '. . . to talk or . . . or help with anything.' On the last she glanced pointedly at the desk to make it clear she was referring to work, and nothing more personal. 'But you have to do this for yourself, by yourself.'

He smiled, in a way she had never seen him smile before. 'Thank you, Rosy,' he said, and he bent forward and brushed his lips lightly against her cheek. It was not a kiss, but a gesture that was no more than would have been given by a fond uncle. Nevertheless, it brought a blush to her cheeks, one that blossomed and turned to magenta, when he lifted both her hands and looked deep into her eyes. 'I understand,' he said, and the depth of feeling in his voice returned the restriction to her throat. 'I want you to understand that I will also be here for you. And that I will be waiting for you, Rosy.'

With that he let her hands go, walked round the desk, sat down and promptly picked up the invoices.

Without speaking a word to him she turned round and walked out, wondering just what she had done!

CHAPTER NINE

1965

'I'm dropping them!' Nicky shouted, more in excitement than in warning, as he fell through the back door, clutching frantically at the pile of logs in his arms. In the next moment he went sprawling across the floor, logs going in all directions.

'You can get them cleared up sharpish!' Nell scolded, as she picked her way carefully over rolling logs. She had been preparing for Christmas and the huge plum pudding in her hands was held high in the air, as if giving it greater height would stop it falling if she tripped over as she took it to the table.

'Come on with you!' Rosy grabbed Nicky's arm and tried to pull him upright. But he was so overcome by giggles that he was a dead weight and, instead of getting him up, she almost fell down on top of him. There was a lot a laughter before he was finally back on his feet.

'Look at the state of you!' Rosy shook her head as she looked him up and down. He was soaked from head to foot. Streaks of dirt covered the front of his green anorak, the knees of his jeans looked as if he had been kneeling in several inches of very wet mud, and his wellington boots were more muddy brown than shiny black. 'I thought Ivan had the logs all chopped and waiting to be picked up?' she said.

'He did,' he said, grinning from ear to ear. 'I helped Joey clean out the drain. It was blocked,' he added unnecessarily.

'The drains!' Nell gasped. The pudding was now standing on the table, by the side of the Christmas cake and a pile of mince pies that looked as if it might weigh several hundredweight. 'Keep away from these!' she cried, holding her arms outstretched and putting herself between him and the table. 'You're filthy. Get out of the kitchen. Now! Go on! Go on!'

'Blaarhhhh!' Lifting his hands above his head he made a grotesque face and advanced on Nell. 'The sewer monster is going to get you!'

'Stop it,' Rosy grabbed his arm and pulled him back, but was having great difficulty keeping a straight face.

'Get him away! Get him away!' Nell's panic-stricken voice rose in volume and she flapped her hands as if scaring off a flock of marauding starlings. 'He'll ruin everything and I haven't got time to make it all again.'

'He'll not ruin anything, Mother,' Rosy assured. 'So calm down and stop panicking.' She turned to Nicky and lifted her finger at him. 'Now behave yourself,' she warned, but there was no anger in her voice and a hint of amusement still tugged at the corners of her mouth. 'And go and get out of those filthy things and get cleaned up.'

'Yes, almost my mum,' he replied, teasing her with the name that had become a joke between them since he was eight years old and had told a new boy at school she was his mum. His excuse had been, 'Well, you are almost my mum!' The name had stuck and was always brought out at his most impish and cheeky moments.

'Get off with you!' She flapped her hand at him. 'And bring those dirty clothes down with you. Don't leave them to fester in your bedroom.'

He gave a cheeky salute, then was gone.

'You're making a rod for your own back with that boy,' Nell chided. 'He should have got a good ticking off for getting himself into that state. Messing about down sewers. You don't know what he'll catch.'

'Oh Mum! Give over.' Rosy had heard it all before and she wasn't any more inclined to believe she was spoiling Nicky now, than she had been when her mother first began suggesting she might be. There was no suggesting now, and there was no longer any 'might be' about it. Rosy was soft and let him get away with murder, and her mother said so . . . very firmly, and very often.

'He needs taking in hand and showing a few manners. Filthy he was, but if I hadn't stood here he'd have had his hands in these mince pies. Then we'd all have gone down with dysentry or something on Christmas Day.'

'He was having a laugh, Mum. He's eleven. And eleven-year-old boys do that sort of thing. He was wet and muddy because it's pouring with rain out there, that's all. He hasn't really been down any sewer. Ivan wouldn't have let him, or Joey either. They'd be clearing leaves out of a grate or something. Nothing more.' At least she hoped it wouldn't have been anything more. But all the same she made a mental note to have a word with Ivan. He had no business letting Nicky and Joey alone with any drains!

Bending down she began to scoop up the fallen logs and toss them into the large wicker basket standing by the fire. Christmas, she thought. It was strange how the festive season could warm even the hardest heart. For fifty weeks of the year Derwent House was more like a mausoleum than a family home. But for the other two weeks it was as if someone had waved a magic wand. Decorations adorned the walls and an air of excitement seemed to permeate the rooms; at least the rooms that Nicky, her mother and herself frequented. Dorothy Hardaker remained the same whatever the season. But the element of expectation Nicky carried around with him did touch his father, making him sit back and take a break from the work that had now become the be-all and end-all of his existence.

The last log fell into the basket and Rosy straightened up. She was about to pinch one of her mother's mince pies, when the postman's delivery clattered noisily to the polished wood floor in the hall. Leaving the pies alone she went to collect the mail. 'Two cards for you,' she said, returning to the kitchen and placing two envelopes on the table next to all the baking. 'And two for our Maggie.' Like her mother's, they were obviously Christmas cards and she stuck them behind the clock on the mantelpiece. Even though they were addressed to the cottage the postman never walked all the way round the back and her mother's and Maggie's mail was always delivered to the house along with the Hardaker's own mail. 'The rest are for him.' She glanced through the pile of business envelopes and inclined her head towards the office, before turning away to take them through to him.

As she walked out, Nell's eyes followed her. When she had gone she shook her head and gave a sigh. The years had been very kind to her youngest daughter. Where Maggie's over-generous curves had become even more generous, Rosy's body was still as slender as when she had been a teenager. She had let her hair grow and now the long, straight, blond waterfall almost reached her waist. But for all her looks she had the awful feeling time was passing her daughter by. She looked down at the two envelopes lying on the table. Christmas cards! They should have been for Rosy, not herself. Rosy was young and should have many friends sending her cards. But how could she have friends when she never went anywhere to meet anyone?

It was this place, she thought bitterly. This house! Rosy was twenty-four years old. She should be married with a family of her own, not looking after somebody else's! But there wasn't much chance of that, living the life she led here: looking after Nicky; helping *him* in the office; running around for *her* upstairs. The occasional nights out with her friend Sue had dried up a couple of years ago and she had never been out with a boy in her life. She'd have had more fun being a nun.

In exasperation Nell picked up one of the freshly cut

logs from the basket and slung it onto the fire with more force than was necessary. It sent a spray of sparks dancing up the chimney, and several more flying out all over the hearth rug. 'Botheration!' she exclaimed, quickly stamping on the sparks, and making Nicky stop in the doorway and laugh, as he caught her in the middle of what appeared to be the Highland fling.

'Go and get your coat on,' she ordered crossly, trying to take the smile from his face. 'I'm going round to the village. You can come with me and help me carry the bags back.'

His face crumpled and his mouth opened on a grumble. But it was quickly bitten back as he thought of the sight that had greeted him when he passed the baker's shop yesterday. 'There's this enormous chocolate log . . .' he began.

Nell was still chuntering about wasting her time doing all that baking as they went out of the door.

Rosy no longer knocked on the office door, but walked straight in. Since the time she had been forced to make John Hardaker see he was heading down the same path as his wife, he had become a changed man. He would now sit in the office all day, and often late into the night as well, working out one new building scheme after another. Apart from the occasional walk he took up the bank, he very rarely left the house, unless he was going to visit a builder to get a job off the ground, or to visit a site to check on the progress of the work. The houses he now had built were all for sale. He still had the rented properties, but he had found it much more lucrative to build them, sell them, and build again. It meant he had much more work to do and it also meant he needed an assistant, a job which Rosy, without consultation, had been fitted into.

At the beginning she had only opened and sorted out the mail for him. But it had not been long before she was back to cashing up and banking the rent money. Now she was in full charge of the cash book and all the invoices and payments. She even had her own desk sitting in the corner by the window.

It was to her desk she now went and began to open the mail. There were several invoices, one statement, a new price-list from a plumber and heating engineer, and an invitation to a cocktail party from the managing director of the builders who were at present constructing his latest development of fifty houses.

'You've got an invitation to a party!' She held the card up. It was blue and gold and looked very posh. 'Duggie Flinders is getting a bit above himself,' she said laughingly, and threw the card so that it winged across the office like an helicopter blade and landed on his desk. 'Or perhaps I should say Mavis is,' she added, knowing it would be Duggie's wife who had organized the party, and the party stationery!

He gave a rumble of laughter and picked the card up. Then, holding it in both hands, stared hard at it for several seconds.

'It's tomorrow evening. You haven't got much time to think about it. Shall I give them a call for you?' she asked, his hesitancy putting a note of hope in her voice. Usually, and much to Rosy's annoyance, such invitations were consigned straight to the bin. He did not have to accept them all, but she wished he would go to the occasional one. Work was now the only thing he made room for in his life and there were times when she regretted having been the cause of him stopping going to the pub. It wasn't good for him to bury himself away in this room for the majority of his waking time. Neither was it good for Nicky; he could go for days without setting eyes on his father. Not that it seemed to worry him, but she knew it wasn't right.

He did not answer immediately, but continued to stare at the invitation card, as if he was trying to will some response out of it. Then he lifted only his eyes and directed them straight at Rosy. 'Will you come with me?' he asked.

Her mouth opened, but no sound came out because her voice, like the rest of her, was too stunned to do anything.

'Would you?' he repeated. He laid the card down flat on the table, made a pyramid with his fingers and watched her over the top.

'I . . . er . . . I don't know.' She gave a nervous shrug. He couldn't be serious, she told herself. But as she looked back into the eyes that were watching her so very carefully, she knew he was deadly serious. His gaze never left her face as he sat there watching, waiting for her response. Just as he had been waiting since the day he asked her to help him and be there for him. The day he had told her he would always be there for her, and that he would always be waiting for her.

It was a numbing reminder, not just the thought, but the fact that she had forgotten all about it until now. He had become so obsessed with work that she had thought nothing else mattered to him any longer. It was so long ago since the days he had pestered her that she had assumed he had forgotten he ever had any romantic thoughts about her.

'I don't think so.' She shook her head and picked up the new invoices and gave them all her attention. 'Good grief! Those boilers we used on the Church Lane site have gone up by twenty per cent,' she said, changing the subject.

As if she had not spoken, he said, 'There would be no problem you coming with me. The invitation is for two and they know I won't be taking Dorothy. There'll be others there who take their colleagues.'

Lifting her gaze from the price list she stared at him blandly. She was thankful he had, at least, had the decency to say colleagues, and not secretaries! 'No!' she stressed pointedly. She was not going to any social function with him as his colleague, assistant, secretary, or anything! She was not, nor was she going to become,

168

an appendage to him, whatever name he cared to put to it.

'So make my apologies.' The card came winging back across the office and dropped onto the desk in front of her, and he immediately returned his full attention to the specification he had been studying when she came in.

'Right!' she snapped tetchily. 'But I don't think it's the right way to go about making business contacts!'

'And just what do you mean by that?' He forgot the specification just long enough to throw a stony glare at her. 'I know Duggie well enough without having to go to his party!'

'Of course you do!' she countered, speaking to the top of his head. 'But you don't know who else is going to be there. You could miss several useful contacts. Remember where you first heard the old mill cottages were coming down and that plot of land was up for grabs!' She laid particular emphasis on the last. It had been several years ago now, when his wife was still attending social functions with him. But it had been at a Christmas party that he had heard the news and she could clearly recall his impatience for the festive season to end and for everyone to get back to work, so he could follow up the lead and get his hands on the prime piece of land.

'I do perfectly all right without having to kowtow to people I probably wouldn't pass the time of day with on the street.'

She gave a humph. He was never on the street to pass the time of day with anybody. 'All of a sudden business is kowtowing . . . is it? Dennis Millward might be there,' she added flippantly, throwing in his arch rival to prod some action from him.

'Well, I definitely don't want to spend any time with him!' he snapped. But he did look up at her, and she had the feeling she was beginning to get there, when he said, 'Perhaps you're right, perhaps it would be silly

169

to miss out on an opportunity to make a few contacts.' But her victory was short lived. In the next breath he said, 'So you can go in my place!'

She clamped her lips tightly together and glared at him for a long, long moment. Finally she said, very stiffly, 'I don't see why I should do your dirty work for you!' She leapt from her chair and swept the invoices up in her hand, marched briskly to the filing cabinet and stuck them away in the file. Then she closed the drawer, very noisily, before turning away and making quickly for the door.

'That's all right, Rosy,' he said, so quietly she could only just make out his words. 'I wasn't thinking. It was not really fair of me to ask you to go alone. Not to a social occasion such as that – where you would be out of your depth!'

She had no difficulty picking up the last and it stopped her in her tracks. The insult sent heat rushing to her face and with cheeks burning she spun round on him, chin jutting out in defiance. 'I'll show you who is out of her depth! If you speak to Duggie before I get the chance, tell him *I* shall be there, representing Hardaker Properties!' Wheeling away she stormed out of the room and slammed the door on him. She did not see the smile she was leaving behind.

'We're supposed to be collecting holly!' Rosy called, as Nicky scampered off through the wood. She knew he was heading for the cottage, he always did. The old derelict building held a fascination for him, much the same as it did for herself.

'We can get the holly on the way back,' he shouted over his shoulder.

She shook her head in despair, but all the same she had to smile. It was pleasing to see at least one person happy, she told herself, as she followed behind, her boots treading carefully through the wet grass and the thick layer of mouldering leaves. Since walking out on

John Hardaker she had experienced many emotions, but happiness had not been one of them. Anger, irritation, frustration, had all been there in great enough quantities to make her grab Nicky the moment she walked into the kitchen, and insist they were going out to get the holly, despite the pouring rain. Now she was reduced to a burning annoyance, accompanied by the embarrassment of realizing what she had done.

John Hardaker had been right and she had been wrong. It had been foolish to stick her neck out and agree to go to the party. She had never been to a cocktail party – she had never been to any party since she was seven – and she *would* feel out of her depth. To make matters worse she hadn't got anything suitable to wear, and it was tomorrow night!

'Come away!' she demanded, seeing Nicky race through the drunkenly hanging gate and go straight up to the cottage window and peer inside. She was not afraid of him finding Maggie there. Maggie was at work, had she not been Rosy would not have allowed Nicky anywhere near the place.

'Why . . . are you frightened of ghosts?' he called cheekily.

'You will be if one sticks its head up at the window,' she teased. 'Now come away.' She flapped an impatient hand at him. 'You don't know how safe the place is.' The wood nailed across the windows was rotten and the frames looked as if they would crumble to dust if you blew on them too hard. But the stone walls appeared to be solid and she did not think there was any real danger of the place collapsing. Nevertheless, she made him come away, wanting to make him recognize the danger of such places which would, hopefully, make him keep away when she was not with him.

The rain had taken a pause and with no thought for the affect of the wet stone, Nicky perched himself on the wall. Rosy had no intention of getting a wet bottom so she stood beside him. It wasn't a very clear view, the grey sky shadowed both village and fields in gloom and a mist clung to the line of the river, erasing the land and all that was on it for several yards on either side of the river bank.

'I want to live here one day,' Nicky suddenly said, taking Rosy by surprise.

'What!' she gasped, unable to comprehend that the heir to Derwent House should consider living in such a pokey little place. 'But it's falling down.'

'I'll have it done up. With a new door and new windows. You can live here with me.'

There was such sincerity in his voice, but the smile slipped from her face, to be replaced by uncertainty. She shook her head. 'You won't want me with you. You'll find someone of your own and you won't want me around.' Sadness rippled through her voice as she acknowledged her fate. Left alone. With no-one. By the time Nicky was old enough to break away in a life of his own, she would be an old maid. Her only comfort would be if Nicky himself had children and she could take over looking after them. But she would never hold her own child in her arms. It was a depressing thought and she was glad the air was chilly enough to give a reason for her watering eyes.

'No I won't!' he replied very emphatically. 'I don't want you ever to leave me. When I'm old enough I shall buy this place and we will live here, just me and you. Who owns it?'

She shook her head. 'I don't know.' She did not refute what he was saying. He was still young and his sterile family life had done nothing to show him anything of the love that would one day come to him. She was confident it would come to him, because he had so much love inside him to give that it would find its mate and be reciprocated. 'It's been empty as long as I can remember.' She turned her mind to the ownership of the cottage and away from the thoughts that emphasized her own sense of loss. 'It must belong to the farm,' she said, just as the rain returned in large stinging drops that pounded against their faces. Quickly pulling their anorak hoods over their heads, they dashed for the meagre protection of the leafless trees in the wood.

'Why didn't we get this before?' Rosy had to shout to make herself heard over the noise of the downpour, as she struggled to get the secateurs round the thick holly stems. If they had collected the holly first they could have run home now. Her thickly padded anorak was already soaked and she could feel dampness seeping through to her neck.

Nicky held his face up and grinned as he left the rain run down his cheeks like tears. 'Because you insisted on going to the cottage first,' he teased cheekily.

'Oh, come on!' She had cut enough holly to give herself two large bunches to carry back and Nicky one bunch. It would have to be enough. She was fed up with the rain and, as she collected the pieces of cut holly from the ground where she had dropped them, her annoyance was directed at John Hardaker, on whom she placed all the blame for them being there and getting wet. If he had not upset her the holly could have waited until tomorrow, she thought irritably, as she started to lead Nicky out of the wood to take the quick route back home down the field. They would be out in the open and at the mercy of the rain, but they were already dripping wet and she just wanted to get home and get into dry clothes as quickly as possible.

But before she had time to move, and, fortunately, before she had time to relay her decision to Nicky, movement caught her eye and brought her up short. It was way down below and it was difficult for her eyes to see through the lashing rain. But someone was coming that way and, although at first she was not sure, it was not many moments before she knew she was watching Maggie walking up the field.

She should be at work, she told herself, staring numbly at the black shape getting ever nearer. She glanced anxiously at Nicky. He was still involved in letting the rain hit him full in the face and was too busy to notice anything else, and she turned back to the fields. The Mill must have broken up early for Christmas, she thought. Maggie had nothing on her head and she was wearing her black leather coat and the knee high black leather boots she had gone out in that morning. She was also carrying the bright orange bag that always went to work with her, filled with all the necessary clutter of brushes, make-up, hairspray and spare pair of tights.

She had come straight from work without calling at home first. Which meant she was coming to the cottage. If they stayed there she would only be a few yards away when she passed by.

'Come on!' she repeated urgently. They did not have a moment to lose and she spun round so quickly she almost lost her footing in the wet grass. Gathering her balance, she forgot her first plan to take to the fields and hurried off into the wood, urging Nicky to stick close behind. If Maggie was heading for the cottage then it would mean someone else was also heading that way. She had no desire herself to see who that someone might be, and she had no intention of letting Nicky be confronted with such goings-on, not at his tender age.

They had walked almost the length of the wood before they saw anyone. A large shape suddenly came into view moving towards them. The breath caught in her throat. Oh no, she thought worriedly – even though she was certain Nicky had not seen Maggie and would have no idea where the man was going, or what he was going for.

Holding her head high, because she was not the one who had anything to be ashamed of, she kept her gaze fixed to the tall beech tree at the point where the path left the wood. She would have walked right past him without looking in his direction, if the man had not spoken. She had not expected him to and, taken by surprise, she stopped in her tracks, then almost dropped one bunch of holly as she spun round to face him and see who it was.

'Mr . . . Mr Hardaker!' she gasped.

CHAPTER TEN

'Was it worth it?' Nell glanced bleakly at the pile of holly on the table. Then she turned to the clothes-horse standing before the fire and holding an array of steaming coats, jumpers and trousers. The rain had gone straight through their top coats and they had been soaked right through to the skin. Their socks and underwear had been tossed straight into the washing-machine, making it plain she was not pleased to be given the extra work on the day before Christmas Eve.

'Anyway, what was he doing going up there on a day like this?'

Rosy gave a shrug. Fortunately not what she had first imagined. 'Getting some exercise,' she said. It had been with great relief that she had found John Hardaker was doing nothing more sinister than taking one of his infrequent walks. She had to admit he had picked a strange time to do it, in a torrential downpour. But he had pushed all her doubts away by not hesitating to turn round and come back with Nicky and herself. For which she had been very grateful. Considering John Hardaker as one of Maggie's men friends disturbed her far more than she was willing to admit.

'Uh . . .' Nell gave a snort of disgust. Then echoing Rosy's thoughts, muttered, 'Picked a fine time to do it!'

Rosy was saved having to reply by the appearance of Dorothy Hardaker in the doorway.

'Where's my green velvet cocktail dress?' she demanded angrily. She was holding her hands out stiffly in front of her and frantically waggling her fingers. It looked as if she was trying to convey some message in secret code, but really she was only drying her scarlet nail varnish.

'It's at the cleaners,' Nell replied. 'You told me to send it.' She did not expect any reply and she turned away and set a match to the grill and the two gas rings with saucepans standing on them.

Dorothy Hardaker breathed a noisy, exasperated sigh, then wheeled round and hurried away.

Nell cast a knowing glance at Rosy.

'I hope we're not going to have a repeat of last Christmas,' she said. Dorothy Hardaker had gone missing from Christmas Eve to Boxing Day. Then there had been an almighty row because she had made no attempt to apologize or offer any explanation as to where she had been. 'Having Christmas without her is preferable. If she'd only have the decency to tell him she is not going to be around.' She was speaking more to herself than to her mother, who was busy laying the gammon in the grill pan. She shook her head, wondering why they allowed the woman to upset things so. Last year John Hardaker had been on tenterhooks the whole time, wondering where his wife was and who she was with.

'I don't think there's much chance of her thinking of anybody else . . . even if it is Christmas,' Nell put in drily.

Rosy gave a humph. 'It spoilt last Christmas for everyone.' By the time she had stumbled over the front doorstep only just managing to keep herself upright as she wobbled up the stairs, John Hardaker had been ready to go for her throat and it had taken the combined efforts of both herself and her mother to keep them apart.

'You're right there!' Nell put in without taking her eyes off the grill pan. Then she looked up, as if a sudden thought had struck her. 'It'd pay us to find out who her current fella is and bribe him to keep her away for a whole week.'

Rosy laughed. But she wished it was possible. It would be heaven to know the woman was going to be out of their hair, and not going to come swaggering home in a drunken haze, spoiling for a fight.

In the next moment the back door was slung open and Dorothy Hardaker was pushed from her mind.

'Bloody weather! Bloody, bloody, buggerin' weather!' Maggie burst into the kitchen, cursing profusely. She tore the shoulder strap off her arm and slung the orange bag across the floor, sending a spray of water right across the kitchen. Then she stopped short, fixing first her mother, then her sister with a teeth clenching glare that have her the appearance of a terrier about to lay into a rabbit.

'What the devil's up with you?' Nell asked, forgetting the gammon to rest her hands on her hips and stare at her daughter in astonishment.

The rain must have dampened his ardour, Rosy thought. She had not expected to see her sister until the usual time, which was still over an hour away. Perhaps the rain put him off and he didn't turn up. Something had obviously happened to put Maggie in such a temper and if her fancy man had not found her allure strong enough to make him brave the rain, that would count as a very big something!

'The weather!' Maggie spat, holding her arms wide to display the water dripping from her leather coat. 'Just look at me!' She had no hat and she shook her head and water sprayed not only over the floor, but also over Nell and Rosy, and a saturated tress whipped round and hit her in the face. 'Oh . . . ! Sod it!' She ground furiously, swiping the hair away.

'Here!' Nell tossed a towel at her. 'Get your hair dried, then get them wet things off! You're dripping all over the carpet. Where've you been to get in that state!'

Maggie grabbed the towel, then paused, looking at

her mother in surprise. 'In the bloody rain!' she stated bluntly. 'Where do you think?'

Where indeed! Rosy thought, deciding she was right about Maggie's partner in crime not turning up. But she could feel no compassion for her sister. If she was daft enough to walk all the way up to the cottage in this weather, just to meet some man, then she deserved all she got.

'Rain isn't red!' Nell pointed out, her shoulders rigid with indignation as she turned her back on her daughter and stuck the pan of gammon under the grill.

'You're home early?' Rosy changed the subject to save her mother wasting her breath. No amount of grumbling or moaning would clean up her sister's bad language.

'They let us finish early. For Christmas!' Maggie added drily, and began rubbing furiously at her wet hair. 'It isn't fit to turn a dog out, but they turn us out – just when the soddin' bus has gone!'

The last was added as an afterthought, Rosy reckoned. Having to wait for the next bus was supposed to be the reason why she was so very wet. She gave an inward grimace. Maggie did not have to explain anything to her, but Maggie did not know she had been seen walking up the fields. The thought irritated Rosy and her voice was harsh, as she said, 'There's a bus shelter. Why didn't you go in it?'

'Me and about fifty soddin' others!' Maggie countered hotly. She stopped rubbing her hair. 'Why am I bothering with this?' She cast a disgusted glance at the window, where the rain appeared like a sheet of silver metal behind the glass pane. 'It's getting worse, not better. I'm going to get drowned again just getting across the yard to the cottage!'

'You can't go in this!' Softening towards her sister, Rosy went and helped her out of her wet coat. 'You're soaked right through.' Rain had run down Maggie's collar and got inside the leather coat and wet her blouse. A large damp patch circled her neck and spread over her shoulder blades and when she pulled her boots off her feet were also wet. 'Come upstairs and you can borrow something of mine. You'll get pneumonia if you stay like this.' She wanted to add you silly fool, because she felt Maggie was an idiot to have got herself into this state for such dubious reasons.

While Maggie stripped off her damp clothes, Rosy sorted through her wardrobe, looking for something suitable. Although Maggie was shorter, she was by far the broader of the two sisters. As her extra girth was a sore point with Maggie, Rosy knew if she gave her something that was too tight it would be taken as a personal insult and Maggie would think it had been done on purpose.

Trousers were no good, she told herself, pushing two pairs of denim jeans, a pair of dog-tooth check hipsters and a pair of white cotton summer slacks out of the way. Neither were straight cut skirts suitable. She passed them by and gave careful consideration to a blue flared skirt. Although it was plenty big enough to go round Maggie's hips, she wasn't sure the fitted waistband would fasten up. It was then she remembered she had another, with an elasticated waist. It was several years old and she didn't wear it much now, but it was perfect for Maggie to slip into until she could go home and get into her own clothes. She rummaged quickly to the back of the wardrobe, knowing it was more likely to be hidden at the back than amongst the things she wore regularly, which were at the front.

There, she thought triumphantly, pulling the wardrobe's contents aside to see the red and black check skirt, not right at the back, but almost. There was only one other thing behind it and, as she pulled the skirt out and saw what it was, she suddenly stopped. It was the black taffeta cocktail dress with the short jacket that had belonged to Dorothy Hardaker. 'Good grief!' she said, finished pulling the skirt out, then lifted the dress and jacket down. Sucking on her bottom lip she looked it up and down.

'You're not giving me that to put on!' Maggie's incredulous voice broke into Rosy's thoughts.

She stared at her sister as if she was not seeing her, then suddenly returned to the moment and realized it was the dress Maggie was talking about. 'Oh no!' she gasped on a laugh. 'No, this is for you.' She handed the red and black skirt over and turned back to the dress and jacket so quickly she missed the way Maggie's nose wrinkled in disgust as she took the skirt.

All Rosy could think about was that if the dress fitted it was just what she needed for tomorrow night. It seemed an eternity since Dorothy Hardaker had thrown it out and John Hardaker had told her she could have it. It must be four, five years. She could not remember exactly when it had found its way into the back of her wardrobe, but it had been there so long she had forgotten all about it.

'Well!' Once more Maggie's voice broke into Rosy's reverie.

She turned and again looked at her sister blankly. Maggie was standing in front of her with her arms outstretched at either side. She had the skirt on, but her top half was bare except for the black lace bra that pushed her breasts upwards and, from the way she was oozing out of the low cut top, appeared to be several sizes too small for her.

'Is this it?' Maggie questioned cynically. Rosy frowned. She knew the skirt was not fashionable, but it was fine as a make-do. It was not until Maggie said, 'Have I got to walk round with my boobs on show?' that the penny dropped.

'Sorry!' She shook herself back to the moment and quickly found a black jumper. It was big and baggy and nothing like anything Maggie would have chosen for herself. Although Maggie didn't say anything when she looked in the mirror, her thoughts were stamped clearly on her face.

'Well, they're dry and will keep you warm,' Rosy said, not knowing what else to say. She would not have thought a change of clothes could so completely turn around a person's image. But Maggie would not have looked odd walking out of some university with a pile of books stuck under her arm. A smile tugged at Rosy's lips but she held it in check. Showing her amusement would only have been greeted by a string of language that would not have got anybody an English degree.

Maggie glanced down at herself, then took another look at her reflection in the mirror. She gave a sigh and a shadow flickered across her eyes, leaving behind a sadness, a resignation.

Resignation seemed an odd word to use about Maggie, who would not have resigned herself to anything she didn't want to do. But Rosy could not think of any other way to describe the strangely intense expression in her sister's dark eyes. Perhaps she had been wrong, she thought. Perhaps the man *had* turned up for their secret liaison, and put an end to the relationship. It would explain Maggie's anger when she arrived home. 'Is something wrong?' she asked, her voice gentle as she offered her sister a shoulder to cry on . . . should she want one.

'I think I'd have been better having that, after all.' Maggie nodded at the cocktail dress still in Rosy's hands. 'What you got that for anyway?'

She did not know if her sister had genuinely misunderstood, or chosen to. But Rosy did not pry. Whatever the problem, Maggie obviously did not want her to know. 'It was DH's,' she said, running her hand admiringly over the sumptuous material. 'She was throwing it out and I thought it was a shame. So I kept it.' She did not tell Maggie about the following night's party. Tact had never been one of Maggie's virtues, and Rosy's self-confidence was shaky enough without having it further deflated by any blunt speaking. She could well imagine Maggie's surprise if she found her socially inept sister was considering going to her first cocktail party . . . on her own!

Leaving the mirror, as if the sight of her reflection had suddenly become repugnant, Maggie lifted the skirt of the black dress and held it out for inspection. 'I didn't know you'd got this. If I had I'd have borrowed it before now.'

You'd never get in it, Rosy thought, looking down at the tightly fitted style and wondering if she was still going to be able to squeeze into it herself. She must have been in her teens when she last tried it on. She grimaced at the narrowness of the skirt. 'Come on!' she urged. 'We'll be in trouble for holding dinner up if we don't hurry.' Sweeping the dress out of Maggie's hands she hung it up on the front of the wardrobe door. She would try it on later. When she was alone.

Christmas Eve proved to be as wet a day as the previous one. It was not actually raining when the taxi arrived to take Rosy to the Flinders', but the air was heavy with moisture and the river was obliterated by a thick wall of rising mist.

When she climbed into the car Rosy turned to look back at the open door of the house. Her mother was standing on the step, framed by the orange glow from the hall light. Her hands, though not actually wringing, were clasped tightly before her and anxiety oozed from every inch of her rigid frame. Nicky was up in his room, too busy sulking to come and wave goodbye. She had half-expected John Hardaker to be lurking around somewhere, checking that she did not chicken out at the last moment. But he seemed to have vanished and had not been seen since teatime.

'Take care,' Nell called, releasing one hand just long enough to lift it in a brief, stiff wave, before it joined

183

the other again, as if the life of each depended on the other.

Rosy shook her head and smiled. 'Stop fretting! I won't be late,' she called through the open window, as the taxi began to pull away. It had been the same all afternoon. Ever since Nell had found out about the party she had been a bundle of nerves. *As if I was fifteen and going on my first date!* Rosy thought, and wound the window up again. Then she settled back in the seat with a sigh and reminded herself she might be twenty-four and it wasn't actually a date, but it was the first real night out she had ever had.

Her thoughts turned to the reason for her cloistered life and, as the car went down the drive, she glanced back at the house. Her mother had not moved from the step but she did not look at the front door, her gaze went to the upper half of the house and the light which burned in the end bedroom. That Nicky had not crept down saddened her. He usually viewed staying in his room as being very close to a prison sentence. But he had stormed up there in a fit of temper at teatime and had not been seen since. She had not expected him to mind her going out and his outburst had taken her so by surprise that she had been lost for words, and she had let him go without uttering one word in her own defence.

Closing her eyes she rested her head back against the seat. Why was she going to the party? Nicky did not want her to go. Neither did her mother. She didn't really want to go herself. If only she hadn't still had the dress! She looked down at the black taffeta and shook her head. If only she had not kept the dress; if only it had not still fitted; if only Dorothy Hardaker had been at home and she had not been able to borrow the shoes, bag and cape.

She gave a sigh and stared out of the window, at the black fields of the meadow passing by. It seemed that fate had intended her to go to this party. Whatever problem had arisen that looked as if it might get in her way had, as if by the wave of a magic wand, been wiped away. The dress still fitted perfectly. Even the shorter length of the skirt had come into fashion since she had first rescued it from the fate of the dustbin. Even leaving trying it on until the last minute had not presented any insurmountable problems. She had not put the dress on until it was almost time to leave for the party, hoping that if it didn't fit it would then be too late to do anything about it. But it had fitted to perfection and the last minute panic, because she only then realized she had no shoes to wear with it, was overcome by her mother's suggestion of borrowing from Dorothy Hardaker.

'I couldn't!' She had been surprised that her mother could even expect her to. Dorothy Hardaker had not returned home last night and they had not seen anything of her today. So it seemed this Christmas was going to be like the last one and she would not come home until the festivities had ended. Even so, Rosy did not like to go poking into her personal things.

'She isn't going to know,' her mother insisted. 'If you are determined to go to this blessed do, you'll go properly dressed!'

Nell had refused to back down and in the end Rosy had given in and they had gone into Dorothy Hardaker's bedroom and sorted through her shoes. Rosy's feet were a size bigger and most of the shoes were too tight and pinched unbearably. But at last she found a pair of black and silver evening sandals which, once she had adjusted the strap round the back of the heel, fitted well and were comfortable. They also had modern cuban heels and were more to Rosy's liking than Dorothy Hardaker's usual choice of pencil slim stilettos.

With the shoes on her feet she had been about to leave the bedroom, when her mother handed her a black velvet cape and a little black evening bag with a pearl and diamante clasp: both taken from Dorothy Hardaker's wardrobe while Rosy had been busy hunting through the shoes. She had been about to protest, but bit the refusal back. Might as well get hung for a sheep as a lamb, she thought, and draped the cape round her shoulders and took the bag. And now she was sitting in the taxi, going to a party she didn't want to go to, dressed from head to foot in someone else's clothes. All because she had wanted to prove something to John Hardaker, and she couldn't even remember what it was she was trying to prove to him.

When the taxi pulled up outside Duggie and Mavis Flinders' large, modern house, her courage was almost lost. The drive was blocked with cars, every available parking space in the small avenue had been taken and they even spilled out onto the road beyond. She had not expected so many people to be there and it was on the tip of her tongue to tell the driver to keep going and take her straight back home. Fortunately, she regained her composure quickly enough not to appear a total idiot and she paid the man, checked he had remembered he was to come back for her at half-past-eleven, then got out of the car.

There was a street light by the side of the Flinders' gate, but it was not really needed. A large brick archway leading to the plain sheet of glass that was the front door was adorned with strings of multicoloured lights. Two tall conifers standing on the front lawn dripped with tiny white lights that flashed on and off like twinkling stars. In front of the trees was a near life-size sledge, complete with a laughing Santa Claus and a Rudolph with a large red nose, which also flashed on and off.

If that was not enough, the lights on the Christmas tree in the hall, visible through the glass door, changed from white to red then back again with a speed that was dizzying. She had never seen anything like it in her life and, as she lifted her hand to press the tinsel-bedecked bell she shook her head: half in amusement, half in wondering if anyone was going to hear her over the din that was coming from inside.

'Mavis never did have any taste.'

On a startled gasp she spun round and away from the sudden voice that had spoken so close to her ear. 'What . . . Oh . . . !' Her right foot collided with her left, she went over on her heel and would have gone crashing into the glass door – had John Hardaker not reached out and caught her.

'What . . . what are you doing here?' she asked stupidly, as he pulled her close and stopped her fall by steadying her against himself. 'Why are you here?' she persisted, though she could see plainly why he was there: the grey velvet jacket and matching bow-tie gave him away, and stopped any illusions that he had come after her because something had happened at the house – to Nicky or her mother. He did not get a chance to reply, or to remove his arms from around her. The door opened and Duggie Flinders was standing there, a pint of beer in one hand, a large cigar in the other, and a twinkle in his eyes that out-sparkled the fairy lights as his gaze settled on the pair of them in what appeared to be an intimate moment.

'Shall I go away and come back later?' Duggie enquired, his dark eyebrows tilting suggestively and vanishing into his shaggy mop of black hair.

Rosy could only stare at him. Partly in shock at being caught out that way, partly in surprise at the way he looked. She had always thought his hairstyle was too young for him and not suitable for someone of his age, and she thought so even more at that moment. The thick gypsy curls were hanging so low over his forehead they almost touched his nose and, along with his two-tone blue velvet jacket with satin collar and a too-large royal blue bow-tie, made him look like an ageing teddy boy. It took a moment before she regained the sense to close her mouth, and several more before she realized she should be pushing John Hardaker away.

But before she could react, he had released his body hold on her, taken her arm and was guiding her into the house. 'You can do what you like, Duggie,' he said calmly, showing none of the embarrassment that was curling Rosy's insides. 'But we're coming to the party!'

When they were in the hall he pulled Rosy round to face him and removed the cape for her, before she had the time to do it herself, and handed it to Duggie. A thousand protests were in her head, but when he took her hand and led her into the crowded lounge she knew she could only follow meekly, like a little lamb: not to the slaughter, she thought mutinously. But there were so many people and to make a scene would only have embarrassed herself. So she kept her lips clamped tightly in the smile she had forced on her face for the benefit of the people they passed that were not strangers to her, and took the glass of wine that was pressed into her hand without comment.

'*John!* You've come!' Mavis Flinders screeched, throwing her gold bangle-laden arms wide and rushing at him the moment he walked through the door. She was wearing a voluminous creation of vivid orange crêpe de Chine and ostrich feathers. It clashed violently with her red hair, the mauve and pink furnishings of the room, and her husband's blue velvet jacket. As she hurried forward she created enough draft to get under the lightweight fabric and inflate it like a balloon.

Mavis carried no weight, but with the dress pumped out all around her it gave Rosy the impression he was about to be attacked by a jaffa orange, and the plastic smile on her face suddenly turned to a real one, but only for a few moments.

When Mavis reached her target she kissed him very noisily on both cheeks, then took hold of his shoulders and held him away, while she gave him a very thorough inspection. 'You're looking good,' she pronounced after several moments. 'Better than I've seen you for a long time.'

'I wonder what his secret is?' Duggie enquired pointedly, coming up behind his wife and wrapping his arms around her waist. Resting his chin on her shoulder he winked suggestively at Rosy. 'Have you been keeping him fit?' he asked.

'Keeping me busy,' John Hardaker put in firmly, as Rosy's face turned crimson. 'Rosy is my assistant now, and a very good one too. I would have missed the Woodland site if it hadn't been for her keen eye!' He laid particular emphasis on the last. Duggie had also put a bid in for the site and had been very put out when he didn't get it. Bringing the matter up had been a bit like throwing the gauntlet down. Fortunately, it was a gauntlet Duggie was only too ready to pick up. The conversation quickly turned to work and he tried to extract a promise that he would be given the contract for the development of the site. Mavis floated off on a sea of tangerine to accost her next victim and Rosy began to relax and feel a bit more at ease, biding her time until her moment arrived.

She did not have long to wait. Duggie got tired of being told the job was going out to tender in the normal way and that he knew the correct procedure for that, and he was soon following Mavis.

'What do you think you're playing at?' The moment they were left alone she turned on John. Her hands were fastened tightly round the coolness of her glass. She had not taken one drink and as she trembled with anger the wine spilled over the rim and splashed her hands and spotted the black taffeta of her dress. 'Oh damn!' she muttered, and began brushing frantically at her skirt.

'I'm not playing at anything,' he assured. 'Here, let me have that before you spill the whole lot down you.' Taking the glass from her hand he put it out of the way. 'It will be dry in a moment – if you leave it alone!'

he added meaningfully, and took hold of her arm and forced her to leave the skirt and return to standing upright. 'Forget it!' he insisted.

His smile, she imagined, was supposed to comfort her, but it only made her feel very stupid and naive. She was making a mountain out of a molehill and his reaction was clearly telling her so. For all Mavis' lack of taste she would never have acted in such an awkward way. Neither would Dorothy Hardaker, she thought dejectedly – except in one of her most inebriated states. It wasn't a comforting thought. Oh why had she come? She looked round the crowded room and realized she was completely out of her depth. She glanced John Hardaker a tight little smile. 'Thank you for coming,' she said. Her sentiments were sincere. On her own she would have been totally lost and she had to admit she was glad he was there. 'Did you know I would make a fool of myself?' She wondered if it had been his own, or her mother's idea for him to come after her.

His smile was warm. 'You are not making a fool of yourself,' he assured.

She shook her head. 'I've looked nothing else since walking in here.' She was sure her uneasiness must have been apparent to everyone else in the room.

It was his turn to shake his head then. 'You have looked nothing of the kind.' His gaze ran down from her bewildered face to the long, slender legs displayed to perfection in the short straight skirt. Dressed as she was, with her hair hanging in her usual blond waterfall down her back, he imagined there could not be many people in that room who had missed seeing her walk in. But he knew for a fact that anyone who had seen anything other than a beautiful young woman must have bad eyesight. Retrieving her glass of wine he returned it to her hand and fixed her intently. 'I came here tonight for no other reason than that I wanted to come here . . . with you!' He stressed the last meaningfully.

She felt the warmth of colour running up her cheeks. But she did not get time to reply, neither did he get time to continue. The sound of the Beatles suddenly cut through the room, far too loud and killing all conversation. Mavis screeched, 'Everybody to the ball-room . . . the dancing has begun!' just in case they hadn't heard the ear-shattering noise for themselves. The next moment Rosy's glass was snatched from her hand and she was being dragged across the room by an exuberant Duggie.

She managed to cast a despairing glance in John Hardaker's direction. Then she was through the door and being taken to another room. It had a highly polished wooden floor and the only furniture was a radiogram in the corner and a small table with two boxes of records standing on it. The walls were covered with garish brown and green patterned paper which put her in mind of a forest of tall trees, and the curtains were the samd vivid orange as Mavis' dress.

This is where she intends to spend most of her time, Rosy thought, watching the female half of her hosts take to the floor in a flurry of crêpe de Chine and ostrich feathers. She wondered where that placed Duggie. If Mavis was supposed to be blending in with the curtains she wouldn't be overly keen to have his garish blue jacket hanging on her arm and spoiling the continuity.

The Beatles were singing 'Help' and Rosy began to shake about in the dance fashion that was popular. But Duggie had other ideas. He pulled her hard against him, wrapping his arms so tightly round her that she had no chance of escape. It was not long before she realized she did not care where his blue jacket placed him in his wife's colour scheme . . . so long as it was not by her side for the rest of the evening. She cast another despairing glance at John Hardaker, who had made his way to the door and was standing there, sipping slowly at his whisky and watching them with great interest.

Fortunately he got the message. By the time the record came to an end he had discarded the whisky. When the room fell into the expectant hush as everyone waited for the next record to begin, he moved quickly between the couples on the dance floor and came up behind Duggie. 'Excuse me,' he said, tapping him on the shoulder, then cutting in and taking hold of Rosy while Duggie was still turning round to protest.

'Come off it!' Duggie moaned, his face crumpling in annoyance when he saw what was happening. 'I've only had one dance!'

'Then you're one up on me,' John replied easily, and whisked Rosy across the floor and away from Duggie before he had time to open his mouth again.

'Thank you, Mr Hardaker,' she said, conveying her gratitude to him for coming to her aid and also for the way he let go of her arm and allowed her to dance freely. She did not think she could have endured another embarrassing bear hug. 'I really should not have come,' she said, regret shadowing her eyes.

'Yes you should!' he replied without hesitation. 'But for heaven's sake stop calling me Mr Hardaker.'

She dropped her head, trying to hide the warmth that came to her cheeks. 'I'm sorry,' she said. Then, annoyed with her silly reaction, she brought her head up, lifting her chin in defiance and having the intention of looking him straight in the eye. She failed, her gaze fastened on a large green leaf on the wallpaper which appeared to be resting on his shoulder – but it was an improvement on looking at her feet.

'I don't think my mother would like it,' she said. Her embarrassment was still strong and her voice contained a stiffness she had not intended. Nevertheless, she managed to bring her eyes fleetingly to his, before returning them to the leaf which grew or diminished depending on whether his shoulder was going up or down as he danced. His smile broadened so much that she could tell he was finding it difficult not to laugh at her. 'Maggie calls me John and your mother has never raised any objections. But I've told you that before,' he pointed out.

She gave a little shrug. 'Mum knows there isn't much point in objecting to anything Maggie does. But I am different.' She realized the last statement had made her seem like a child still tucked under her mother's wing and her voice fell away embarrassedly. Perhaps it was because she felt inside that she was still that child, she thought. Or perhaps it was just that she knew Maggie would not have been out of place there. In fact Maggie would have been in her element and vying with Mavis for the centre of attention role of leading lady.

'You are most definitely different,' he agreed, openly laughing now and lifting her chin and making her look into his face. 'But I don't see that should make any difference to what you call me.'

'Perhaps not,' she replied, not willing to commit herself. At that moment, with the laughter in his eyes making him look half his age, she could not find one good reason why she should adhere to her mother's Victorian values. He might be her boss, he might pay her wages, but that did not stop him also being a friend. A rather attractive friend, as well!

She had always thought he had a nice face. He was the type of man who looked good in anything, but the grey velvet jacket he was wearing made him look very elegant and was a far cry from Duggie's rather tacky attempt at sophistication. A sprinkling of grey now streaked the hair at his temples, but that seemed to add to his attractiveness.

If only he was not married. The unexpected thought took her by surprise and she smiled uncertainly. He was watching her oddly, intently, almost as if she had been speaking out loud. She was still trying to fathom out the reason for the strange path her mind had suddenly taken, when the music changed tempo. The sultry voice of Nat King Cole replaced the Beatles, and when he held his arms out to her she slipped into them and coiled her arms round his neck without any hesitation.

It seemed so right being held by him, being close to him. Nat King Cole's treacle smooth voice droned in her ear, implanting suggestions of love and togetherness. All her earlier embarrassment disappeared. There was a warmth running through her, a contentment which made her conveniently forget he was a married man. All she knew was that she was enjoying herself in a new and unexpected way; in an adult way. She was not squealing with laughter as she raced across the fields with Nicky, but she was still experiencing a thrill of joy. Maybe not in the same way, but the feeling was very real. Everything was new, strange and intoxicating; from the clothes she was dressed in to the people she was with. She was sampling things she had never sampled before . . . and she liked them.

When he looked down into her eyes and asked, 'Happy?' she readily nodded her head.

'Yes, John,' she replied, speaking his name with unashamed confidence. No scarlet flush rushed up her cheeks as his arms tightened round her and when his smile deepened she responded with one of equal warmth.

As the evening wore on she forgot the passing of time and it came as a shock when Duggie called out that her taxi had arrived. Nothing was said. They both took it for granted they were going home together. He helped put the cape round her shoulders, they said goodbye to a very red faced Duggie and a very tousled Mavis, then walked silently to the waiting car.

'I'll give you a call about the Woodlands site,' Duggie called after them. 'We can work something out. Don't you worry.'

'You do that, Duggie,' John returned, laughing

quietly as he slid onto the back seat next to Rosy and closed the door on Duggie's reply. 'He can't give it a rest,' he said, clasping her hand tightly in his own and laying them against his thigh.

They fell into silence then. Rosy gazed out of the window. Surprisingly the air had cleared. A band of cloud hung over the horizon but up above was a clear, perfect half-moon and a sprinkling of stars. What would they do now, she asked herself, as she stared at two closely aligned stars which seemed to be chasing one another across the sky? Would she tell her mother? Would he tell her mother? Was there anything to tell her mother! Was she going to be like Cinderella, the moment she took off her ballgown it all ended? Her chest lifted on a silent sigh and she cast him a sideways glance. He was staring out of his window and she could not see much of his face. But he was still holding her hand, she reminded herself, looking down at their clasped hands on his thigh.

He turned then, catching her out. She did not blush. Thankfully something had happened during the course of the evening to put an end to that particular affliction . . . in his company, at least. But her eyes were wide and uncertain as they stared at him.

'It's a nice night. Will you come for a walk with me?' he asked.

'A walk?' she questioned incredulously, as visions of the pitch black wood and eerily shadowed fields flashed through her mind.

He nodded his head. 'Not far,' he assured. 'The car can drop us at the bottom of the drive and we can walk up it . . . that's all.' He moved closer, bringing his face right up to hers. 'You know as well as I do your mother will be waiting in the kitchen for you.' His eyebrows tilted and his mouth twisted ruefully.

Rosy had to smile. Not so much at his reaction, as at the picture in her mind of her mother standing on the doorstep, anxiously watching the taxi going down the drive. 'Wild dogs would not drag her away,' she said.

'I know,' he replied, with quiet certainty. 'But I would like to have you all to myself for just a little while. For just as long as it takes to get from one end of the drive to the other,' he added persuasively.

He reminded her of Nicky trying to wheedle another ice-cream out of her, and her smile broadened. She gave a little shrug. 'All right,' she said. It wasn't an unreasonable request and she could see no reason to refuse. And the idea of being alone with him did rather excite her. She must have drunk too much wine, was the only explanation she could find for having thoughts more suited to their Maggie than herself.

His hand tightened on hers, giving a possessive squeeze. Then he settled back in the seat and did not speak again until they reached the gate at the entrance to the house and he told the driver to stop there.

As the car pulled away, leaving them in the moon's silvery half-light, he took her hand and pulled her into the shadows of the gatehouse cottage. She did not resist and when he pressed her against the wall and brought his head down she lifted her mouth, eager to receive his kiss. The whisky he had been drinking all night still clung to his lips. It tasted nice, warm and mellow, and as his lips worked gently against hers she was incited with an uncommon boldness.

Pushing her hands inside his jacket she ran her fingers over his shirt, up to his shoulders, down to his waist.

'Rosy!' he growled, again and again, as his mouth left her lips and moved down her neck and over her throat. Then he stopped, cupping her face in his hands he gazed into her eyes with an intensity that even the darkness could not conceal. 'I've wanted you for so long,' he said, his voice gravelly and uneven. 'Come into the cottage with me – please!'

She needed no persuading. Since she had left the

house to go to the party she had experienced another life, another world full of new and exciting things, all pleasing. In one evening she had learned so much, but she was not satisfied. She wanted to know it all. She was twenty-four years old and it was well past the time she should have learned about love and thrown off that last vestige of girlhood – her virginity.

When he took her hand and led her round to the front door there were no doubts in her mind. If their Maggie could have a little love nest at the cottage on the hill, then she could have one in the gatehouse, she told herself. It wasn't until he took the key out of his pocket and unlocked the door that she remembered the cottage was now Joey's den.

She rested her hand on his arm before he could lift the latch. 'What about Joey?' she asked.

'He hasn't been working today. And even if he had he wouldn't still be here at this time of night.'

She smiled embarrassedly. 'I know. But . . . do we have a right to go in? Aren't we invading his privacy?'

'It's only his shed. Besides, I do own the place!' He smiled at her concern. 'He's taken his rabbits home with him for the holiday, if that's what's bothering you.' Bending his head he planted a gentle kiss on her lips. 'So we won't be spoiling their beauty sleep.' The last was said with affectionate teasing and, not listening to any more protests, he opened the door and stepped inside.

The cleanness of the place never failed to amaze Rosy and was obvious even in the limited glow of the moonlight. Joey's collection of boxes and jars were all packed tidily together on the table, and there was no animal smell, which she had expected.

'We mustn't move anything so he knows we've been here,' she said, worried that Joey might be upset to think they had been prowling round his territory. She knew how precious his den was to him.

He smiled and shook his head. 'He won't know a

thing.' He held out his hand. 'In here,' he said, going to the door that led into the tiny front room which Phoebe had always had stuffed so full of furniture you could hardly more round it. The moon was on the other side of the cottage and, while the kitchen had been filled with a reasonable light, this room was very dark. As Rosy stepped inside she could make out the black outline of one large armchair. Joey had made himself a real home from home, she thought with a smile. There was a shape by the fire which she took for a small table, a cube shape which she thought must be a cardboard box, and what looked like a pile of old clothes lying up against the corner of the far wall.

'There are some candles, somewhere,' John said.

'How did Joey get candles?' She turned to him with a frown. But it was too dark to see anything of him other than a tall, black shape moving across the dark square of the fireplace.

'I gave them to him,' he said, as he felt carefully along the mantelpiece, trying to find the candlestick.

'Was that wise?' Her deepening frown was lost in the darkness.

'Joey is quite capable,' he assured. 'Ah . . . got it.' He sounded victorious and she knew he must have found the candle.

'Dare we?' She looked round, her voice filled with the question he could not see in her eyes. She could just imagine her mother's reaction if she saw light coming from the cottage windows. She knew she would be bobbing up and down at regular intervals to look out of the window to see if she was on her way home.

'I'll draw the curtains,' he said, and made her laugh as he rummaged in the dark for a piece of cloth she had not noticed lying on the floor beneath the window.

'Is it thick enough?' she asked, worried that the police were going to burst in on them at an intimate moment, because her mother had reported they had intruders in the gatehouse. 'There's some more down here.' She bent down, reaching into the pile of old clothes. Her hand touched something cold. It felt strange. It felt like . . .

'What's down there?' John asked, as a sickening feeling hit Rosy in the stomach and with a shudder she pulled her hand away and jumped back, as if she had touched a scorching brand of red hot metal. She did not reply. Her voice was lost in the horror of what she had been touching, a horror that was so great she was frozen to the spot, her gaze fixed onto the darkness that concealed its ghastly secret.

'What is it?' John repeated, as he touched a cigarette lighter to the candle standing on the mantelpiece. He had his back to Rosy and his body was shielding both her and the room from the first flickering glows of the light.

When he picked the candle up and turned around, Rosy had her worst fears confirmed. She had been touching the cold, lifeless arm of a dead body.

As the candle's glow grew and extended to reach the furthermost corner of the room, she found herself staring into the glassy condemnation of Dorothy Hardaker's unseeing eyes.

CHAPTER ELEVEN

Rosy heard a scream – a terrified, horrible sound that echoed through the neglected cottage and rattled inside her head like a siren warning an imminent explosion. She was not aware the scream was coming from herself.

She clapped her hands over her ears to shut out the noise, but any other movement was lost to her. She was frozen, her gaze pinned to the piercing eyes that glittered and seemed to come to life as the candle's glow was reflected in their icily dormant depths.

'*Bloody hell!*' John's eyes widened as his gaze fastened on his wife's body. For a moment he froze. In the next he dropped the candle, grabbed Rosy and dragged her out of the room. The sudden movement at least stopped the screaming but her hands remained fastened to her ears, as if she feared the noise was going to start up again at any moment.

They were out of the cottage, through the gate and clear of the tiny garden before he stopped. 'It's all right! It's over! It's in there . . . not out here!' His unsteady voice gasped out a steamy breath-cloud in the cold night air. He pulled her into his arms, felt the trembling of her body, and held her tightly to him.

Her gaze lifted slowly, wide, fear-filled eyes resting uncertainly on his face. She had almost expected to find she was once more looking into the inanimate gaze of his wife. She shuddered, recalling that stare: so hard and reprehensive, as if Dorothy Hardaker had been casting the blame where she knew it belonged.

'Oh no! No!' Her head wagged from side to side as guilt took over from the previous terror. Her hands finally left her ears but John was holding her so tightly she could not bring her arms down and so could only rest them on his shoulders. 'Did she know I was going to the party?' Her voice was filled with the anxiety mirrored in her eyes. 'What if she knew I had borrowed her clothes!' It was too awful to contemplate. 'She might have come back to the house after we'd gone and . . . and . . . seen I'd taken her clothes.' She hesitated, her eyes widening so far they looked as if they might pop out of her head. 'She could have known we were both at the party . . . together!' Having Dorothy Hardaker dead was bad enough. Having her dying with the knowledge that Rosy had been rifling through her things, before spending the evening with her husband, was twice as bad.

'Of course she didn't know! But what does it matter if she did?'

'It does matter. It does!'

'*No it doesn't!*' he snapped, giving her a shake. 'Stop it! You've had a shock but you've got to pull yourself out of it!'

'Pull myself out of it?' she repeated incredulously.

'Yes,' he replied bluntly. 'Unless you want everyone to know we went into the cottage together, you've got to forget what you've seen.'

'You can't . . .' she began. Then she let her words trail away as she realized what he was saying. If they said they had seen the body everyone would wonder what they had been doing in the cottage at close on midnight. No, not wonder. They would jump to the conclusion – the correct conclusion!

Her mother would never forgive her! 'But . . . ?' she questioned, staring at his face with resignation.

'I'll come down tomorrow,' he promised. 'All you have to do is put on an act for a few hours. Will you be able to manage that?'

'Yes,' she replied flatly, even though she did not know how she was going to do it. She just knew it had to be done or the truth would cause her mother indescribable hurt. At that moment it was her mother who was giving her the most concern. The full implications of the situation had not occurred to her and she did not care if the rest of the world knew she had been keeping the night watch with John Hardaker, so long as her mother never found out. 'It will be Christmas Day,' she pointed out unnecessarily.

He gave a bleak nod. 'I'll say I was checking Joey had not forgotten to take his rabbits home.'

Rosy looked doubtful. Joey would never have forgotten any of the menagerie of birds or animals that he constantly took under his wing to nurse back to health. But she remained silent, unable to come up with a better reason to visit the cottage on Christmas Day. 'Joey!' she gasped, her hand flying to her mouth. 'Thank goodness he wasn't the one to find her!'

John did not reply. He was too busy peering over her shoulder at the watch on his wrist. He had to turn his arm first one way then the other, before the moonlight shone directly on the dial and he could see it was ten minutes past midnight. 'It's already Christmas Day,' he said, his voice lacking the joy of the announcement.

'Merry Christmas,' she quipped mirthlessly, and took a great breath, drawing courage into herself along with the air she sucked into her lungs. She pushed him away, suddenly embarrassed to be in his arms. 'We'd better get going. Before . . .' She came up short, her mouth falling open and her voice trailing away. 'The . . . the cottage,' she cried, her arm flying out in panic.

He spun round. 'Oh God!' he exclaimed, seeing the flickering orange glow of fire coming from the front room window. 'The candle! I forgot the bloody candle!' For a moment he froze. Then he leapt to life. 'Wait here!' he ordered, and hurtled back through the gate and through the door he had so recently bundled her out of.

Not knowing what else to do, Rosy obeyed and stood

there. But the orange glow in the window did not diminish and after what seemed like an eternity she could stand impotently by no longer.

'John,' she called. 'John! John!' There was no answer and she raced to the cottage door. Again she called his name, again there was no reply. She stepped inside. The kitchen was full of acrid smoke that got up her nose, in her throat and stung her eyes. 'John!' she called. The door to the front room was open and she could hear the crackling of the flames and see their glow flickering and leaping up the dingy walls. But she could not hear or see anything of him.

Fear for his safety gripped her insides like icy fingers. She turned back to the dark night air in the open doorway and took a large gasp, filling her lungs in preparation for what she knew she had to do. For her own peace of mind she could not stand there feeling useless a moment longer. She had to get across the smoke-filled kitchen and look inside the blazing room to find out what he was doing, if he was safe.

When her lungs were filled she turned back, ready to make a frantic dash. But as she took the first step a large flame licked through the front room door and set fire to the peeling paint on the kitchen ceiling. It brought her to an abrupt halt. *John! Where was he?* she screamed inside, her voice locked in a terror that made sound impossible.

She was fearing the worst, just as a loud bump came from upstairs. The place was falling down around her ears! Her gaze leaped anxiously round the kitchen. Flames from the front room now filled the doorway and she could not have got near. She glanced round at the back door, flame free, the black oblong of night seeming to be the only safe haven in a sea of thick, burgeoning smoke and fire. In the next moment she turned and ran.

When she was outside she paused long enough to kick Dorothy Hardaker's strappy sandals off her feet and hitch the tight fitting skirt up over her thighs. Then, not stopping to look back at the burning cottage, she raced up the long drive to the house, faster than she had ever raced up it before.

She had summoned the fire brigade, ordered a bewildered and anxious Nell to stay in the house with the sleeping Nicky, and was racing back to the cottage before she realized her fears that John had perished in the fire had been unfounded.

A great cloud of smoke was rising skyward and the front of the cottage was now burning well. The orange glow of the flames lit up the dark night and illuminated the grey stone walls of the little building, and she was only halfway down the long straight drive when she saw him scrambling across the roof towards the back where, for the moment, the flames had not reached.

Her feet stopped abruptly. 'John!' she cried, staring at the hunched figure doing a crab-like crawl across the grey slates. In an instant she was racing towards him, feeling a rush of gratitude that replenished her lungs and gave renewed strength to her legs. She reached the cottage just as he reached the edge of the roof and lowered himself carefully down onto the flat top of the coal house, which made a suitable landing stage not quite halfway between roof and ground.

'Are you all right?' she asked, prancing beneath the coal house wall like a nervous fawn.

'I will be if you get out of the way.' His voice was sharp and had her moving quickly back, giving him a clear space as he once more lowered himself over the edge. But this time the height was greater and his feet did not touch solid ground and he had to let himself drop the last few feet.

With legs buckling and the breath punched out of his lungs, he hit the ground on a noisy gasp and rolled backwards.

'Are you all right?' She knew she was repeating herself but was too concerned to stop. 'Are you?'

Rushing forward she grabbed his arm and helped him up, and breathed a whole lot easier when she saw his legs could still support him.

'I'm fine.' Straightening himself out, he turned and looked at the cottage. The tongues of flame licking from the windows and through the door could not be seen from there, but the orange glow lighting the night sky and hanging over the roof like a halo was enough to know the front of the building was well alight.

'What can we do?' Rosy asked.

He shook his head. 'Nothing. I only just got out and I'm certainly not going in again. Besides . . .' he added, not looking at her and beginning to walk round to the front to see just what was happening, '. . . we know she was dead.'

Rosy gave a bleak nod. Dorothy Hardaker had most certainly gone from this life. But it still didn't seem right to leave her in there, she thought, and followed him round the burning building. She had no real wish to stand and watch the devastation which he seemed unable to look away from, but at that moment she did not want to be left alone. Smoke swirled all around and the night was filled with the smell of burning wood and plaster, as well as a pungent stench she had no wish to identify.

'I've called the fire brigade,' she said, as she rounded the front corner of the cottage and the heat hit her sharply in the face. Yet despite that heat she shivered: partly from imagining what the long, licking flames could have done to John; partly from the memory of a glassy eyed stare, and what the flames *were* doing to Dorothy Hardaker.

He lifted his face to the glowing sky and gave a sigh. 'We'll have to tell them the truth then,' he said baldly.

Before she could say anything or consider the implications of what had to be done, a mighty crack sent them both leaping quickly away to a safer distance. The flames had burnt through the wooden rafters and part of the roof collapsed in a shower of slates, sparks and burning wood.

'Oh no!' Rosy gasped, not aware she was actually speaking. Some of the debris had fallen on the ground around her feet, but it was not her own safety she was concerned about. Most of the slates had fallen inwards, right on top of where Dorothy Hardaker was lying and, though she knew it was too late to worry about the woman's well-being, it was painful to consider the lifeless body was now getting pummelled and broken.

Fortunately, the sound of a heavy motor put an end to her mental torment and she looked up to see the fire-engine speeding down the lane. 'Thank goodness,' she murmured with feeling.

John turned to her. 'Let me do all the talking,' he said.

She gave a nod, only too ready to let him have the responsibility.

'What a night!' Nell piled the last bacon sandwich onto a plate. Her face was red from standing over the stove cooking all the bacon. Strands of hair had escaped from her bun and hung down, tickling her hot cheeks. 'They should fill a small hole,' she said, studying the food as she pushed her untidy hair away from her face.

Rosy glanced at the two trays. One was packed with rows of steaming mugs of tea, the other piled high with sandwiches. 'A small hole!' she repeated. 'I think you've made enough to fill a crater.'

'She always has been of the opinion that the way to a man's heart is through his stomach,' Maggie put in, as she lit a cigarette, then took a long draw followed by a big yawn. She had arrived home just after the fire-engine, sat herself down in the chair in front of the fire and lit her first cigarette. And that was all she had done for the rest of the night: light up one cigarette after another and wait for any news. She had not lifted

206

a finger to help her mother with the sandwiches and tea, except to drink a few cups.

'It's better than thinking it starts from the bit you aim for!' Nell cast her eldest daughter a disparaging glare and dropped her hands with a gesture of defeat. All the loose strands of hair immediately fell round her face again, and caused another glare to be directed at Maggie, as if she was to blame for that, as well. 'You'll end up sitting in a cowpat one day, Miss. Just you mark my words!'

Maggie did not reply. She returned her mother's withering glance. Then she turned back to the fire, stuck the cigarette between her scarlet lips and took another long draw, which was noisy enough to speak for her.

For several seconds the only sounds in the room were the crackling fire, boiling kettle, and hiss of the gas ring. Nell was bristling with silent indignation. Maggie was sitting very still and staring into the fire and sucking on the cigarette, which never went very far from her lips.

Rosy stood by and watched, and pondered on her sister's unusual behaviour. It was not like Maggie to ever hold her tongue. But at that moment she felt the need to bring harmony back to the kitchen was greater than the need to know the cause of Maggie's odd behaviour. So she turned the subject round and went back to the beginning, as if the short exchange between her mother and sister had never happened.

'They'll need a good feed . . . after that!' she said. 'They've got a job on, some of them.' She could recall the sickness she had felt in the pit of her stomach as she watched the firemen sifting through the smouldering debris of the cottage. She had wanted to move, to turn away and not watch. But she had been frozen to the spot, begging and praying for them to make the grisly find. She kept on telling herself that it was not possible for every trace of Dorothy Hardaker to have burnt away. But the flames had been very hot and she was petrified they would have turned the woman's remains to dust. She had the feeling if they did not find anything left to take away, Dorothy Hardaker would stay there, haunting that patch of land for ever. If that happened she would never walk easily past the spot again.

Fortunately, shortly after the church clock struck the hour of three, the firemen reached what was left of the body.

Over one hour ago, Rosy thought, glancing at the clock on the mantelpiece and seeing the hands lying at four-thirty. It seemed more like an eternity. Turning to the window she gave a sigh. The firemen were coiling the hose back onto the engine and now a police car stood at the bottom of the drive. Uniformed men seemed to be everywhere.

'Nicky will be cross he's missed this,' she said flatly, then suddenly turned to her mother. 'You haven't heard him, have you?' she asked, a note of anxiety entering her voice.

Nell shook her head and attempted once more to make her messy hair stay put.

Rosy turned back to the window, sending up a grateful thank you. As soon as they found the body she had left the cottage and come up to the house, expecting to find the noise had woken Nicky and that he would be in the kitchen with her mother and Maggie. She had been surprised to find he was not there and she went straight up to his room, and was even more surprised to find he was fast asleep. She had then fetched his Christmas stocking from the side of the large marble fireplace in the drawing-room and placed it at the foot of his bed. She hoped, if he did wake up, it might keep him occupied and away from the window.

'Isn't anybody coming yet? This bacon will turn to lard if they don't hurry up,' Nell chuntered.

'The first ones are coming,' Rosy said, peering into the darkness at two large figures striding up the drive. 'It's Kev Cauldwell and Dave Morris,' she added, when they came into the beam of the light at the corner of the house. All the local firemen were from the village and she knew both men fairly well. She watched until they turned up the path to the back door, then she left the window and went to the table. 'I wish Jo . . . Mr Hardaker would come, as well,' she said.

Nell's eyes narrowed. 'Yes,' she said pointedly. 'I imagine you do wish *Mr Hardaker* was here!' She laid extra emphasis on the name, making it clear she had not missed the slip. It was bad enough one of her daughters being too familiar with the man. But not both! 'A fine kettle of fish this is,' she muttered with feeling. 'What's it going to look like? You and him out together . . . finding her like that!' She gave an exaggerated shudder of disgust, and missed the way Maggie's head had spun round, her mouth half-opening as if to speak, then closing again.

Neither did Rosy see her sister's reaction. 'Oh Mum!' she began, then was cut short when the door opened and Dave Morris stuck his blond head and grimy face round.

'Can we come in?' he asked.

'Come on!' Nell urged impatiently. 'I thought you were coming before now. I had this tea poured ages ago. Still, I've got another pot that will be mashed by now, so you can have a fresh one after.'

Dave stopped in front of the table, his smoke reddened eyes widening in appreciation in his blackened face. 'Bacon butties! You're a saint, Nell,' he declared with feeling, and took the mug of tea she offered and poured it down his throat in one go. 'I needed that,' he said, unnecessarily.

Rosy smiled for the first time since close on midnight. 'How's it going, down there?' she asked. She had wanted to ask what John was doing, and how he was taking it all. But she thought better of it in her mother's presence.

'It's a bit grim,' Kev replied honestly, as he combed his fingers through jet black hair that his helmet had flattened to his head. Pausing, he loosened the neck of his heavy fireman's jacket and gave himself more freedom to eat and drink. Then he picked up his tea and dived into the sandwiches, and said knowledgeably, 'Then it always is when there's bodies concerned.'

'It's not that bad!' Dave shot his younger colleague a warning glare: to shut him up before he said too much. 'We've seen a lot worse.'

Having her mind turned back to Dorothy Hardaker and those cold, staring eyes put a tremble in Rosy's limbs. She wrapped her arms tightly around herself to keep them still, then turned away from the men and stared into the fire. But the flames leaping up the chimney only reminded her of the other flames she had seen that night – much larger flames. She gave a shudder and spun away and grabbed one of the mugs of tea for herself, and took a large steadying gulp.

'Now I'm one short,' Nell scolded.

Rosy did not reply. She knew it was going to be impossible for her to do anything right in her mother's eyes, at least until the events of this evening had faded into history.

At a quarter-to-five an ambulance turned up to take Dorothy Hardaker's remains away. Rosy wondered how much there was left to remove and if an ambulance had been really necessary, but she did not ask anyone. Her imagination could provide vivid enough pictures for her to cope with and she had no wish to add fact to them.

After Dave and Kev had finished their tea and gone back outside the other firemen had come up in relays, until the only reminder of the sandwiches was a few crumbs, and the teapots were drained dry.

'That just leaves the policemen,' Rosy said flatly, and returned to the kitchen window to see what was going off at the bottom of the drive. Watching from a distance, she told herself with self- reproach, feeling as if she was a snooper, a peeping Tom. But she knew she did not want to go down there again, not until Dorothy Hardaker had been taken right away, and she did not know what else to do. So she wrapped her arms tightly around herself, chewed on her bottom lip, and watched the dark shadows scurrying round in the glow from the gate lamps.

'I'm going to get some shut-eye,' Maggie suddenly announced, and stood up, scraping the chair noisily across the quarry tiles, in a manner befitting the belligerent glare she passed over her sister. Then she walked out of the door without speaking another word.

'What's the matter with her?' Rosy asked.

Nell gave a grunt. *You've pinched her fella,* she thought. But she would not say that, even though the last thing she wanted was to see Rosy with John Hardaker. He wasn't right for her. But if she spoke out on the subject she would do more to make Rosy want to prove her wrong, than make her see she could never be happy with the man. Besides, she didn't think there was any need for her to get accused of poking her nose in. Maggie would not lie down and take it and she knew Maggie had set her cap at him long before now. Confident Maggie would soon put her twopenn'orth in. She said, 'I don't know. Perhaps she was just tired.'

Rosy wasn't convinced, but she did not want to add any more worries to the one already pressing heavily on her mother's shoulders, so she kept quiet.

It was a few minutes before Nell stopped doing the washing-up and looked at Rosy again. 'Why don't you go and try and get a couple of hours sleep yourself?' she suggested.

Rosy smiled thinly and shook her head. 'I couldn't sleep. Besides, I expect they'll want to talk to me before they go.'

'Oh yes!' Nell's head bobbed up and down as if she had only just remembered.

'And I've got to go and take a look at Nicky in a bit,' Rosy quickly added, wishing she had not mentioned the forthcoming interview with the police and wanting to take her mother's mind off in another direction again.

But Rosy did not go to Nicky. Her mother returned to the washing-up and she remained standing at the window, not making any sound until she let out a great sigh of relief when the ambulance finally went out of the drive.

It was only another few minutes before the last two firemen jumped into the cab and the fire-engine also moved away. Then the policemen jumped into their car and John climbed into the back. They were taking him away, she thought, her hand flying to her mouth to catch the frightened whimper that rose in her throat. But instead of going out of the gate the car turned and came up the drive. She was so relieved she actually laughed; she couldn't stop herself, it just slipped out.

'Whatever's the matter with you?' her mother asked, the rebuke of her voice and the accusation of her gaze making it clear she thought mirth was out of order.

'Sorry, Mum.' Rosy flashed her a grimace of apology. 'They're coming up,' she added, inclining her head towards the window.

'Thanks be for that!' Nell said with feeling.

Rosy silently agreed. She wanted this night over and done with as much as her mother did.

John was the first to get out of the car when it stopped by the front door. But he did not immediately come inside. Stuffing his hands into his trouser pockets he stood in the shadow of the big dark house and turned to the river and stared woodenly at the grey carpet of water rolling past.

His shoulders were slumped and he had such an air of sadness about him that Rosy's heart went out to him. Even though there had been no love between him and Dorothy at the end, she imagined he must be remembering the beginning. The happier times when they had been close and had meant a lot to each other: their courtship; the first days of marriage; the birth of the twins.

Her chest lifted on a silent sigh as her thoughts turned to Nicky. She knew she should go up to him. He might be wanting her, needing her. But still she stood there, staring out of the window at the man who had almost made love to her last night. How differently things had turned out, she thought.

It felt like an eternity before John moved. So long, in fact, that Rosy had begun to have the disturbing feeling he might be considering throwing himself into the river which seemed to be taking all his attention. She was only glad the policemen were out there with him. They were standing by the car and obviously giving him the few minutes they felt he needed, until, finally, he turned around and lifted his head to look up at the hazy ball of the sun in the dawn sky. Then he spoke to the policemen and they all walked slowly to the door.

'Have you got the kettle on, Nell?' John asked, as he came into the kitchen. The policemen followed, taking their hats off as they came into the room. One was a sergeant with a flat cap, the other had the helmet of a constable, and the rather innocent face of someone fairly new to the force. They placed their hats on the dresser, then stood in the middle of the floor, their tall, broad bodies seeming to fill the room.

John seemed to have forgotten they were there. He pulled a chair from beneath the table and sank onto it with a weary sigh. Then he rubbed his dirty hands over his smoke smeared face.

Rosy's heart turned for him. She thought of how much guilt and regret she herself was feeling for the circumstances in which they had found his wife's body. She could not begin to imagine what he was going through.

'Do you want anything to eat?' she asked, feeling the need to do something for him, to care for him. He had not had anything to eat or drink since leaving the party. Her mind turned briefly to the music and dancing and laughter they had left behind at Duggie's and Mavis'. It seemed like a million years ago now.

He shook his head. 'But perhaps these two gentlemen would like something.' He waved his hand at the uniformed men.

'It's all in hand,' Nell interrupted, bustling to the stove and pulling yet another plate full of bacon sandwiches out of the oven, where they had been keeping warm. She put them on the table. 'You'll have to eat some,' she told John, in the manner of a stern mother chastising a naughty boy. 'Or they'll go to waste.' She turned to the two policemen. 'Sit yourselves down,' she ordered, pulling a couple of chairs out for them. 'And get tucked into these. You'll be needing something after spending the night out there when you should be in your beds. Christmas Eve an' all.'

'We'd have been on duty anyway,' the sergeant replied in a friendly manner. He was the older man by several years. He had a large, bushy, silver moustache which gave the impression he had a permanent smile on his face. Rosy wondered if it was to make up for the lack of hair on his head, the top of which was totally bald and shone as if regularly polished.

'These are just the job.' The constable's young face crinkled in a grin of pleasure and he dived into Nell's sandwiches as if he hadn't eaten for a month. He had single-handedly cleared the plate before the sergeant instructed him to get out his notebook to take the statements they had come for.

Oh dear, Rosy thought anxiously. How did it go: something about what you say being taken down in evidence? And worse than that – having to say it in front of her mother! The last thought lifted her gaze to her mother's back, as Nell once more had her hands in water, washing-up.

Fortunately, John looked up at the same time and saw the action, and read her mind.

'You can leave that now, Nell,' he said. 'We won't need you again until the morning. So go and get some rest.'

'Oh no . . .' Nell began.

'Yes!' He cut her off, insistently but kindly. 'We'll have to try and make it some sort of Christmas for Nicky, and that means you'll be required to cook the turkey and all the trimmings. We don't want you collapsing on us through lack of sleep.'

Nell hesitated, turned to Rosy and looked as if about to speak, then changed her mind. 'All right,' she finally said, the stiffness of her voice making plain her disapproval. 'You know where I am if you want me.' She tossed the tea towel onto the draining-board and was at the door, before she added, 'But I'll not sleep, so I might as well not be going!'

'Goodnight, Nell,' John said. He got no reply and he glanced knowingly at Rosy. She smiled her thanks and sat down at the table, thinking she might at least make herself comfortable in body, because she certainly was not going to be comfortable in mind until this was over.

Taking Nell's departure as his cue, the sergeant leaned on the table and clasped his hands before him. 'Can you tell me exactly what happened?' He turned to John. 'Perhaps you could begin first, sir.'

John took a deep breath and fixed his gaze on his

own clasped hands. 'Rosy and I had been to a party,' he began. Rosy felt warmth creeping into her cheeks and dropped her gaze and stared at the cleanly scrubbed tabletop. 'We had a taxi bring us home and it dropped us at the bottom of the drive.' All the time he was speaking the constable's pencil scratched at his notebook.

'Why didn't the taxi bring you up the drive?' the sergeant questioned, his narrow-eyed gaze never leaving John's face.

'We asked to get out at the gate.' Despite the intense scrutiny his voice remained steady. 'We knew Rosy's mother – Nell . . .' he inserted in explanation, '. . . would be waiting up to see us get home safely, and we wanted to be alone.' His head shook with regret. 'I would never have taken Rosy in there if I'd known what we were going to find. But . . .' he continued on a sigh, '. . . I did take her into the cottage.'

As the conversation became more personal, Rosy chewed hard at her bottom lip.

'Do you do that very often?' The sergeant looked from John to Rosy, causing her cheeks to turn the colour of the berries on the holly she had collected the previous day; which now looked very out of place in the tense kitchen.

'No,' John replied easily, drawing the policeman's attention back to himself. Rosy glanced at him. Her face was on fire and she could only wonder how he could remain so calm and collected. 'It was the first time,' he continued without embarrassment. 'It was dark when we first got inside and we couldn't see anything.' He hesitated, glanced across the table at Rosy as if uncertain about something, then turned back to the sergeant. 'I . . . I knew there were some candles somewhere. The cottage was used by Joey Fletcher. He works here, doing odd jobs. He used the cottage for his shed.'

'Isn't it a bit strange to use a cottage for a shed?' the sergeant questioned.

John rubbed wearily at the back of his neck. 'It wasn't really a shed. It was just for Joey to potter about in. He called it his den.' He looked up, fixing the sergeant with a direct gaze. 'You see, Joey's brother, Ivan, is our real gardener and handyman. Joey just helps him. He's mentally retarded and . . .'

'No!' Three pairs of eyes pivoted to Rosy as the word screamed from her lips. She experienced a moment's embarrassment that she had spoken out so forcefully, but then it was gone and she shook her head fiercely, knowing she could not sit there and let it pass by. 'Joey isn't mentally retarded,' she insisted. She hated the word retarded. It made him sound as if he should be locked up. 'He's just . . . just . . .'

'Just what, Miss?' the sergeant enquired, with a note of exasperation in his voice.

'He's a bit slow . . . backward. That's all.'

The sergeant eyed her for several seconds and she felt colour bursting into her cheeks once more. 'A bit slow? Backward?' he repeated carefully.

'Yes,' she said.

'So he is not normal? Mentally he is not normal?' he added pointedly.

She hesitated. 'No,' she finally replied, her voice little more than a whisper. Then she fell silent, knowing she was making matters worse instead of better.

The sergeant immediately turned his attention back to John. 'So you were looking for a candle,' he prompted.

He gave a nod. 'I searched around and finally found one. But by the time I'd got it lit Rosy had already discovered there was something in the room. She was naturally upset. I went over to her with the candle to see better.' He hesitated, dropped his head in his hands and gave a groan of remembered horror. Then he scraped his fingers all the way through his hair to the back of his neck, leaving them clasped there. 'My wife was lying propped up in the corner,' he finally said.

'And where was your wife supposed to be? Should she have been at home?'

With a heavy sigh John released his hands and sat back in the chair. 'No, sergeant,' he said, shaking his head in regret. 'To tell the truth I didn't know where she was. She had not been home the night before.' He exhaled noisily, before saying, 'My wife was an alcoholic. She led her own life and there wasn't much anyone could do about it.'

'So it wasn't unusual for her to be away from home. And she would go out drinking?'

'Every night she went out drinking.' There was resignation in his voice.

'How did you come to drop the candle?'

Rosy looked round in surprise, wondering how they knew the candle had been dropped. Then she remembered they had been outside for some time and that these would not be the first questions John would have had to endure.

'When I saw Dorothy there . . .' he began easily enough, then he hesitated, his head shaking with regret, '. . . I dropped the candle and grabbed Rosy and dragged her out. My concern was for Rosy and I'm afraid I never thought about where the candle landed. Or what the consequences would be.'

'And you are sure your wife was already dead?'

'Without a doubt, sergeant,' he replied.

'But you did not touch her?'

He shook his head.

'I . . . I did.' Rosy's voice was little more than a whisper and she shuddered with the recollection. It was the last thing she wanted to talk about, and remember.

'You did!' The sergeant did not attempt to conceal his surprise, and the young constable also looked up, his pencil taking a well earned rest.

Her head gave a taut nod. 'Yes,' she said. 'Before the candle was lit. I thought it was just a pile of old rags in the corner.' She did not explain why she had put her hand into a pile of old rags. They could, and would, jump to their own conclusions and she no longer cared. She just wanted it all over and done with. 'I reached down and . . .' her voice faltered as she recalled the feel of death and she grasped her own arm, needing the touch of something warm and alive to wipe away the memory. 'I reached down and my hand touched her arm,' she completed hurriedly. She wrapped her arms tightly around herself and closed her eyes, trying to wipe out the images, trying to forget.

'And she was cold?' the sergeant persisted.

Her head moved in a second taut nod. 'Yes,' she said, the words rushing from her lips on a noisy breath. 'Yes, she was cold. Icy cold!' She gave a great gasping shudder and pressed a hand over her mouth. She had the feeling if they made her say any more she would be physically sick. She could feel the bile rising and bitterness scorched her throat and soured her tongue.

John jumped up and rounded the table to go to her side. Wrapping his arm around her shoulders he pulled her against him. 'Please!' he begged, his imploring gaze moving from one to the other of the two policemen. 'Can't she go? There's really nothing more she can tell you.'

'That's all right, sir.' The sergeant pushed his chair back and stood up. 'I don't think we need trouble either of you much longer.'

Rosy did not know if it was a reaction to the relief at knowing the police were leaving, or if her body just chose that moment to give in to extreme tiredness. But she put her arms on the table and dropped her head onto them with a groan that echoed her pain. She ached all over, as if she had undergone some great physical task that had left her bone weary. She felt spent, empty. Somewhere inside her head a little voice told her she should be crying. She had not shed one tear for Dorothy Hardaker and she could not now. She regretted the way the woman had met her end, but she could not deny that a part of her was feeling a sense of release, as if a dark cloud had been lifted off the house and now the sun was going to be allowed to shine in.

Lifting her head she looked up to find the policemen had gone. She had not heard them go out of the house but the only other person with her was John. His arm was still lying across her shoulders and he was looking down at her with concern. 'What will happen now?' she asked.

He gave a negligent shrug. 'I want to get out of these clothes and have a bath before I do anything else,' he replied, deliberately misinterpreting the meaning of her question. Then his gaze took on an intensity she did not understand, and he said, 'I would not have taken you in the cottage if I had known Dorothy was there.' He hesitated. 'You do believe that . . . don't you?'

Her smile was uncertain but she nodded her head. 'Of course I do,' she assured, wondering why he had found it necessary to repeat the words she had already heard him speak to the policeman.

But before she could question his reasons he returned to the previous subject. Lifting his lapel he gave it a sniff. 'I smell more like November the fifth than Christmas,' he said.

Thankful he could find some humour in the situation, she pushed her doubts aside and returned his smile. But then her gaze ran over the velvet jacket and her smile turned to a grimace. It was now dulled from the effects of smoke and smeared with grime, and there were several damp patches where the pile had been flattened down. The quick escape from the burning building across the roof had left his trousers scuffed and torn. His hair had lost its chestnut gloss beneath a layer of grey and his face and hands looked more befitting to a chimney sweep.

His appearance reminded her that she had not changed out of the black taffeta dress and jacket either and that her clothes were also entirely unsuitable to the occasion. She wondered what the firemen had thought, seeing her dishing out tea and bacon butties in a posh frock. Even if they had not had to admit to going into the cottage and starting the fire, it was obvious from their clothing that she and John had been out together. As her mother had said earlier: a fine kettle of fish! With a yawn John wiped a hand tiredly over his face. 'I think we should go and try and get some rest. Dave Morris said a couple of them would be back later in the morning to check the cottage over again, and I want to be around when they do.' He stood up and pulled Rosy to her feet. 'Dave didn't know who it would be. I think it was a matter of which two drew the shortest straws. It being Christmas Day,' he added drily.

She gave a nod. 'Santa is supposed to come on a sleigh, not a fire-engine.' She made a bleak attempt at humour as she went and turned the key in the lock of the back door, then followed him out of the kitchen switching the light off as she went.

He was waiting for her at the bottom of the stairs. As she reached his side he took hold of her arm. 'Don't leave me now, Rosy.'

She stopped in her tracks, shook her head. 'You can't mean . . . No . . . No!' Instantly recoiling from the suggestion she pushed his hand away.

'Please, Rosy. Just be with me. I won't touch you . . . not if you don't want me to. But I don't want to be alone.'

The pleading in his voice was almost her undoing. She could understand perfectly what he was saying – the prospect of being alone was not very pleasing to her either, especially lying in bed. She knew the images that would haunt her: the blazing cottage; the staring eyes; the smell of smoke and that other, sickeningly acrid stench which she did not want to put a name to. But she would not go to him now, not like this, not to have the memory blighted by horror. 'No!' she insisted,

221

and freed her arm from his grasp and hurried past him and up the stairs.

She could hear his footsteps following closely and when she reached Nicky's bedroom door, she stopped and grabbed the knob. 'I'll check he's OK,' she said, and without turning to look at him pushed the door open before he could stop her.

Nicky was wide awake, sitting up on the bed, the contents of the Christmas stocking spread all over the blue counterpane.

'Good morning,' she said, her voice brittle with tension as she stepped inside the room, quickly closed the door and leaned back against it – as if she expected his father to try and hammer it down to get at her. She only realized how near to the truth she had been, when she heard the footsteps on the other side of the door moving away and she let out the breath she had not been aware she was holding.

Collecting herself, she pushed away from the door. 'What are you doing?' she asked. Her voice was now as relaxed as the smile she settled on him as she watched him playing with a set of toy soldiers complete with two tanks, an armoured car and a first aid post.

He was in the process of aiming the gun of one tank at a pack of playing cards. Not until there had been a noisy discharge, and a lot of spitting from tightly pursed lips and over-inflated cheeks, did he look up. 'Hello,' he said simply. He looked her up and down. 'You're dirty,' he added, and immediately turned back to the khaki plastic army.

'Yes,' she agreed, then hesitated. 'He didn't miss you out then?' she said half-heartedly, as she crossed the room and perched herself on the edge of the bed. Then wondered how she was going to begin to tell him about his mother.

'Nah!' he said, looking up with a grin. 'He even brought them up here instead of leaving them downstairs. He must have got his reindeers to stop outside the window.'

'Yes.' She smoothed a hand fondly over his brown curls. She hoped these were not going to be the last joyful minutes of Christmas for him. This year the festivities had been doused, and the happy times of future years would be blighted by the memory. She gave a sigh, summoning up the courage to begin. 'The gate cottage burned down last night,' she said.

'I know,' he replied, without looking up at her.

It had not been the answer she had been expecting and her mouth fell open. 'You know?' she repeated cautiously.

He gave a nod, as he steered the armoured car over the rocky terrain of a packet of marshmallows, two chocolate bars and a bag of peanuts. 'I saw it.'

'What?' she gasped. 'You saw the fire.'

His head nodded again. 'I watched it all through the window.'

'*All?*'

'Until the flames had gone. By then I was dropping to sleep so I got back into bed.'

She gave a gasp of diebelief. 'I thought you'd slept through everything. I thought you were sleeping well!' she added drily. It was no wonder she had previously found him gone to the world. He had only had a few hours sleep and he must have been getting back into bed at the time he more usually woke up on Christmas morning. 'Why didn't you go downstairs to my mum?'

'I could see better from up here,' he stated matter-of-factly. 'Did you enjoy the party?'

She did not miss the tightening of his voice on the last. The excitement had not made him forget his anger with her for going out without him. 'Yes, thanks.' She kept the reply brief and turned the conversation in another direction. 'How many soldiers have you got there?'

'Twenty-five. There's fifteen there and ten over here.'

'That's a bit uneven, isn't it? This lot won't stand a chance.' She waved her hand at the under-manned group of ten miniature soldiers.

'No it isn't. They're the British! And they're better than anybody else. So they always win!'

'Oh,' she replied feebly, wondering where he had inherited the bulldog spirit from. 'Nicky . . .' she began, hoping the same spirit would see him through what she had to say, '. . . you saw the fire-engine, but did you see the police car and the ambulance?'

'I saw the police car.' He did not look up. The outnumbered British Army was knocking seven bells out of their opponents, and was of far greater interest to him.

Rosy gave a sigh. 'Nicky . . . look at me!' Her voice had been harsher than intended, but she still had to repeat, 'Nicky!' and take hold of his shoulders and make him look at her, before she got his full attention. 'There was an ambulance, as well!' she said. She hesitated, wondering just how to lead up to it. There was no easy way, and she said straight out, 'Your mother was in the cottage, Nicky. I'm afraid she's dead.'

The tank being steered over the bag of peanuts stopped abruptly. For several moments he stared at the counterpane. Finally the tank began to move again, over the peanuts, over the chocolate, finishing off by going over each member of the opposing army and crushing them fiercely into the blankets. 'Did she burn to death?'

Such a brutally blunt enquiry had not been expected and Rosy was unable to hold back a gasp of shock. 'No . . . she . . . I mean, no she didn't burn to death. She was dead before the fire started.' She spoke gently, thinking he must share her own horror of burning flesh.

But then he lifted his head and looked her straight

224

in the eyes and she knew she had been wrong. 'I wish she had burnt,' he said, and the coldness in his voice sent a shiver through her.

'Oh Nicky!' She pulled him into her arms. 'Don't . . . don't say that. You don't mean it. You're hurting, but it will go away and then you'll know you didn't really mean what you said.' Whatever the woman had been she had been his mother.

He did not speak. His arms went round her waist and he buried his face against her chest and clung to her. She expected him to begin crying but there were no tears, no shuddering sobs. His body remained so still he could have been sleeping as deeply as when she had looked in on him in the early hours.

She heard his father's footsteps going from the bedroom to the bathroom. She could hear the sound of water running from the taps and filling the bath, before he finally lifted his head and fixed his gaze onto hers with an intensity she had never seen in him before. It was part pain, but it also contained something she found disconcerting in one so young. 'You won't ever leave me, will you?' he said, his voice now filled with all the emotion she had expected from him before.

'Not willingly,' she replied, as she looked down sadly into his pleading brown eyes.

'I don't care about anybody else as long as *you* stay with me!' he said. Then his arms tightened around her waist with such force she had the feeling she was being enclosed in a band of metal.

CHAPTER TWELVE

It was the day after Boxing Day when the police returned. Rosy was in the conservatory, playing with Nicky on the new train set his father had given him after Christmas dinner. It was a massive layout which circled the room and twisted in and out of the table and chair legs and round the potted plants that gave the room its tropical aura.

The Flying Scotsman was just hurtling nonstop through the station, pulling a wagon filled with the khaki plastic army, when the door opened and Maggie stuck her head round. 'The next train leaving this station is bound for plodsville,' she announced drily.

Nicky was too busy to take any notice and did not lift his head to acknowledge her presence.

Rosy did look round. 'You coming to have a play?' she asked, her voice enthusiastic to the point of pleading. Despite his unexpectedly cold first reaction, his mother's death had not left Nicky untouched. No-one had been very jolly over the holiday, but it had been most noticeable in him, and she had gone out of her way to try and create a friendly atmosphere for him. But it was difficult on her own and she was hoping Maggie would come and join them.

But she did not get her wish. 'No . . .' Maggie replied bluntly. '. . . you are!' She inclined her head towards the kitchen. 'With the boys in blue.'

'The police!' Rosy gasped, as the penny finally dropped, making her forget about Nicky and concern herself more with self-preservation. 'What do they want?' she asked. Maggie's tilted eyebrows and tight-lipped grimace told her just how stupid the last question had been. 'I mean . . . why do they want to see me? We told them everything the other night.'

'Then I imagine they want you to tell them everything all over again.' Maggie's voice was edged with the impatience that had been with her since the beginning of Christmas.

Rosy frowned at her sister, but before she could say anything she was being pushed towards the kitchen. Then urged to hurry up by her mother, standing in the hall, a bright yellow duster dangling from hands clasped tightly at her waist.

'We shall be in the drawing-room,' Nell pointed out. '*If* we are wanted!' The last was stressed with great meaning and Rosy did not need any more pushing forward. She was only too grateful to get to the kitchen and leave her mother's and sister's censure behind.

Maggie had been wrong, Rosy thought, as she walked through the door to see the men sitting round the kitchen table – large, steaming mugs of her mother's tea standing in front of them. They were not the boys in blue, they were the boys in plain clothes. Detectives! In sombre grey suits that went well with their serious expressions. She forced a welcoming smile to her face, even though it was a million miles from her real feeling. John was standing in front of the fire, his hands stuffed deep into his trouser pockets. His head was bent and he stared pensively at the floor. Rosy took one look at him and her smile slipped from her face.

'What is it?' she asked anxiously.

He lifted his head but before he could open his mouth the more senior of the two men spoke.

'Would you sit down please, Miss Smith. We want to ask you a few more questions.' His smile was pleasant but the way he had called her 'Miss Smith' sent shivers of doubt racing through her flesh. The shivers increased dramatically when he turned to John and said, 'Would you leave us, sir.' Rosy had the feeling that if a chair had not been within her reach, so that she only had to sink onto it, she might have ended up on the floor. For her legs turned to jelly and she had to press her arms against the table and clasp her hands tightly together, to stop their shaking becoming too evident.

She did not look at John as he walked slowly across the room. She kept her gaze fastened on her hands and only sensed the moment of hesitation before he finally went through the door, closing it behind him.

'Now then, Miss Smith, don't look so frightened. We don't bite.' It was the older man again, who drew her gaze upwards and put an uncertain smile on her lips.

'I'd . . . prefer it if you called me Rosy,' she said, her voice beginning on a whisper but finding strength towards the end, as she gained courage from the upward tilt of his mouth and the eyes that danced kindly at her.

His smile broadened. 'All right, Rosy,' he said. 'And I am Detective-Inspector Donaldson and this is Detective-Sergeant Evans. Now, we just want to go over a few points again.'

Her nervousness immediately returned and she feared she had been gullible and allowed herself to be blinded by a friendly smile.

'Tell me what happened on Christmas Eve. In your own words,' he quickly added, as he saw doubt forming on her face. 'We've only heard Mr Hardaker's side so far. We'd like to hear yours. Just in case you remember something he has forgotten.'

She took a deep breath. 'Where . . . where do you want me to begin?'

'You went to the party together and left in the taxi which dropped you at the gate.'

She gave a nod.

'Then begin from there.'

228

It took a few moments. Several times her troubled gaze swung between the Inspector's smiling face and the quiet watchfulness of his younger colleague, who was waiting with notepad and pencil poised, ready to make notes – just as before. On a sigh she dropped her eyes and toyed with her fingers. 'We got out of the car . . .' she finally began, in an uncertain whisper.

The pencil scratched noisily as each word she spoke was hurriedly scribbled down. But neither of the men spoke until she was almost at the end. She was relating how she had reached down into what she had thought to be no more than a bundle of old clothes, when the Inspector suddenly said, 'You live here, don't you, Rosy?'

'Yes,' she replied, wondering where the question was leading.

'With Mr Hardaker and his son?' She gave a nod, a frown forming on her face. 'But your mother and sister don't live here?'

'They live in the cottage behind,' she replied cautiously, suddenly seeing exactly where the questions were leading. But nothing could have prepared her for the blunt enquiry that followed.

'Are you Mr Hardaker's mistress?' the inspector asked.

Without so much as batting an eyelid, she thought, her mouth dropping open. Her silence did not prompt him to repeat the question and for several seconds the only sound in the kitchen was the crackling of the fire. Finally she shook her head. 'No,' she replied, in little more than a whisper. Then, the impertinence of the question lighting her fury, she lifted her chin and stared straight into the eyes that no longer danced, but looked back at her with an astuteness that would previously have made her shiver. 'No,' she repeated, her voice growing in strength along with her manner. 'I am *not* Mr Hardaker's mistress and never have been. I look after his son. I have done since he was a baby. That is why I live in the house.'

Her cool gaze flicked across to the younger officer, who suddenly seemed to be finding his notes very interesting and, for the first time, was not looking at her. She turned back to his superior and her voice was stiff with offence, as she added, 'If it has any relevance to Mrs Hardaker's death!' She felt they were taking liberties. Her personal life had nothing to do with Dorothy Hardaker drinking herself to death. But the Inspector did not agree.

'It could have, Miss . . . er . . . Rosy,' he said. Then he stood up and, with hands clasped behind his back, walked across to the fire, paused for a moment, then walked back again. He stopped right behind her. 'If you and Mr Hardaker were in a long-time relationship . . .' he began, the excessive severity of his voice sending a shiver down her spine, '. . . it could have been very useful for you to have got rid of Mrs Hardaker.'

'What . . . !' she gasped, almost falling off her chair as she spun round to look up into his face as he towered above her. 'You can't be serious!' she glanced across at the sergeant. He was looking extremely serious now, and so was the inspector. Her head began to wag from side to side, then suddenly stopped and, shock widening her eyes, she said, 'Are you trying to tell me her death was not an accident? That . . . that she was murdered!' It was unthinkable. Dorothy Hardaker had been a drunk and she had drunk herself to death. Nothing else.

But then the inspector moved round the table and sat down once more, and when she looked into his face, now touched with a concern she had not previously seen, she knew the unthinkable had happened.

'But who . . . who would want to kill her?' As the question left her lips she knew exactly where the finger of suspicion would point. John! But he had not done it. She knew he would not, could not have been capable. But she knew in the eyes of the world he had good reason to want to be rid of the woman who had made his life hell.

'That is what we want to find out,' the inspector's voice had become gentler.

Rosy responded with a smile that came out more like a grimace. 'Are . . . are you sure?' she asked. 'It wasn't unusual for Mrs Hardaker to get very drunk. She could have fallen or . . . or something.' Her voice diminished at the end.

The inspector shook his head. 'Despite the fire Mrs Hardaker's body was not so badly burnt.' Rosy gave a little nod, at least grateful for a small mercy. Though Dorothy Hardaker had been dead long before the flames got to her she was thankful the woman had been spared something. But then the inspector continued and she thought the word 'spared' had been out of place.

'When part of the roof collapsed it landed on top of the body and protected it from the flames.' Clasping his hands on the table he watched her intently. Looking for clues, she thought, feeling something heavy sink in her stomach. 'One side of the body was burnt . . .' he continued, '. . . and naturally the falling slates did quite a bit of damage so the body was very battered, but mostly on the bottom half.' He paused and took a deep breath. 'We know Mrs Hardaker had drunk a considerable amount.' His voice softened again, but there was no softening in the shrewd eyes, as he said, 'But there is evidence of bruising round her throat that was nothing to do with falling over. It suggests she was strangled.'

Rosy's own throat went dry and her mouth dropped open. 'No! No! No!' She whispered the word over and over again, until it rattled inside her head like a crazy tom-tom. She clapped her hands over her ears but that only trapped the sound inside and when she continued to insist, 'No! No! No!' she did not know if she was still trying to deny the way in which Dorothy Hardaker met her death, or if she was now trying to demand the noise to stop.

It was the feel of the inspector's hand, settling on her shoulder, that brought her back to sanity. 'Do you want a drink of water?' he asked.

She shook her head, but this time the action was slow and controlled. Taking a deep breath she straightened herself up in the chair and laid her hands palm down on the table. 'I'm sorry,' she said, feeling an apology was needed. Such crazy displays could only persuade them she had some part in it, she warned herself.

'What can you tell me about Joey Fletcher?' Letting go of her shoulder he walked round the table, but did not sit down again.

'Joey wouldn't have anything to do with it,' she said, quick to leap to his defence. 'He wouldn't hurt a fly.' She recalled the time she had watched him feeding the baby birds with live worms and his genuine concern for the worms.

'Can you think why Mrs Hardaker would have gone into Joey's shed?'

'No,' she replied, her head moving from side to side once more. Taking a deep breath she forced her head to be still, telling herself if it didn't stop rolling around she was going to make herself seasick. There was no reason for Dorothy Hardaker going into Joey's den. The woman avoided him like the plague. Had avoided him like the plague, she amended. 'She had many men friends. Maybe she went in there with one of them.' But even as she spoke she could not imagine Dorothy Hardaker, at her most inebriated, going into the dingy cottage for anything. It was the lady of the house they were talking about, she reminded herself, not their Maggie. Or herself, she added sadly, knowing full well that, had fate not stepped in, she would have sunk to her sister's level.

'Did she have a key to the place?'

Rosy gave a shrug. 'I don't know.'

'But there were no signs of any forced entry into the cottage?'

'I don't think so. I didn't see any. I don't know!' Her hands came up to catch her head, as it flopped forwards. 'I don't know,' she repeated, her voice dulled with despair. At that moment the only thing she was sure of was that she wanted the questioning to end and this all to be over.

In the next moment, as if some good fairy suddenly waved a magic wand above her, Rosy got her wish.

The inspector sat down again. 'I don't think we need you any more just now. On your way out will you ask Mr Hardaker to come back in.'

She did not need telling twice. She was on her feet and out of the door before Detective Sergeant Evans had time to put his pencil down.

'Whatever's going off in there?' Not for the first time Rosy walked to the drawing-room door and gazed anxiously across the hallway to the closed kitchen door. John had been with the two policemen for one and a half hours.

'You'll know soon enough,' Maggie replied sharply, lifting her gaze from the pages of a magazine to glare at her sister. Her irritability with Rosy had increased as she had watched her pacing up and down the room and had had to endure her constant moaning. 'Now for heaven's sake sit down and shut up. You're wearing a hole in the carpet and you're getting right on my nerves.'

'I'm worried!' Rosy spun round angrily. 'And if you don't like it you can always go home!' she added pointedly. Maggie had spent all of Christmas at the house, moping round, smoking one cigarette after

233

another. She had not even made her evening trips to the pub. And the feeling was mutual: she was beginning to get right on Rosy's nerves.

Maggie gave a snort and returned to the magazine.

'Shut up the both of you!' Nell demanded, glancing round as, for the third time, she studiously polished a bronze stallion which stood on the windowsill. 'It's coming to something when all you can do is go at each other. At a time like this!'

'I want to know what's going off in there.' Rosy stabbed a finger towards the kitchen. 'Doesn't it concern you that they've had him in there for over an hour. What are they asking him? How much longer are they going to be?'

'I'd like to know the answer to that one,' Nell put in, moving on from the bronze to an ivory samurai warrior, which had also been treated by the duster several times before. 'I should have started on dinner half an hour ago. It'll be cold cuts again.'

'Does dinner blasted well matter?' Rosy fumed, releasing her frustration on her mother. She let out a long groan. 'For heaven's sake put that blessed duster down!'

Nell's lips compressed into a tight line and she turned on her youngest daughter. 'I'll thank you to moderate your language, madam. And in case you'd forgotten, just you remember whose stupidity it was that started all this!'

Rosy's mouth dropped open, but only for a moment. The next she was fighting back. 'It isn't my fault that Dorothy Hardaker got herself murdered,' she hissed. '*We* had nothing to do with it. We only found the body. That isn't a criminal offence. Or do *you* think we had something to do with it, as well!'

'I should hope not!' Nell managed to get every ounce of indignation contained in her short body into the four words.

'Leave it will you!' Tossing the magazine aside,

Maggie glared at first her mother, then her sister. 'There's two coppers still over there.' She cocked her thumb towards the kitchen. 'Do you want them to hear all this?'

Nell gave a snort and turned back to her polishing.

'I want them to come out and let John go,' Rosy said with feeling. Nell gave another snort; Rosy imagined at the way she had referred to him only as John. But what did it matter? What did anything matter? In a manner that echoed her despair, she flopped into the chair by Maggie's side. 'Will they know about the time he hit her?' she asked, her gaze settling bleakly on her sister's face as she recalled the day Dorothy Hardaker had stubbed her cigarette out on her hand, and her husband's retribution. If only he had kept his mouth shut, she thought. But he had had to go blabbering to Doctor Hampson, letting him know exactly what had happened . . .

Maggie gave a shrug. 'It all depends on whether Larry Hampson told the hospital the truth. If he did I imagine they will have dug her records out and . . . yes . . . they will know.'

'Oh . . . !' It was half-cry, half-groan and Rosy dropped her forehead into her hand and let out a shaky sigh. 'I should go and see Nicky.' It was obvious from her tone of voice that she had no intention of doing so.

'He's all right with his trains,' Maggie assured. 'If he wasn't you'd be hearing about it.' Rosy did not reply. She wasn't convinced. Being quiet was not natural for him. But she was too worried about John to force her body to go and check on his son, and for several moments Maggie silently watched the changing emotions of her sister's face. Finally, she said, 'Do you really think that much of him? John, I mean?'

Rosy looked round. It was only a moment before she said, very simply, 'Yes . . . I think I do.'

Another snort of disgust came from Nell at the

window. But Rosy was too busy trying to work out the emotion on her sister's face to take any notice of her mother. For a moment she thought Maggie was angry, then she realized it was sadness her sister was feeling. 'What is it?' she asked, reaching out and placing her hand on top of Maggie's as it lay on the arm of the chair.

Maggie gave a little shrug. Then she broke into a smile that was not completely devoid of the previous emotion, but it was a smile and it had a certain amount of warmth about it. 'Trust you,' she said with feeling. 'The first fella you have!'

Rosy smiled, even though she was not sure she understood exactly what it was that Maggie was saying.

Another snort came from the window, much louder than all the previous. 'You should be ashamed of yourself!' Nell declared. 'You're both as bad as each other. I'm glad your dad didn't live to see this day!'

Before either of her daughters had time to reply, the kitchen door opened and John Hardaker came out, followed by the two detectives. Without acknowledging the three faces watching from the drawing-room, the men walked down the hall and went out of the front door, got into the police car and drove away.

'*You didn't take them to Joey!*' Rosy's disbelief and anger tore from her. She paced across the office, stopped at the door and spun round on him. 'You can't seriously think Joey had anything to do with it! He wouldn't hurt a fly. You know that as well as I do.' She paced back across the office, this time going to the window and staring out on the frosty fields and riverbank, yet could not see any of the beauty before her. Her mind was too locked on the horror of what John had done. Instead of trying to keep Joey out of it, he had taken the police round to Joey's home and helped them question him.

'My hands were tied, Rosy. What could I do?'

She spun round on him again, folding her arms and sticking her hands tightly away beneath her arm-pits, fearing that if they were free she might just set about him. 'You didn't have to go with them!' she blazed. 'You didn't have to show Joey that you were of the same opinion as the police. That you thought he had . . . had . . . !' Her voice trailed away and her head fell forward, her chin resting on her chest. 'He couldn't have done it! Joey couldn't have done it!' she moaned.

'Rosy!' He came to her side and pulled her into his arms. 'I don't believe he did it, either. But I couldn't refuse to tell the police where Joey lived and I thought it would be better if I went with them. I thought he wouldn't be so frightened if there was someone there he knew.'

It took several moments, but Rosy finally accepted defeat, realizing she had allowed emotion to override reason. It would have been impossible to keep Joey out of the police investigation and had two strange policemen turned up to question him he would have been terrified. 'This is so awful,' she said. 'I wish it was all over.' Even in death Dorothy Hardaker was causing turmoil in their lives, she thought.

'So do I!' he agreed with feeling. 'But it will be, one day. Then we'll be able to get on with our own lives again.' Lifting her chin he brought her face up to look at him. 'Just be with me when that time comes,' he said, his voice and eyes filled with pleading, 'I need you more than ever now. Marry me, Rosy? I don't mean straight away. But just say you will.'

Her smile was tight and uncertain. She recalled the feel of his arms and the way he had kissed her on Christmas Eve, before they had made the fateful mistake of going into the cottage. But it did not seem right to be talking this way, not at the moment, and she pushed his hand from her chin and turned away.

237

'Don't turn your back on me, Rosy.' The pleading was still there, but there was also a spark of anger, and he reached out and grabbed her arm to stop her going and his fingers bit into her flesh more tightly than was necessary.

She turned slowly, his force putting a determination in her that could not be coaxed by soft words. 'I won't do anything that will add further scandal to this house,' she said. Neither would she do anything that would cause her mother any more distress than was necessary. Nell was not pleased with the association between them. But if they did anything to make it public before what she considered to be a suitable time of mourning had passed, she would never forgive them.

His smile instantly vanished, for a moment anger flashed across his face, then it was replaced by a hurt that would have been more appropriate on a little boy who had had his sweets taken from him.

Rosy immediately softened and a smile came to her lips. But she felt too uncomfortable with the conversation to prolong it. She could not forget that somewhere lay the meagre remains of Dorothy Hardaker and, at times like this, she felt angry that John appeared to be able to forget them so easily. 'I should go and find out what Nicky is doing,' she said, and turned for the door before he had time to object.

Nicky was doing what he had been doing every waking minute since Christmas afternoon – playing with the train set his father had given him. He did not look up when she walked into the conservatory and sat down in the bentwood rocking-chair by the side of a large Swiss Cheese plant, and watched him silently.

He did not acknowledge her presence and, when finally she asked, 'Would you like to go for a walk?' he shook his head. 'A swim?' she offered hopefully, only to have that also turned down in the same voiceless manner.

'Nicky!' Her voice was filled with concern and, leaving the chair to rock gently without her, she crossed the room and knelt down by his side. 'Let it out.' She pressed a hand to his shoulder. His emotions were so mixed up that he was afraid to let them show. He had not meant those first harsh words on his mother's death. But he did not know how to admit that, even, she suspected, to himself. Because of that he was not giving himself the chance to get rid of the hurt building inside him. 'Come on, love,' she urged. 'When things happen that frighten us we sometimes say and do things we shouldn't. But we don't mean them.' She paused, giving him the time to speak. He did not, and she said, 'It's perfectly all right to let people know you are missing your mum.'

His gaze left the moving train and fell to a spot on the carpet close to his feet. 'I don't miss her,' he said, his voice filled with pain. 'She didn't love me. Why should I miss her?'

Rosy wanted to tell him his mother had loved him, but she did not want to lie to him. Instead she said, 'Your mum was ill, love.' Reaching out she brushed a hand over his soft brown curls. 'She wasn't herself these last years. But that doesn't mean she didn't have any feelings for you. Or Guy, when he was here.' She gave a thin smile. Then, hoping to comfort him, unthinkingly said, 'They'll be together now.'

But there was no comfort for him. 'No!' he cried, turning on her like a wild animal. 'Guy isn't with her because he isn't dead!'

It took all her strength to catch and hold his flailing arms. 'I'm sorry. I'm sorry. Nicky, please!' she begged. He had never accepted his brother was dead, or had time for her argument that, if Guy was still alive, they would have found him by now. But now was not the time to force the issue, so she continued to hold onto him until the tension went from his arms and his body sagged, as if in resignation.

'All right?' she asked, peering into his face with concern. She would rather have seen him cry, but fighting his emotions out was better than nothing.

He looked up at her, his distraught features a parody of his usual smiling face. 'Do . . . do they have gin in heaven?' he asked.

His voice was so serious and Rosy looked both surprised and confused at the unexpected enquiry. 'I shouldn't think so,' she replied.

'Then she won't be very happy . . . will she?' he said, and fell against her and gave way to the tears he had been holding back.

'Come on!' Rosy tugged at a reluctant Nicky's arm, to get him over the wall into the field below the wood. 'You'll stagnate if you don't get any fresh air.' Even after getting him to give way to his emotions, he had still remained cooped up inside all over Christmas, never wanting to leave his train set, and she had been determined he was going for a walk. All his groans and whines had been ignored and she forced him into his coat, stuck his woolly hat on his head and dragged him out of the house, not exactly screaming but making an awful lot of noise.

'I've had some fresh air,' he complained. 'Now I want to go back.'

He looked so miserable, she had to smile. It was so unlike him not to want to get out and about. She could not be sure if it was still reaction to his mother's death, or if it was nothing more than his father having made the right choice of Christmas present. Fortunately, a grey squirrel chose that moment to jump over the wall and race across the field in the direction they were going.

In an instant Nicky had forgotten his moans and was chasing after it. 'Can I keep it for a pet,' he called, as his Wellington boots slipped and slid in the long, damp grass, and the squirrel got further and further away.

'If you can catch it,' Rosy replied, though not loud enough for him to hear. She was only too pleased to find something had diverted his attention away from trains and soldiers. And the squirrel was in no danger of having its liberty curtailed.

The squirrel was obviously of the same opinion, or it was enjoying the race. For it went deep into the wood, passing the refuge of many tall trees, before it sprinted up to the top of an oak tree and stood on a branch looking down, giving the distinct impression it was laughing at them.

'I'll get you next time,' Nicky warned. He turned to Rosy with a grin. 'I nearly got him,' he said proudly.

She laughingly agreed. Then she lay her arm across his shoulders and turned him away. 'Come on,' she urged. 'Leave it in peace.'

The excitement of the chase had returned Nicky's enthusiasm for the great outdoors and it wasn't long before he was racing off in front. Kicking up the thick carpet of dead leaves he raced round tree trunk after tree trunk, making a noise that Rosy could only describe as the call of a demented wolf. He was being so noisy that she almost missed hearing the gentle sobbing coming from behind a large rhododendron bush standing at the edge of the wood, where the grassy bank came up to meet the trees. The evergreen was still clustered with leaves, making it impossible to see through its branches. She crept round the side, quietly pulled a large protruding branch out of the way, and peered round to the front.

The sight that met her eyes instantly tore at her heart. Joey was sitting on the trunk of a fallen tree. His head was slumped forward, his large hands hanging impotently between his knees, tears ran freely down his cheeks, and his big shoulders were shaking with uncontrollable sobs.

'Joey!' she gasped, rushing round the bush and dropping onto the trunk by his side. Grasping hold of one of his hands she clasped it tightly between both of her own. 'Whatever is it?' It was a stupid question. She could guess why he was upset – the visit from the two detectives. 'Oh Joey! Don't take on. They had to ask us all questions. It wasn't just you. They weren't picking on you.' She knew that words were hollow after what he must have gone through but she did not know what else to do to comfort him. 'Don't, Joey,' she said gently. 'Don't upset yourself.'

Slowly his head turned, his wide tear-filled eyes settling miserably on her face. 'They think I hurt Mrs Hardaker.' His head shook and a fresh spurt of tears rushed down his cheeks. 'I wouldn't do that, Rosy. I wouldn't never hurt nobody.'

'No, Joey! It isn't just you. They've been like that with all of us.' She was repeating herself, saying the same things all over again, words that had been no comfort to him the first time. But she did not know what words to speak to ease the burden that his broad shoulders should have been able to take, but his young heart could not. 'Oh Joey!' she gasped, her own emotion rising and threatening to choke her. Forcing it back she threw her arms around his great shoulders and pulled him close to her. 'Don't let them do this to you,' she said, her voice little more than a whisper.

But his sobbing increased, making speech impossible. His head fell against her neck and he cried like the little boy he really was, trapped inside a man's body.

Knowing he would eventually cry himself out, Rosy fell silent and allowed him to sob into her neck. It was several minutes before Nicky, realizing he had lost her, came back to investigate and found them sitting there.

'What's wrong with Joey?' he asked, his face filling with concern. 'Have his rabbits died?'

Rosy shook her head. 'His rabbits are fine,' she assured. 'He's just got himself upset. He'll be all right in a minute.' She imagined Nicky would find out sooner or later that the police had been questioning Joey in regard to his mother's death, but she did not want to tell him while Joey was there. He would never have believed his friend could have done it, but it would have upset him to think others could think it and that would have upset Joey even more.

Not content with her meagre explanation, Nicky took hold of Joey's arm and began to shake it. 'What's the matter with you?' he demanded. 'Have you hurt yourself? Is it your rabbits? Is it?'

'Don't, Nicky!' Rosy tried to push him away. She had wanted him back to normal, but for the moment she wished he would go quiet again. But Nicky would not be moved and kept a tight hold on Joey's arm.

'Come on, Joey! What's wrong with you?'

Joey lifted his head then. 'Me rabbits are all right,' he said, but his voice was flat and there was none of the joy that would usually have accompanied the statement. 'An' so am I.' He dashed his hands across his cheeks, wiping away the trails of tears, but leaving behind black smudges from his dirt-smeared hands. Then he gave a large snuffle and wiped his nose with the back of his hand.

Rosy fished in her pocket and found a clean handkerchief. 'Here,' she said. 'Use that.'

'Thank you, Rosy.' The pale blue handkerchief seemed to vanish in his large hands, which Rosy had always thought should have belonged to a bear. But it was big enough for him to blow his nose on, which he promptly did, before giving the handkerchief back to Rosy.

'It's a good job it was Christmas and you'd taken the rabbits home with you, or they might have got killed in the fire.' Nicky, in his innocence, set the tears rolling down Joey's cheeks all over again.

Before she had to put her hand in her pocket and bring the wet, soggy handkerchief out again, Rosy quickly cut in. 'Does anyone know you're up here?' she asked. Ivan and his mother knew well enough how recent events had upset him and she could not imagine they would have allowed him to come out on his own.

Proving her correct, he shook his head. 'I nipped out the front door when Mam went out the back to get the coal in.'

'Wasn't Ivan in?' They had not returned to work yet after, what was supposedly, their Christmas holiday.

She turned immediately to Nicky. 'Run down and let Ivan know Joey's all right. Tell him I'll bring him down to the house and he can fetch him from there.'

'Why can't Joey come with me now?' He looked greatly put out.

'Just do it will you!' she snapped. She could imagine the panic they would be in on finding Joey gone. 'And stop asking so many questions.' The outward curl of his bottom lip and the mutinous glare had not been necessary to tell her she had been out of order with the last. He had not bombarded her with questions when she knew there was plenty he was wanting to know. His concern for his friend had kept him far quieter than normal. 'Sorry.' She laid her hand on his arm and gave him an apologetic smile. 'We'll talk later, all right?'

The bottom lip still protruded, but the corners of his mouth lifted in a grudging smile. 'I'll go home with Ivan, shall I?'

'Yes,' she said, and he turned and ran off down the hill, as if once more in pursuit of the squirrel.

Rosy watched him go. When he had reached the bottom of the field and climbed over the wall onto the lane, she took hold of Joey's large, paw-like hand and pulled him up off the tree trunk. When he was standing upright he towered above her and a poignant smile stretched her mouth. Life was so unfair, she thought. He should be protecting her, looking after her, not the other way round.

'Come on,' she said, giving a little tug at his hand. 'Let's get you home.' His tears had dried up but his reddened eyes were flat and empty, as if the spark of life had been drawn from him. The dirty smears across his cheeks only added to his misery and she tightened her grip, giving his big hand a reassuring squeeze. 'It'll be all right. Just you wait and see. In a couple of weeks it'll all be over and you'll have nothing left to worry about.'

When Rosy had spoken those words to Joey, she had not known how prophetic they would turn out to be.

Every day for a whole week the police returned. Each day they questioned her and John . . . and then Joey.

'It can't go on,' she said worriedly, and scraped her fingers through her hair and bunched it into a ponytail. Then she picked up a rubber band from the pot lying on John's desk and stuffed the blond bunch into it.

'Don't do that.' Looking up from his chair he cast a disapproving scowl over the restricted hair. 'I don't like it.'

She gave a groan. 'Does my hair really matter at a time like this?' She planted her hands on the desk and returned the scowl. 'We were talking about the police,' she said. 'They can't keep questioning Joey this way. It's worrying him sick. He doesn't understand and his mind can't handle it.'

'There's nothing I can do!' John lifted his hands, opening them wide before him. 'The police have their work to do and no-one can stop them. If they want to ask questions we have to let them.' His hands dropped to the desk with a thud and he gave a sigh. 'Don't you think it's getting on my nerves, as well? Besides, there's nothing to worry about. I've told you before, if the police really thought any of us had anything to do with it they would have hauled us into the station and really interrogated us.'

Really interrogated us! What did he think they had been doing? Her head dropped forward and she stared bleakly at the cluttered desk top. 'It isn't me I'm worried about. It's Joey. The police don't seem to accept he isn't able to understand like you or me. This morning they kept on at me about his size, about him being big and strong and had I ever felt threatened by him.' Her head shook in disbelief. 'Threatened by him! Joey! They could not have suggested it if they had known just half about him.'

'Rosy!' He left his chair and came round the desk, and took hold of her hands. 'It will all be over soon. There's been a murder committed and the police have to find the culprit.'

'Yes,' she said baldly. 'But the right culprit.'

'They will,' he assured. 'I have faith in them.'

At that moment she could not agree with him. But his mouth came down to muzzle at her neck. 'And when it's over just think what we have to look forward to,' he said, and she forgot about Joey and the police.

'Stop it!' she insisted. 'What would happen if someone saw us? The police could even be snooping around. They would take great delight in having their theory about us proved correct.'

He shook his head. 'You're worrying too much. When this is all over . . .'

'Don't make it more difficult than it is.' She cut him off mid-speech and pushed him away, knowing he was going to tell her how wonderful life was going to be for them.

'Rosy, it doesn't have to be difficult,' he insisted, his voice weary with exasperation. 'As soon as this is over we'll get married. But we already live in the same house. Who is there to know if we share the same bedroom now?'

'Share the same bedroom?' she repeated in disbelief. That was new. She shook her head very determinedly.

'You don't mean that.' Her hand went up in front of him, as if she expected him to grab her and carry her off to the suggested room they share. 'Your wife has not been buried yet! It's wrong to speak of marriage.'

Before she could say more he had pushed her hand away and taken hold of her arms, pulling her upwards and forwards, so that her face was close to his and her toes had almost left the floor. 'Rosy . . .' he said with great feeling, '. . . I love you. Now tell me you don't have any feelings for me. Tell me you don't want to be my wife.'

For a long moment she could only stare bewilderedly into his eyes. 'I . . . I can't,' she finally said. 'I do want to be your wife and I do have feelings for you. But it isn't right . . . not at the moment.'

'Who would know?'

'Nicky,' she said baldly. 'We have to consider Nicky. Let him get adjusted to one thing before we go changing anything else for him.'

'Changing what!' His voice was sharp and a spark of anger glittered in his eyes. 'Nothing would be changing for him.'

'Maybe not,' she replied, and forcing herself out of his grasp, went over to her own desk by the window and sat down, wanting the conversation brought to an end. 'But I still think we should wait.' Picking up the cash bag from the corner of the desk she opened it up and tipped the rent money out in front of her. There were a couple of one pound notes, several ten shilling notes and the rest was in change. She began counting it out into piles of silver and copper. There was a regiment of half-crowns, two and one shilling pieces, sixpences and threepenny bits standing in front of her, before John finally returned to his own chair and stopped staring at the back of her neck in a way that made her feel she had icicles growing there.

When the money was all counted and entered into

the cash book, she got up from the desk and quietly left the office. He did not speak, but she could feel his eyes following her all the way to the door.

Her mother was bent over the fire, throwing logs onto it, when she walked into the kitchen.

'That needs filling up,' Nell said, putting the large brass bucket aside and straightening her back with a bit of difficulty. 'Where's Nicky?' The groan she had tried to conceal was evident in her voice.

Rosy did not mention her mother's stiffening spine. She knew it would not have been well-received and so she kept to the subject of Nicky. 'Where do you think!' she said drily. He would sleep in the conservatory with his train set if she let him. She could not imagine what would happen next week, when he had to go back to school. She picked up the empty bucket. 'I'll do it,' she said. Although keeping the coal scuttle and log bucket stocked up was really Nicky's job, she had the feeling a bit of physical activity would help take her mind off John, and his suggestion of sharing a bedroom.

The weather was not kind. A brisk wind whistled through the yard, whipping the fine drizzle into her face and eyes. Bending her head she ran across to the old laundry, where Ivan chopped and stored the logs. Her head was still bent as she lifted the latch, took one long stride over the raised step and turned to close the door against the harsh elements behind her. As she turned back onto the old laundry she was hit in the face and sent stumbling backwards into the door.

It took a moment to regain her balance. Then her mouth fell open but no sound came out, as her wide-eyed gaze fixed on the pair of legs swinging in the air and the large boots that had administered the sharp kick to her chin and cheek.

Her gaze pivoted upwards. On the ceiling was a large metal ring which was part of an old pulley system.

From the ring was suspended a thick rope. From the rope was suspended . . .

'Joey!' she screamed, leaping forwards and grabbing his legs and trying to take the weight of his large body. 'No! Please, God, no!' she begged, as she clung to him with all her might, trying to push his heavy weight upwards and take the strain off the rope. Then, lifting her voice as high as it would possibly go, she screamed again. This time for Ivan.

CHAPTER THIRTEEN

The weather was no kinder for the day of Joey's funeral than it had been on the day of his death. As they stood by the grave, on top of the hillside which swept down field after field to the valley below, the wind lifted Rosy's hair and whipped it across her face, and tangled her coat around her legs.

Although at first the rain had held off, it began as they were leaving the cemetery. Nicky was clinging to Rosy, as he had done since leaving home, and she pulled him closer into the protection of her body to stop him getting soaked. He had been inconsolable since the day they had found Joey hanging in the old laundry. The train set had not been touched and his eyes had never been dry for more than a few minutes at a time. Joey had been his friend and he had cried for him in a way he had not cried for his mother, in a way Rosy had never seen him cry before.

Fortunately, Ivan had been in the garage when Rosy had begun screaming out his name and he had immediately heard and raced to her aid. Unfortunately, so had all the other occupants of the house. There had been such panic to get Joey down and try and revive him, that Rosy had not noticed Nicky standing there watching it all, until it was too late. She had tried to take him away, but he had refused to move and had stood frozenly staring at his friend's body lying on the cold floor. Then he had seen the cardboard box.

'His rabbits!' he cried, diving across the floor and falling to his knees and pulling the lid open. He lifted first one, then the other squirming bundle of grey fur, followed by a sheet of white writing paper. He had read it before Rosy got to him. When she reached his side he leapt up, spun round and buried his head against her shoulder, and with the wriggling rabbits trapped between their two bodies, shed his first tears for his lost friend.

Rosy had to gently prise the paper from his grip, before she could hold it up above his head to read the untidy, childish scrawl. It was addressed to Nicky, and in one long line, without any punctuation, it read: *Deer Niky plees luk afta them fer me til thay big anuff ter luk afta them selfs lov Joey.*

Rosy's own tears flowed freely then and they clung to each other and cried together, until John forced them apart and took them back to the house.

'Well, that's that!' Nell pulled a chair from beneath the table and sank down on it with a weary sigh.

'Yes, that's that,' Rosy echoed with equal weariness. The funeral was over and it had been a very depressing occasion. Although they had not said as much, it was obvious the police had come to the conclusion Joey's suicide was a declaration of his guilt. They stopped the persistent questioning and permission was given for the burial of Dorothy Hardaker's remains. To Rosy that meant the case was now closed. She had the vivid image of the file with Dorothy Hardaker's name on it being shut away in a drawer marked *Unsolved – Insufficient Evidence*. In other words the culprit had died before confessing.

'I felt really sorry for the Fletchers,' Maggie said, as she slipped out of her black leather coat and draped it over a chair. 'Especially Ivan. He holds himself responsible.'

'But it wasn't his fault!' Nell said, shocked by the suggestion.

'We know that, Mum,' Rosy put in. 'But Ivan blames himself for not watching Joey more closely.' Her voice fell away at the end, as she recalled Ivan's slumped shoulders and bowed head throughout the funeral.

The door opened and Nicky came in. When they arrived home he had not come to the house, but gone straight from the car to Ivan's store, where the rabbits had been housed in a proper wooden hutch. He was carrying one furry bundle and was followed a few seconds after by his father, carrying the other.

Rosy glanced at her mother. Nell did not speak but her expression said it all. She did not like having the animals in her clean kitchen. But the rabbits had given Nicky something to think about other than his own misery and Rosy had persuaded her to put up with them for the time being, for Nicky's sake. 'Keep them away from the table,' she warned, seeing John heading in that direction. Having them on the floor was one thing, but having them running around her scrubbed table really would be beyond the limit for her mother.

'Ooops!' he said, smiling knowingly, before spinning round and going to where Nicky was sitting on the floor, by the side of a cardboard construction that turned the far corner of the kitchen into a good-sized rabbit pen. The floor inside was covered in straw. There were two dishes, one for food, one for water, and several toys and bits of wood erected for the rabbits to climb or jump over.

John crouched down and placed his rabbit gently in the pen with the other one. He stayed in that position and watched his son playing with the active pair, and pride grew slowly over his face.

Rosy's heart went out to him and an emotional smile lifted the corners of her mouth. She wished it could be this time next year and the bad memories had been put behind them. Then they could be together in the way he wanted. There were times when she felt she was wrong to hold him back, times like this, when all she could see in him was the caring father and his bad moods were forgotten. And she had to admit she had been grateful to have him there during the past few days. Joey's death had affected her badly and she had not only allowed John to hold her tightly, but at times had gone to him, seeking the reassurance of his closeness.

Her smile expanding on the memory, she turned away from the two men in her life towards the two women in her life.

It was not such an appealing sight and she gave an inward sigh. Her mother was still sitting at the table, a faraway look in her eyes. Maggie had taken up her usual position in front of the fire, smoking a cigarette. There was something about her position that looked very permanent and Rosy had the sinking feeling that they were all going to hang around like wet weekends for the rest of the day. 'Are you going back to work for the afternoon?' she asked, hoping to prompt some action out of her sister and, if Maggie had not thought of returning to the mill, putting the idea into her head. 'There's nothing much to do and it seems silly to lose a whole day's pay when you don't have to.'

Maggie took a draw on the cigarette, then glanced round, fixing Rosy for several seconds, before finally speaking. 'I don't suppose this is the right time, but you've got to know.' She hesitated, and sucked noisily on the cigarette.

'I've got to know what?' Rosy's voice sharpened with irritation, as she came to the conclusion Maggie had no intention of returning to work. She gave another sigh, this time audibly. She wanted them all to get back to normal, herself included. That was not going to happen with Maggie sitting under their feet, chuffing away.

'Not just you . . . all of you.' Maggie's gaze passed over her mother, who still seemed to be in another world, then moved on to John, who was standing up now and giving her all his attention. 'I'm not going back to the mill. I gave my notice in last week. So I've left now.'

'You've left!' Nell was suddenly back with them, her stunned gaze pivoting to her eldest daughter.

'Given up your job!' Rosy gasped. 'You can't have. What are you going to do?'

'You needn't think I'm going to support you,' Nell snapped irritably. 'I haven't got money to go throwing away on drink and cigarettes!'

Maggie's face tightened. 'Did I ask you to?'

Nell looked indignant.

'Be quiet, Mum,' Rosy insisted, having the impression there was more to this than met the eye. She went to her mother's side and laid a comforting hand on her shoulder. 'Let's hear Maggie out.' She looked at her sister. 'What are you going to do?'

'I'm going to Bournemouth.' Ignoring the astonished gasps coming from both her mother and her sister, she said, 'I've got a job in a hotel. Waiting on.'

'At this time of year!' Nell could not contain her disbelief. It was clear in the sharpness of her voice, as well as in the frown that creased her eyes into a multitude of tiny bewildered lines.

'Yes,' Maggie returned bluntly. 'It's one of those big ones that has conferences and things all year round.'

'And what would you know about conferences?' Nell enquired pointedly.

'As much as I need to know to be capable of serving them with food and drink!' Maggie took another long, noisy draw on the cigarette, then tossed it angrily into the fire.

Attempting to calm the situation, Rosy tightened her grip on her mother's shoulder, hoping to convey the message to leave it alone. 'When are you thinking of going?' she asked.

'Tomorrow.'

'*Tomorrow!*' Rosy and Nell chorused together.

For several moments silence hung heavily in the room. Nell dropped her head into her hands and stared at the table top. Finally, Maggie's head began to nod slowly. 'Yes, tomorrow,' she repeated flatly, her manner so bleak that Rosy's shock immediately turned to concern.

'Oh Maggie!' Letting go of her mother she dropped her hands impotently to her sides. 'You can't mean to go! Why? Why so quickly? Why didn't you tell us before?'

Maggie gave a negligent shrug. 'There was so much going off. Besides, it all happened very fast. They're desperate to get staff and wanted me to start straightaway.' Turning back to the fire she pulled her packet of cigarettes from the breast pocket of her blouse and lit another one up. She looked round, meeting Rosy's bewildered gaze. 'I need to get away. I need a change. If I don't break away now I'll be doing the same things day in and day out until I retire. Or die!'

'But you can do something else here,' Rosy pleaded. 'Without going away.'

Maggie sucked thoughtfully on the cigarette. Then she shook her head. 'There's nothing left for me here. Not now!' she added pointedly, letting her gaze move to rest briefly on the silent, unmoving figure of John, before returning to Rosy's face and breaking into a smile. 'Stop looking so worried. I'm a big girl now and can take care of myself.'

'But why Bournemouth? It's miles away!'

Maggie's smile increased, though not with amusement. 'Maybe just because it is miles away,' she said, tossed the second cigarette, unfinished, into the flames of the fire and jumped up from the chair. 'I'd better go and start packing.' Her voice was far too light and flippant and she grabbed her coat and walked out, leaving them to gaze after her with open mouths.

'She can't go!' Rosy turned imploringly to John. 'Do something to stop her. Tell her she's being foolish.'

'What can I do?' His hands swept wide and he looked at her blankly.

'You could at least try,' she snapped, infuriated by

his lack of concern. 'She can't just be allowed to go off to heaven knows where. She hasn't even seen the place, she can't have. It could be a real dump.'

'Rosy! Rosy!' He came towards her and took hold of her hands. 'Maggie is twenty-seven years old. She isn't a young girl. She's old enough to make her own decisions.'

'You can't just stand there and watch her walk away!'

'No,' he replied baldly, dropping her hands in a way that made her feel she had been tossed aside. 'I'm not going to stand here and watch her walk anywhere. She isn't my concern.' With that he turned away and went towards the hall.

'Where are you going?' she demanded.

'To do some work,' was his short reply, as he kept on walking.

With a snort of fury Rosy turned on her mother. 'Surely you aren't just going to sit there and do nothing?' she demanded hotly.

Nell lifted her head and looked up into her beloved daughter's eyes, a strangely twisted smile pulling at her lips. 'If Maggie has made her mind up nothing is going to stop her,' she said, her voice dulled with resignation. For years she had longed for this day, the day Maggie would leave home and leave her in peace. Yet now it was happening she did wish she had the power to stop it and to keep her wayward daughter there. She shook her head. Had the situation not been so serious she would have burst out laughing. She had been relying on Maggie to sink her claws into John Hardaker and refusing to let him go. She had been relying on her to let Rosy know she was stepping on her toes where the man was concerned. But, Maggie, who had always done the wrong thing, who had never put anyone else above herself, who had always gone out to get exactly what she wanted without a thought for putting anyone else's nose out of joint, had, just when it mattered most, backed off and let her down.

John had been in his office for over an hour before the door opened. Dropping the letter he was reading he looked up with a smile that was full of the confidence of victory. He had expected Rosy to be standing there, an apology in one hand, a cup of tea in the other.

But it was Maggie who came through the door and the smile slipped rapidly from his face, leaving behind a thunderous scowl. 'What do you want coming in here?' he enquired, a hardness in his voice that matched perfectly the look in his eyes.

She tossed her head and sent her black curls shivering and her lips twisted in a bitter smile. 'I want to have a little talk,' she said, and not put off by his manner crossed the room, dragged a chair up in front of his desk, and sat down.

'I've got nothing to say to you.' Picking the letter up again he made clear it was more deserving of his attention than she was.

'Oh yes you have!' She snatched the letter from his hand and tossed it across the desk, sending it, along with several other documents scattering across the floor. 'I'm pregnant,' she hissed when his mutinous glare lifted to hers.

His momentary discomfort soon passed. 'So what do you expect me to do about it?' he asked, his voice devoid of all emotion.

She smiled bitterly. 'It's your baby so I expect you to pay for it. If I go away I need some money to go with. I expect you to give it me.'

He gave a derisive snort. 'You don't really expect me to believe it's mine!'

'*Yes!*' she hissed, standing up and pressing her hands against the desk and leaning over so their faces were only inches apart. 'The baby is yours! If you don't believe me . . . Rosy will!' The last was stressed meaningfully.

One corner of his mouth began to twitch and Maggie

sensed victory, but felt no glory in it. She would rather have been dragged over hot coals than ask him for anything, but she needed the money if she was to go away, which she felt she had to do. She'd seen that look in her sister's eyes and she knew, if Rosy was not already involved with him, it would not be long before she was. 'Give me the money and I'll leave tomorrow, as planned. And no-one will be any the wiser. Don't give me the money and I stay right here. Rosy will be the first to know!' She was confident that he also wanted Rosy – and would do anything to get her.

'You bitch!' he snarled, leaping up and pacing across the office. 'You'd do that,' he said, turning to her with a contemptuous sneer. 'You'd hurt your sister without batting an eyelid.'

For a long moment she stared at him, her expression unmoved. No, she thought, she wouldn't hurt her sister. If she had wanted to do that she would not have considered going away. But she would hurt him, without any qualms whatsoever. She walked slowly towards him, not stopping until she was so close they were almost touching. 'I'm doing this for Rosy.' Standing on tip-toe she brought her face close to his, so he could feel all the force of her anger. 'If I wanted to hurt her I'd stay around . . . and let her see *your baby* . . .' she stabbed a finger hard into his chest, '. . . growing inside me. Before she has to watch it grow up. The decision is all yours. It's you that will decide if she gets hurt or not. Do I make myself clear!'

He opened his mouth to speak, then changed his mind. Wheeling away from her he rushed to the desk and yanked the top drawer open so violently it almost came right out and fell on his feet. Pulling a cheque-book out he slapped it down on the desk, grabbed his pen and scribbled an amount.

'This means don't let me see your face round here again,' he growled, tearing the cheque out of the book and thrusting it at her. 'It also means get rid of it!'

Her lips tightened but she did not tell him exactly what she thought of him. She glanced at the cheque. Her eyebrows lifted in surprise; firstly that it was legible after the speed it had been written; secondly at the amount – £300. She had expected a paltry fifty. He really did want her out of the way!

As if to confirm her last thought, he grated, 'Now get out and don't come back.'

She was halfway to the door, before he again said, 'Get rid of it! I don't ever want to find that you let it be born. Do I make myself clear?' He laid particular emphasis on repeating the words she had spoken to him.

She stopped in her tracks, turned slowly to him. 'Oh . . . you make yourself very clear!' she said, her voice as brittle as ice. Then she was gone.

Knowing nothing of the meeting between John and her sister, Rosy tried her best to persuade Maggie to change her mind and not go. But Maggie remained true to her promise to John and caught the Bournemouth train the following morning.

Much to John's annoyance Rosy made him drive her and Maggie down to the station. Then he had to stand on the cold, drafty platform until the train pulled away. Nell said her goodbyes at the house and was surprised to find she felt saddened that her daughter was leaving, and not just because of Rosy and John Hardaker.

For the next six months Nell held her tongue, hoping that Rosy would see the light for herself. John Hardaker was twenty-five years her senior and Nell could not see what attraction a fifty-year-old man could have to someone half his age. She knew if she opened her mouth on the subject Rosy would tell her she was worrying over nothing and, worse than that, accuse her of interfering and dismiss whatever she had to say without giving it any consideration. So she kept quiet and hoped and prayed for Rosy's infatuation with the man to fade. She knew it could only be infatuation, and infatuation never stood the test of time. It was the hot and stormy month of August, before she realized how wrong she had been.

'Why don't we go and see Maggie?' Nicky suggested, as they collected tomatoes from Ivan's greenhouse. He had the air of someone who, although only just having had the idea, considered it to be brilliant.

Rosy's responding laugh was fond and affectionate. It was holiday time again and Nicky's main choice of subject was why they were not going on holiday. 'Next year will be different,' she promised, but did not explain why it would be different. She had not told him she would be marrying his father at the beginning of the following year. February they had decided on. Just a little over a year from Dorothy Hardaker's death, and long enough for her mother not to object on grounds of what was right and proper. It was because of her mother she had not told Nicky. She feared he might let it slip before she was ready to tell her herself.

'But if we said we were going to see Maggie no-one would know we were really going for a holiday,' Nicky persisted. He knew Rosy's current excuse was they should not be seen going off and enjoying themselves so soon after his mother's death. 'Just you and me could go. We could get the train ourselves and Dad wouldn't have to come.'

'Have you got that basket filled yet?' she asked, changing the subject, even though her mind was considering the idea. Maggie had not made any visits home since she had gone to Bournemouth and the letters she had sent regularly to begin with had become very scarce of late. And they never filled more than one side of a sheet of writing paper. It would have been nice to see her, to see where she was living and working and to make sure she was all right. It would also be an ideal visit for just the two of them to make.

'We don't have to go for a whole week . . . if you don't want to!'

'All right! All right! I'll think about it.' Her voice was stern but there was a glimmer of a smile in her eyes.

'For a whole week!' he said, looking very excited.

'I thought you said we didn't have to go for a whole week,' she reminded him pointedly. His excitement was instantly squashed into a grimace and she regretted her bluntness. Her voice softened. 'Maybe two or three days,' she said. 'We'll have to find out about the trains first.'

'Don't be silly!' Rosy looked aghast. John stood stiff and unrelenting in front of the drawing-room's large marble fireplace. She had just told him she was considering taking Nicky to visit Maggie, and he was not very pleased about it. 'It will make up for him not having a proper holiday,' she persisted. 'And it will only be for a few days.'

'No!' he replied bluntly. 'If you want to go away I'll come with you. But not to see Maggie. We could go anywhere in the car and . . .'

'No!' she returned with equal bluntness, cutting him off before he could finish speaking. 'I'll not go away with you before we are married.' She recalled the time before, when she had wanted to go away with Sue. He had stopped her going then, supposedly because he was going to be away for the same week; it turned out his week had been one-and-a-half days. At the time she had been annoyed, but she had thought it was just one of those things. Suddenly she was not so sure. She was now more inclined to think it was because he didn't want her going anywhere without him, and she did not like the idea that he was not willing to let her out of his sight.

'For heaven's sake, Rosy!' he stormed, lifting a hand and dragging it frustratedly through his hair. 'Don't be so bloody Victorian.' He gave a sigh of exasperation. 'If that's all that bothers you let's bring the date forward. I, for one, am sick of waiting.'

She tilted her chin and glared at him defiantly. 'If something is worth having it is worth waiting for. And I'll be as bloody Victorian as I want to be. But I will *not* be anybody's mistress!' She knew deep down that was the real reason for his anger. He had never been able to understand why she would not allow him into her bed at night. Maybe if he hadn't pushed so hard she would have been more willing. But he had gone on and on about it, continually pressuring her to do it.

Her unexpected forcefulness took him so much by surprise that for a moment he could only stare at her. When finally he regained his voice, it was to growl, 'How the devil can you and Maggie be sisters?'

'I don't know,' she retaliated coolly, too angry to read any real significance into the statement. 'But I'll ask her for you when I take Nicky down to Bournemouth!' Not giving him time to reply, she whirled away and out of the room, thrusting the door open so fast that it almost knocked her mother flying, as it caught her standing on the other side.

'What!' Rosy gasped in surprise. It only took a moment to realize her mother had not been about to come into the room, but had been standing at the door, listening. And, from the tightly clamped lips and stony gaze, had heard every word. Having no intention of conducting a second argument overheard by a third person, Rosy spun away and hurried to the kitchen. The smell of roasting chicken filled the air but her lips and nostrils were too tightly clamped in anger to notice the delicious aroma. The only thing she was aware of was her mother following closely behind.

The kitchen door was securely closed before Rosy turned to her. 'Well?' she enquired pointedly.

Nell gave a disgusted snort. 'It's coming to something when you have to listen at keyholes to know your own daughter is getting wed.'

'Oh!' Rosy groaned in exasperation and settled her hands on her hips and fixed her mother with an accusing glare. 'So you admit you were snooping.'

Nell's spine stiffened and her chin came up. 'Yes! I was snooping! Because it seems snooping is the only way to find anything out round here. Getting married! He's twice as old as you. He's older than me!' Anger ran hot in her cheeks and she stabbed her finger viciously at her own chest, making her ample bosom wobble visibly. 'If he wants anybody it should be me he's looking at. Not a young girl who hasn't had enough experience of life to know what she does or doesn't want.'

'That is not true!' Rosy was greatly offended at her mother's poor view of her capabilities. 'I am twenty-five, not fifteen. I know enough to know I love John and want to be his wife.'

'How can you know?' Nell's hands spread wide and she lifted her gaze heavenwards, as if seeking divine assistance. Then, as if all the strength suddenly drained out of her, she pulled a chair from beneath the table and sank onto it. 'Oh Rosy!' Her voice was tight with anxiety. 'Think what you are doing. You don't have to accept the first man that asks you to marry him. There are plenty of young men out there.' Her arm made a weak gesture towards the window. 'But you have to go out and find them. They'll not come to you while you keep yourself a prisoner in this house.'

'I'm not a prisoner. I go out.'

'Into the village or for a walk up the bank,' Nell said

drily. 'If you think you'll find yourself a husband in the Co-op, you're gravely mistaken.'

'Oh Mum!' Rose dropped to her knees by Nell's chair and took hold of her hand. 'I *have* found a husband. Despite what you think, I do know what I'm doing. I know I want to be John's wife. Please be happy for me.'

Nell shook her head. 'How can I be happy? I saw his first marriage, remember! It wasn't a raging success!'

'Oh come off it!' Rosy leapt to his defence. 'It wasn't his fault Dorothy turned to drink. He did his best for her. He stuck by her. Many men would have thrown her out.'

Nell gave a snort of disgust. 'Throw her out! He couldn't throw her out!' Her hands went out and swept round the room. 'You don't think he'd have willingly lost all this . . . do you?'

Rosy fell silent, gazed uncomprehendingly at her mother.

'Oh no!' Nell shook her head in despair. 'You must have known it was Dorothy who had the money to buy this and start him up in business.'

Rosy shook her head. 'I know he started from nothing.' It had never been a secret that he came from humble stock. She hesitated uncertainly. There was suspicion in her voice, when she said, 'You told me often enough that his father had been a bricklayer. Why didn't you tell me this, as well?'

'He was proud of having built up a business from nothing. When it first got going he was always telling people himself. But he didn't go telling them about the money, and it wouldn't have done my job much good if I had, now would it?'

'Oh Mum!' Rosy went to her and wrapped an arm around her shoulders. 'I love John, the John I know. It doesn't matter about money, or what he did or didn't do.' She was hurt that there was something she did not know about him, but it was silly to expect to know

264

every little thing. There must be plenty he did not know about her. They would find all that out later, when they were married. Besides, she didn't believe he had only stuck by Dorothy for her money. He'd made plenty for himself now.

'When do you intend for this wedding to take place then?' Nell asked, resigning herself to the fact that she was powerless to stop it happening.

'We thought February.'

'You'll be in your prime when he's an old man.'

Rosy laughed, and attempted to lighten the moment, by jokingly saying, 'Well, you know what they say, "Would you rather be an old man's darling or a young man's slave!" '

But Nell was not in the mood for frivolity. 'It's no good being anyone's darling if they're infirm, incontinent and gaga,' she said bleakly.

'Well, if that happens I shall look after him just the same as I'll look after you . . . when you reach your dotage!'

'I'd better be getting dinner,' Nell said, as if Rosy had not made the last comment, and went to the stove and began rearranging the saucepans. She was not happy, but she was only making matters worse. The more she spoke out against him the more Rosy leapt to his defence. All she could hope was that something would happen to change Rosy's mind, before February arrived.

Later in the afternoon Rosy and Nicky went to the pool for a swim. Nell could not get her daughter's impending marriage off her mind and, seizing her chance, decided she would speak her mind to John Hardaker.

She rubbed her hands over her hair, attempting to tidy the wayward strands. As usual, the strands lay flat while her hands held them down, then sprang to life again the moment she let go. But she did not seem to notice the inefficiency of the action and she squared her shoulders, smoothed down her apron, and went to the office. It was time for a bit of straight talking. Well past time, in fact.

The office was empty, but she found him standing by the fireplace in the drawing-room. He had one hand resting on the mantel and a rather petulant gaze fixed woodenly on the space behind the tapestry screen concealing the empty grate. With the warm weather fires were not necessary.

'I need to talk to you,' she said, her voice stiff and holding a quality that refused to be ignored.

He looked round but did not speak.

'I won't beat about the bush,' she continued bluntly. 'I don't want you marrying our Rosy. She's far too young for you. You'll ruin her life.'

He gave a sarcastic grunt. 'I wasn't aware it was any of your business,' he replied haughtily. 'Rosy is old enough to make her own decisions about her own life. I haven't heard her complaining that I am ruining anything!' He turned back to the empty grate, as if that held more interest than she did.

'No, you wouldn't have.' Scorn filled Nell's voice and she folded her arms tightly beneath her rounded bosom. 'She's too besotted to see straight. That's all it is . . . besotted! But how besotted will she be when she's forty-five and you're seventy? You know it can't work. Why can't you be man enough to admit it and let her go.'

'Never!' he snapped furiously, not looking round at her. 'Now I suggest you get out of here before we both say something we'll regret.'

Nell's nostrils sucked in a deep, noisy breath. 'I'll tell her,' she hissed. 'I'll tell her about Maggie. Don't think I don't know what went off. Oh, I know all right! I've seen the pair of you coming down the bank often enough – one taking one path, one the other.' Her lips curled with disgust and her shoulders trembled with the contempt that filled her voice. 'As if our Maggie ever went walking for the good of her health!' she spat derisively.

By the time she had finished speaking, he had turned round and was facing her squarely. He gave a rumble of dry laughter. 'Go on and tell her,' he said, with a lack of concern that was deliberately taunting. 'Tell her I had an affair with her sister. But don't think you're blackmailing me. It will be Rosy you are hurting.'

Nell lifted her chin and glared at him. 'And how do you make that out?' she enquired pointedly.

His eyes lit with a gleam of victory. 'If you tell her, she will know Maggie only went away because she could not stay here and see me married to someone else.' He spoke with an arrogance that made Nell want to lash out at him. 'She will then refuse to marry me . . . thinking it her duty not to hurt her sister. Then what would she have?' He took a significant pause, giving Nell a chance to come up with some answer. When she did not he supplied one for her. 'Nothing,' he said bluntly. 'All that knowledge would have made her life here miserable, yet she could not leave.'

'She might,' Nell countered. But even as she spoke she knew the words were feeble. So did he, as the ironic lift of his eyebrows told her. Rosy would never have left Nicky, not for anything. She would have put up with any amount of misery just to be with him. Nell's head fell forward and she gave a great sigh. She had marched in there so full of determination, yet he had snatched it all away, and so easily. He had put her in the position of blame. She was now the one with the power to make or break her daughter's life. If she spoke out Rosy would be shattered, but if she kept quiet . . . what? John Hardaker lifted his wrist and took a cursory glance at his watch. 'Isn't it dinner time?' he asked pointedly.

Nell did not immediately reply. Her gaze hardened

on his contemptuous face. The air between them crackled with ice; had anyone held a thermometer to it the mercury would have rapidly dropped below freezing point. 'I'll never forgive you for this,' she finally said. 'Not until my dying day!' Then she turned towards the smell of roasting chicken, and left him standing there.

CHAPTER FOURTEEN

'I'm going into the office this morning,' John announced the following day. 'Do you want to come with me?'

He was meaning the office in Derby and sometimes Rosy took the chance of a lift to do some shopping while he was there. But today she declined the offer. She was determined not to let him have his way over her suggestion of going to see Maggie and, if he was going out, he was giving her the perfect opportunity to phone Maggie, without having the worry that he was going to walk in and catch her. She wanted it to be a firm arrangement when she told him.

But when she telephoned the hotel where Maggie should have been, it was to be told that she had stopped working there six weeks before. She telephoned the house where Maggie had been renting a room, again she was told Maggie had moved on, and they did not know where.

Rosy gazed at her mother in bewilderment. 'She's vanished,' she said numbly. 'Why would she move without letting us know?' Letters from her sister had been few and far between, but she could not believe she would just up and go, without letting them know where to.

Nell stopped scrubbing the table top and, for a long moment, returned Rosy's gaze. Finally she said, 'I don't know.' She had returned to scrubbing, before saying, 'Maggie always was a law unto herself.'

'Oh Mum! Do you think she's all right?'

Nell hesitated a moment, then nodded her head. 'Yes . . .' she replied thoughtfully, '. . . I imagine she will be. She just won't have thought about anybody else but herself. Some man will have come on the scene and she'll have forgot she's got a family.'

Rosy fell silent. She had the feeling the last comment had been aimed at herself, as well as her sister. Her marriage to John had not been mentioned since yesterday, but her mother had been very brusque with John for the rest of the day and again this morning.

'I think I'll go and cut some fresh flowers for the drawing-room,' she suddenly said, thinking it best to get out of the way before they began a discussion that ended in an argument.

The day was very hot and by the time she had the trug piled high with geraniums, gypsophila and wallflowers, Rosy was hot and sticky. As she walked back to the house the swimming-pool looked very inviting and when she reached the kitchen to be met by her mother coming out, she knew exactly what she was going to do next.

'I'm going round the village,' Nell said, stopping on the step and inspecting the flowers. 'And I'm going to call on Madge Fletcher. So I don't know when I'll be back!' The last was said with extra meaning.

Rosy gave a nod of understanding. Madge was Joey's mother and his death had hit her very badly. Some days she shut herself away and would not see anyone, other days she was glad of the company and wanted to talk and talk and talk.

'Don't worry about dinner,' she said, standing aside to let her mother pass. 'I'll see to John and myself.'

Nell's gaze pivoted to her face, but she made no comment. Instead, she asked, 'When's Nicky due back?'

Rosy gave a shrug. 'We won't see him before teatime.' At the least, she thought. During the long school holidays it had become the habit for his friend Gordon's father to take the two of them with him, when he had a long journey to make in his haulage lorry.

Today they had gone to Manchester and yesterday she had overheard Nicky and Gordon planning how to get Mr Gregory to make a short detour, and take them to Belle Vue Zoo for the afternoon.

'I imagine *he* will be back before long.'

Rosy did not need to ask who he was. The tightening of her mother's lips told her exactly who she was referring to. 'Yes . . .' she replied meaningfully, '. . . *John* will be coming back for dinner.' She did not point out that they had plenty of chances to be alone, without having to wait until the house was empty.

Nell did not reply. She nodded at the flowers. 'Get them put in water before they wilt.' Then she marched across the courtyard and out onto the drive, the basket held rigidly at her side, with the tension Rosy knew she had put there.

Oh Mum, she thought. Would she ever accept John as her son-in-law? Try as she might, at that moment, she could not see it happening. All she could see was herself stuck between the pair of them.

'Oh, damnation!' she muttered with feeling, and pushing the uncomfortable thoughts away, stuck the flowers in a vase and hurried to the swimming-pool.

She did not usually swim on her own and it seemed strange to have the large pool all to herself, with no splashing and shrieks of laughter. She swam around for a while, then she slipped onto her back and floated. She was still floating when she heard the door opening, followed by John's voice.

'I didn't know where you were!' He sounded annoyed, and his heels clicked with an angry urgency as he walked down the side of the pool. 'The back door is wide open but the house is empty. I thought you'd been abducted.' Coming to a standstill he looked down at her with a tight-lipped glare that closely resembled that of her mother, as she had left the house.

Rosy laughed, it was all she could do as, once

more, she saw herself as pig-in-the-middle between two warring factions, but his expression did not alter. 'It was too hot to close the door,' she said, continuing to float. 'Ivan is in the garage. No-one would get past him.'

'I didn't see him!'

'Well, I bet he saw you.' Her voice sharpened with exasperation. 'Oh, stop being an old grouch!' She lowered her legs and stood up and gave him an exaggerated scowl. 'You're back early. I didn't expect to be interrupted.' She was too busy pulling her hair over one shoulder and squeezing the water out, to see the way his gaze rested on her chest.

He watched the droplets of water running down her breasts and disappearing beneath the low cut neckline of her lavender swimsuit. It was a moment, before he said, 'Where's your mother?'

'Gone to see Joey's mum. Thankfully!' she tossed over her shoulder, as she walked to the steps and climbed out. 'She's not in the best of moods and I was glad to get her out of the house.'

'What's wrong with her?'

As she took the last step out of the water onto the tiled surround, she cast him a glance that said, need you ask?

He smiled grimly. Then he came towards her and pulled her into his arms.

'I'm wet!' she gasped, unnecessarily. She was dripping and the moment her body touched his shirt the water soaked right through to his skin. 'I'll spoil your suit.' She tried to push him away.

'To hell with my suit!' he growled. He pulled her tightly against him and she fell silent and became still. 'Oh Rosy,' he said, gazing down at her with the open longing she had come to know so well. 'I want you so much.'

His body felt very hard against her and the swimsuit suddenly felt very insubstantial. Fear rose in her and she braced her arms against his shoulders, to hold him back.

Then he said, 'I have an admission to make.'

Uncertainty overcame her fear and the tension left her body. 'What?' she questioned cautiously.

His mouth twisted in a crooked smile, which would have looked more fitting coming from Nicky, trying to persuade another biscuit out of her. 'Come on!' she prompted impatiently, when he remained silent.

It was several more moments, before he said, 'I haven't been to the office.'

She looked bewildered, wondering why that should concern her.

'I've been to see Reverend Bowles.'

She was even more confused now. He had never shown any interest in religion. The only times he saw the inside of a church were births, deaths and . . .

'Why?' The word was little more than a whispered breath. Even before he spoke she knew the answer.

'I want to know you are mine, Rosy. I know we'd planned to wait until next year. But . . .' His chest lifted on a sigh. 'I'm worried your mother's anxieties will rub off on you. I don't want to wait any longer.' He paused, as if uncertain, but there was no uncertainty in him, when he said, 'I've booked the church for the twenty-second of next month.'

'You can't have!' Her eyes widened and her jaw dropped open. She would have turned from him then, but he held her more tightly and grasped her chin, forcing her to look at his face.

'I have!' he insisted. 'I have booked the church. We are getting married!'

'But it's too soon. My mum . . .'

'To hell with your mother!' he ground. 'It isn't about what she thinks. It's what you think that matters. Do you want to marry me?'

She hesitated. 'Yes . . . but . . . your wife has only been dead for seven months.'

'Over half a year.' Releasing her chin he curled both arms round her again. 'You can't let your mother dictate to you. You're an adult. Act like one! Do what *you* want to do.'

'You make it sound so easy,' she said, the hurt of his accusation dulling her voice.

'It is easy,' he replied with confidence, unperturbed by her reticence. 'All you have to do is get a dress. Or whatever you want to wear.'

And tell my mother, she thought, and was surprised to find her mind working in that way, instead of raising more objections. But the charge of letting her mother dictate to her had gone deep, hitting a nerve. For a long moment she sucked on her bottom lip. Then she looked him in the eyes, and said simply, 'All right.'

A smile stretched across his face. 'You'll make me the happiest man in the world,' he said, and lifting her chin kissed her long and hard.

Not until his hand slipped beneath her shoulder strap and began to slip it down her arm did she move.

'No!' she insisted, her tone brooking no refusal. Once again she realized she was at a great disadvantage dressed only in a swimsuit.

'Rosy!' he pleaded, his voice a mixture of hurt and anger. 'Your mother wouldn't know.'

'I would know!' she replied, with blunt determination, and disentangled herself from his grasp and stepped away from him. 'Now look at you.' Her hand went out, waving up and down the length of him. His shirt front clung damply to his chest and damp patches darkened his pale grey jacket and trouser legs. 'Your clothes are ruined.'

He did not reply, but let his gaze move up and down her body in much the same way her hand had done to him. 'Never mind what I look like,' he said, his gaze lingering on the long slender legs, then rising to her breasts. 'You look good enough to eat.'

Her hands went up, covering her breasts, as if they

were suddenly naked to his sight. The wet swimsuit displayed her body far too intimately and she had the desire to jump back into the pool and let the water spoil the image. But she had the feeling if she did he might follow her. So she remained where she was, but only long enough to say, 'I'd better get dressed. I don't think mum will be much longer now and we don't want to go upsetting her. Before we tell her!' The last was stressed meaningfully. Then, before he had time to speak, she turned and hurried down the side of the pool to the changing-room. She did not think her mother would be back for ages yet, but hoped thoughts of her imminent return would be enough to stop him following her.

There was no lock on the changing-room door and she had been standing with her back pressed to it for several long seconds, before she heard his leather soled shoes clicking against the tiles. She breathed a sigh of relief when she realized he was going in the opposite direction.

Madge Fletcher had been in a talking mood and it was well into the afternoon before Nell got home.

Despite the lateness she walked into the kitchen to find Rosy in the middle of washing up the dinner pots.

'You're late with them!' she said bluntly, as she put the basket down on the table.

Rosy did not miss the rebuke in her voice. Nell was a creature of habit and meals were always served at a certain time, and cleared away with the same punctuality. 'John did not get back until late,' she said, considering a small white lie to be better than the truth. She could just imagine the reaction if she explained that they had taken a long time over dinner because they had been discussing wedding plans.

She gave an inward sigh. John had been discussing plans, she corrected. She had been nothing more than a listener as he told her what he had *already* arranged.

It seemed everything had been seen to: church, reception, cars. Only the honeymoon had still to be booked. But he had it all worked out. He was going to take her to Spain.

Or so he thought.

Rosy had other ideas and she dug her heels in, insisting she was not going away without Nicky. He would be back at school by the time of the wedding and she was not going to agree to taking him out of school so soon after the long summer holidays. So they had to wait and go somewhere special next year.

John was not pleased. But he finally accepted he was not going to move her, and so he agreed.

He was only happy when he was in charge and getting his own way, she told herself, as she picked up the last dirty plate. It was a disturbing thought. 'How was Madge?' she asked, turning her mind in another direction and glancing over her shoulder at her mother.

'Not good.' Nell paused with a tin of salmon in her hands as she unpacked her basket. Eggs, bread and apples were already laid on the table. 'She blames herself and Ivan blames himself. I told her they couldn't have watched over Joey twenty-four hours a day. But she feels he was her little boy and she should have taken more care of him.'

As Rosy picked up the tea towel and began drying the pots, she recalled the day she had found Joey in the wood, sobbing his heart out. He had been a little boy then and she could understand exactly what Madge was feeling, because she felt she shared the blame; that they were all guilty by neglect. They should have done more to help him through the police interrogations. John had gone that once, but that was all. Then they had left him to face it alone. And it was too late now.

'I've got some news for you,' she suddenly said, leaping to a happier subject, but then she hesitated. John wanted, or rather had insisted that he be with her when Nell was told, and she really should go and fetch him from his office. He had also told her she should pick her moment very carefully, and blurting it out was not picking her moment. But her mother was now looking at her expectantly and she did prefer to be alone to tell her. Just as she opened her mouth to speak, the hall door opened and John appeared.

'You're back then, Nell,' he said, easily enough. But the look he gave Rosy told her clearly he was aware of what she had been about to do. It made her wonder if he had been listening at the door.

Annoyed by his manner, she put down the tea towel and cup she had been drying, and said pointedly, 'I was just telling mum I had some news.'

For the briefest of moments anger sparked in his eyes. Then he broke into a smile and turned to Nell. Rosy saw what he was going to do and lifted her hand to stop him. She wanted to be the one to break the news to her mother. She would know the right words. He wouldn't.

But he waved her away, and said bluntly, 'We're getting married next month. On the twenty-second. It's all fixed up.'

Rosy did not miss the glee in his voice, especially on the last. And neither did her mother. Her initial shock soon turned to tight-lipped anger.

'It's at the church,' Rosy put in, hoping to offer her mother some consolation, but her voice was far too light and displayed all her anxiety. Then she made matters worse, by saying, 'We've got plenty of time to prepare.'

Nell gave a snort of disgust. '*Time to prepare!*' she spat. 'Prepare for what? The wedding . . . or the reason for all the rush?'

Rosy's mouth dropped open and she could only stand and stare at her mother, as she turned on John.

'You should be ashamed of yourself!' she blazed. 'Or was that the only way you could make sure of getting her? Were you frightened she'd come to her senses and run before you got a ring on her finger.'

'*Mum!*' Rosy cried, grabbing John's hand, as if he needed her protection. 'Stop it! Stop it!' She glared at Nell in furious accusation. 'I'm not pregnant. I'm not having a baby. I can't believe it. How . . . how could you even think that?'

Nell fell silent, for a long moment was overcome with guilt that she could have considered her youngest daughter capable of such deceit. Her head sank forward and wagged from side to side. 'Then why the hurry?' she asked, her voice weary with concern. 'Everyone will think it's a rush job.'

'Well, time will prove them wrong.' It was John who spoke, his voice vibrating with barely concealed anger. 'Won't it?' he added pointedly, bringing Nell's gaze pivoting to his. 'In nine months time they'll know they were wrong.' He wrapped his arm round Rosy and pulled her to him, making it clear where she belonged. 'We are getting married, Nell,' he said, in a manner that brooked no argument. 'And I shall be too proud at being Rosy's husband to give a fiddler's cuss to what anyone else might be thinking on the subject . . . *that isn't any concern of theirs in the first place!*'

'John!' Rosy's voice was an insistent whisper and she squeezed his hand tightly, trying to convey the need to him to keep quiet and not make matters worse. 'It's all right, Mum,' she said, turning a tight smile on Nell. 'There isn't anything to worry about. I'm marrying John because I want to. Nothing is making me do it.'

Oh yes there is, Nell thought, looking right at it. *He* was making Rosy marry him. She didn't know how because she could not believe her daughter could love him. He was old enough to be her father and, as if that wasn't enough, he had a temper like a bear with a sore head. She had to admit he had kept his looks, but even so he could not compare to a young man.

In growing despair she looked at her daughter: a young girl, wrapped in an old man's arm, and she wished she could have taken a photograph to show to her. But even if she could have done, she doubted Rosy would have seen exactly what she was seeing. It was all Maggie's fault, she told herself. If Maggie hadn't given in and run away, none of this would be happening.

'I'll go and see if Ivan's got a cucumber ready,' she suddenly said, and walked out, leaving the basket and the shopping where it stood on the table.

Nell was very quiet for the rest of the afternoon. She made an egg and bacon flan and prepared a large bowl of salad for dinner. Then she excused herself on the pretence of a headache and went over to the cottage earlier than she had ever done before.

It was six o'clock when Nicky arrived home, having spent the entire afternoon at Belle Vue Zoo. Rosy and John heard all about the monkeys and elephants before they sat down to tea. The hippopotamus and giraffes came before he picked up his knife and fork. But when they began eating and reached the reptile house and he began to talk about snakes sliding out of their skins, John put a very firm stop to it.

Rosy laughed, first at John's squeamishness, then at Nicky's confusion as to what he had done wrong. 'We'll hear all about them later,' she said. 'Besides, we have something we want to tell you.'

'What?' he asked, too busy tucking into his flan and chips to look up at her. He was not very partial to salad so Rosy had cooked the chips specially for him.

But before she could reply, John took over again. 'Rosy has agreed to be my wife,' he said. 'We will be getting married next month.'

Nicky's head snapped back on his neck, his eyes pivoted to Rosy, mouth dropping open to display a mush of half-eaten chips blood red with tomato sauce.

Her heart lurched. She reached across the table and placed her hand on his arm. 'It's all right,' she assured.

'It won't change anything. We'll still live here as we've always done. It will just make your "almost mum" into your mum for real.'

The mention of his joking title for her did not bring the expected lightening of his countenance. His disbelieving gaze remained fastened on her face. His mouth closed but there was no chewing action to get rid of the chips.

'Empty your mouth,' she suggested gently. 'Or you'll choke.'

It was not exactly what she had intended, but in the next moment his mouth was empty: the full contents having been spat back onto his plate and the surrounding table.

'*Nicky!*' his father scolded angrily.

Rosy flashed John a warning glare to back off. His son's reaction to the news had also taken her by surprise, but she knew the answer to it was not in force. It was just the suddenness, she told herself. If John had held his tongue and let her lead up to it gently, instead of blurting it out like that! She tried to redeem the situation by picking up Nicky's glass of orange squash and holding it out to him. 'Here,' she said, using the gentleness that his father should have used before. 'Have a drink to clean your mouth out.'

He stared at the offered glass, but did not take it.

'Go on,' she urged.

Slowly his eyes left the orange liquid and lifted to her face. His head began to shake. 'No,' he finally said.

'Take the drink,' John insisted, with more force than was necessary, earning himself another warning glare from Rosy, and a murderous one from his son. 'Rosy and I are going to get married,' he said, his voice strained as he fought to control his anger. But then impatience took full reign, and he snapped, 'I would have thought you, at least, would have been pleased about it!'

'Stop it!' Rosy stared at the tabletop, refusing to

look at either of the stony glares slicing across the table from one side of her to the other, and seeming to collide in a ball of tension right in front of her nose. 'Let's calm down . . . before we talk about it again!' The last was stressed pointedly, and aimed mainly at John, hoping he would get the message to let the matter drop for now.

But he either did not, or chose not to understand. 'What is there to talk about?' he questioned mulishly.

Ignoring him, Rosy turned to Nicky. 'We'll talk about it tomorrow. Or later, if you want,' she said, her voice filled with the suggestion that 'later' meant alone, without his father.

He did not reply. He dropped his head and stared at his messed up meal.

It was John who broke the silence. 'The wedding is fixed for next month,' he put in on a determined growl. 'It will not be put off. I will not . . .' He was not given a chance to finish.

'Shut up!' Rosy's voice shot across the space between them like a flung dagger. Then, clamping her lips tightly together, her gaze defied him to utter so much as one more word of protest. His momentary surprise turned to a dark glower, but his lips stayed clamped as tightly as hers. When she was sure he was going to remain that way, she turned to Nicky. 'Do you want any more to eat?' she asked, even though she could see what was left on his plate was spattered with half-eaten chips, made worse by the addition of red splodges of sauce and was now unpalatable.

He shook his head.

'Well, take your drink with you,' she insisted. 'And go into the conservatory and play with your trains. I'll come in and see you in a bit.' The encouraging smile she gave him was not reciprocated. As he got up from the table he did not look at either her or his father and he went silently out of the room – leaving the glass of orange squash standing there.

For a time the kitchen was filled with a silence that was as stunning as the beating of a great gong. It was Rosy who spoke first. 'Why?' she said simply, repeating the word twice over, each time with more force. Balling her fists she pressed them into the tabletop. 'First my mother. Now Nicky,' she ground, looking at the walls, the ceiling, anywhere but at him. 'Why couldn't you lead up to it gently? Or have left it to me?' Her gaze pivoted to him then, full of the anger that vibrated in her limbs and stiffened her voice. 'Instead you go charging in. Couldn't you have shown a little more understanding?'

For a moment he looked about to come back at her with equal fury. Then his shoulders slumped and he seemed to be diminishing in the chair right before her eyes. He dropped his gaze and stared at his untouched meal lying before him, and his features softened and looked almost regretful.

Regret was not an emotion she was accustomed to seeing on him, but regret was the only name she could put to the sadness clouding his eyes. 'I don't want anything to get in the way of our happiness.' There was something in his voice that made him sound very like his son, and put a thin smile on her face.

'It won't,' she assured. 'Mum will come round. And Nicky needs to be allowed his own time to get used to the idea. So much has happened recently. He *is* only twelve and he hasn't yet fully recovered from the loss of Joey and his mum. I shouldn't be at all surprised if he isn't worrying that one of us is going to be next.'

He looked up then. 'Do you really think so?' he asked, a note of amazement in his voice.

'Yes,' she said confidently. 'He's frightened because of all the changes that have been forced on him. He sees our marriage as yet another change and he's baulking at it because he wants everything to go back to the way it was.' She hoped she was right. Oh, how she hoped she was right. She felt there was truth in what she was saying, but she had thought Nicky would be so pleased she was going to become his mother that nothing else would have mattered to him. That she had been wrong had stunned her. 'Do you want the flan warming up?' she asked, glancing at his half-finished plate as she got up and put Nicky's messed up meal out of the way on the draining-board. 'Or have you gone off your food, as well?' she added pointedly, and wiped the table clean.

'No,' he assured, breaking into a brief smile before falling serious again. 'Are you really going to be able to put up with us?' he asked.

'What do you mean?' As she returned to sit at the table she looked at him oddly.

'It isn't going to be easy, living in the same house with two men who both want you all to themselves . . . and who are both insanely jealous about you!'

'I've managed it for the last few years,' she replied on a laugh. She turned quickly to her own plate and began to eat. Getting the meal over suddenly became a priority. She wanted it out of the way so she was free to go to Nicky.

He was sitting on the floor in front of the window, arms wrapped tightly round his bent legs, his gaze fixed firmly on the blue Pullman as it hurtled beneath the overhanging leaves of a fern. He did not look up when the door opened and Rosy walked in.

'Are you all right?' she asked, the gentleness of her voice displaying her concern. He did not reply and she crossed the tiled floor and was standing next to him before she repeated the question. Again there was no response.

'Nicky!' she said, sitting down on the floor by his side. 'Talk to me. Tell me what's worrying you. I thought you would be pleased. I thought you would like the idea of my becoming your mum.' On the last her voice weighed heavy with her sadness. She had expected his reaction to be something in the line of a whoop of joy.

His head dropped forward onto his knees and for several seconds he stayed that way. When finally he looked up, it was to ask, 'Are you pleased about it?'

'Yes,' she replied, taken by surprise by the unexpected question and her voice showing uncertainty. 'Yes!' she repeated more strongly, forcing the lost confidence back. 'I am pleased about it. I love you, Nicky. I want us all to live here like a proper family. And, more than anything, I want to be your mum!' She lay an arm across his shoulders. At first his body stiffened, rejecting the touch. Then he suddenly turned and threw himself at her and clung to her with all his might. He did not cry, as she had thought he was about to, but just remained still and silent, his face pressed so tightly to her chest that fear for his ability to breathe, finally made her lift him up and hold him away. 'There's absolutely nothing to worry about,' she assured, a thin smile tugging at her mouth, as she peered into his eyes and the sadness in him touched something deep within her. 'You're not losing anything. You'll still have me and you'll still have your dad.'

'But you . . .' His voice diminished. 'But you'll be with him,' he completed in little more than a whisper. 'You won't be here with me any more.'

'Of course I will.' She pulled him into her arms again and held him close. She had laughed at his father's suggestion of jealousy between them, not taking it seriously. But it was true. There was a rivalry between them that made both frightened that the other was going to come first in her affections. She had not seen it before, but it explained John's brusqueness with Nicky. It also threw light on his reaction to her mother. The same emotion obviously affected him when he was faced with anyone she loved. She gave an inward sigh and tightened her hold on Nicky. 'I'll still love you as much as I've always loved you,' she assured.

'But it will be different,' he said flatly.

'Not so different. In fact, it's more likely to be so much the same that you'll forget I'm not still the hired hand.'

'You never were the hired hand to me.' His head snapped back, his worried gaze leaping up to her. 'He won't get another nanny to look after me?'

'Oh no! No!' she assured. 'That would never happen.' He was too old now to need a nanny, but even if he had not been she would never have allowed anyone else to look after him. She loved him too much to risk putting him in the hands of a tyrant like the old Nanny Richardson again. Smiling sadly on the memory of the peculiar woman who had cost his twin's life, she laid her cheek on the top of his head. 'Don't be frightened,' she said. 'Things will be better, not worse. Just you wait and see.'

He did not reply and they remained sitting there, clinging to each other. It was several minutes before he moved. 'It's getting late and I haven't shut the rabbits up,' he said, and stood up.

She gave a nod, then watched him walk slowly out of the room, his shoulders dipping in an unusual slump. *Things will be better, not worse*, she repeated to herself, and hoped it would be true. Oh, how she hoped it would be true!

When the wedding took place the oppressively hot days of August were a thing of the past. The weather was still warm, but now pleasantly so. Rosy wore a pale pink and white mini-dress with white lace tights and white shoes. Her pale hair hung down her back, free of any adornment. At Rosy's request only a handful of guests were invited, so she had not considered a full, flowing wedding gown to be necessary. She was only carrying the small bunch of pink and white roses because Ivan had picked them out of the garden, bound the stalks in white ribbon, and stuck them in her hand as she came out of the front door to get into the car, which he had become the driver of for the day.

Nicky accepted she was to be his father's wife. But accepted was all she could say he had done. There was a sadness in his eyes when he looked at her, a look almost of bereavement. He would change, she assured herself, several times a day. When life had settled down and he realized her new status had not affected their relationship or her feelings towards him, he would see his fears had been silly and he would return to his happy self. Oh yes, she was sure he would change.

'I wish you had let me take you away,' John said, as they sat in the kitchen waiting for Nicky to return after putting the rabbits to bed for the night. 'This all seems rather . . . ordinary!'

Rosy laughed. She had refused to give way over a honeymoon and after the reception they had returned to Derwent House. 'It is ordinary,' she agreed. 'But ordinary is just what I want.'

He laughed then. 'You're a strange one Rosy . . . er . . .' he gave a crooked grimace, '. . . Hardaker! It doesn't have quite the same ring about it as Rosy Smith.'

'Rosy Hardaker.' It was the first time she had spoken her new name. In fact it was the first time she had put both the names together. She had thought of herself as becoming Mrs Hardaker, but not Rosy Hardaker. And he was right – they didn't go together very well. She thought about when she had signed the register with her new name. Only that had been Rosetta, not the more familiar Rosy. 'Rosetta Hardaker,' she said. It sounded very grand and made her laugh. 'Don't try saying that if you've had one over the eight. Oh dear! It was all right my father insisting on something fancy to jazz up Smith, but I really should have put more thought into who I married.'

'No you should not!' he insisted, a look of hurt coming to his face that she felt was not totally feigned.

She laughed again, and wanting to lighten his mood reached across the table for his hand and pulled it towards her. 'Perhaps I'll have to change my name to something like Elizabeth, or Matilda.'

It brought a smile to his lips. 'Or I could always change mine to Smith,' he suggested teasingly.

Their heads were close together and they were still laughing when Nicky came back through the door, the sight of them bringing him up short.

'Are the rabbits all right?' Rosy asked, and went to him and wrapped an arm about his shoulders.

He did not immediately reply, and when he did it was only with a short, stiff, 'Yes.' Then he shrugged away from her and hurried across the room and out of the door, before racing up the stairs at great speed.

Rosy bit down on her bottom lip. Perhaps they should have gone away on honeymoon, she thought, and turned to John and gave a telling shrug. 'I think he's a bit embarrassed with the situation.' He was about to face the biggest change; of knowing she was sleeping in the same room and the same bed as his father. 'I'll just go and make sure he's all right,' she said. But before she could move John had grasped her wrist and his fingers were biting into her flesh as he held her back.

'No!' he insisted, in a manner that brooked no refusal. 'He is a big boy now and can look after himself. Besides . . .' he added, his voice dropping meaningfully, '. . . I have waited long enough for this moment, I'll not wait any longer!' Standing up he pulled her towards him, so close that even daylight was too large to get into the space between them. 'You're mine now, Rosy. And no-one is going to stop me having what is mine.'

He kissed her then, with a gentleness that was alien

to his previous words and manner. It stilled the doubts that had jumped up like demons right in front of her eyes, and her arms went willingly round his neck and her lips parted hungrily when his tongue snaked out to possess her mouth.

'Come,' he said, finally releasing her from the embrace and taking her hand and guiding her towards the door. 'Come with me to *our* bed.'

Without any doubts and with her affection for him smiling from her eyes, she followed him out of the kitchen and up the stairs.

CHAPTER FIFTEEN

'I know where the school is! I am capable of finding my own way!' Nicky insisted vehemently, grabbed up his satchel, tossed it over his shoulder and stormed out of the door.

'I was going to the shops,' Rosy said lamely, the words dying on her lips as the front door closed noisily behind him. Turning to the window she watched him run down the path, leap over the steps and race down the drive. As if the hounds of hell were after him. Going to the kitchen she sank onto a chair at the table and let her head flop defeatedly into her hand.

A month ago, before she married his father, he would not have considered going to school alone. He would have insisted she go with him. Even now he had moved away from the junior school to the local grammar school he had never thought having her there made him appear childish. He had wanted her there, had liked being seen with her and had enjoyed their conversations as they walked over the meadow and down the lane. Now he didn't want her with him. The last time she had gone to meet him out of school he had turned round and gone back inside. Then he had come out by another door and hurried home without her.

And it was all her fault. *I wish I'd listened to you, Mum*, she said inwardly. If she had only waited longer before marrying John! Perhaps it would have been better not to marry at all!

Oh no! she thought, angry she could allow her mind to work that way. She looked down at the large diamond on her finger, thought of the matching earrings in the bedroom upstairs. Then there was the long gold neck-chain and matching bracelet, handbags, shoes, and enough clothes of every description to enable her to start up a shop. Since the day they had fixed the wedding date John had spent a small fortune on her. She had not wanted him to. He had either turned up and presented her with the things, or taken her into a shop and been so insistent that he was buying her something she had agreed just to get out again and save herself embarrassment.

Feeling torn between guilt and regret, she pushed herself up from the chair with a sigh, just as John came through the door reading the morning newspaper.

'That sounded extremely weary,' he said. 'Is something wrong?' He stopped and peered over the top of the paper at her.

She shook her head. 'I've got to go round to the village and I don't feel very energetic.' She considered a little white lie to be better than the truth – he had little patience with Nicky's moodiness and only got angry with him. Their arguments were getting more and more frequent and she was often put in the invidious position of mediator, while trying not to show she sided with either one or the other.

The newspaper was suddenly folded up and tossed onto the table. Then he came up to her and took hold of her hands. A smile spread across his face which made him appear as if he had just won the football pools. 'I know just the thing,' he said excitedly. 'I was looking at it yesterday and I almost bought it. But you can't drive and I wasn't sure if you had any desire to learn.'

'What?' She tugged her hands free and held them up to silence him. 'Wait a minute. Just what are you talking about? You almost bought what?'

'A car!' he declared proudly. 'A Triumph Herald. It would be just the job. I should have got it for you. We'll go and get it today.'

'We will not!' She turned away, wrapped her arms around herself and dropped her head forward and stared into the flames.

'What's wrong? You'll be able to learn to drive easily enough.'

She glanced round at him. 'Stop it, John!' Her voice was full of warning. 'Maybe I don't want to learn to drive.' Tightening her arms she returned her gaze to the fire. In truth she had never given a thought to learning to drive, but everything was about what he wanted, she thought. All his gifts, even the ones she had been taken to the shop to buy, had been of his choosing. Whether she liked the things or not never came into the conversation. They were what he wanted her to have and so she had been made to feel it was her duty to accept them.

Now he wanted her to have a car! Well this time he was going too far. 'There's no reason for me to have a car,' she said, her voice softening but still with the firm edge that would not be disregarded. 'I only go round the village. If I want to go further you take me.'

'But if I'm not available?'

'Ivan can take me,' she returned instantly. She had not stopped to think if John was not available it would most likely be because he was out, and if he was out he would be in the car, so there would be no car for Ivan to take her in.

Fortunately the thought also escaped his mind. Instead of pointing out her error, he said, 'If you had your own car you'd have something to go and pick Nicky up in when the weather was bad.'

She almost laughed out loud. *And have him walk straight past me!* She kept the thought to herself. She had not told him of the day Nicky had avoided her and left her standing there. 'You'll have me getting fat and lazy,' she said, attempting to turn the conversation into a joke.

'Never!' he said with feeling, his gaze running up and

down the length of her and pausing on the long, slender legs he loved so much.

It was a look she knew only too well, and before he could reach out for her she hurried to the pantry and grabbed the shopping basket. 'I won't be long,' she said, and went out of the door without looking back. Sex was his panacea for everything. He never stopped to consider if she was willing or not. She was his wife and that meant she should be available whenever he wanted.

For the next months life ran in a pattern, the same one that had been brought into force from Rosy's wedding day. John was still prolific with his gifts; to the point where she became frightened to open her mouth because she only had to mention something in passing and it arrived the very next day. The constant supply of presents increased her guilt over the feelings she had about the demands he made on her in bed, and so she continued to hold her tongue and put up with it.

Nicky did not improve either. His moodiness increased and he became more and more distant. He suddenly found places to go to every evening and he was away from the house more often than he was at home. What time he did spend at home was either cloistered in his room or out with the rabbits. He did not sit with Rosy any more as she prepared and cooked the meals and he no longer shared his accounts of the daily happenings at school with her. In fact, he did not speak to her at all unless it was unavoidable.

It was Nicky's attitude that saddened Rosy most. She never went to meet him from school again but she tried timing her trips into the village so that on the way back she would bump into him as he crossed the meadow. The first time she had done it he had walked silently by her side and she had seen that as a good sign. It was only a matter of time before she got him talking, she told herself. But she had now lost count of how many times she had 'accidentally' bumped into him, and the response was exactly the same as the first time: he would walk by her side but he would not speak, other than the odd grunt in answer to some question she put to him.

John was no help with Nicky either. He just put it all down to the boy's age, telling her he was growing up, and bound to resist parental control and the feeling that she was trying to smother him.

'I am not trying to smother him!' she retaliated hotly. I only want to mother him, she thought sadly. All the years she had been a mother to him and now, when she had a right to the position, he did not want her. The realization lay heavy on her and many times John had walked into the kitchen to find her sitting in front of the fire, staring into the flames, the weight of her thoughts creasing her brow.

It was one such occasion at the beginning of March, six months after their wedding day. John had been out all afternoon looking at a plot of land that had come on the market. 'What's wrong?' he asked. 'You look . . . ill.' His voice was uncertain. He was not sure what name to put to the emotion he could see troubling his wife. When she turned to him he could see she had been crying and he was immediately full of concern. 'What's happened?' He hurried to her side and took her hand in his. 'What is it?'

She gave a grim smile, but shook her head. 'Nothing much. At least I hope not,' she added, with a negligent shrug. Pulling her hand free she got up from the chair and picked the kettle up and stuck it under the tap. While the water was gushing into it, she said, 'I've had a phone call from Mr Woodward. The headmaster at Nicky's school,' she added, the reluctance in her voice clearly discernible. She did not want to tell him this, but if whatever Nicky had done was important enough to be called to the school, he was going to find out eventually. If he also found out it had been kept from him his fury would be doubled.

'I do know who Mr Woodward is!' There was more than a touch of irritability in his voice at the suggestion he might not. 'Why did he phone? What does he want?'

She put the kettle on the stove and lit the gas ring. Then she turned to him and folded her arms, fearing if she left her hands free they might start shaking. 'He wants to see me.' The headmaster had actually asked to see both of them. But she felt the matter would be better dealt with by herself alone.

'And that has made you cry?' There was amusement in his voice. 'Being summoned in front of the head-master!'

It put a watery smile on Rosy's lips. She shook her head. 'No,' she said. It was a lie: she had sat and broken her heart over Nicky and for all that she had lost with him. She felt that whatever sin he had committed she was to blame. But again she felt it was better to keep those thoughts to herself. When it came to his son John now steamed in like a battleship with all guns blazing. 'It was just that I got thinking and one thing led to another and . . .' She gave a sigh. 'Well, I was thinking about Maggie.' That was not a total lie. Maggie had crossed her mind, which she did more and more often of late. There had been no letters and even Christmas had gone by without a card from her. 'What if some-thing awful has happened to her? We haven't done anything to find her – or find out if she is all right.'

'You've written.'

Many times, she thought, recalling the numerous envelopes she had dropped into the mail box in John's office, which he would take to the post office every evening along with his own mail.

'And because I've got no reply I've left it!' Her frustration over Nicky now turned to anger aimed at herself and she began pacing the floor. Nicky! Maggie! It seemed she was very good at failing to do the best for the people close to her. 'Besides, what's the point of sending letters! I know she doesn't live there any more. Why should I think they might get passed on? I don't know anything and I haven't done anything!'

'What can you do?' he questioned baldly. 'Maggie can look after herself. Why . . . she could have found herself someone and be married and settled down by now.'

'Married!' Rosy stopped pacing, her astonished gaze pivoting to his amused features. She shook her head. 'You can't . . .'

'Why not?' he questioned. 'You are and she doesn't know it.'

'But she's only been gone . . .'

'Fourteen months,' he inserted, while she was still trying to work it out.

Fourteen months! Over a year. Enough time for someone like Maggie to have got through a list of men as long as your arm. Her concern increased and so did her frown.

He gave an affectionate laugh and went to her and laid his arm round her shoulders. 'Stop worrying about Maggie! If she was in trouble, or needed anything, we would be the first to know. No news is good news, remember.'

She did not reply. The touch of his hand had wiped all thoughts of Maggie from her mind. Fortunately, the kettle chose that moment to boil and gave her reason to move quickly away from him. But before she could drop the tea-leaves into the teapot he was right behind her.

'Leave that,' he insisted, taking both caddy and spoon out of her hands and laying them aside. Lifting her hair he placed a kiss on the back of her neck, then another, and another. All were gentle, warm, affectionate, the same as when he turned her round to face him and kissed her on the mouth.

If only he was like this all the time, she thought, as

his lips ran softly, lovingly over her skin, and his arms held her firmly yet gently. But she knew that when the bedroom door closed behind him he became another person. He was not brutal, but hard and demanding. As if he was driven by a passion that was too big for him, which took him over and made him unaware of all else until it had been sated.

When he lifted his head he took her hand and led her to the door. As they walked up the stairs he made jokes about the imminent interview with the headmaster and ran his hand fondly up and down her forearm. But the moment the bedroom door closed she was dragged round to face him. His fingers bit into her flesh and his mouth became hard and unyielding, crushing her lips against her teeth so that she was surprised not to be tasting her own blood. In that position she was steered across the floor to the bed.

'Please, John!' she said, forcing herself to sound calm, when really to beg would have been more in tune with her emotions. She put her hands on his face, cupping his cheeks and trying to hold him back, trying to slow him down, trying to return the embrace to the gentleness of his first kisses. She was not afraid of intimacy and she wanted to be loved by him, but this was not love. At least, not what she called love.

But he was beyond response to anything other than his own lust. He did not even have time to undress her properly. When he began hammering into her, with no consideration for whether she was ready for him or not, her blouse and bra were shoved up round her neck and her skirt was rucked up round her waist. When his body stiffened in the thralls of an ecstasy that was a mystery to her, she had the terrible thought she knew why Dorothy had turned to drink.

The grammar school was close to the village centre. It took Rosy only half the time to get there that it would have taken to walk to the old junior school at the other end of the village. At the gate she stopped, stared at the long flat-roofed building and wondered what was waiting for her inside. Please don't let it be too serious, she begged. But she knew if it had been only a minor offence she would not be standing there now. With a heavy heart she forced her feet to move and carry her down the path.

Mr Woodward's nickname was 'the Beak'. When Rosy entered his small, book-lined study and saw him sitting behind the cluttered desk that was almost as big as the room itself, she could fully understand why. He was a tall, fleshless man with a thinning head of hair of indeterminate colour sitting on a skeletal face and a long, scrawny neck. Two beady eyes peeped over the top of a pair of half-moon spectacles perched halfway down the only part of his body that was firm and fleshy: his large, hooked nose. He looked exactly like a vulture. His manner also resembled one, she thought, when finally he spoke.

'Sit down,' he said, his voice as tight as a newly stretched drum.

Pulling the old leather-backed chair as far away from the desk as the wall behind allowed, Rosy sat down. She bit her lip against reminding him she was not one of his pupils there for a ticking off.

'Now, Mrs Hardaker.' He leaned back in his chair, the hawk-like eyes fixing her steadily. 'You are here to see me about Nicholas?'

Nicholas! It was a long time since she had heard his full name. She did not like it. It sounded cold and unfriendly. Neither did she like the man's superior attitude and her spine stiffened and she sat more erect in the chair. 'That was what *you* asked me to come here for!' she replied pointedly.

'Yes.' He dragged the word out meaningfully and glanced down at a sheet of paper lying on the desk in front of him. 'I think, actually, I asked to see both yourself and Nicholas' father.'

The sarcastic reprimand was not lost to her. But her expression gave nothing away. 'He is a very busy man,' she returned, the words shot as if from a gun. 'And I am quite intelligent enough to understand anything you have to say!'

'Yes. Yes. Quite. Quite,' he spluttered, experiencing a moment's discomfort. But it was soon gone and his composure returned, as he said, 'I only thought it would be best for his father to be present seeing that you are not his real mother.'

Again there was no hesitation before her reply was flung like a dart across the space of the desk. 'I have looked after Nicky since he was a baby. I have been more of a mother to him than his real mother ever was!'

He looked confused and she remembered he had only been at the school for a few years, and obviously did not know the full story. 'I have been Nicky's nanny since he was two. We have always been close.' Until now, she thought regretfully. 'So what was it you needed to see me about?' she asked, wanting to get on with it and get it over.

Taking her cue for speed, he said, 'Nicholas has become a bully. He has become the leader of a gang who regularly pick on and terrorize the other children.'

She was too stunned to speak. Her hand went to her forehead and for several moments she could only stay that way. Not Nicky, she thought. Not her kind, considerate Nicky. He had got into fights before, but only with others who also wanted to fight.

'You must understand bullying is something we will *not* tolerate!' Mr Woodward said, when she remained silent longer than he expected her to. 'Nicholas' behaviour over the last few months has been totally unacceptable. We have to make a stand over it or the other children will think it is something we condone.'

She looked up then. 'What . . . what do you intend to do?' she asked, anxiety filling her voice as her mind filled with the vision of a cane. Her gaze quickly searched the overcrowded study but could not see the implement of torture resting anywhere amongst the clutter, and she breathed easier.

'I'll be quite frank, Mrs Hardaker.' The beady eyes smiled at her in a way that told her he expected gratitude for what he was about to say. 'The school does not want children who behave the way Nicholas is behaving. But . . .' his scrawny hands lifted and made a benevolent gesture, '. . . as this is not the way he has always acted, I am willing to be lenient. I am suspending him for a week in the hope that during that time you and your husband will be able to get to the root of the problem, and talk some sense into him. If, when he returns at the end of that week, there is no change in his behaviour, then I will have no alternative than to expel him.'

'Expel!' she repeated stupidly.

'Yes, Mrs Hardaker. I will not go into a catalogue of his crimes. I think it is sufficient to say he has been the perpetrator of acts of particular cruelty to other children, both boys and girls, and including ones smaller and younger than himself.'

'Including? You mean he doesn't always pick on weaker victims?'

The skeleton-like head moved from side to side. 'No,' he said, his thin, colourless lips puckering up in a thoughtful purse. 'He has terrorized at least one boy who is almost twice his size. It could be more. Unfortunately, male pride could have stopped others coming forward to complain.'

'Has he just picked on them and taunted them? Or has he actually used physical violence?' She had to ask the question, but was not sure she wanted to know the answer.

'The mother of one girl brought her daughter to me to show me the bruises on her legs where he had kicked her. Apparently he did it every time he set eyes on the unfortunate child.' He hesitated uncertainly, before adding, 'I could find no reason for this action. Nicholas would give me none.' The scrawny hands made a wide, sweeping gesture. 'I do not know if it is significant, but now I have seen you, I realize the child he picked on looks very like yourself, Mrs Hardaker. Do you think that could be by accident or design?'

She felt heat rushing to her face and she dropped her head, for the moment unable to look him in the eye. 'I don't know,' she finally said, her voice devoid of all strength, her hands nervously clasping and unclasping in her lap. 'It could be.' She had no intention of going into any details and offered no more explanation, and he did not ask for any.

He stood up and went to the door and asked the secretary sitting at the desk outside to go and fetch Nicholas. Then he closed the door but remained standing by it and did not return to his chair behind the desk. 'I will leave the problem with you now, Mrs Hardaker.' His voice had softened slightly but there was still that air of authority about him that she did not like. 'Nicholas will come home with you now and I do not want to see him until one week today. If you feel after that time you have not got anywhere, then I must ask you not to let him return to school. If you feel you are making progress but, perhaps, you need some extra time or some outside assistance, then let me know and I will see what I can do to help. Is there anything else you would like to ask before he arrives?'

She shook her head. There were probably one hundred and one questions she would think of later, but for now the only thought occupying her mind was that Nicholas had attacked the little girl . . . in place of herself.

'Come in, Nicholas.' Mr Woodward held the door wide and a belligerent Nicky, with squared shoulders and cocky chin, stepped inside. But his confidence left him the moment he saw Rosy sitting there.

'What . . . !' he gasped, his gaze swinging from her to the headmaster then back again. In an instant his chin fell onto his chest and his stature seemed to diminish by several inches, and he fell silent.

He looked so young and vulnerable and defenceless. All Rosy could think was that she had brought him to this and a lump closed her throat and she could not speak.

Mr Woodward, however, was not affected by the same malady. 'I told you the last time you were summoned to this study that it was your final warning.' He spoke very clearly and precisely, glaring down his huge nose at the petrified boy. 'Since then you have done nothing to show me you have taken any notice whatsoever of my warnings, so I have been forced to take the gravest measures.'

Nicky's chin remained fixed to his chest, the only acknowledgement to the man speaking was the nervous flicker of his eyelids with every word. Rosy bit down on her bottom lip. She wanted to go to him and put her arm around his shoulders and assure him everything was going to be all right. But she knew she had to be firm, show the headmaster that she was capable of carrying out his orders. If he thought she was so soft she would let Nicky get away with it all, he would give up on him completely and expel him right here and now.

Adding credence to her last thought, Mr Woodward continued, 'I am sending you home now. You are suspended for a full week. At the end of that week you may return *if* you have mended your ways. Do you think that is possible? If you do not then tell me now and we can finish with the matter completely.' He paused significantly. 'Well,' he prompted, when there was no response. 'Do you think you are capable of mending your ways?'

The bowed head began to nod slowly, but did not look up.

Mr Woodward turned to Rosy. 'It is in your hands now,' he said, and opened the door and held it open for them to go out. And without speaking another word made it very clear he was glad to be washing his hands of the matter.

They were through the glass entrance door and halfway down the path, before Rosy spoke. 'Oh Nicky!' she said. 'Why did you do it?'

He did not look at her. His gaze remained fixed to the ground and he kept on walking. She had to repeat the question before there was any response, then only a small, noncommittal shrug of the shoulders.

In despair she matched his silence, over the meadow, the railway bridge, then the river bridge. She recalled how he had feared the river when he was younger, how she had done everything in her power to make him lose that fear. She had succeeded. It had been several years since he had skipped from one side to the other to keep her between himself and the water. Oh yes, she had succeeded there. But she had failed him in all else.

It was that sense of failure which, when they turned through the gate to Derwent House and passed the burnt out ruins of the old gate cottage, made her reach out and lay her hand on the back of his neck. 'I've got enough love for both you and your dad,' she said. 'If only you would let me show it.'

He stopped and turned to her and lifted his head and looked in her eyes with a bleakness that wrenched at her heart. Then his shoulders began to shake and before she could open her arms to him he had thrown himself at her.

'Oh Nicky,' she gasped. 'Nicky! Nicky! Nicky!'

He clung to her and sobbed as if his heart was breaking. She made no attempt to still his tears. She had the feeling he needed the release. Besides, she needed the feeling of his closeness, which she had missed so much. It was so long since she had touched him and she was not going to cut the moment short of her own free will.

When finally he looked up his eyes were red and swollen and his face all pink and blotchy.

She smiled fondly. 'All right now?' she asked.

He gave a nod. Then snuffled loudly and wiped his nose on the cuff of his blazer. 'Is dad in?' he asked bleakly.

'I'm not sure,' she said. 'He wasn't, but he might be back now.' Her heart filled with compassion for him, but meeting his father was inevitable and the sooner it was over the sooner he could relax. 'Come on,' she said, putting her arm round his shoulder and urging him onward. 'He'll be mad, but he'll get over it. And I'll be with you. If you want me to be with you,' she added, suddenly wondering if their present truce was only temporary.

She had no need to worry. He nodded his head and when he looked at her his watery features formed a smile that belonged to the old Nicky, the one who had returned all the love she had given to him. He returned it now, by curling his arm around her waist and clinging to her tightly, as they walked up the rest of the drive.

'Don't you go through that door!' John's mouth set in a mutinous line. His fingers tightened on the marble mantelshelf and he glared at his son, before his head spun away again, as if he could not bear to look at him. He had been given only half the facts and yet had still gone off like a volcano in full eruption. Nicky had responded with equal force and for several minutes full-scale war broke out in the drawing-room.

Rosy tried to remain neutral, knowing that to side with Nicky would have further inflamed his father. But when he threatened to take a strap to him, she could keep out no longer.

'Stop it,' she insisted, firmly, but keeping her voice

303

low in the hope of controlling the situation rather than adding to it.

'*Stop it!*' he repeated incredulously. 'Why shouldn't I give him a taste of his own medicine?'

'That isn't the way, John.' Her gaze fixed him pointedly. 'And you know it!' She turned to Nicky and, her voice softening, said, 'Go to your room. I want to talk to your dad.'

His expression was belligerent and she was reminded of his hostile entrance into the headmaster's study. 'Go on,' she insisted, when he did not move. It took another few seconds, but finally he went slowly from the room. She listened to his heavy footsteps taking him to the top of the stairs, before she turned to John. 'I've got a suggestion,' she said. He had still been out when they got home and she had had plenty of time to think and consider what to do. 'I think a few days away would do Nicky good.' John looked surprised, but he did not speak, and she said, 'The main reason for his odd behaviour is he's missing the closeness he and I shared.'

'Rubbish!' he spat, his surprise turning to annoyance. 'You're still here with him . . . aren't you?'

'Hear me out . . . please!' she insisted, and fixed him with a determined glare. 'I'm sure if we had a bit of time to ourselves I could . . .' She got no further.

'You mean the two of you!' he spluttered, an angry flush running up his cheeks and the fingers that had been resting on the mantel curling into a tight fist that looked as if it was about to thump the marble. '*Without me!*' Condemnation dripped from his voice and hardened the eyes that sliced into her.

'He needs me,' she persisted. 'I think . . .' Again she was not allowed to finish.

'I need you!' He stabbed a furious finger at his own chest. 'It was me you married, not him!'

She refused to be put off and squared her shoulders. 'We have to do something. We can't let things go on as they are, trusting that he won't do it again because he's said he won't. We need to find the real reasons for it and sort it all out. But that won't happen with you around.' The last was stressed meaningfully. At the moment John and Nicky only had to look at each other to begin snarling. It was impossible for them to have an intelligent conversation. 'Besides, going away will kill two birds with one stone. It will give me a chance to go and find Maggie.'

'*No!*' The word slammed round the room like a clap of thunder. He wheeled round on her, his eyes blazing. 'You will *not* go and look for her! I forbid it!'

Rosy's spine stiffened yet again and her chin tilted a little bit higher. 'If I want to go and look for my sister . . . I will!'

'You will not!' He stuck his hands deep into his trouser pockets and began to pace across the carpet in front of the fire, one way, then the other. 'You are my wife and you'll do as you're bloody well told!'

'I'm damned if I will!' She tossed her head in defiance. 'I am your wife. But that doesn't mean you own me. You don't think or breathe for me, never have done and never will. And you will *not* stop me finding my sister.' With that she spun away from him and hurried from the room, ignoring the angry demands that she return this minute.

She rushed into the kitchen to find Nell busy folding a pile of freshly laundered towels. She stopped what she was doing and looked round, her expression saying, I told you so.

'Oh don't you start!' Rosy snapped and, seeing the biscuit tin lying on the table, dived in and began taking her fury out on a digestive.

'I wasn't going to open my mouth,' Nell replied blandly.

'Good!' Rosy returned.

Then the kitchen fell silent.

The towels were put away and Nell was pairing up

a pile of socks, before Rosy said, 'I am going to find Maggie.'

Nell looked up, her eyebrows tilting wryly. 'Haven't you heard the saying about letting sleeping dogs lie? If Maggie wanted us to know where she was she'd have got in touch.'

Rosy heaved a sigh, then went to the window and fixed her gaze on the murky river. She knew what her mother was saying. She had herself begun to believe Maggie had found a better life and wanted nothing more to do with them. But it had now become a matter of principle.

She turned back to Nell and folded her arms about herself. 'I can't let him win,' she said baldly. 'If I do he'll suffocate me.' She bit down on her lip. She'd have to take Nicky, she realized. John would be so mad and he would take it out on his son. She couldn't let that happen.

Without saying any more she hurried out of the kitchen. In the hall she hesitated and peeped round the door to make sure John was still in the drawing-room. Her luck was in. Not only was he there, he was sitting with his back to her, his head stuck in the evening newspaper. Holding her breath she crept quietly up the stairs.

When she reached the top of the stairs she went straight to the boxroom at the end of the corridor and took out two small suitcases. She took them to her bedroom and quickly packed a few essentials in one of them, she didn't need much because they were only going for two or three days.

The next part was the most dangerous and she hesitated at the door, gathering her courage. She had to get down the corridor to Nicky's room and hope John would not come up the stairs and catch her.

Taking a deep, steadying breath she went through the door. Once out of the room there was no time to lose and she hurried fast as she could without actually breaking into a run that would sound on the ceiling downstairs. Putting one suitcase down she turned the door knob. He was sulking and the door was locked. 'Nicky! Nicky!' she called in an urgent whisper. 'It's only me! Let me in. Quickly.'

He did not take long to get the key turned and the door opened. But to Rosy, standing outside in fear of John appearing at any moment, it seemed like a lifetime. 'Thank goodness!' she breathed, as the door closed behind her and she leaned back on its support.

'What are you doing?' Nicky's gaze fell on the suitcases in her hands and panic filled his eyes. 'Where are you going?'

'Don't worry,' she hurriedly assured, reading his mind. 'You are coming with me.' She shoved the empty suitcase at him. 'Get that packed, then get them both out of sight.'

'Where are we going?' He stared at her bewilderedly.

'Bournemouth. To look for Maggie,' she replied without hesitation. Then she paused, considering the wiseness of her decision. 'Your dad doesn't know. And he isn't to know!' she added meaningfully.

'I won't tell him. Cross my heart.' His hand made quick slicing motions over his chest.

She smiled at the childish gesture, then fell serious. 'He'll be mad. So we'll have to creep out.'

'In the middle of the night?'

He sounded so excited, as if it was a real adventure. Rosy suddenly lost heart. 'Perhaps we should forget it,' she said, staring bleakly at her suitcase. But then she thought of Maggie and knew she had to go. It had gone on for too long and she'd never get any rest if she didn't do something to try and trace her.

She gave a nod. 'All right,' she agreed, talking more to herself than to Nicky. She glanced up at him. 'Not in the middle of the night, but early in the morning. I'll come and get you about half-past-five.' John didn't usually wake before six-thirty, so she felt that was a

307

safe time even though creeping out like thieves was not a pleasant prospect. But she wanted to be gone before her mother came over from the cottage. That way John could not lay any of the blame on her. If they vanished during the day he would insist Nell had played a part in it.

'Are we going tomorrow?'

For a long moment she fixed her gaze on his face, brimming with anticipation. Then she gave a nod. 'Yes, we'll go tomorrow. Get everything you'll need ready tonight. But keep it out of sight,' she warned, then left him to it and hurried downstairs, working out in her mind what she would put in the letter she was going to leave for John.

CHAPTER SIXTEEN

Rosy slid out of bed at five o'clock. Picking up the clothes she had left ready on the chair, she crept silently across the floor. She held her breath, fearing even that meagre sound might distract her ears, which were tuned intently to the heavy, rhythmic breathing coming from the bed. Luckily the carpet's pile was thick and muffled her steps, but still she glanced nervously at the shadowed figure of her sleeping husband. His breathing remained constant and he did not move, and she gave an inward prayer of gratitude as she reached the door.

Not until her hand went out to find the doorknob was the silence shattered. In the darkness she misjudged the position and the back of her hand hit the heavy brass ball with a thud that seemed to echo not only in the bedroom, but through every other room in the sleeping house.

Her heart leapt against her rib cage and she froze. She held her breath even tighter than before, fearing the violent pounding inside her chest was noise enough alone to snap John into wakefulness. But he only grunted, snuffled, grunted again, then turned over and fell back into the steady pattern of breathing. A great shuddering breath of relief welled up inside her. In the nick of time she caught it back. Then, taking a careful hold of the doorknob, turned it silently and slipped quickly out of the room.

In the corridor she pulled on her underwear, followed by the black slacks and grey sweater she had initially chosen for their warmth. Now she began to wonder if their colour had also played a part. Had she gone for the dark tones so that, like a villain, she would hopefully pass undetected in the darkness? It was a chilling thought. As she crept to Nicky's bedroom door, she began asking herself why such drastic measures were necessary. Because she had to make John realize she would not be dictated to, came the reply.

Nicky was ready for her. A small battery-operated lantern cast enough orange glow for her to be able to see him clearly when he sat up in bed, fully clothed. She closed the door quietly behind her and lifted a finger to her lips, ordering silence. 'Where are the cases?' she asked, in a whisper so low she doubted he would be able to hear her. But his arm shot out and he pointed to the bottom of the wardrobe, and saved her having to repeat herself.

She took a case in each hand. 'Come on,' she instructed, and he followed her out of the bedroom and down the stairs. In the hall she put the suitcases down and, leaving Nicky standing there, went into the kitchen and placed the letter for John on the table. It didn't say much: *Gone to Bournemouth. Will be back by the weekend. Love Rosy.*

As they made their escape it was almost as if the old house was on their side and held itself stiff and still until they were safely outside. Rosy could not believe their luck that the stairs, which could groan and creak, had remained strangely silent. When the key turned in the latch with only the faintest of clicks and the heavy door swung open without so much as a squeak, she was sure some guardian angel must be standing by her side.

'It's very dark,' she said, anxiety creeping into her voice as she looked up at the black sky. A thick layer of cloud obliterated any stars and any moon that might still have been hanging around.

'It will keep us hidden if anyone is looking out of their windows,' Nicky replied, the excitement in his voice making it obvious he was finding it all an adventure and had no qualms about sneaking out behind his father's back.

Rosy gave a nod. 'But keep close,' she ordered, as they began to hurry away. She was not sure if she needed him close for his safety, or for her own.

They kept to the bank by the side of the drive so the grass deadened their footsteps. Not until they reached the gate and turned out into the lane did she relax. She now admitted to herself she had not expected to get out of the bedroom without John knowing, and she put down the cases and turned to look back at the dark outline of Derwent House – her home. Perhaps they should go back, a small voice said. It was a moment before she found the courage to reply with a very determined, *No*!

'Come on!' she insisted, grabbing up the suitacses and turning to hurry down the lane. 'I hope you're fit for walking? There'll be no buses at this hour.'

The Bournemouth train from Derby did not leave until twenty-past-ten, giving John plenty of time to find the letter and get to the station to stop them. But sleep had not come easy to Rosy last night and she had got it all worked out that it would be safer to take a train from Nottingham. John would not think of looking there, not considering her to be so devious. So, when they reached Derby, they went straight to the bus station and got on the first bus to Nottingham.

'Does it suit?' Rosy asked, smiling at Nicky's childish excitement as he stood on the balcony of their room in the very large hotel. The sea view was something he had personally ordered. Not knowing where to go she had asked the taxi driver to take them to a hotel. Nicky had very quickly added, 'On the seafront,' to the instruction. But it was good to see he was once more the old Nicky. The sullen, moody boy whose bullying had caused them to be there was gone.

'It's great!' he replied, glancing a grin at her that made her feel sure his bad behaviour was going to be a thing of the past. She was still smiling as he turned back to the sea that fascinated him so much. His arm shot out, thrusting a finger towards the horizon. 'Look . . . there's a big ship out there!'

She went to look, just as she had looked at the several yachts, fishing boats, one speed boat and a black buoy he had thought was the head of a seal. All she could see was a black speck, but she did not want to squash his enthusiasm. 'It's probably a tanker,' she said, and did not go back inside the hotel room that was to be their home for the next days, but stood by his side and also looked out over the great expanse of grey water. She wondered what John was doing, and felt the sinking feeling of guilt and regret, which she had experienced many times on the long train journey. She glanced round into the room, considered the cream telephone standing by her bed and thought perhaps she should call him. Leave it till tomorrow, when he would have calmed down a bit, she told herself, and turned her mind to Maggie. Where was she? Would they find her easily, if they would find her at all? She hoped they would, because she could not imagine what she would do if it turned out Maggie had disappeared off the face of the earth.

As soon as they had eaten breakfast the following day, they set out to look for Maggie. The receptionist at their hotel gave them details of how to get to both the hotel Maggie had been working at and the address she should have been living at; the one where Rosy had been sending all her letters. Although the phone calls there had proved useless, Rosy was hoping there would be someone around who knew where she had moved on to.

It turned out that the hotel was only a little way further along the front from their own hotel, so Rosy decided to go there first. Unfortunately, the mouse-like woman on the reception desk, dressed in a grey suit a size too big for her small frame and looking as if she would not hurt a fly, turned out to be very closely related to Attila the Hun. Magdalena Smith had left, she said, peering down her short, pointed nose. And they were not in the habit of giving out the addresses of their staff to just anyone! The 'just anyone' was stressed very plainly.

Pointing out she was Maggie's sister and that she had been aware she was no longer employed there had no effect whatsoever. The woman was unyielding and, realizing she was not going to get past her to talk to any of Maggie's ex-colleagues, Rosy grabbed Nicky and walked out.

'What was wrong with her?' he enquired, as he was bustled out of the door. 'Grumpy old hen!'

Very much a grumpy old hen, Rosy thought. 'I think she had toothache,' she said. And if she didn't she should have had, she thought rebelliously. She wondered why she had not thought of coming to stay at this hotel, instead of asking the taxi driver to find one. If she had been a resident the female gorgon could not have stopped her talking to the staff. And she would have had to be polite to her herself.

The second address was a long bus ride away to the outskirts of the town. As the bus approached the stop and they stood up to get off, Rosy hoped Maggie had not moved on. Or if she had, that the neighbours were not going to be as uncooperative as the hotel staff had been.

But when they got off the bus her heart sank. It was not the most salubrious area she had ever seen. The street, though not exactly dirty, had a dejected and unkempt aura to it, as if no-one really cared for any of the tall, dark-bricked terraced houses. It was a far cry from the plush hotel they were booked into. *Oh Maggie!* she thought, and suddenly changed her thinking to hoping her sister *had* moved on. It was not a place she would like to think of her living.

'Is this it?' Nicky asked, when Rosy came to a stop and stood staring up at the dismal building of number seventeen: at the peeling paintwork and tatty curtains.

His obvious doubt that this could be the correct address made her grimace. 'I'm afraid so,' she said bleakly. 'So . . .' She gave a sigh. 'We had better go and find out if she is still here.'

She was looking for 17E and on the front door were the numbers 17A, B and C. A roughly painted white arrow on the brickwork, pointed round the corner and down the arched entry between the house and its neighbour, indicating 17D, E and F were round the back.

'Come on.' Summoning up all her courage she grabbed Nicky's arm and pulled him towards the entry. The passage was dark and had a damp, musty smell that wrinkled her nose. They hadn't gone far when she realized the ground was covered in dog dirt. 'Oh!' she groaned in disgust. 'Watch where you're walking.'

More by luck than judgement, they got down the passage and out the other end without getting any mess on their shoes. Some people lived like pigs, she thought, as they walked up the five steps to the back door. There was no bell so she knocked. A dog began barking but no-one answered. She knocked again. The only sign of life was the insistent yapping and after knocking for the fifth time without any response, she opened the door and stuck her head round. 'Anyone there?' she called dubiously, into a small, dark hall with a steep, equally dark staircase coming down to it.

On the right was a door with the number 17D daubed on it in a garish orange paint. It was where the yapping was coming from and Rosy was pleased to find the dog was fastened securely behind it, and not about to leap out of the darkness at them. 17E must be on the next floor, she told herself, grabbed Nicky's arm again and dragged him inside and up the first flight of stairs.

The interior was even more shabby than the exterior and the pungent smell of boiled cabbage and greasy chips filled the air, seeming to come from the very walls themselves. The place was so awful. When they reached the small landing where the stairs did a sharp turn and the door numbered 17E stood, and the sound of a crying baby came from inside the room, Rosy let out an audible sigh of relief. If there was a child there it could not be Maggie, she told herself.

'Is this it?' Nicky repeated the question he had asked outside, this time with more incredulity.

Again she gave the bleak reply, 'I'm afraid so.' Then she knocked on the door, hoping that whoever lived there would know something of where Maggie had gone to.

The location of the house had been a shock, the condition more so. But when the door opened nothing equalled the stunning sensation that widened her eyes and froze her mouth in a stupid half-open gape. It was several seconds before she managed to gasp, 'Maggie!'

The woman at the door was her sister, at least what was left of her. She looked like a skeleton, her rounded curves had gone and she was nothing but skin and bone. Her face had a gaunt, haggard look about it, her cheeks were pale and sallow, dark shadows smudged her eyes and her black hair hung lank and lifeless.

On seeing Rosy standing there Maggie's eyes closed and for a long moment her forehead fell into her hand. Not until she looked up again, did she utter a lifeless, 'Hello.'

Like her appearance, the flatness and resignation in her voice was so unlike Maggie. Before she had left home she would never have been seen dead in such scruffy clothes. And the colour of the trousers! Maggie went for bright colours, or plain black. She would never have chosen the dull, muddy-coloured brown.

Realizing there was something very wrong, Rosy gathered herself and took control. 'Can we come in?' she asked, stepping forward and dragging Nicky with her, not giving Maggie a chance to object. 'We've come a long way,' she added jokingly, hoping it might ease the tension a little.

Maggie gave a weak smile, just as a loud wail brought Rosy up short and diverted her attention to a sickly coloured pink cot standing in the corner. She turned to her sister, a questioning frown in her gaze. Maggie gave a shrug. Then, as if realizing there was no point pretending, seemed to come to life and crossed the room with the swift confident steps of someone saying, 'See if I care!'

A tight smile tugged at Rosy's lips. At least the old Maggie had not vanished completely. She found a certain comfort in the knowledge. The pathetic figure that had met her at the door had been so alien she had thought her sister might have been lost to her for ever.

When she reached the cot Maggie bent over the side and lifted the occupant up in her arms. She turned to Rosy. 'Meet your niece,' she said simply.

It had been an unnecessary statement. Had Rosy had any doubts before that the noisy baby belonged to Maggie, she could not cling to them any longer. The child was almost an exact miniature of her mother. The jet black bubbles of curls and the big dark eyes, staring at her widely, were a perfect imitation of Maggie's. At least an imitation of how they used to be: bright and smiling; not dull and lifeless like now. 'What . . .' she began, then hesitated uncertainly. 'A little girl?' she said, for the moment too taken by surprise to think what else to say.

'A girl,' Maggie replied, rubbing her hand fondly over the silky black curls. 'Her name's Charlie.'

'Charlie!' Rosy could not conceal her surprise, or amusement.

'Well, Charlotte really,' Maggie explained. 'But I'm going to call her Charlie.'

Rosy wanted to ask if 'Charlie' was perhaps the baby's father, but thought it best to put such pertinent questions off until later. 'Why didn't you let us know?' She looked round the room which was kitchen, living-room and bedroom all in one. The furnishings were cheap and sparse but, unlike Maggie's own appearance, were neat and tidy. It was obvious she had made the effort to get the room as clean as it was possible to get such a place. 'How have you managed on your own?' Rosy's gaze pivoted to her sister. 'You are on your own?' she added pointedly.

Maggie gave a nod. 'Yes . . . I am on my own,' she replied flatly.

For a moment Rosy gave no reply. Well it serves you right, leapt to her mind, but she would not speak so harshly. Besides, from the state of things, she imagined Maggie already knew that for herself. 'How are you managing?' she asked, and settled herself down on the small sofa that was the room's only comfortable seating. The only other seat was a wooden stool by the side of a small gas fire fixed directly to the wall. Knowing Maggie's habit of sitting in front of the fire she imagined that must be where she usually sat. Nevertheless, she indicated to Nicky to go and sit on the stool, leaving the other half of the sofa free for Maggie, if she chose to sit down. 'I was meaning how have you managed about money,' she said. 'You can't work with a baby, can you?'

'I manage. I've paid my share of insurance stamps in my time. They can't begrudge me having a bit back. And it is a bit!' she added bitterly.

'That's what I mean!' Rosy put her handbag down on the floor and fixed her sister with concern. 'You can't be getting much! *How are you managing?*' She hesitated. 'Who is the father? Is he paying you anything?' Her tone was cautious. She was not sure how her sister would react to such a forthright question.

'Nobody you know!' Maggie replied bluntly. 'And no he isn't paying me anything!'

Rosy gave a sigh. 'Well, don't you think he should be?' she said, even though she was wondering if Maggie knew exactly *who* she had to send the bill to. Charlie was so like her mother that her appearance gave no clues away.

'No, I do not!' Maggie replied with the same bluntness.

Which means she doesn't know which one it was, Rosy told herself. But it was only a moment before she had to take back the unchivalrous thought.

'He gave me some at first,' Maggie said.

'What!' The word slipped out on a surprised gasp before she could pull it back. 'You mean . . .' She brought herself up short.

'Yes!' Maggie replied meaningfully, as she carried Charlie over to a cheap plastic table by the sink and poured a small measure of orange juice into a cup which had a top with a drinking spout. 'I do know who he is.' She glanced round at Rosy, her eyes relaying in no uncertain terms that she knew exactly what was going through her mind.

'So what's happened to him now? Where is he?'

'Where he has always been. At home!'

With his wife, Rosy thought. 'So why doesn't he still give some money towards Charlie's upkeep?'

'He gave me a lump sum and . . .' Maggie's voice failed and her arms tightened round Charlie and she pressed a pale, sunken cheek to her daughter's plump rosy one. It was several moments, and one very deep breath, before she said. 'He gave me a lump sum and told me to get rid of her.' The words were spat like bullets, as if knowing if she did not speak them quickly they would stick in her throat and choke her.

'Oh!' It was all Rosy could utter. She would have

liked to have put into words exactly what she thought of the low-down skunk. But those thoughts were not suitable to be uttered in front of Nicky. Neither was the rest of the conversation, she reminded herself. He had sat so quietly since entering the room she had almost forgotten he was there.

It seemed, once again, Maggie was reading her mind. After following Rosy's glance to the boy on the stool, she changed the subject herself. 'Anyway, what are you two doing down here?'

'We came to find you.'

Maggie gave a disbelieving snort. Then she lifted the baby's cup and held it to Charlie's mouth, before she said, 'Come off it! I don't hear from you for months, then you expect me to believe you came to see me.'

'What do you mean?' Rosy frowned. 'What do you mean?' she repeated, as she watched Charlie holding the cup herself and tipping it to her mouth like an expert, and realized the child was older than she had first imagined.

Maggie did not reply. She went back to the cot and put Charlie down in it again. For several moments the child sat there quite steadily, the cup continuing to go backwards and forwards to her mouth. Then she pulled herself up by hanging on to the side of the cot, held the cup out to Maggie, and said very clearly, 'Gone.'

But before Rosy could voice the question on her lips, Maggie had turned on her with her own question glaring coldly from her eyes. 'Your letters dried up months ago,' she said, putting all thoughts of the baby's age from Rosy's mind. 'So just why have you come?' Sarcasm entered Maggie's voice. 'Have tongues been wagging? Is that it? Somebody's been down here and seen me and come back with a tale you felt you had to check up on. Well, if you've only come to poke and pry you can go back now. Because I don't want you.' On the last she turned her back on Rosy and fastened her gaze on her daughter. 'We can manage on our own.

Thank you very much,' she added, with great bitterness.

At first Rosy was bewildered. She could not understand what Maggie was talking about – letters dried up months ago! She had sent them regularly. Until Maggie had stopped replying. Maggie had been the one to stop the communication. 'No-one has told me anything,' she insisted. 'But I sent letters regularly until you stopped writing. Even then I kept trying. Are you telling me you got none of them?'

'The last letter I got from you was back at Easter.'

Rosy shook her head. 'No,' she muttered. It wasn't possible for all the letters to go missing. 'Would that dog downstairs eat them?'

Maggie grimaced. 'I don't think he'd eat all of them. He might chew them but we'd see some evidence.'

Rosy wasn't so sure. It had sounded an unruly animal, and it was the only explanation she could find. 'Then you don't know I got married to John,' she finally said.

Maggie shook her head. 'I didn't know for sure. But I guessed you would have done by now.' Her voice was flat and she did not look at Rosy. It was a long moment, before she said, 'Are you staying on the front? If you are I'll come back with you and take Charlie for a walk. I like her to get some fresh air everyday.'

'We're right on the front,' Rosy replied, albeit a little uncertainly. If she lived in this place she would have wanted to get Charlie out of it as much as possible, but she suspected Maggie's motives. She had the feeling she was more interested in getting them away from there, rather than it having anything to do with her daughter's well-being.

The sky was cloudless as they walked along the top of the cliff with the beach and the sea down below. Had it not been for the biting wind that made them huddle deeper into their coats, it could have been a summer day. They said very little. Rosy tried to break the silence every now and then. But Maggie's replies were short and stilted and made it clear she had no intention of getting into any lengthy conversation.

Rosy found it disturbing that her previously ebullient sister had been brought to this and she began to wish she had not brought Nicky with her. She thought perhaps his presence was putting Maggie off. If they had been alone she might have opened up more to her.

It was dinner time and Nicky's hungry moans had become too persistent to ignore, before they left the front and went into the town. They found a cafe and ordered chips, eggs and beans for Nicky, a boiled egg for Charlie, and a plate of sandwiches and a large pot of tea for themselves. Rosy would have dearly liked to put a big meal in front of Maggie. She had the feeling eating was something her sister had not done much of lately. But she had thought better than to continue pressing, after Maggie's second, very blunt refusal.

They were on the second cup of tea, before Rosy asked, 'How did you manage with the birth, on your own? I trust you went into hospital?' she added, suddenly wondering if Maggie had taken to shunning all human life, and it wasn't just them, her family, that she had taken against.

'Of course I went into hospital.' There was a sharpness in her voice that reminded Rosy of the old Maggie, and put a smile on her face. 'I was in for four days.'

'When was it? How old is she?'

'Ten months.'

'Ten months!' Rosy gasped, as she hurriedly made the quick calculations in her head. If Charlie was almost one year old it meant Maggie had been pregnant before she left home – very much pregnant. 'You must have been six months gone when you were at home.' Her voice echoed her incredulity. 'Why didn't anyone notice?'

'Five,' Maggie corrected. 'I found a good pair of corsets,' she added drily.

'Oh Maggie!' Rosy bit her lip from saying more. One thing she had learned was that Maggie had no shortage of love for Charlie. The baby was everything to her and she guessed she already knew wearing a tight girdle during pregnancy could have hurt both herself and Charlie. Reaching out she ruffled the black curls and smiled fondly at the big brown eyes as they turned towards her, wide with wonderment. 'Well, no harm done,' she said with feeling, casting a telling glance at her sister.

Maggie did not reply and there was a long silence, until Rosy said, 'I must know her father then?'

Maggie shook her head. 'He was just somebody I met at the Locarno. Nobody you knew.'

The local dance hall, Rosy thought drily. In that case it was more than a wonder she knew who he was.

'How long are you staying?' Maggie asked.

The obvious change of subject tightened Rosy's smile. 'I don't know,' she replied. 'John didn't know we were coming.' She explained how they crept out before dawn, in the hope of curing him of his possessiveness.

Maggie's head shook in despair. 'You want your head looking at. He'll be raging mad and you'll pay for it.'

Rosy grimaced. 'I know. I should have telephoned him this morning, but I didn't.' The receiver had been in her hand, her finger poised to dial. But she feared he would say something to make her rush out and get the first train home, before having time to begin looking for Maggie. So she had put it off again. 'I'll do it as soon as we get back to the hotel,' she said, making the promise as much to herself as to Maggie.

'You do that,' Maggie replied drily.

After leaving the café they went down to the beach. Their feet sank into the soft, damp sand at the water's edge and Rosy had to take the front of Charlie's pushchair and carry her across.

Despite the coolness of the day and the even cooler water, Nicky had soon pulled off his shoes and socks and was paddling in the sea. As they watched him kicking up the spray and dodging the big waves, Rosy turned to Maggie. 'Come back home with us? You can't be happy here.'

Maggie's gaze was fixed on a point on the far horizon. It was several moments before her head began to shake. 'I can't,' she said sadly. Then forced herself to sound brighter. 'Beside, I've made the break and I'm not going back. This is my life now.'

'Rubbish!' Rosy snapped. 'This isn't any life. What has Charlie got here?' She paused, before adding a very insistent, '*You!* But nothing else. Come home where she'll have a grandma, as well as an aunty and uncle and cousin. She'll have a family up there. And a proper home,' she added meaningfully, recalling the one cramped room she had found them in.

But Maggie refused to be persuaded. 'What we have is nothing to do with anyone else,' she replied impatiently and, sending up a dust of sand as she turned the pushchair round, began to struggle to get it moving back the way they had come. She didn't get very far. The more she moved the deeper the wheels went.

'Oh come here!' Rosy gasped in annoyance, and hurried after her, to overtake and grab the front of the pushchair and hoist it in the air again. It was on her tongue to point out that she couldn't even get across the sand without another person's help. Knowing that would have been petty she held it back. 'It's you that needs your head looking at.' She tossed Maggie's own charge back at her. 'You could have everything at home. Instead of nothing!'

'We get by all right,' Maggie returned sharply. 'I might not have much. But what I've got is mine!'

Rosy did not miss the knock at herself in the last. 'Well, if it bothers you that I've got more than you, then I should have thought you'd want to come back and get your hands on a piece of it.'

Maggie's fierce gaze pivoted to her face. Her mouth opened, as if about to speak, then she changed her mind, closed it and turned away again.

There was so much hurt in her. Rosy immediately softened. 'Oh Maggie!' she exclaimed with feeling. 'Don't let's argue. I came to find out if you were all right.' She gave a weary sigh. 'I wouldn't have bothered myself if I hadn't been worried about you. Now I've seen you I'm more worried about you. I can't go back leaving you in that . . .' she hesitated, seeking a word that was not as derogatory as hovel '. . . that room,' she concluded lamely.

They had reached the bottom of the steep steps up to the road at the top of the cliff. 'You've got to go back and leave me,' Maggie insisted.

Rosy shook her head as she put the pushchair down for a few moments rest before climbing the steep slope. 'No!' she replied with feeling. 'I'm not going till you agree to come with me. You owe it to Charlie to give her the best start she can possibly get. And one room and very little money is no start at all.'

She had hit a nerve. Maggie's face clouded as she positioned herself to carry the pushchair backwards up the steps.

Rosy looked round at the sea then. 'Nicky!' she called, waving her hand to beckon him to follow. He was still paddling, but he instantly obeyed and ran out of the water, grabbing his socks and shoes and carrying them across the sand.

She turned back to Maggie and took hold of the pushchair again. 'Mum would love to have Charlie living with her. And Charlie would love to have her grandma around. You have no right to deprive either of them of that.'

She could see her point had been hammered home, even though Maggie did not reply. A sadness came to her face and, as they silently carried Charlie up the steps, Rosy was sure the glitter of tears was in her sister's eyes.

'I wouldn't want to do this many times a day,' Rosy said, as she reached the top and anxiously watched Maggie struggle up the last steps. The climb had not really been any trouble to herself, she had only made the comment to make Maggie feel easier, because she could see she was struggling.

'Me neither,' Maggie confirmed, stopping when she reached the top to gather her breath and give her aching legs a moment to recover.

'You've got to take more care of yourself.' Rosy noted the laboured rise and fall of her chest and the unhealthy flush that now flamed on her previously alabaster cheeks.

Maggie shook her head. 'I know. But . . .' Her voice trailed away and Rosy nodded her head, understanding what she had been trying to say: the shortage of money made it difficult.

'Well, the first thing is to feed you up.' Laying her arm on Maggie's shoulder she turned her towards the shops. 'We'll come back and have tea with you.' Before Maggie could voice her protest, Rosy said, 'We'll go and buy something and at the same time stock up your store cupboard.' She knew Maggie would be too ashamed to admit she had nothing to give them, so she kept on talking, not giving her time to raise any objections.

By the time they got on the bus to take them back to Maggie's they were all loaded with bags of groceries along with some new clothes for Charlie – Maggie had drawn the line at letting Rosy buy anything new for her. But, despite all the food, Rosy's plans for tea never came about.

When they got off the bus it was to see a police car standing outside the house where Maggie lived. The occupants, two uniformed men, were sitting inside, as if waiting for somebody. On seeing them walk up the road the policemen got out of the car and waited.

'Mrs Rosetta Hardaker?' The shorter and more senior looking officer asked as they reached the house.

'Yes,' she said bewilderedly, her anxious gaze flicking from one to the other of the stern expressions focused firmly on her face. 'Is . . . is there something wrong?' Her voice almost failed and came out in nothing more than a squeaky whisper. All she could think was that something had happened at home – to her mother or John.

The officer looked at Nicky. 'Am I right in thinking you are Nicholas Hardaker, young man?' he asked, his voice noticeably softening.

Nicky closed in on Rosy and nervously grasped her arm. She did not know if he was offering support or seeking it, but she placed her free hand on his arm in a gesture of comfort. 'Yes, this is Nicky,' she answered for him, lifting her chin and facing the officer squarely. 'Is there something wrong?' she repeated, forcing her voice to a confidence she was far from feeling.

'Would you please accompany us to the station, Mrs Hardaker,' he said. 'We have been informed by the Derbyshire Constabulary that you should be here. We have also been informed that Nicholas has been reported as missing.'

'What . . . what do you mean?' Her bewildered gaze moved from one policeman to the other, taking in their sombre faces, yet not able to fully comprehend what was being said. 'I . . . I don't understand.'

'Abduction, Mrs Hardaker,' the policeman replied baldly. 'Your husband has made an allegation against you, with regard to the abduction of his son.'

CHAPTER SEVENTEEN

Rosy lifted her eyes from the cream formica topped table and gazed bleakly at the young policeman standing by the door. He reminded her of the young officer who had come to the house when Dorothy had been found dead. He still had the thinness of youth about him and an innocence that looked out of place for the job of policeman. Had he not been in uniform she would have judged him too young to be out of school.

Her constant staring did nothing to attract his attention. His eyes remained pinned to the opposite side of the room and she slowly followed his gaze, wondering what he found so interesting about the grubby cream wall.

'Where's Nicky?' she finally asked, not looking round at him. It was not the first time she had asked the question. She had been at the police station for half an hour, but it felt more like several hours. The table and two grey plastic chairs were the only furnishings in the small, windowless room, which would have given the most confident of people a feeling of claustrophobia. Thankfully, two long fluorescent tubes gave ample light and alleviated her feeling of being totally incarcerated in a dungeon. 'Where have you taken him?' she persisted, bringing her gaze to the young officer. She knew he would not tell her, but the silence was driving her mad.

As on all the previous occasions, the policeman's eyes turned to her and his shoulders made a token gesture of lifting. 'I can't tell you anything,' he said. His gaze returned to the wall in front of him. It was several seconds before he glanced back and with a sudden surge of pity for her, said, 'But wherever he is he'll be safe. They'll take care of him.'

A weak smile was all the thanks she could muster. Her head dropped forward and she stared at her hands, lying clasped tightly together on the oddly clinical table. She could not believe John had done this to her. She had known he would be angry, so furious in fact that she would not have been surprised to find him standing outside Maggie's waiting for her. But not the police!

It was all like a bad dream, she thought, and clasped her hands tighter and tighter so that the fingers became white and bloodless and the skin between felt it was being torn apart. But the pain did not make her wake up to find none of this was real. When she lifted her head she was still in the small, airless room, the young policeman was still guarding the door, the charge of abducting her stepson still hung round her neck like a heavy iron yoke.

Fifteen long minutes passed before a sound in the corridor outside made her look up.

The door swung open and the sergeant who had been waiting for her at Maggie's walked in. 'I'm sorry about the delay, Mrs Hardaker.' Coming to the table he sat down on the chair across from Rosy. 'Would you like a cup of tea?'

Her mouth and throat were dry as sandpaper, but she had expected to be shackled in handcuffs at any moment and the unexpected concern for her welfare took her so much by surprise that she could not immediately find a reply. When she did it was only a hurried, 'Yes . . . Yes, please,' and that only because she feared if she hesitated any longer the offer would be withdrawn.

The sergeant gave a nod to the officer by the door and, without speaking, the young man turned and went out of the room.

The sergeant then folded his arms and leaned back

in his chair, fastening his gaze on her face. Assessing her, she thought, taking his silence for the worst. 'What . . . what's happening?' she asked. As if she didn't already know! She was being charged with stealing Nicky away from his father, she reminded herself bitterly. 'Is he all right? Nicky?' she asked, scraping anxious fingers through her already dishevelled hair. 'He was very frightened.' She could not rid her mind of the picture of Nicky being forced to let go of her arm when they reached the police station. She could see clearly his terrified face as she was taken away from him and he was told to wait with Maggie. She was grateful they had, at least, let Maggie stay with him.

'The boy is fine,' he assured. 'He and your sister have been taken to the canteen and are being fed.'

'Thank you,' she said, her lips stretching in a thin smile of gratitude. Putting food in front of him would lessen Nicky's anxiety.

He leaned forward then, resting his arms on the table. 'I've been so long because I've been on the telephone to the Derby police.' He paused and sucked on his bottom lip. 'You and Mr Hardaker are legally married, aren't you?'

'Yes,' she replied simply.

'But you have never adopted Nicky as your own.'

'No.' Her head shook with regret. 'I didn't think there was any need. His real mother is dead and I am now married to his father. That makes me his stepmother!' she stressed pointedly. 'Surely that gives me the right to bring him away for a few days break. At least I thought it gave me the right.' Her voice diminished on the last and her head fell into her hands.

It was an action of weariness rather than distress, but the officer obviously thought she was about to break into tears, for he said, 'Don't upset yourself, Mrs Hardaker. It does give you the right. But Mr Hardaker being the natural parent has more rights. So we had to listen to him.'

She lifted a bleak gaze to his face. 'Has my husband tried to suggest we are not married?'

The officer shook his head. 'I'm only trying to get all the facts straightened out. The Derby police are a bit muddled about things because your husband went storming in this morning like a raging bull. He told them you had run off with his son and that he was coming down here to get you back. But he wanted them to pass a message to us to hold you until he got here. Then he raced out before they could question him further. They've had to fall back on your mother to fill in some of the cracks. But she didn't know where either you, or your husband had gone.'

Oh, Mum! she thought, imagining the panic she would be in on finding them gone. And it sounded as if John hadn't helped matters much. He'd obviously fumed for a day, then rushed out this morning without letting her mother know. A sigh of regret lifted her chest. 'We'd had a silly argument. Nicky and I crept out before my husband had woken up, or my mother come over to the house. I only did it to teach him a lesson,' she admitted lamely, and rubbed tiredly at her forehead. 'But he knew I'd only come down to . . .' she hesitated from saying, try to find my sister, '. . . to see my sister,' she completed, feeling it better if the police did not know she might have been coming on a wild goose chase.

'Don't worry, Mrs Hardaker. With him knowing where you would be the Derby police recognized it as . . . shall we say, "a domestic". But with a child being involved they had to follow it up, and we had to make sure.'

'Yes . . . yes of course,' she said, as the door opened and the young policeman came back, balancing a large plain white cup and saucer in each hand. He put them on the table and slipped a sheet of paper into the sergeant's hand. Then he went back to his previous position of standing by the door.

The sergeant glanced at the note. Rosy was sipping gratefully at her tea, when he looked up and said, 'Your husband has just arrived. Is there anything else you'd like to say before we bring him in?'

She shook her head, returning the cup slowly to the saucer. She would have preferred to meet John in private, but that was obviously not to be. 'I've told you everything,' she said, and sat back and, with sinking heart, watched the sergeant turn to the young policeman and lift his hand. Obeying the unspoken command the young man turned and walked out.

He was back in no time at all. John was right behind him.

But while the young policeman came right into the room and took up his position by the door, John stopped just inside the door and did not immediately come towards her. 'Hello, Rosy,' he said.

There was none of the expected anger in his voice, but still she could not immediately respond. Her voice was locked away in the tightness of her throat, brought on by the increasing anger of knowing that he had tried to treat her like a criminal. Finally she managed, 'Hello,' in a hoarse, barely discernible whisper.

'Are you all right?'

'What?' she enquired incredulously. Her head came up then and she faced him squarely. 'Of course I'm not all right,' she snapped, her voice finding its full strength. 'Don't pretend you really care whether I am all right or not! Because the reason for me not being all right is all down to you.'

'Oh Rosy!' He came forward then, took hold of her hands and held them clasped in his own in a way that made them both appear to be in a position of prayer. 'What happened to you? What made you run away?'

Her eyes widened and her mouth dropped open as her disbelief grew. She shook her head, denying what he was trying to say, yet unable to find the words to do so. 'I was not running away.' Her voice was forced through her teeth. 'And you know it!'

'I didn't, Rosy. I was worried about you. I thought something had happened to you both.'

'Stop it,' she demanded, dragging her hands away from him. 'You'd found the note. You must have done to know we had come down here. So don't give me any bunkum about being worried. There was nothing to worry about.'

John did not reply, but turned to the sergeant. 'Can I speak to my wife alone, please?' he asked, very politely.

'Well . . .' The sergeant hesitated. 'I suppose you can have a couple of minutes,' he finally agreed, and got up from the chair. 'But then I want to get this sorted out. So we can get down to some real work!' The last was stressed very meaningfully, before he walked out, taking the young policeman with him.

The moment they were alone John moved towards Rosy, his arms open to take hold of her.

'Don't you dare touch me,' she warned, backing quickly away.

'Rosy!' There was a pleading in his voice she had never heard before. 'Don't be angry.'

'Don't be angry!' she repeated incredulously. 'You make accusations that get me dragged in here like a common criminal. You've made a fool of me! And of yourself!' Folding her arms she turned away from him. 'Heaven knows what the police must think of us.'

'I don't care what the police are thinking.' His voice hardened and filled with the proprietorial quality she knew so well. 'You are my wife, Rosy. You had no right to go without telling me.'

She gave a snort of disgust. He hadn't once mentioned the son whose disappearance had, supposedly, made him beside himself. 'I did tell you – in the letter! And if it hadn't been for just the sort of attitude you are now displaying, I could have told you to your face.'

'Is everything all right?' the young policeman poked his head round the door to ask, making it obvious he had not gone with the sergeant but was standing outside.

'Yes,' John quickly assured. 'My wife is a bit upset. But she'll be all right.'

Without turning to look at the young man, Rosy said, 'I think it would be best if you fetched the sergeant back now and let us get out of your hair.'

'Right you are,' he replied, and vanished.

'That's if they will let us go.' Her gaze pivoted to John's. 'After the way you've acted I wouldn't be surprised if they locked us both up and threw away the key.'

'Of course they will let us,' he assured confidently.

Only because they'll be glad to see the back of us, she thought.

Twenty minutes later the police did let them go. John turned on the charm and proved just how accommodating he could be, along with explaining that Rosy had not really been herself since being unfortunate enough to find the body of a young man they had had working for them, who had committed suicide on their property.

Her eyebrows tilted slightly on the last, but she did not open her mouth to deny the fact. She just wanted it all over and to get away and see Nicky and assure him that everything was going to be all right. She knew he must be as worried about her as she was about him. So she remained silent and let John provide all the explanations, before the sergeant gave a long lecture on the folly of taking domestic problems too far and wasting police time. They were then sent away with a stern warning that *next time* they would not be dealt with so leniently.

'She's not coming!' John blazed, raking furious fingers through his hair. 'Maggie has made a life for herself

333

down here and it's not up to you to go poking your nose in and telling her what to do!'

'A *life* down here?' Rosy's voice was full of scorn and she threw Nicky's clothes into his case with undue force. She had just informed John that they would be taking Maggie and Charlie back home with them, and he was not pleased about it. 'Maggie has *no* life!' she persisted. 'I am not going to leave her down here. She has the baby and she needs help.' She suddenly stopped what she was doing, straightened up and turned on him squarely. 'What sort of life is Charlie going to have? Maggie can't afford to keep the both of them. Charlie's father wants nothing to do with her, so we are the only relatives the child has any chance of ever knowing. We owe her that, at least!'

'I will not take Maggie back with us! I will not have her living with us!'

Rosy fixed her angry glare on the remaining items of clothing lying strewn across the bed. 'She is my sister! And doesn't have to live with us. She'll move back in with Mum.' She spoke slowly and purposefully, making it very clear she was not going to give in. 'I will not leave her, or her baby, to starve.'

'Starve! Don't be so bloody silly! They might be a bit hard up but they aren't going to starve.'

'You haven't seen the conditions she's living in.'

'I don't need to see where she's living to know . . .' he began, but was cut off by a burst of anger that was as unexpected to Rosy as it was to himself.

'But you have seen Maggie!' she retorted, her fury hissing through her lips like the spit of an angry cat. 'You've seen the difference in her. You know what she was built like before. Now she's like a skeleton.' Scooping the last of Nicky's clothes from the bed she threw them into the case and slammed the lid shut. 'I am not going without her!' Her voice brooked no refusal. 'You either take us all or you go alone and we'll make our way way.' Despite the lack of sleep she had got up that morning with a clear head. It had not been Nicky he had raced down here to get back, it had been herself. She was not, as she had imagined, a lowly pawn in the game, but the queen, with all the power.

'How?' he demanded.

'The train. The same as we got here. But if it's the train I shall be going back to the cottage *not* the house!' she added pointedly.

He fell silent. Needing the time to accept defeat, she thought, until he spoke and proved her wrong.

'Maggie is not your responsibility,' he said, making it clear he was still not ready to back down. 'I don't want you getting landed with her mistakes.'

'Don't be silly.' She was so full of disbelief that she almost laughed. 'Why should taking Maggie back home mean I get landed with her mistakes?'

'You're better off without her. It would have been better if you'd never found her.'

There was such a peevish quality to his voice it brought Rosy up short. She went very still, glared at him, first in uncertainty, then in icy disbelief. 'Maggie never got my letters,' she finally said, her voice strangely quiet. 'Why?' she questioned, not sure she really believed the way her mind was working.

His mouth puckered in a mulish pout and he remained silent.

'Because you took them!' she answered for him, her chest rising and falling with the force of her anger. 'You took them out of the mail.' And she had been happy to blame the yappy dog. Her lip curled and her voice filled with contempt, as she said, 'How could you?'

He remained silent, but his glare turned mutinous.

'You did! For God's sake why?' she demanded furiously. 'What earthly good did keeping her in the dark do you?' Although she was saying these things there was still a part of her telling herself he could not have done it. 'Why? Tell me why, John?' It was so ridiculous, so childish, to have taken the letters out and thrown them away when he took the mail to the post-box. But that is what he must have done. The odd one could have gone missing in the postal system, but not all of them. They had been taken, deliberately, and by him. It was the only explanation.

'You were better off without her,' he replied baldly. 'She was nothing but a nuisance to you before. I knew if she came back she'd be the same again. And she still will be and that's why I won't take her back with us.'

Rosy's head wagged from side to side, in bewilderment, confusion and rage. 'Maggie was never a nuisance to me! I don't know how you could even suggest she was.'

'I want you to come home and be the same as before.' He spoke as if she had not said one word. 'I don't want your sister hanging about the place all the time.'

He sounded like a petulant child and Rosy grimaced, at both his manner and the words he spoke. The last thing she wanted was to be 'the same as before'. But she did not tell him that. 'How could you have been so mean?' Her voice hardened. 'Because of you Maggie had to go through the traumas of childbirth on her own. She didn't have anyone to hold her hand, or talk out her worries with.' She picked up the closed suitcase and swung it off the bed and onto the floor by the side of the other one that was already packed. John had come down in the car, in such a hurry he had only the clothes he stood in. 'Well!' she questioned pointedly. 'Is it the car or the train?' The reasons why he had cut the link between herself and Maggie could wait until later, when they were at home.

'Oh Rosy . . . !' His open hands came out to her and he looked at her with pleading.

'I'm not going without her. Especially now!' She set her hands on her hips and fixed him purposefully. 'And don't try and threaten me with Nicky. It isn't Nicky you want, it's me!' The quiet certainty of her voice lifted his eyebrows. 'Yes,' she said, staring calmly into his surprised eyes. 'You're not fooling anyone, John. Unless it's yourself.' She hesitated only the briefest of moments, then said, 'The only way you can take me back home is by taking Maggie and her baby with us. The choice is yours.'

'Oh Rosy!' he repeated.

She could not tell if the sigh accompanying his words was one of resignation or exasperation, and she had to wish to find out. 'Well!' she prompted again bluntly. 'Which is it to be?'

His gaze fell to the carpet and he looked so distant that for a heart-stopping moment she thought she had got it wrong and he was going to refuse. Then he looked up and the sadness in his eyes stabbed at her.

'I want you all to myself, Rosy. I can't bear to share you with anyone. Is that so wrong?'

There was no contrition in his voice and she shook her head, more in disbelief than denial, amazed that after all that had happened he could still speak in that proprietorial way. 'It's only wrong when you take it to extremes.' Her gaze fastened bleakly to his and her voice was weary. She was wasting her breath and she knew it. He could not, or would not see that he was in the wrong. 'But let's call a truce now,' she said. 'It was a stupid argument that started all this so let's have done with it.' She still had no agreement from him to take Maggie home and, at that moment, that was the priority.

'Just come back home with me,' he said, and moved towards her.

'And Maggie,' she said, not moving away from him, but lifting her hand to hold him back until she had got her answer.

For several moments his gaze cut right into hers, as if he was trying by some form of magic to melt the steely determination he could see there.

She stood her ground, not even blinking. 'I will not

go without her,' she said. When he did not immediately reply she swept her hand out over the suitcases. 'There are Nicky's things. Don't forget to put them in the car before you take him home.' She was clutching at a straw, one she expected to break. He would never believe she could leave Nicky and she was sure he would call her bluff, or laugh in her face at the very idea. But fortunately her iron-willed gaze did not let her down and he saw nothing of the rapidly thumping heart in her breast. For, finally, she got his agreement.

'All right,' he said, if somewhat grudgingly. 'You win. We'll take Maggie home with us. But she must go to your mother.' Before she could speak her thanks she was pulled roughly against him and his mouth came down on hers in a kiss that was hard and un-yielding. It reminded her of his roughness in bed and sent a shiver through her body, but not one of passion.

Fortunately, Nicky chose that moment to come back with the newspaper he had been sent to get.

'We are having breakfast before we go?' he questioned seriously. His voice and his eyes still held signs of the anxiety that had been in him since leaving the police station. She could tell he was worried that at any moment his father was going to remember that he and his bad report from school, was what had started all this. But his anxiety was not enough to conceal the fear that he might be expected to leave without first being fed.

'Of course we'll have breakfast,' Rosy assured, moving away from his father, relief shining from her smile that, for the time being, she had been saved. 'We'll go down now,' she quickly added, taking hold of Nicky's arm and guiding him back out of the door he had just come through. She shared his concern that John was going to suddenly remember she was not totally to blame for their present situation. At least

338

the problem of Maggie had made him forget. But she knew that would not go on indefinitely. Nicky would, sooner or later, get the rough edge of his father's tongue. She only hoped the moment could be put off until they were in the privacy of their own home.

CHAPTER EIGHTEEN

'Get off the bloody road, bloody idiot!' John mouthed furiously, as the Rover raced round the traffic island without any consideration for anything else that might be using the highway, and almost collided with a Bird's bread van.

The irate driver shook his fist and cast a very stony glare at the car.

'Maniac!' John responded through his teeth and returned his gaze to the front and his concentration to driving only just in the nick of time. Instead of going round and round in circles, as Rosy imagined they were about to do, he managed to swerve the car off the roundabout at the correct exit.

'Uh . . . !' Rosy folded her arms across her chest and fixed her husband with fermenting anger. 'It was *your* fault!' she pointed out with feeling. 'If you don't calm down you're going to kill us all!' She had forced him into bringing Maggie back and he was really letting her know it was under duress. He was totally overreacting and getting himself into a right state. She was not sure how they had made it back to Derby without having an accident. The entire journey had been a catalogue of minor skirmishes, with drivers who took exception to his arrogant attitude that his was the only vehicle on the road not failing to let him know it. All because she had put her foot down, she thought!

'I am perfectly well able to control a car!' He flashed her a thunderous glare and she saw that his previously pale cheeks were now dotted with angry red patches.

'We're almost home.' Maggie reached over from the

back and placed a restraining hand on her sister's shoulder, just as Charlie began to grizzle.

'For Christ's sake keep that kid quiet,' John snarled. 'She's done nothing but blubber since leaving Bournemouth.'

'*She has not!*' Rosy retaliated hotly, leaping to the child's defence. 'We didn't hear a peep out of her until well past Birmingham. And the way you've been throwing the car around it's a wonder she hasn't been sick every half hour.' She cast a despairing glance over her shoulder at Maggie.

Maggie gave a grimace and lifted Charlie from her knee and settled her over her shoulder, and looked intensely relieved when she immediately fell silent. 'She's ready for something to eat,' she said in explanation.

She isn't the only one, Rosy thought. Her own throat was parched and screaming out for a drink and, despite Nicky having sat silently throughout the journey, she knew he would be thinking he was on the verge of starvation after the long drive without so much as one stop. The break for lunch she had suggested, when they were passing through Northampton, had been refused so bluntly she had not bothered to repeat the suggestion. It's a wonder Charlie wasn't screaming at the top of her lungs, she thought, turning away from John to gaze out of the side window and send up grateful thanks that they were only a couple of miles from the end of their journey.

'Home!' Maggie breathed, as she stepped through the door into the kitchen of Derwent House, and into the overwhelming smell of onions. She came to an abrupt halt when she saw her mother standing there.

'Well . . . !' Nell gasped, too stunned to say more as she looked up from chopping the offending vegetables, to find her much changed elder daughter standing there with a child in her arms.

341

'This isn't home!' John put in bluntly, hurrying through the kitchen and dumping Rosy and Nicky's suitcases none too gently in the hall. 'Home is at the cottage!' he pointed out, as he made the return journey with equal haste, to begin unloading Maggie's belongings from the car.

Rosy flashed him a glare, then turned to her mother. 'Look what we found,' she said. 'You didn't know you were a grandma, did you?'

Nell was speechless. *But who's the father*, she wondered, and did not like the answer she came up with.

As if to confirm her worst fears, John gave a snort as he went out again.

'Uh . . . I didn't know if I'd still got *any* daughters.' Nell found her voice and hoped she did not sound as disturbed as she felt. All she could see before them was trouble. 'I thought the one I did know about had been put in prison.'

'Put the kettle on, Mum,' Rosy said drily, ignoring the dig. 'We're all spitting feathers.'

Nell humphed, but put the vegetable knife down and went to the kettle. 'I suppose that's telling me to mind my own business!' she said, her voice as stiff as her shoulders. Trouble, she thought. With a capital T!

'I think it would be best if we went straight over to the cottage.' Maggie's voice was filled with the uncertainty Rosy could see in her eyes. 'I don't want to cause any more trouble between you and John.' She glanced down at the top of her daughter's bent head. 'And she desperately needs changing.'

'But Mum hasn't seen anything of Charlie yet,' Rosy began to protest. Then she changed her mind. 'All right, if you prefer,' she agreed. If the only problem had been the state of Charlie's nappy, it could have been dealt with there just as easily as at the cottage. But she knew that wasn't the real reason Maggie wanted to get over to the cottage. It was this house that was bothering her . . . and its owner! After finally

342

getting him to agree to bring Maggie, Rosy had thought she was home and dry. But getting Maggie to agree to come, had been twice as difficult. Even when she had successfully persuaded Maggie it was the best thing to do for herself and Charlie, persuading her that John gave his blessing was a totally different matter. But she had finally managed it; only to have all her good work ruined by his bad humour throughout the journey back.

Now Maggie was a bundle of nerves, obviously thinking it had all been a big mistake.

'It's me he's angry with, not you.' Rosy spoke with the confidence of someone who knew what they were talking about. 'But if it makes you happier . . . come on, I'll take you to the cottage.' On an afterthought she turned to Nell. 'Unless you want to go with her?' She had no qualms that her mother would object to Maggie moving back in, not after seeing the state she was now in, but the cottage wasn't really anything to do with her and she didn't want her mother to feel she was poking her nose in and taking her home over.

Nell hesitated, then shook her head. 'You go and I'll come over when I've got these done.' She would dearly have liked to go and get to know her granddaughter, but it was obvious John was not in the best of moods and he would be wanting a meal after the long journey. If she vanished it would only make him more irritable. 'I was going to make some soup,' she added, hoping her disappointment didn't show. 'But now you're back you'll be wanting a good meal.'

Rosy smiled, but remained silent. A 'good meal' to her mother was home-cooked and something that was impossible to find anywhere but at home. She turned to Maggie and jerked her head towards the door. 'Come on,' she said.

But Maggie did not move. Charlie had fallen asleep on her shoulder and she pressed her chin against the back of the child's tiny head. 'I'm so sorry,' she suddenly said, causing Nell to look round, wondering just what had happened these last couple of days, and how much Rosy knew of Charlie's parentage.

Rosy's expression remained blank. 'There's nothing to be sorry for,' she replied, even though she was not sure if Maggie was apologizing to her, or to Charlie.

Nell breathed a silent sigh, then wondered why she should feel any relief. Rosy might still be in the dark about her husband's affair with her sister, but the truth would come out – one day.

Maggie shook her head and tears sparkled in her eyes and ran slowly down her cheeks. She gave a loud snuffle. 'I'm causing trouble between you and John,' she said.

It was Rosy's turn to shake her head then. 'Don't be daft,' she returned fondly. 'I'm only too pleased to have you back. He'll get used to it sooner or later,' she added confidently, pressing a handkerchief into Maggie's hand before taking her arm and steering her towards the door.

In the courtyard John and Nicky were busy ferrying bags and boxes over to the cottage door, where they had piled them on the ground. 'They want taking inside,' Rosy said, her tone clearly showing she could not understand why they had not done so.

'We didn't know where you wanted them,' John replied shortly, and Nicky cast them a telling glance.

'Well, they want taking inside,' Rosy insisted.

'They'll be all right there,' Maggie put in, her gaze telling Rosy to let it be. 'I can carry them inside.'

But Rosy had not been prepared to back down over Maggie and she would not back down now, either. 'Bring them in and put them at the bottom of the stairs,' she instructed. 'He isn't used to being told what to do,' she whispered to Maggie, as they reached the cottage door. Well, he'd have to get used to it, she told herself. It was a long time since the days when she had had to chivvy him into seeing sense and get on with his work. Since then he had taken over everything . . . including herself. And it was going to stop. It had to stop, if they were going to make anything of their marriage.

'Do you want this taking upstairs?' Nicky asked, as he came through the door with Maggie's one suitcase.

'Leave it there. I'll see to it.' Maggie flashed him a watery smile of thanks. Then she looked round the little living-room with its well-used furniture and array of pot animals strewn everywhere, and drew a deep breath. 'It's so good to be back.' Her voice trembling with the force of her feelings.

For Rosy it was the first real evidence that she had done the right thing and a thin smile pulled at her lips as her sister's emotion also touched her.

It was then that the doorway darkened and John's body cut out the light. 'By the stairs,' he said huffily, dropping the selection of carrier bags before anyone could answer. There was a clatter of pottery.

'Be careful,' Rosy warned.

But he did not stop to listen and Maggie rested her hand on Rosy's arm and shook her head, once more telling her to leave it be. Then when he had gone back out of the door she dropped her hand and went to the old sofa and lifted up the red tartan blanket that covered all the pulls on the worn moquette. She laid Charlie gently down and placed the blanket over her. 'I'll leave her to sleep while I get sorted out,' she said, straightening up and turning back to Rosy who now had Nicky, plus a large cardboard box, standing by her side.

'Where?' he asked.

'Put it all together for now,' Rosy said, giving a nod towards the rest of Maggie's luggage. Two boxes, several bags and the one suitcase, which had been got especially for her to go to Bournemouth with. It must have been stored away carefully, she thought. It still looked brand new. She gave an inward grimace, considering the incongruity of the contents: the scruffy clothes and meagre selection of babywear. 'We'll go shopping tomorrow and get you kitted out,' she said.

'There isn't any need. We can manage,' Maggie protested.

'Magdalena Smith, stop being too independent for your own good,' Rosy teased. Whether Maggie liked it or not, tomorrow they were going shopping for clothes for both herself and Charlie, and food for the pantry. Nell only kept a very meagre supply, because she ate all her meals over at the house. But she knew now that the more she went on about it the more Maggie would protest so she would present her with a *fait accompli* in the morning. 'You'll need something to eat now . . . unless you're going to come over to the house?' The last was added dubiously, knowing, even before Maggie shook her head, that she would not want to come and eat where John might be.

'If you could send Nicky over with a bit of bread and a tin of baked beans, that will do us.'

Rosy grimaced at the humble request and the modest way it was spoken. *Oh, Maggie!* she thought sadly, gazing at the drawn features and fleshless body and wondering where her confident sister had gone. She would never have thought it possible that she could miss the brash hussy who had paraded round the house as if she owned it. But she would have given anything now to see the loud, garishly painted Maggie come bouncing through the door, swearing fit for a trooper, and with breasts like a pair of bazookas, aimed at anything that got in their way.

'I'll send something over,' she said, her voice flat with her concern, and she coiled her arm through Nicky's and stopped him passing as he was on his way out again. 'Come and get some food for Maggie and sort the rest of the things out later,' she said to him. He didn't need telling twice, as soon as he thought food was on the agenda he was one step ahead of her.

When they got back the kitchen was filled with the smell of frying onions and bacon. The soup obviously forgotten, Rosy thought. 'Are you doing any for Maggie?' she asked, peering over her mother's shoulder as she shuffled the bacon round in the pan.

Nell shook her head. 'I thought it best not to.'

Rosy gave an understanding nod. She was pleased her mother had not gone and prepared extra food. Sending Maggie unprepared food was getting herself into trouble, but not involving her mother – which was exactly how she wanted it to be. Picking up the pack of remaining bacon lying by the gas stove, she placed it in her mother's shopping basket, followed by half a loaf, butter, tea, sugar, six eggs, a bottle of milk, packet of biscuits, and the requested tin of baked beans. 'That will see her through until tomorrow,' she said, handing the basket to Nicky, just as his father came through the door.

'What's in there?' he demanded darkly.

'Food!' she replied, in the manner of someone stating the obvious, fixing him with a glare that dared him to object.

Unfortunately it had no effect. 'Didn't she bring any food back with her?' He paced across the floor, scraped a chair noisily from beneath the table and threw himself on to it, his jaw vibrating to a frantic rhythm that Rosy hoped dearly was not in tune with his heartbeat.

'A bit,' she replied. 'She didn't have much. So I'm helping her out!'

'I am to feed them as well as house them?' he questioned sarcastically, causing Nell's shoulders to sink lower over the stove and Nicky to make a very hasty exit with the basket, before it was taken off him.

'Yes!' Rosy returned bluntly. 'Until Maggie has got herself sorted out. While Mum works here the cottage is hers and it's no skin off your nose to have Maggie and Charlie living in it, as well.' She heard the clatter of Nell's bacon fork hitting the floor. Oh Mum! she

347

thought, thinking it had only fallen because Nell was getting worked up about what she was saying. She felt like getting up and going to her mother and telling her, no matter what she said, there was no fear of him throwing her out. But with John in the room she could not explain that he would put up with Maggie in the cottage in just the same way he had put up with bringing her home: because his insanity of the last two days had proved to her he would go to any lengths to keep her. It was not exactly a comforting thought. It made her feel no better than a chattel that he thought he had the right to do whatever he pleased with. But for now she had to put Maggie and Charlie before herself and put up with it, and hope that in time she could change him.

'I had been thinking of bringing your mother over here . . . to live in the house,' he said, fixing a meaningful gaze to Rosy's face. 'I thought it would be better for her, and that Ivan might like to take on the cottage.'

Nell looked round in shock, then spun back to the bacon and prodded it round the pan with more zeal than necessary.

Rosy's bottom jaw dropped open in amazement. 'And why would Ivan want to take it on?' she questioned, her voice incredulous.

'He might want a place of his own!' he snapped back.

'Don't be ridiculous!' she spat. 'Since Joey's death Ivan hasn't dared leave his mother alone for any length of time. He pays Elsie Lomas to spend the day with her while he's at work.'

'I'm not being ridiculous!' He leapt up so violently the chair toppled backwards. But he did not stop to pick it up. He came forward, advancing on her with blazing eyes and the ruddy spots on his cheeks seeming to explode as she watched, until his face was suffused with a magenta glow. '*I don't want your sister here!*' he snarled. 'You've forced me into it . . . and I won't let

348

you forget that! But I will not be forced into keeping her and her brat!'

Stretching her spine to its greatest extent, Rosy thrust her chin out and squared up to him. 'You needn't worry, Maggie might be down but she is still too proud to accept charity. She'll make sure she's looking after herself soon enough. But until that day comes *you* . . .' she thrust her finger into his chest, '. . . will look after her. Because she is my sister and I look after my family, and while I am your wife you will also look after my family!'

His arms came up and she thought he was about to strike her. But then he grabbed hold of his head, a strange guttural sound bubbled in his throat and his legs buckled and he sank slowly to the floor.

'John!' she said. But her voice had lost all its strength and she was not sure if she was actually speaking or not.

'Oh my God!' Nell exclaimed, spinning round from the stove, the bacon suddenly forgotten. 'Whatever's the matter with him?'

'I don't know.' For a long moment Rosy could only stare into her mother's anxious face. Then she suddenly leapt to life. 'John!' she cried, forcing a modicum of reason back into a brain that seemed to have forgotten how to work. Falling to her knees she scooped him up into her arms. 'John!' she repeated, her lips unable to form any other word than his name. Her anxious gaze washed over his hotly flushed face. Terror seized her as she saw the drooping corner of his mouth and looked into his eyes to see that only one was looking back at her: the other was a big, dark, unseeing circle, where the pupil had expanded to completely obliterate the pale grey iris. 'John! John!' she cried, and lifted her gaze to look down the length of his inert body, just as a dark wet stain grew over the front of his trousers.

Nell hurried over and sank to her knees on the

349

opposite side of him and Rosy's frightened gaze pivoted to her face. 'What is it, Mum? What is it?' Her voice begged her mother to contradict the other voice at the back of her head, that was telling her exactly what had happened to him. But even before Nell had a chance to open her mouth, her arms had tightened round him and she pulled him closer and rocked him like a baby, and cried his name over and over again.

'Let him have some air,' Nell insisted, gently prising her daughter's arms apart. 'He'll not come round if he can't breathe. You need plenty of air when you've fainted.'

'He hasn't fainted!' Despite wanting to be proved wrong she did not like her mother thinking her stupid enough to believe he had done nothing more than had a blackout, and her voice was spiked with a harshness heightened by panic. 'He's had a stroke,' she snapped, forced to accept what she did not want to admit.

'The doctor's the best person to make a diagnosis like that!' Nell returned, a sharpness in her voice put there by her own fear. 'I'll go and phone him.' Pushing herself to her feet she hurried to the door. 'You loosen his tie and open his collar,' she instructed, before going into the hall. It was what they always said; loosen any tight clothing. In this case she didn't know if it would do any good or not, but she had the feeling Rosy needed something to make her feel she was helping him.

But Rosy had no power to obey her mother's instructions. 'John! John!' she said, over and over, her voice little more than a murmur as she looked down on his lifeless face. She could not recall ever being so frightened in her life as when she had seen him falling, and had thought he was dying right there and then. Those few moments had wiped away all the anger, accusations and bad moods of the last two days. All she knew was that she was to blame. She should have listened to him and not gone off without him. She should not have insisted Maggie come back with them. She could have given her the train fare and told her to come the following day, or the next, giving him time to get used to the idea. She could have. But she had not.

Pulling him closer she pressed her lips to his temple. 'I'll never leave you again,' she promised, feeling her love for him in a way she had never felt it before.

As they reached the bottom of the stairs, Larry Hampson turned to Rosy. His ginger eyebrows lifted apologetically, and vanished beneath his mass of equally bright hair. 'He could improve. But don't go thinking I'm making you any promises. We'll just have to wait and see. He's had quite a severe stroke and, at the moment, we just have to be glad he's alive.'

Glad he's alive! Rosy pictured the pathetic figure lying on the stretcher the ambulance men were taking out of the front door. He had no use all the way down one side of his body. His crooked mouth made his chin appear so lopsided it looked as if it had been knocked sideways. The only noise he could make were guttural grunts that sounded like a hoarse dog. She could find nothing in his condition to be 'glad' about.

'Is he in pain?' she asked.

Larry Hampson shook his head. 'No,' he said simply.

'Good.' She clasped her hands nervously before her and gazed bleakly down at them. All she could think was that she had brought her husband to this. 'He's only fifty-one,' she finally said. 'He's too young for this.'

Larry nodded in understanding. 'But I'm afraid it happens.' For a long moment he gazed down at her with compassion in his eyes. She was the one who was too young for this, he thought.

'Yes . . . it happens,' she repeated flatly. 'Will they keep him in hospital long?'

351

Larry gave a shrug. 'If he goes on all right he could be home in a couple of weeks.'

She gave a nod, regret and guilt weighing heavy on her.

'Don't worry. If it's necessary I'll get the nurse to come in and help with him,' Larry said, misunderstanding her emotion.

Her head began to shake, then fell still. She could not explain to Larry the events of the past days and how she felt responsible. 'Thank you,' she suddenly said, and hurried out of the house and jumped into the back of the ambulance, leaving Larry Hampson to do the explaining to Nicky, Maggie and her mother, who were all waiting anxiously in the kitchen.

John did stay in hospital for two weeks and he made an improvement. The drooping corner of his mouth returned to almost normal, so that unless you were looking for it you did not notice there was anything wrong. His speech came back, unless he was getting tired, when he tended to stutter and stammer a bit. He regained the use of his arm but not his leg. Walking was impossible without the aid of a couple of sticks and most of the time he had to resort to a wheelchair.

For six weeks after his return home Nurse Ida Baker became a regular visitor to the house. Ida was a tiny little woman, but what Ida lost in height she made up for in personality. Yet despite her friendly disposition and a smile that was contagious, John did not like having a 'stranger' as he called her, messing around with him.

Rosy pointed out that Ida may have been a stranger on her first visit but after visiting him three or four times a week they had all got to know her very well. But he still insisted he wanted her visits stopped. He liked Nicky to sit and talk to him, but when it came to looking after him Rosy was the only one he wanted near him, and he made it perfectly obvious.

'We need some more help in the house,' she said to him one day, as she pushed the wheelchair down the drive. It was a lovely warm sunny day and, though at first he would not go out of the house at all, as the weather had improved she managed to persuade him to let her take him out for walks in the wheelchair. Now she often took him down the drive and a little way along the lane. But not into the village. His condition was still too new and he was very sensitive about being seen by many people.

'I don't want another nurse.' He glanced round at her. They were on the way back and crossing the railway bridge for the second time. 'I won't have a stranger moving in with us.' The panic in his voice was not completely drowned out by the thunder of a train passing beneath them.

Rosy smiled and took her hand briefly from the wheelchair handle and laid it on his shoulder. He was so changed and, when she saw that look of fear in his eyes, she was reminded that she was responsible for his condition. Maggie, her mother, even Larry Hampson had tried to tell her that it had obviously been going to happen and it would have happened sooner or later, with or without her help. But that did not alter anything. It had happened because she had made him angry and she felt a tremendous weight of guilt.

'There is no need for anyone to move in with us,' she pointed out. 'And neither do we need to have a stranger.'

He glanced round again.

'Maggie is going to help. I've . . .'

'No! No! No!'

She gave an inward sigh. 'Please, John!' The plea in her voice quietened him down and his expression became sullen. She stopped pushing the wheelchair and moved round to the front so he could see her better. 'Mum needs help. I can't give her any because you want me to be with you all the time.' Even when

353

she wasn't doing anything for him he insisted she sit with him and be there for him, every waking minute of his day, either just talking or, of late, reading to him. She only hoped his pressure on her would lessen when he got more used to his new condition and realized he wasn't so helpless, after all. She often tried to persuade him into the office. He was still capable of sitting at his desk and doing some work, but he had lost interest even in that, preferring to leave Bill Cowlishaw to take the reins of the business and run it for him. 'Maggie won't be working all the time, she couldn't possibly do it, not with Charlie to look after. But she can put in the odd hour here and there. And she needs the money!' she stressed meaningfully.

'I don't want Maggie round me!' he insisted, childish petulance tightening his mouth.

'Oh, John!' She tried never to lose her patience with him but at times it was very difficult. Especially times like now – when Maggie came into the conversation. She could never get to the root of his dislike for her sister; Maggie was no help either. It was always apparent she kept out of his way but when questioned about it her reply was simply that it was because he did not like her. 'Well, if it's any consolation, she isn't very keen on you, either.'

He gave a grunt.

'Come on, John!' Placing her hands on the wheel-chair's arms she leaned forward and brought her face level with his. 'I've had a devil of a job persuading Maggie to do it. I only succeeded in the end because she realized she wasn't going to get offered anything else, not without having someone to look after Charlie for her.' His hands were clasped on his lap, his thumbs twirling erratic circles round each other. She laid her hand on top, stilling his thumbs with an affectionate squeeze. 'Don't let me down by being stubborn about it,' she said. '*I* need this. I need to know Maggie is there to help mum, so I don't have to worry about her

354

and can give you all my time and concentration.' He got all her time and concentration now, but she realized she had to resort to bribery. And any suggestion that he might not be getting all of her was the only persuasion she knew would work on him.

For several moments he remained stubbornly silent and he refused to look into her eyes. Then his mouth relaxed and his gaze met hers. 'To help you,' he said, his head nodding a slow agreement. 'But I don't want to see her . . . or her brat,' he added mulishly. 'And I won't have her doing anything for me.'

Rosy's lips curved in a fond smile. 'I wouldn't think of letting anyone, only a trained nurse, do anything for you,' she said, and planted a tiny kiss on his forehead, before standing up and beginning to push the wheelchair again.

'I don't want a trained nurse, either,' he put in.

She gave a grimace at his continuing petulance. 'So long as I'm free to help you there won't be any need for one,' she assured.

He glanced round at her, the familiar fear filling his eyes. 'I never want anyone else doing things for me, Rosy. Only you.' He lifted his hand up to his shoulder, reaching out for her.

She smiled and slipped her hand into it. 'Don't worry, I'll always be here,' she promised. For as long as you need me, she thought, confident that the day would come when he realized he was not as reliant on her as he imagined himself to be.

CHAPTER NINETEEN

1973

As the car turned the corner Rosy saw the figure tripping down the lane, a loaded shopping bag in each hand. She smiled, and was grateful to find she still had the ability. Nowadays there seemed very little to smile about.

Her smile broadened as she got closer and could see the rhythmic swing of the well-rounded backside, covered by a skimpy red mini-skirt. It was good to see her sister back again. It had taken a long time, but over the past year Maggie had returned to what she had been before she left home. Rosy suspected it could have something to do with the Derwent's new landlord, Roy Parker. He was a widower in his early forties and since his arrival Maggie had taken to visiting the pub more regularly again. But Maggie wasn't saying anything on the subject, so Rosy could only come to her own conclusions.

'Get in,' she called, drawing up by Maggie's side and leaning across the passenger seat and pushing the door open for her. 'I'm going home.'

'I timed that nicely.' Maggie gave a sigh of relief as she stuffed the shopping bags under the dashboard and inserted her legs one on either side.

Rosy looked down at the overflowing bags and shook her head. 'I really don't know why you haven't learnt to drive.'

'Cars are anti-social,' Maggie declared. 'You don't meet people when you're driving past them.'

'And you don't break your back when you can throw the bags into a car,' Rosy replied, even though she knew she was wasting her breath. She had tried to get Maggie to have driving lessons when she had hers, almost six years ago. But Maggie had refused then and she had continued to refuse, preferring to turn her jaunts to the village into social occasions.

'So . . . who are all these people you've met while you weren't driving to the village?' she asked, knowing she was beat and giving in gracefully.

'Freddy Baker, Joe Hetherington, Franny Hallsworth.'

'I'll bet that was exciting,' Rosy responded drily. Freddy and Joe were both retired from the railways and as inseparable as Siamese twins. Their conversation was equally limited, covering the weather, the war, and their confident insistence that the bomb was going to be dropped at any minute – the constant worry of the latter making it necessary for the daily consumption of enough mild ale to have kept the Titanic afloat.

'I don't think Franny is very keen on retirement,' Maggie said, brushing her chaotic curls away from her hot face.

'We said she would regret it,' Rosy replied, as they crossed the railway bridge. 'That pub has been her life for twenty odd years.' Franny's announcement to leave the pub and move into a cottage at the other end of the village had taken everyone by surprise. She had been landlady of the Derwent for so long she had become part of the fixtures and fittings. 'It's bound to take her a time to get settled down. But her going has brought a bit of new blood into the village,' she added mischievously, and glanced round to see if there was any reaction.

There was none. Maggie's face remained bland, her gaze never leaving the road ahead.

'Perhaps he could let Franny work as barmaid a couple of evenings a week,' Rosy persisted. 'The new landlord. Roy . . . is that his name?'

'You know very well it is.' Maggie flashed Rosy a telling glance. 'And while we're on the subject . . .'

Rosy's ear pricked up in expectation.

'He's offered me a job as barmaid at the weekends.'

'Oh!' Rosy's disappointment was clear. Then it changed to a mixture of surprise and confusion. 'You?' she questioned. 'A barmaid? You don't need a job. If you're short of money you only have to ask.' The last was spoken with annoyance as she experienced a stab of jealousy towards her sister. She suddenly saw her enjoying the life that was passing her by. It was an odd thought. She had never yearned for the type of social life Maggie had gone after, but now anything would be preferable to what she had. It was over six years since John's stroke and in all that time he had made little improvement. The rapid progress in the first weeks had been very misleading. He could do nothing now that he couldn't do on the day nurse Ida Baker had made her final call. Day in day out life was the same for him . . . and for her.

Maggie grimaced. 'Maybe I want to earn my own money for a change.'

'You do earn your own money. You work for what I pay you.'

Maggie's head wagged from side to side and she turned her gaze to the window and watched the hawthorn hedge going swiftly by. 'I do part-time work and get full-time pay. It isn't that I'm complaining about it, but there are times when I feel I'm being bought, when you appear to be of the opinion you own me – *like now!*' she added meaningfully.

'I do not!' Rosy snapped, and turned the old Rover so violently into the drive she almost scraped the front wing on the stone gatepost. 'Damn!' she muttered. It had been a very rare occasion for her to leave the house on her own. John did not like her out of his sight for longer than a few minutes at a time. She had only managed it today because she had been to see the doctor, but even so she had been enjoying the taste of freedom and had felt in a much better frame of mind than when she had gone out. Now Maggie, with her selfishness, had spoilt it all.

Maggie's gaze hardened on her sister's face. 'I just fancied the idea. I wasn't aware it would be putting your nose out!'

'You aren't putting my nose out!' Rosy insisted, but nevertheless swung the car into the courtyard and stamped on the brake so hard it came to an abrupt halt. Then she leapt out and was at the back door before Maggie had retrieved the shopping bags from round her feet. When Maggie finally caught up with her she was standing by the kitchen fire, the fingers of one hand drumming frustratedly on the mantel, as she stared into the black, unlit grate.

'What's wrong?' Nell asked, coming up short as she came into the kitchen from the hall, duster in hand, and saw Rosy standing there. She knew she had been to see the doctor but she did not know why, and her concern was immediately evident.

'Nothing!' Rosy snapped. 'Absolutely nothing.'

Nell's reply was cut off by Maggie rushing through the door. 'Just what's rattled your cage?' she enquired pointedly, glaring at her sister as she dumped the shopping on the table with more force than was necessary. There was an ominous crunching sound. 'Bugger!' she exclaimed expressively. Rosy looked round to see the cause of her distress. 'What is it?' she asked wearily. There were some parts of her sister she wished had not returned.

'The eggs!' Maggie gave a groan and pulled a bottle of lemonade out of the shopping-bag, followed, very carefully, by a sorry-looking brown paper bag with orange yolk stains seeping through it. 'The bloody pop bottle fell on it and crushed them,' she said, her nose turning up in disgust.

Holding the mess suspended in both hands stuck out

in front of her, she hurried it over to the sink. She wasn't aware she was laying a trail of dangling egg white, until it fell against her bare legs. 'Oh sod it!' she said with feeling, as the cold stickiness trickled down to her feet. She chucked the bag and its contents into the washing-up bowl as if it had turned to poison. 'Now look what you made me bloody do!' she said angrily.

'Me!' Rosy looked amazed.

'Stop it . . . the pair of you!' Springing to life Nell tossed the duster onto the table and went to the sink to get a cloth to begin wiping the mess up from the floor.

'Yes . . . *you*!' Maggie returned, taking no notice of her mother. She flapped her gooey hands in the air as if she did not know what to do with them and glanced down at the mess on her legs, her nose curling with repulsion. Then she turned on Rosy. 'Anybody would have thought I was telling you I was going to rob a bank. I know you pay me well. You keep me and Charlie but that doesn't mean you sodding well own me body and soul!'

The last hit a nerve deep in Rosy. She did not need Maggie to point out she was being unfair. She knew it for herself. Her own self-pity had blinded her to all else. 'Oh Maggie,' she began, going to the table and sinking down on a chair and dropping her head into her hands. 'I'm sorry. Take the job if you want to, it's nothing to do with me.'

'What job?' Nell looked up with a frown.

The sadness in Rosy's gaze and the sound, almost of fear, that vibrated in her voice, brought Maggie up short. For a long moment she stared in bewilderment at her sister.

'What is it?' Nell asked, her brow crinkling in a frown and the floor, and the job, forgotten.

'Is there something wrong?' Maggie's concern now equalled her mother's and she quickly ran the tap and rinsed her sticky fingers. 'Has something happened?

Where've you been?' She stopped and looked up as she was about to wipe her legs with the dishcloth. When Rosy did not reply she picked up the tea towel and hurried to her side, drying her hands as she went. 'Whatever's brought this on? It's not like you.'

Rosy grimaced. No, it wasn't like her. People often commented on how wonderful she was with John: never leaving him alone; never letting it get her down. What they didn't know was that the smile on her face was plastered there each morning when she put on her make-up. A sweep of lipstick lifted the corners of her mouth, a dab of eyeshadow added a sparkle to empty eyes, and it stayed there until she went to bed. No-one saw the real Rosy any more, not even Maggie. No-one knew what she really looked like and no-one heard her screaming inside: screaming for a moment's release; to be herself; to do something that was not for someone else, but just for her.

In the next moment she broke down and sobbed, the emotion she had felt mounting inside her for several weeks suddenly getting the better of her.

'Rosy! Rosy!' Forgetting her wet legs Maggie slung the tea towel down on the floor and pulled Rosy into her arms. 'What's happened? Is it John?' She knew well enough he was not easy to live with. He had always been a jealous and possessive man, but now he never gave Rosy a moment to herself. On the rare occasions she had tried to go anywhere he had kicked up such a fuss that she had been forced to back down, fearing he would get himself into such a state he would have another stroke.

'What is it, love?' Nell pulled a chair up by the side of Rosy and sat down. 'Is it something the doctor's said?'

Rosy did not reply immediately, but continued to sob with her head pressed tightly against the swell of Maggie's breast. Not until she felt dampness against her cheek did she finally move. 'Look what I'm doing,' she said, pushing away and staring bleakly at the wet patch on her sister's red and white striped top. It made an almost perfect circle on the end of her breast and, with a nipple prominent in the centre, gave the impression of a dartboard. 'You look ready for target practice,' she pointed out flatly, unable to find the amusement she had aimed for as she brushed her tears away from her cheeks.

Maggie looked down at herself with a grimace. 'It could be my lucky day if somebody gets bull's-eye,' she joked.

Nell glanced her a scowl, but was too worried about Rosy to tell her off for being rude.

Maggie's humour had a bit more affect than her own. The corners of Rosy's lips lifted, but only slightly.

'That's better,' Maggie said with feeling. 'This old thing won't hurt for a few tears.' She stretched the tight fitting top out in front of her, then let it go, so that it leapt back and clung to her curves with the intimacy of a nylon underskirt filled with static. 'And it could have been worse,' she added knowledgeably. Rosy looked puzzled, until Maggie said, 'It could have been your suit you got wet, not just an old rag.'

Rosy's head shook stiffly from side to side. 'No,' she replied flatly. 'This is an old rag. I've had it for seven years, like most of my clothes.' Lifting her hand she waved it up and down the length of her sister. 'You look normal, ordinary.' That wasn't quite true. Whether people approved of her or not, Maggie had the power to turn heads wherever she went and could never be called ordinary.

'Well, you haven't got two heads,' Maggie replied, folding her arms under her generous bosom, and frowning as she tried to decide if she was being complimented or insulted. 'And you've always looked nice in that outfit.' Her gaze ran over the brown checked jacket and plain brown skirt which covered her sister's slender body. 'It's smart.'

'I know it's smart. It's also seven years out of date.' Rosy sat back in the chair and rubbed her hands over the smooth cap of hair on top of her head. As her hands ran down the back of her head her fingers met the soft bump of the bun she had taken to wearing, so her long hair didn't get in the way when she was bending over John. 'And so is this,' she snapped, and tugged angrily at the pins to release it. 'But it isn't me . . .' Her voice trailed away on the last, because she was wrong – it *was* her! She might not like it but it was what she had become. Old and frumpy! As her long blond hair slowly uncoiled down her back like an awakening python, she dropped her head into her hand and gave a groan. 'I've let myself go and I don't think I've got the confidence left to find myself again.'

'Is that what the doctor said?' Nell questioned, her concern not lessened. She could not believe her daughter's troubles were all to do with her appearance.

Rosy looked up at her mother and gave a thin smile. 'Not in so many words. But I know it's all part of it. I've got to break free, Mum. If only for half an hour a week. Larry said if I didn't get a break from John I'd likely have a breakdown.'

Nell's incredulous gaze swung from Rosy to Maggie and back again. 'I've been telling you that for ages,' she said, folding her arms tightly and appearing greatly offended. 'But would you listen?'

Rosy's head shook with her despair. 'How can I? John needs me. He gets frightened when he's on his own.'

'He wouldn't be on his own!' Nell countered, the anger she was feeling towards him being aimed at the wrong person.

'Mum could sit with him,' Maggie put in. 'And I'd be here.' She gave a telling shrug. 'I know that wouldn't exactly put a smile on his face, but what I mean is I'd be here in case of emergencies.'

Again Rosy shook her head, just as an insistent

hammering began on the ceiling. Three pairs of eyes lifted upwards. Maggie grimaced, Nell groaned, and Rosy gave a resigned smile.

'I'd better go up before he brings the place down round our ears,' she said, but her attempt at humour fell flat on its face. Neither Nell nor Maggie responded and she got up and walked out.

She could not understand why he had insisted on staying upstairs while she was out. He spent most of the time with her in the drawing-room, but after sulking for most of the morning he had left it until the last minute before insisting she take him up to the bedroom before going. He had been extra awkward, as well. 'It was only one leg,' she had reminded him, when she had her arm round his waist practically carrying him up the stairs, as he did his best to drag both legs.

It was only one leg! She had said exactly the same to Larry Hampson, when she was sitting looking across the big mahogany desk in his surgery.

He had nodded his head. 'In body,' he said. 'But in his mind . . .' His voice trailed away and he lifted his hands palm upwards and spread them wide. 'To be truthful, I don't really know.'

'Could he be putting it on?' she had asked. Larry had been good to her throughout John's illness and she had not wanted to put him on the spot, but of late she was coming to believe John could have done much more for himself, if only he had tried. Or was it just that she was so tired of it all that she had no patience left and was trying to blame him for her own failings.

'I don't know,' he replied. He had often questioned himself as to the extent of John's disability. He had not been old when the stroke hit him and, in truth, he had expected him to make an almost complete recovery. It was usually only the elderly who were left with the bad lasting effects. Or multiple stroke victims. But he had to admit John baffled him. There were times when he definitely thought he was putting it on. But then he only had to look at Rosy to make him change his mind. He could not believe any man who had such a beautiful young wife would willingly choose to turn himself into an invalid.

At the top of the stairs Rosy paused. Promise yourself a break from him every day! She heard Larry's voice in her head as if he was right there with her. *How?* she asked herself, in just the same way she had asked Larry. How could she be expected to turn her back on John, when just the mention of her going anywhere caused him to get so heated she expected one day to see steam coming from his ears?

She was no nearer finding an answer when the banging began on the bedroom floor again.

'I'm coming,' she called, and hurried across the landing and down the corridor.

He was lying on top of the bed, the walking stick resting across his legs as if it had never been picked up.

'You've been a long time,' he said, fixing her with a glare of tight-lipped accusation.

'No I haven't.' Going to the bed she sat down on the edge and took hold of his hand as it lay limply against his thigh. 'I've been gone no more than forty-five minutes.'

'Over an hour!' he insisted.

'No I haven't.' Before visiting Larry she would have agreed with him and made the excuse her watch must have stopped, in order to keep him calm. But Larry had told her to be firmer with him. 'I've been gone forty-five minutes.' She spoke slowly and precisely, as if speaking to a child.

'It doesn't take forty-five minutes to get to Larry's surgery.' Pulling his hand away from hers he folded his arms across his chest in a belligerent manner. 'I don't believe you've been there,' he said. 'There's nothing wrong with you. If you'd really wanted to see him you could have sent for him to come here.'

And have you insisting on being with me when I spoke to him, she thought bitterly. 'Larry is far too busy to come visiting people who are well enough to get to him.' She refused to reply to his suggestion that she had been lying about where she had been, and she got up from the bed and walked across to the window. The sun was high in the sky and sparkled off the river's surface like dancing diamonds. A pair of moorhens were busy foraging by the bank and a female mallard swam proudly upstream, six fluffy ducklings following erratically behind her. At some point in every day she stood and looked at that river, and had the feeling she was watching her own life, slipping slowly away from her and out of reach. It was even more depressing at this time of year, when the new-fledged young were being paraded in front of her. The mothers always looked so superior, as if they were saying, 'Look what I can do that you can't.'

And those snooty ducks knew the truth. She couldn't do it. She had left it too late. When she first married John she had thought there was plenty of time before she began planning a family of her own. But time had been snatched away from her. It was not true that John's leg was his only disability: since his stroke he had been unable to make love to her.

She turned away from the window, casting her painful thoughts aside. John's head was averted but she could see enough of his face to know the mulish expression had not gone. 'Well . . .' she said, fixing him with a questioning gaze, '. . . aren't you going to ask why I went to see Larry?' In his anger and sulking he had not bothered to ask.

His gaze pivoted to hers and the frightened look was back in his eyes. It had obviously not occurred to him that she might have something seriously wrong with her, and guilt stabbed at her for putting the thought into his head. 'It's nothing major,' she quickly assured, returning to sit on the bed. He did not unfold his arms so she lay her hands in her lap and did not attempt to take hold of his. 'I've been getting tired just lately, even though I'm not exactly rushed off my feet.' It was true. Although John took up all of her day, the most part of it was only sitting with him, talking, watching television or reading to him.

'You don't have to go into hospital?'

She smiled at the concern she knew was more for himself than for her. She shook her head. 'No. I don't even need any pills. Larry told me to take a bit more fresh air every day.' That wasn't exactly what he had said, but taking a walk would get her out of the house and away from John and give her the short breaks Larry had prescribed.

'We can go for two walks then,' he suggested, looking greatly relieved. 'One every morning and one every afternoon.'

It was a moment before her head began to shake in refusal. 'On my own,' she said, keeping her voice as gentle as she could, knowing what she had to say was going to hurt him. But it had to be done. It had taken her weeks to gather up the courage to go to Larry. She would not back down now she had set the stone in motion. 'Just on my own,' she repeated, and her head dropped forward and she stared at her hands. 'Just walking. Not pushing the wheelchair.' She hoped the last would suggest it was the strain of pushing the chair that was the most trouble to her.

But if John picked up the hint he chose to ignore it. 'So it's me that's making you ill?' he said, his voice as tight as the belligerent pout that returned to his lips.

'Don't be silly.' She smiled as she spoke, even though she felt more like screaming. 'You always have a little rest after dinner. I'll go then and you'll hardly miss me.'

'I will miss you.'

She reached out to him but his arms remained stubbornly folded and so she dropped her hand and rested it on his thigh. 'And I'll miss you.' It was no lie. She would be worrying and wondering about him every step of the way. But if she refused to back down and made it a regular part of the day, he would eventually get used to it and she would be able to go with a clear conscience. 'It will only be for a few minutes. Half an hour at the most.' To begin with, she thought. She hoped that she could extend the time as he got more used to her being away from him.

'I might be ill. I don't want to be left alone.'

'You will not be left alone.' Impatience began to creep into her voice. 'Mum will be here. You'll only have to knock if you need her.'

'I won't have Maggie coming up to me.'

She bit her lip from telling him Maggie would be the last person to answer any call from him. 'There won't be any need for you to see anyone,' she insisted, and jumped up from the bed, folded her arms and walked across the floor, hoping to assuage the anger his stubbornness was lighting inside her. 'I shall only be gone a short while,' she pointed out, releasing one arm and sweeping the hand out before her. 'I'll make sure you have anything you might need before I go.' Folding her arms again she fixed him steadily. 'I do think you are being unreasonable,' she said.

'Am I unreasonable to expect you to look after me?' he demanded bitterly. 'You're my wife and you're supposed to be here with me . . . not out with some other man!'

'That is not fair.' She had thought she was prepared for his anger, but to hear him make such an unfounded accusation was too much. Something snapped inside her. 'How dare you even suggest it? I have been at your beck and call for the last six years. I am not complaining about that, or condemning you for it. All I'm asking is that you give me a bit of consideration and accept that I would like a little time to myself.' She began to pace across the floor to the window, but when she reached it she immediately turned round and paced the other way again. She was close to the foot of the bed when she stopped, and said, 'This is the first day I have been out without you since I can't remember when, and you accuse me of seeing another man! I've been to see Larry this morning because I felt at the end of my tether and I needed someone to talk to.'

'So . . . it's Larry, is it?' he questioned sarcastically. 'He is to provide a shoulder to cry on. And what else . . . I wonder?'

That his accusations not only hurt her, but could have done irreparable harm to Larry's professional standing, caused a rage to ignite inside her that was so fierce she knew if she stayed there any longer she would have lashed out at him. With her hands stuffed tightly under her arms to stop them taking on a will of their own and attacking him, she spun round and rushed from the room.

Only when she was safely on the landing, with the bedroom door closed behind her, did she pause long enough to release the breath that had been held in her lungs and was almost choking her.

CHAPTER TWENTY

Rosy paused and took a deep breath. The smell of sun-warmed vegetation and new-mown grass floated through the trees, trapped by the thick overhead canopy of leaves. After the argument and John's unreasonable reaction, her senses revelled in the aroma and the freedom that went with it and she shook her head and enjoyed the feel of her hair hanging freely down her back.

She should have done this long before now, she told herself, and began walking along the shadowed path leading through the wood. The suit she had worn for the visit to Larry had been far too heavy for the warm weather and she was pleased she had regained enough control of her anger to stop and change. She felt good in the simple, daffodil yellow cotton sundress she had retrieved from the washing basket, where it had been waiting to be laundered. A few splashes of spilt tea on the hemline were preferable to going back into the bedroom, and John, to get something clean.

In the abundant foliage she could not see the derelict cottage until she had almost reached it, and then only a fleeting glimpse here and there between the branches. But it was enough to fill her heart with the memories of contentment sitting on the wall had brought to her in years gone by.

Leaving the path she stepped carefully through the sea of ferns which stood between herself and the edge of the wood. When she reached the far side both trees and fern came to an abrupt end, opening out onto a field of buttercups that shone like gold in the intense sunlight.

The light was dazzling as she came out of the shadows and she lifted her hand to shade her eyes and paused to take in the beautiful sight. She tried to recall the last time she had been up there, but it was so long ago she could not remember the exact occasion. She smiled as her mind dragged up the memory of peeping through the cottage window and seeing Maggie performing with some unknown man.

Maggie's love nest, she thought, and began to wade through the carpet of buttercups that came up to her knees. She had to go some way before the front of the cottage came into clear view. Then she came up short.

'What!' she gasped, her hand flying to her mouth to catch the sound. A mucky, mustard coloured pickup truck stood by the garden wall and the crumbling dwelling of her memory had, at least partially, been transformed. The boarded up holes of the windows were now glazed, newly so, she guessed, from the putty fingerprints covering the glass and the bare unpainted wood. And instead of the rotting front door was a solid wooden structure, also lacking paint.

She walked slowly forward. A miniature five bar gate was propped against the garden wall, obviously waiting to take the place of the drunkenly hanging remains of its predecessor. Beyond the gate the brambles had been cut back and no longer overran the path. But the rest of the garden's natural wildness had not been touched.

The last pleased her and without any thought for whether she had the right, she walked through the gate. There was no sign of life and she made a complete circle round the cottage and back again, at times, struggling to get through thigh high nettles and grasping brambles.

It was odd, she thought, that no-one had mentioned anyone moving in. It was even more odd that they had missed the sale. News like that usually set the place on fire.

When she arrived back at the gate she rested her

hands on top of the wall and stood staring at the cottage. Her place of refuge. Now it belonged to someone else. She felt a mixture of annoyance and sadness, and an inexplicable feeling of resentment towards the new owners. The feeling grew and she wondered where they were. She glanced at the scruffy truck and realized she had no business to be nosing around someone else's property. Reluctantly she turned away, thinking the day was going from bad to worse. One of her fondest memories was of walking up here with Nicky and she had promised herself that one day they would do it again. It might not have been until Nicky himself was a father and they had a third, or even fourth member to the party. But it had been hope for the future and something she had clung to in her darker moments. Now it was gone, washed away by intruders.

The quickest route back to the house was diagonally across the buttercup field, but the weather was too beautiful and she did not want to get back before her half an hour was up. John had been at the bedroom window when she walked down the drive and she knew he would still be there when she walked back up it. And he would have timed her to the second. If she only took twenty minutes today he would expect her to be no longer than that every other day. So she set off in a straight line down the edge of the field, where the truck's tyres had flattened a track in the tall grass and flowers.

She walked slowly, pondering on the cottage and its mysterious occupants.

'*And such a sight beheld my eyes that I could scarcely speak. An angel slipped from paradise with flowers around her feet.*'

Rosy stopped short, spinning round in the direction of the unexpected voice. 'Oh!' she gasped, her hand flying to her throat as her gaze settled on the smiling eyes watching her from the other side of the wall.

He was wearing black cowboy boots with black jeans and a sleeveless T-shirt. He had blond hair which, though not as long as her own, reached his shoulders and hung in the same centre-parted style. He was sitting in the grass, his back leaning against the withered remains of a victim of Dutch elm disease, an opened can of lager clutched in his hands.

'You startled me,' she said, unable to take her eyes off him as he stood up and came towards her. He was tall, exceptionally so, and had the willowy build of someone in their early twenties. But as he got closer she could see she was mistaken with the last. He was still smiling and tiny lines fanning out from the corners of his eyes put him in a much older age bracket. Around forty, she guessed. 'Who said that?' she asked, feeling inexplicably silly and not knowing what else to say.

'I did,' he replied, his lips stretching in a deeper smile.

'I know that.' Embarrassment put impatience into her voice. 'But where are the words from?'

'Out of my head,' he replied simply. 'I made them up when I saw you. You look like the buttercup fairy.' The hand with the lager can made a sweeping gesture up and down the length of the yellow dress that blended perfectly with the flowers she stood in. 'But an angel dropping from paradise sounds much nicer than a fairy. Unless you'd prefer to be a fairy?' A dark blond eyebrow arched in enquiry.

Rosy gave an inward sigh. She wished she was a fairy, with a magic wand to wave and make him vanish. She didn't know who he was and if he thought irritating her was good sport, she had no wish to find out. She should go, she told herself, but did nothing to put the order into motion. 'I didn't think there was anyone around,' she said, suddenly annoyed that he had the power to embarrass her and hardening her voice in an attempt to prove he had not.

'I know that,' he finally said, his mouth twitching

with amusement. 'Or do you make a habit of being nosy?'

Heat flooded into her cheeks, leaving behind a colour too strong for even the overpowering glow of buttercups to conceal. He had seen her snooping round the cottage, his cottage, she corrected. 'I take it you are the new owner,' she said, glancing back up the hill to the newly renovated cottage. It had been a stupid thing to say. It was obvious who he was.

'Yes,' he replied simply.

She looked sheepish. 'I haven't been up here for some time. How long have you been here?' She forced herself to sound calm and take control of the situation, before making an even bigger fool of herself.

'A couple of days. What you can see is all that has been done. The inside is still like a cave. I'm living in fear of being captured by a troll at any moment.'

'You're doing it yourself?' She made no attempt to conceal her surprise. He looked like a pop star or a hippy, not a painter and decorator.

He smiled knowingly and gave a nod.

'I didn't know it had been sold. What made you buy a place in such a lonely spot?'

'I want the isolation. I'm a writer,' he explained, when she looked puzzled. 'I wanted somewhere I could lose myself and get on with my work. And it hasn't been for sale and I haven't bought it.'

'*You're not a squatter!*' she gasped incredulously.

'Good grief no!' He threw his head back and laughed, sending his hair shimmering round his shoulders like the mane of an arrogant palomino. 'This place has been in my family for several generations. My great uncle was the last to live here. He died just after the war and it's been left to rot since then.'

Her mother had once told her who had lived there, but Rosy could not remember much about it. 'What was your uncle's name?' she asked, to see if that spurred her memory.

'Tom Bridges.'

Rosy shook her head. 'I remember the Bridges family who lived up Hazelwood Road. But they moved away several years ago.'

'They were the same family,' he said. 'Did you know them well?'

It was Rosy's turn to laugh and shake her head. The Bridges had lived in a very grand house and had not been in the habit of consorting with the likes of the Smiths. 'And they were related to the man who lived here?' she said, unable to conceal her amazement. She found it difficult to believe the little cottage could have belonged to the same family.

He nodded his head and laughed. 'Is it really so strange?' he asked.

She felt a renewed surge of embarrassment, as if she had been speaking out of turn. 'So what made you suddenly decide to move in?' She ignored his question but needed to keep talking to hide her discomfort.

'I'd have been here before if I'd known the place existed. But I didn't know about it until I happened to mention to my mother that I needed somewhere quiet to escape to and she said, if I was really desperate to be a recluse, I should move into Tom's old place. She was joking,' he added laughingly. 'Even now I don't think she really believes I have actually done it.'

'She obviously doesn't think it's good enough for you.' Rosy's tone was dry. She suddenly wondered why she was standing there listening to a complete stranger's life story. Especially one that seemed beyond belief and, suddenly, just a touch too perfect. A writer indeed! He was a squatter. He had moved in on the quiet because he was not supposed to be there. 'How many people live with you?' she asked.

He inclined his head and grimaced in a way that told her he had not missed the accusation in her voice. 'I live here alone. So you needn't worry about loud parties, naked rituals and pot smoking. Although . . .'

375

he paused and looked around the empty fields, '. . . if I wanted a nice little sideline I could always plant some cannabis. I believe it can be quite a lucrative commodity.'

Her mouth tightened in anger and her chin lifted in challenge, before his dancing eyes told her he was laughing at her again.

She gave a sigh, her neck immediately shrinking as it relaxed once more. 'Sorry,' she said, grimacing apologetically. 'It just seems so strange to have some-one turn up after the place has stood empty for so long.'

'I can understand that.' He placed his free hand on his heart. 'But I assure you this place belongs to my family and I have every right to be here.'

She gave a little nod. 'All right . . . I believe you,' she said, breaking into an uncertain smile.

'Thank goodness for that.' He swept imaginary sweat from his forehead with the back of the hand holding the lager can. 'For a moment there I had awful imaginations of the vice squad arriving to drag me out of bed one night.'

She gave an apologetic shrug. 'It's just odd to find you here and no-one knowing it. Haven't you done any shopping or anything yet?'

He grinned broadly, lifted the lager can and waggled it against his ear. 'That was the last of the supplies, so I shall be presenting myself at the local pub this evening.'

Rosy smiled. Then everyone would know about him. Because if no-one else took any notice of him, Maggie would be there, and she'd be all eyes. 'Will you live here all the time? Or just when you're writing?'

'Yes to both, because I write all the time. I've only stopped now to get this place in order. As soon as it's finished I shall be up to my neck in manuscript, trying to catch up with my deadline.'

'Well, if you're busy, I won't keep you,' she said, grateful to have found a reason to walk away, yet unable to explain why she felt she had the need of an excuse to get away from him. 'I won't come snooping again,' she assured, and began to walk quickly down the hilly field.

'That's all right. Feel free to drop in anytime you're passing,' he called after her.

'And muck up your deadline!' she replied pointedly, without turning back to look at him.

As Rosy had expected, John was at the window watching for her. At first he stood very still, his gaze glued to her as she took each step. Not until she was halfway up the drive did he move. Then only to press himself up against the side of the window so he could see round the corner and down to the gate and the lane beyond.

Rosy came to an abrupt halt. He was looking to see if there was a car there, she realized angrily. He still thought she had been out to see another man. Resting her hands on her hips she glared at him meaningfully, and shook her head at him. You stupid fool of a man, she was thinking, just as the sound of a noisy engine put all other thoughts from her mind.

'What the devil?' she said aloud, and turned towards the gate as the throaty sound got closer. 'Oh no!' The sight that met her was not one that pleased her. A large gleaming black and chrome motor cycle, with two black leather clad riders, was coming up the drive.

'Nicky!' she gasped, and spun round and cast a furious glance at the figure still lurking at the bedroom window, making clear that she held him responsible for this. Earlier in the year Nicky had pestered his father for a motor cycle and, despite her protests, had got one. At the time his lack of a full licence had prevented him having a large machine. But now he had passed his test the same rules did not apply, and he had obviously brought her worst fears to life.

As the bike went by it slowed and he turned and grinned at her.

'Oh Nicky!' she muttered in exasperation, before hurrying after him as he turned the bike into the courtyard.

When she caught up with him the noisy engine had stopped but he had not got off. A black leather clad leg was positioned stiffly on either side, to keep the machine upright as he pulled off his gauntlets and silver crash helmet, then straightened his hair. Going up to the front of the bike she looked him straight in the eye, shaking her head. 'Tell me you've just borrowed it,' she said, a plea in her voice that she knew was useless.

'It's mine,' he replied, with a grin from ear to ear and little concern for her distress.

'Oh no!' Her hand came out in front of her, grasping at thin air. 'Why?' she questioned angrily. 'Why a bigger bike? Why not a car? Your father would have got you one if you couldn't afford it.'

'I know,' he beamed proudly. 'Dad bought me this.'

Rosy was struck dumb. She was angry and hurt with both of them: John for not telling her; Nicky for doing it behind her back. And when it had been done she did not know. It must have been arranged in a snatched few minutes here and there – in the space of time it took for her to make John a cup of tea or tell her mother what he wanted to eat. Which made it all the more furtive. 'Why didn't you tell me?' Her lips tightened and she glared at him accusingly. 'You knew I wouldn't want you to have one of these. That was it, wasn't it? You knew I'd try to stop you. Or if not you . . . your dad knew I would try and stop him paying for it! Oh Nicky, how could you?' On the last she wheeled away and hurried back to the house, too enraged to say any more.

It was several minutes before he finally came in. Rosy's temper had not subsided, but she had managed to bring it under a certain control, knowing that an out and out slanging match would get them nowhere.

'Well!' she asked, without looking round at him,

when he had closed the door and come right into the room. 'What have you got to say for yourself?' Even with her hands pressed against the tabletop her arms trembled from the force of her emotions.

Coming up close by her side he laid an arm across her shoulders. 'I've got a motor bike. That isn't a crime. Is it?' he questioned, making her turn to see the plaintive look on his face, that under other circumstances would have made her laugh. Her stony features didn't even twitch.

'It could be a lethal weapon in the wrong hands,' she said meaningfully. She wasn't sure why she had said that. It wasn't that she thought his hands were the wrong ones. After his suspension from school and their trip to Bournemouth he had returned to his lessons as meek as a lamb. There had not been one bad report about him since then and his final two years at school had been exceptional; a fact the redoubtable Mr Woodward put down to *his* right and proper action when the need arose. But motor cycles meant gangs and she was frightened he would get himself into a situation where he had to take risks, or lose face in front of his friends. A smaller bike could only go as fast as its engine would allow. The one standing outside was a big bike . . . with an enormous engine. She dreaded to think what speeds it was capable of.

'Don't be silly!' He tossed his head and rested his hands on his leather clad hips. 'You can have a fatal accident in a car. Or even walking down the road. Besides, that wasn't the only thing I've brought home to show you.'

Rosy looked uncertain. He looked amused. Then he inclined his head towards the door, directing her gaze to the second leather clad figure, silently standing holding the matching helmet, gauntlets and goggles.

Rosy turned. 'Oh . . . !' she gasped, her hand flying to her lips as her eyes settled on a pretty blonde girl with enormous eyes, looking very ill at ease. 'Oh I'm sorry,' she said, hurrying to take the girl's hand and bring her right into the room. 'Trust him to leave you standing there.' She flashed Nicky a glance of admonishment. She had not taken much notice of the pillion passenger, thinking it would be his friend Gordon. Nicky was now being tutored by Bill Cowlishaw to take over the running of his father's business when Bill retired in a couple of years, and Gordon was working at Rolls Royce, but they spent all their spare time together. She could now see that the black leather covered a very definite female shape – at first glance she had assumed it was Gordon.

'See what I mean,' Nicky said, wrapping his arm round the girl's shoulders. 'I told you she was a tyrant.'

The girl coloured shyly and Rosy flashed him a scowl. 'Well, aren't you going to introduce us,' she asked pointedly.

'This is Cassie,' he replied without hesitation. 'Short for Cassandra. If her father's about you have to call her Cassandra.'

'Hello Cassie.' Rosy took the girl's hand for the second time, wondering if the bit about her father was important. Had it just been a passing comment? Or did it mean their relationship was serious enough to involve a meeting of the parents. The last thought unsettled her, yet she did not know why. He was only nineteen. He wasn't old enough to settle down yet, she told herself, unfortunately finding no comfort in the theory. He was old enough to be married and have a family, a small voice at the back of her head inserted. 'Well . . .' she was suddenly nervous and showing it. 'Do you want a cup of tea or something?' she asked, her hands flapping erratically in front of her.

'No,' Nicky replied. 'We've come back to go for a swim. We'll have something after.'

'You're going in the pool?' she said, unable to keep her shock to herself. There was something a bit too intimate about them going swimming together. 'But what . . .' Her disturbed gaze ran down the matching suits of leather to the knee high boots. 'Where is Cassie's swimsuit?' she asked, her voice sharper than intended.

Cassie coloured and Rosy's lips tightened and she had fixed Nicky with burning disapproval, before he could say, 'I thought she could borrow one of yours.'

He returned her gaze with one that said, 'So take that look off your face.' And her anger melted and she felt very unchivalrous. 'Yes . . . yes of course,' she stammered embarrassedly. 'I'll show you where they are.'

Nicky opened his mouth to point out he knew where they were, then thought better of it. He could see Cassie had come as a big surprise and he now wished he had said something about her before, and not just turned up with her this way.

'Gordon will be here soon,' he said, as he took Cassie's hand and they followed Rosy to the swimming-pool. 'He's bringing his girlfriend, as well,' he added meaningfully. 'So we'll need to borrow a couple of costumes, if you don't mind.'

Rosy didn't mind. She didn't mind at all. Four of them in the pool was a lot more to her liking, and her expression relaxed and the smile she cast over her shoulder was genuine.

'I think this should fit you all right.' Rosy held up a plain black swimsuit. It had a low back, but a high front that came right up to the neck. She glanced Cassie up and down. They were the same height, but Cassie's figure still had the willowy slenderness of youth, while her own shape, although nothing like the voluptuous Maggie, now had more womanly curves. 'Go and try it on.' She pointed at the two cubicles at the end of the changing-room, making it obvious she was staying there to approve the fit.

Nicky picked up his swimming trunks and took them to the other cubicle. He did not say anything to Rosy, even though he was well aware she was only hanging round because she did not want to leave them in the changing-rooms together.

It didn't take him long and he was soon out again, the black leather and the blue jeans he had been wearing underneath left hanging over the cubicle's door. 'Let's leave her to it,' he said, winding his arm through Rosy's and leading her out of the changing-rooms. He knew she wouldn't mind going, as long as he went with her.

They were standing by the side of the pool, when he said, 'I'm not a little boy any more you know.'

She looked up at him with a tight smile, thinking that must have been one of the understatements of the year. He was several inches taller than her now and, standing there in a very brief pair of red swimming trunks, appeared to be all chest and legs. He was built just like his father and there was not one thing about him she could have put the label 'boyish' to. Nevertheless, she said, 'You're still my little boy. And always will be.' *And the only one I'll ever have*, she thought sadly.

He smiled then, with all the love and affection he felt for her. 'And you'll always be my mum. But I want other things as well now.'

'I know,' she replied, fondly patting his arm. 'You'll just have to give me time to get used to it.'

Before he could reply, Cassie came out of the changing-rooms and Rosy's heart dropped. She had deliberately chosen the high-necked swimsuit, not wanting to give anything too revealing that would show off the girl's figure. But it had not been a wise choice. The swimsuit could have been made for Cassie. It emphasized the length of her legs and displayed her slender curves to perfection. With her long blond hair hanging round her shoulders and her big, innocent blue eyes, she looked good enough for the front cover of any magazine.

You're jealous, she told herself, stunned by the realization. And, as Cassie tactfully walked down to the other end of the pool and did not intrude on them, to try and prove herself wrong, she looked up at Nicky and said, 'You've got yourself a very beautiful girl.'

He lifted his gaze across the pool and fixed it on Cassie, and his smile told Rosy far more than his words, as he said simply, 'I know.' It was a moment before he looked down at her again, and with emotion clear in his voice, said, 'I only hope she has a sister somewhere that Guy might find.'

Rosy hesitated, feeling his emotion transferring to herself and clogging her throat. It had been a long time since he had mentioned Guy. She had thought he had finally come to terms with the fact that his brother must be dead. Shaking her head she turned to gaze out of the window and up the bank towards the wood, and did not look at him, as she said, 'You still think he's alive then?'

'Yes,' he replied, with a confidence that frightened her: for if he was ever proved wrong she felt it would destroy him. 'I have these feelings inside me,' he continued. 'I can't explain it. But I'm sure if he was dead I would know it. The feelings would be different.'

She did not reply. She had long ago stopped going over the events of that day and telling him how she was sure she had seen Guy's coat being washed down the river. And that if she had seen his coat it was reasonable to believe he had been in it. He was obviously still clinging to the dream that one day they would find each other again, and she did not want to be the one to squash his hopes.

It was then that the sound of another motor cycle was heard coming into the courtyard. 'That will be Gordon,' Nicky said, unnecessarily.

Rosy glanced round at him. 'You find a swimsuit for his girlfriend,' she said. He gave a nod and she turned and walked away without saying anything else. As she went through the glass door and lifted her hand in acknowledgement to Gordon and the unknown girl across the courtyard, both also clothed in black leather and very closely resembling spacemen, it was not the loss of Guy that was filling her mind. It was her own loss, first of John, and now of Nicky. He had grown into a man and she had no choice but to let him go. But, oh, how she was going to miss him. In reality she had lost John a long time ago and so Nicky was really all she had left. And all she would ever have, she thought sadly, and entered the kitchen just as Nell came in from the other side. Her face was all red and her hair escaping her bun and flying out in all directions as she came bustling through the hall door with Nicky's bedroom curtains in her arms. 'What's going off?' she asked. 'It sounds like Brands Hatch out there.'

Rosy gave her mother a very brief description of events. She did not have time to go into too many details. She knew John would be even angrier with her for not going up to him the minute she got back from her walk. She was also eager to question him on the matter of the new motor cycle. And leaving her mother with several questions on her lips, she hurried out of the kitchen and up the stairs.

She had been right about his anger. As she stepped through the door his furious glare hit her in the face and stopped her in her tracks.

'Well?' he questioned bluntly.

'You might ask "well"!' she countered, pulling herself back together and going towards the bed. He was sitting propped up against the headboard. His arms were folded and his affected leg was stretched out on the bed, but his good one was hanging over the edge, the foot touching the floor. He had been at the window, watching for any sight of her, she told herself in despair. 'What about that motor cycle?' she demanded, thrusting an angry finger in the direction of the courtyard. He opened his mouth, but before he could speak, she went on, 'Don't try and pretend you don't know what I'm talking about. You saw him coming up the drive on it. When you were spying on me!' she added meaningfully, for once too angry to take his health into consideration.

'I was not spying on you. You are my wife and I have every right to know what you are doing.' Lifting his bad leg with his hands he put it over the side of the bed and picked up his walking sticks, as if he was going to stand up. But he remained sitting on the bed, glaring up at her. 'And I wasn't going to pretend anything. If I want to buy my son a motor bike, I damned well will do!'

'Bur he could kill himself on it!' Emotion clogged her throat and she folded her arms tightly about herself and went to the window and gazed out, to keep the sparkle of tears in her eyes hidden from his view. But he could hear them in the tremble of her voice, as she said, 'He could be hurt badly. Even maimed.' It hurt so much to see John reduced to half of what he had been. She could not have borne to see Nicky's life and vitality taken from him, as well.

'Rosy!'

The way he spoke her name brought her head round and her gaze pivoting to his. It had been a long time since she had heard him speak to her with such tenderness and concern.

He held his hand out to her and she willingly slipped her own into it, and he pulled her down to sit by his side. 'Nicky is sensible enough to know what he's doing on the bike.' Cradling her hand in both his own, he gazed into her eyes with a feeling she had thought long gone from him. 'It was better I pay for him to have the best, than let him go getting a second-hand one that might have something wrong with it.'

'But why didn't you tell me?' she asked, bending her head and staring at their clasped hands and thinking, if only it could be like this all the time.

385

He shook his head regretfully. 'I don't really know. I knew you'd be upset.' He wrapped one arm around her shoulders, but still kept his other hand holding onto hers. 'I was frightened,' he finally admitted.

She looked up, meeting his gaze. 'I don't understand?'

'You've been different recently. I thought I was losing you.' He hesitated a moment, before saying. 'I knew getting the bike behind your back would hurt you. And I wanted to hurt you.'

'Oh John!' It felt so good to have his arm around her and be close to him, and she dropped her head onto his shoulder and, without thinking, said, 'You're not losing me. It's just that my biological clock is ticking away.' She turned her head, burying her face against him. 'Oh, I wish we hadn't put off having a child as soon as we got married.' They had agreed to wait a couple of years before beginning a family of their own. At least, she had put a time limit of two years on it. John had not committed himself, saying only that he did not want to share her with anyone else. At the time she had been confident she would change his mind, when he came to realize the joy of having their very own baby. But fate had taken away her chances of doing anything to change his mind.

In an instant she felt his body stiffen. His arm slipped from her shoulders and he dropped her hand and moved away from her.

'John!' she said, unable to understand what she had done to cause his sudden change.

'We don't need children,' he snapped, all the old anger back in his voice. 'We've got Nicky. Or isn't he good enough for you any more?'

'John!' she repeated, reaching out for his hand. But he pulled his hand back and shrugged away from her like a moody child. 'Of course Nicky is good enough for me,' she said, and let her hand drop defeatedly to her lap. But, love Nicky as she did, he had not come from her body. Her natural desire for procreation had never been attended to and had, for the past year, been gnawing away at her insides like a hungry rat. But she did not speak those thoughts. She had already said too much and hurt him by making reference to things that reminded him of his impotence. 'I'm sorry,' she said. 'I didn't mean . . .' her voice trailed away. His back was to her, making it obvious he did not want to hear anything she had to say.

With a heart made heavy with regret, she pushed up from the bed and walked out of the bedroom. She was going down the stairs before she realized he had let her go without demanding to know where she was going, or how long she was going to be.

Nell was busy in the washroom with the curtains, but it was close enough to the kitchen for the questions still on her lips to be heard. Where did Cassie come from? Who were her parents? But Rosy was in no mood to talk about Nicky and she took herself out into the garden and, keeping right away from the swimming-pool, began picking strawberries. Almost an hour later she had two large bowls overflowing and the only fruit left on the plants was green and unripe.

Nell was still busy when Rosy went back into the kitchen. Not wishing to endure another barrage of enquiries, she left the strawberries on the table and went quietly out again and up the stairs.

But when she reached the bedroom she got a shock. 'John!' she called, finding the room empty. She rushed to the bathroom, but he was not there. Nicky's bedroom was empty and so were all the others. 'John! John!' she called, again and again, her panic growing. At the top of the stairs she stopped. He couldn't get down on his own. She was about to turn round. But the bedrooms were all empty. She had checked them all, she assured herself, and leaping back to life raced down the stairs and into the drawing-room.

She had only stepped through the door when she came to an abrupt halt. 'John!' she gasped, her hand leaping to her throat and the blood draining from her face, as her gaze met and locked with his lifeless eyes. He was lying like a limp rag doll, his body hanging drunkenly over the side of an armchair. One arm dangled down to the floor, the other lay uselessly in his lap, and a pinky purple flush gave his face the appearance of a boiled beetroot.

For several seconds she stood there, unable to move, not knowing what to do. Then suddenly she was racing out of the room and screaming for her mother. But she did not go to the washroom. She dived for the telephone in the hall and snatched up the receiver.

'What is it?' Nell cried, as she came running to her daughter's aid.

Rosy did not reply. Her shaking fingers were stumbling over dialling and getting the correct number was taking all her concentration. Somehow she managed it and in only moments Larry Hampson's comforting voice was speaking in her ear.

'It's Rosy Hardaker,' she gabbled, her voice leaving her lips with the speed of an express train. 'You must come quickly. John's dead!'

'Oh my God!' Nell gasped.

CHAPTER TWENTY-ONE

Rosy looked sheepishly at Larry. 'I'm sorry,' she said.

He shook his head with a smile. 'Think nothing of it. At least your mistake was genuine. You weren't someone making things sound worse, just to get me out to give you an aspirin so you didn't have to go and buy one. Besides . . .' he added with feeling, '. . . it was a damned stupid thing to do in his condition.'

Rosy nodded her head and turned her gaze on the inert figure of her husband lying on the bed. Dead, she had thought. Dead drunk! In her panic she had not seen the cocktail cabinet door was open, or that there was an empty glass and bottle lying on the floor by his feet. The bottle had been full of whisky. He had drunk the lot. He was out cold. It had taken Larry, Nicky, Gordon and herself to carry him up the stairs and put him to bed. And it was all her fault, she thought. If only she had kept her mouth shut. She had known it was beyond his capabilities to give her a baby now and she could not understand why she had brought the subject up.

'He'll have a hell of a headache until he's slept it off,' Larry said, drawing her mind away from her guilt. 'And that could take him a day or two.'

She gave a nod as Larry picked up his leather bag. 'Will he be all right?' She could not believe he could have taken that much alcohol without having another stroke.

Larry's shoulders lifted slightly. 'I think he should be. But we'll have to wait and see. I'll come and check on him tomorrow.' Swinging the bag from one hand to the other he led the way out of the room and down the stairs.

After showing him out, Rosy went to the kitchen. Gordon and his girlfriend had gone now. But Cassie was still there. What an introduction to the family, she thought, as she sank down on a chair at the table and let her gaze take in the three anxious faces already seated, watching her expectantly.

'Is he all right?' Nell voiced the question on all their lips.

Rosy gave a shrug. 'We won't know for sure until he's come out of the alcoholic haze. But Larry's happy that he's stable for now.'

'What caused it?' It was Nicky who spoke and the cautious tone of his voice made Rosy frown.

She shook her head. 'He was just fed up.' She could not tell them the truth. It was John she was protecting, not herself. He had forbidden her even to mention his impotency to Larry. To tell anyone would cause him more pain than she had already done.

'But why?' Nicky's hands swept out before him, as if trying to catch the elusive answer. Then he scraped his fingers through his hair. It was when he finally said, 'What made him fed up? What happened? Why today?' that she realized his nervousness was because he thought it could have been him, bringing Cassie home, that had tipped his father over the edge.

'It was between your father and me.' Rosy was quick to put an end to his concern. 'We had an argument,' she added, when they all remained silent, obviously waiting for more. Then she jumped up, bringing the subject to an end. 'You'll have to excuse me now. I should go back to him.'

There was no change and she wondered why she had come back to the bedroom. But as she sat by the bed and watched his sleeping face, she knew that she could not have stayed downstairs a moment longer, and not just because Nicky was asking difficult questions. She felt responsible and she wanted, needed, to be with him, to make sure he kept on breathing.

'I'm sorry, John,' she said, and feeling she had to do something physical to help him reached over and picked up the Alastair Maclean novel her mother had got from the library for him. He liked to hear her reading to him. So she opened the page where the bookmark lay and began to read, even though she did not know if he could hear her or not.

'Charlie wants to go and see *One Hundred and One Dalmatians*,' Maggie said, as she spooned mincemeat into pastry cases, reminding Rosy so much of their mother. 'It's on at the Regal over Christmas.' She glanced up at her, as she sat across the table. 'Why don't you take her? You could do with a break.'

Rosy smiled weakly and shook her head. John would not have approved and she would not leave him. He had not been the same since the day of his drunken binge, but she could not make out if it was the after effects of the alcohol, or the effect of her pointing out his lack as a husband. Whichever it was his frustration had become more intense and on several occasions, where he would have snapped at her with his tongue, he now lashed out with his hand. He had struck her twice, causing bruising to her arms. After that she had learned not to get too close when he was grumpy, or be ready to spring away in a moment.

But this new development in her husband had only made Rosy more aware that she had been the one to bring him to this. And, instead of following Larry's advice to get a break from the constant strain of John, she returned to being constantly by his side – which now meant she never got out at all. He stubbornly refused to be taken out in the wheelchair anymore and spent his days in the bedroom, only allowing her to bring him down to the drawing-room on the evenings he decided he wanted to watch the television. The only time she got a break from him was like now, when he had a sleep after dinner. But she never went further than the kitchen for fear he should wake up and bang on the ceiling for her.

'Oh Rosy!' Maggie chided. 'You're going to be ill.' She fixed her sister pointedly. Her face was pale from lack of fresh air and sunlight and her cheeks were sunken and gaunt. 'You look awful.'

'I haven't been sleeping well these last few nights,' she replied. 'That's all it is.'

Maggie gave a snort of disbelief. Even her sister's voice had lost its power. She never said much nowadays, but when she did there was no life in her voice and it was as if it was an effort to her. 'If he's going to act like a complete invalid, why don't you ask the doctor about fixing a nurse up,' she suggested. 'If you only had somebody two of three days a week it would give you a break.'

'I will not have him looked after by anybody else!' she retorted.

There was more fire in her voice than Maggie had heard in a long time. But her first response was a disgusted grunt. 'You mean he won't have anybody else looking after him!' she said. 'If I was you I'd get a nurse and make him put up with it.'

'I will not! There's no need.'

'*No need!*' Maggie was incredulous. 'Take a look in the mirror and you won't say that. It's ridiculous, Rosy. What are you trying to do . . . wear yourself into an early grave?'

'Don't Maggie.' Rosy's gaze was bleak as the cold grey weather outside. 'I have to do it. You know I have to do it.'

'I know nothing of the sort.' Maggie plonked the empty mincemeat jar down with undue force and grabbed up another full one. But she did know what Rosy was meaning: that she had to be there for John because if she hadn't gone to Bournemouth the stroke

392

would never have happened; and if they had not had an argument about whatever they had an argument about, he would not be acting as damned awkward as he was doing now. Well she had told Rosy right from the start that any theory that she was to blame held no water whatsoever. 'John demands twenty-four hour nursing, I know that,' she said, and screwed the top off the mincemeat jar as if she was wringing someone's neck.

'So I can't leave him,' Rosy put in.

Maggie gave a sigh. 'Even if he really needed it no one person can provide twenty-four hour anything.' She chucked the lid across into the rubbish bucket with so much force it hit the side and bounced out again and fell on the floor, where it got left. 'It isn't humanly possible to do what you are doing for very long. In fact, I would say you'd already been doing it too long. I've been expecting you to collapse on me for several weeks now.' She rested her hands on her hips and fixed Rosy determinedly. 'You've got to ease off and let somebody help you. Or you'll crack up! Then where will John be?'

Rosy dropped her head and toyed with her thumbs. 'But he wouldn't like anyone else looking after him. He'd be . . .' Her voice diminished and she held the unchivalrous comment back.

Maggie had no such sensitivity. 'He'd be what?' she questioned. 'Upset? Annoyed? Or were you going to say awkward? Because . . .' she continued pointedly, as Rosy dropped her head further to conceal the embarrassment running red up her cheeks, '. . . that is what he'd be. You know it! I know it! So let's be honest. He would be bloody awkward! Wouldn't he?' She paused and waited. '*Wouldn't he?*' she repeated, before Rosy finally lifted her head and looked at her.

'Yes,' she replied simply. 'But he *is* ill. I don't think he realizes what he's doing,' she quickly added in his defence.

'Bah!' Maggie uttered with feeling. 'He knows exactly what he's doing . . . running you in circles. And he takes great pleasure from it.' She had been about to add, the only time Rosy got any rest was when he was asleep, but a sudden banging, coming from upstairs, cut her short.

'He's awake,' Rosy said, immediately standing up and lifting her eyes heavenward.

As if she was talking about God, Maggie thought. 'Yes, he's awake,' she repeated drily. 'So you'd better get your running pumps on. If you're not up there in ten seconds he'll have the ceiling down.'

'Oh, Maggie!' Rosy hesitated and turned to her. 'You don't understand,' she said, before hurrying from the room.

Don't I? Maggie thought, as she listened to her sister's urgent footsteps running up the stairs, obeying the command!

'Where's grandma's present?' Charlie demanded, looking excitedly round the drawing-room.

'Grandma is busy getting the dinner ready,' Maggie replied. 'She said you'd got to open the others first. You've got to wait for her's until she can come and watch you open it.'

Grandma's presents were always the best and Charlie showed her disapproval at having to wait for it with a pout. But the next moment she forgot her problems and tore into the blue and red wrapping paper of the largest present under the Christmas tree. When the paper was nicely scattered all over the floor, her mouth dropped open and her big eyes looked about to pop out of her head.

It was several seconds before she turned to her mother. 'Look!' she said in wonder. 'Look what Auntie Rosy's given me!' She held up the large cardboard box with a transparent front, so her mother could see the baby doll, dressed in a white broderie anglaise nightdress and nestled inside a pink-lined crib. 'It's the dolly I wanted. The one I really wanted,' she gasped, her voice bursting with glee. She gazed at the doll for another long, wondrous moment, then took a deep breath and threw herself, and the box, at Rosy. 'Oh Auntie Rosy! It's the bestest doll in the world. I love her. I really do!'

'I'm pleased to hear it,' Rosy smiled fondly, as she cuddled her little niece to her. Tears came to her eyes as she recalled a Christmas long ago, when she herself had woken to find a doll sitting by her bed – a large pot doll wearing a blue romper suit, knitted by her mother. It had been nothing compared to Charlie's lifelike baby, but how she had treasured it.

Rosy's eyes were still watery a few moments later, when Nicky walked in. He was dressed in his boots and leathers and her heart dipped. 'Are you going so early?' she asked. He was spending the day with Cassie and her family. He had asked Rosy if she would mind him not being there for Christmas Day. Of course she had minded, but she had told him she didn't and had given her blessing for him to spend the day with Cassie. But as she saw him standing there, all ready to go, she wished she had asked him to stay at home for Christmas dinner and go to Cassie's later in the afternoon. If Nicky had been there she might even have got John to come downstairs and eat at the table.

She gave a weary sigh. Who was she trying to fool? John would not come out of the bedroom if he'd had an invitation to the Last Supper. Christmas dinner was not going to stir him. She'd only managed to get away from him now because she'd told him she was going to the toilet. When he realized she had been gone too long, he would start banging on the ceiling.

'Look at my dolly,' Charlie put in. She thrust the baby doll, now released from its box, at Nicky.

He smiled down at the little girl, in a way that reminded Rosy of the child he had been. If only they could be back there again, with John whole and happy, she thought, and a lump clogged her throat and she turned away.

'She's all right,' Nicky said, a laugh in his voice that increased Rosy's emotion. She heard the squeak of his leathers and knew he was crouching down to the little girl's size, and large tears rolled silently down her cheeks and the vivid scarlet poinsettia she was staring at on the marble mantelpiece blurred and went from view. She fumbled surreptitiously in the pocket of her jeans for a handkerchief. She did not want to spoil Nicky's day by letting him see her tears. He might think they were because he was going out. They *were* because he was going out, she told herself, but she still didn't want him to see her and change his plans just because she was being emotional.

After several moments of fruitless searching for a handkerchief, Maggie was suddenly by her side. She did not speak, but gazed at her pointedly and thrust a paper serviette into her hand.

Rosy responded with a thin smile and Maggie turned away. 'You've got more presents under the tree,' she pointed out to her daughter. 'Don't you think you should open those, as well!'

Charlie immediately stuck the baby doll back into its crib, which was lying on the floor by the side of the now empty box. Then she raced over to the large Christmas tree standing by the window. 'Have I got one from you, Nicky?' she called excitedly, and dropped to her knees and pulled all the gaily wrapped parcels out from beneath the tree.

'You'll have to find out by reading the labels,' he replied. 'You can read, can't you?' he teased, and the creaking of his leathers indicated to Rosy that he had stood up and was following Charlie across the room to the tree.

As Charlie was insisting she was a very good reader, Rosy dashed the serviette across her wet cheeks and blew her nose as quietly as possible, and silently thanked her sister for drawing attention away from her. She knew Maggie had purposely steered Charlie to the tree on the opposite side of the room, and away from her.

'Be careful! They're not all for you,' Maggie warned, rescuing some of the smaller parcels from her over-excited daughter.

'I want to read them. Let me do it!' Charlie insisted, as Rosy turned round and found the forced smile on her lips suddenly become real at the sight of her niece's little outstretched hands, like a pair of crab's pincers, grabbing for the presents her mother was holding high above her head and out of reach.

'Only if you promise to be gentle,' Maggie insisted. 'You don't know what they are. They might break.'

'I will! I will!' Charlie cried. But it was not until Nicky joined her on the floor and offered to do it with her, that Maggie relented and released the gifts.

'This one is for you.' Charlie thrust a small square parcel, neatly wrapped in glossy red paper, into Nicky's hands. Then she quickly went on to the next, until all the presents had been sorted into piles, and she was free to tear into the biggest pile; which belonged to herself.

Rosy did not begin to open her own presents, but stood watching Nicky. He remained kneeling as he opened the glossy red package and took out the gold watch his father had chosen from a catalogue Maggie had brought back specially from the jewellers. Taking the watch from the box he held it in his hand and stared at it for a long moment. It was obvious from the expression on his face that he knew just how expensive it had been.

It was odd, she thought. John always had to get the best for Nicky, yet he would not come down and eat his meals with him, or try to join in the ordinary things of life with him.

She was fighting the second lump in her throat when Nicky looked up at her, with a long searching look that seemed to reach right inside her and tug at something that was sore and tender. 'Thank you,' he said, and all she could do was nod in response. He smiled knowingly and stood up and came to her. 'Aren't you going to open yours?' he asked, turning her attention to the selection of packages Charlie had put on the coffee table by her side.

Taking a deep breath, she picked up the one with the card signed by him and carefully unwrapped the snowman bedecked paper to reveal a blue box with gold scrolling embossed around the edge. Inside, on a bed of blue satin, lay a gold locket. It was oval in shape and was engraved with a rose which had a tiny diamond at its heart.

'Oh, Nicky!' she gasped. It was the most beautiful present she had ever been given.

'I wanted you to have something special to remember this Christmas,' he said.

For a moment she could only stare at him, not understanding. Then suddenly the penny dropped. 'You mean . . . you and Cassie?'

'Hush! Cassie doesn't know herself yet, so don't let the others know.'

He was getting engaged. Planning to marry. She really was losing him altogether. The lump in her throat threatened to explode and choke her. Her head wagged from side to side. She managed to say, 'I'm so pleased. Be happy.'

Fortunately, at that moment Charlie screeched, 'Look! Nicky's got me a watch. A proper one that goes.' And Nicky turned away, giving his attention to the little girl, and Rosy had time to take hold of herself before she found herself begging him not to leave her. 'Come here,' Nicky said, holding his hand out to Charlie. 'Let's see if it fits.' He sat back on the heels of his boots and pulled her onto his knee. Then he took the

Cinderella watch from her hand and fastened the pink leather strap round her wrist.

He will make a wonderful father, Rosy thought, just as the banging began on the ceiling. 'I think I've been missed,' she said, and with the locket clutched in her hand ran from the room, for once happy to obey the command.

'Come on!' Rosy urged, as she held a spoonful of Christmas pudding to John's lips. 'You've got to eat something.' He had refused to eat and in desperation she was trying to spoon feed him. But his lips remained clamped together and, despite striving to keep her composure, her voice now had an impatient edge to it. He had refused to get out of bed, either to stand with his sticks or be helped into the wheelchair, while she straightened the bed for him. Her suggestion that he should come downstairs and sit at the table with them for dinner, had brought on a reaction she had feared would end in another stroke. Now he was refusing to eat.

With a sigh she returned the spoon to the dish. She stared defeatedly at the tray on her knee: asparagus soup, turkey with all the trimmings, plum pudding and brandy butter. Surely there was one thing there he liked!

She gave another sigh and reminded herself he liked it all. Whatever she had put before him would have received the same reaction.

'Shall I read to you?' she asked, reaching over to place the untouched tray on the bedside table and picking up the new Tom Clancy novel she was reading to him. Listening to her reading was one of the few times she was sure he was getting some pleasure out of something, and was usually greeted favourably.

But he was not in the mood for even that. 'No!' he insisted baldly.

'All right,' she said, and put the book down and

picked the tray up again to take it over to put on top of the chest of drawers by the door, where she usually left it for her mother to come and pick up. But it was Christmas Day and her mother had spent all morning cooking in the kitchen, so she said, 'I'll run downstairs with this. I won't . . .'

Before she had time to finish saying 'I won't be long,' he had caught her a swinging blow to the side of the head. Bright lights flashed past her eyes. The tray fell from her hands and hit the floor as she went crashing into the chair she had previously been sitting on.

She wasn't sure how long she had been on the floor. All she knew was that she suddenly woke up to find her head was making circles round her eyes, which were going in the opposite direction. She clutched her forehead and groaned, at least she thought she groaned. The revolving of her head slowed down so she knew she must have hold of it, but she was not sure if the noise she made actually came out or just rolled around inside.

It was several seconds before her senses returned to normal. Then she felt the pain in her thigh and looked down to see the chair leg she had landed on snapped in two. The sharp end had torn ight through her skirt and into her flesh. Blood was running down her leg from a jagged cut which had large splinters of wood sticking from it like hedgehog spines.

She looked up at her husband, lying in bed glaring at her with no sign of remorse, no attempt at apology. Amongst all the confusion she was feeling, one emotion was coming to the surface strong and powerful: hate. For in that moment, for the very first time, she hated the man she had married.

Using the toppled chair to heave herself upright, she stood up. For a long moment she returned his glare with equal intensity. This morning she had not been able to bear the thought of Nicky leaving her to a life with John, but now the thought was doubly unbearable. Her husband had turned into a monster.

'You would do very well to remember who it is that looks after you . . .' she finally said, her voice stiff with the bitterness that was curling her insides. 'Who feeds you . . . cleans you . . . and tried to make life as pleasant as possible for you.'

He gave a snort and flapped his hand at her.

'You're my wife. It's your duty.'

She shook her head, very slowly, for fear the spinning would come back. 'Oh no. It isn't my duty to sit here day in and day out trying to amuse you and keep you happy, while getting nothing but insults and unkindness in return. I've had enough. It's Christmas Day and I am not going to spend it with someone who does not appreciate my company.' She turned away from him and picked up the broken chair and propped it up against the wall. Then she walked to the door. 'I shan't be coming back up here before teatime,' she said, without turning to look at him. 'If you feel hungry or thirsty I suggest you scrape some of that mess up off the floor. Because I won't be doing it. You can bang on the ceiling all you like. It will be ignored!'

CHAPTER TWENTY-TWO

'He wants a bloody good slap himself!' Maggie fumed, as she watched her mother cleaning Rosy's leg while she lay on the kitchen table. Nell was having to pluck small splinters of wood from the wound with a pair of eyebrow tweezers and had found it very difficult to get at them with Rosy sitting in a chair. 'And I'd be just the one to give it him!' Maggie added, rolling her sleeves up and looking ready for action. She was seething with anger. When Rosy had appeared in the kitchen with her face deathly white and blood running down her leg, she had only just stopped herself racing straight upstairs and knocking hell out of him. It was only knowing that would have upset Rosy more that had held her back.

'You sit yourself down and keep out of it!' Nell warned, flashing her daughter a glare that said very clearly: *or else*! And made Rosy look up in surprise. She was used to hearing Nell bickering at them, but there had been something very forceful about the order.

Maggie recognized it too. 'Keep your hair on,' she said, and flopped moodily onto a chair and folded her arms tightly across her chest, as if needing to keep them under control.

'There, that's all clean.' Nell stood back and studied her work. 'It isn't so bad now. I think a tight plaster will hold it in place without having to go and get it stitched.'

'A plaster will be fine,' Rosy insisted. 'It won't show so I don't care if it does leave a scar.'

'It will show if you wear a swimming costume,' Maggie put in.

Rosy gave a snort. 'I only wear one here. So who's going to see me?' Holidays were not on the agenda, not with John! If it wasn't for the swimming-pool she would never have got the chance to swim.

'Can you walk?' Charlie asked, her big eyes full of concern. She had stood very quietly, watching everything Nell had done.

' 'Course I can,' Rosy assured, running her hand fondly over the top of the bubbly black curls. The action suddenly brought to mind her own father, the little girl's grandfather, who had been the benefactor of the thick black hair. It was strange, she thought, her lips stretching in a thin smile. Maggie had their father's colouring and their mother's rounded figure, while she had inherited their mother's colouring and their father's taller, more willowy build. But Charlie was all Smith. There was still nothing to indicate who her father might have been.

'What's the matter with you?' Maggie asked, eyeing her sister oddly. 'Is it hurting?'

Rosy shook her head. 'No. I was just thinking,' she said, as the pounding began on the bedroom floor. She looked upwards and gave a sigh. He must be psychic, she thought. It was as if he had known Nell had just finished dressing the wound and she was free to go running up to him. Or mad, she added, deciding that was nearer the truth. Because he had to be mad to think she would do anything for him after the way he had just treated her.

The banging continued and she looked bleakly at her mother. 'I'm going out,' she said. 'I'm sorry, but I can't stay here with that going on. And I'm not going up to him again!'

Maggie gave a nod of approval. At last her sister was learning some sense.

'All right,' Nell replied. 'You take yourself off. Leave him to me.' She hesitated. 'But where will you go . . . with that leg?'

'I won't go far. I'll be all right. If it hurts too much I'll turn back.'

'You can't mean you're going walking!' Maggie looked astonished. She had thought Rosy was going somewhere in the car, not on her own two feet. The cut on her thigh had not been as bad as she had first expected, after all the blood had been cleaned away, but it certainly wasn't something she would have prescribed walking for.

'It will be all right,' Rosy insisted. 'A bit of exercise will stop it stiffening up.' She looked apologetic. 'I won't be long. But if you prefer to go over to the cottage until I get back, I won't mind.' Her gaze took in both her mother and sister. She could not stay and listen to John's banging on the ceiling, but she would not expect them to, either.

Maggie was the first to shake her head. 'We'll stay here even if mum wants to go.' She could put up with his banging, but she knew Rosy could not put up with knowing he was on his own. 'He won't bother us,' she assured, and he would soon give up when she appeared at his bedroom door to inform him he had been left alone with her. The prospect was rather pleasing and she was disappointed when Nell also agreed to stay.

Five minutes later Rosy had changed from her torn skirt back into the pair of blue jeans she'd thrown into the laundry basket, pulled on tan knee-high boots, slipped into her sheepskin jacket, and was leaving the house. She had no plans as to where she was going. It was force of habit that turned her towards the bank.

It wasn't a very pleasant day for walking. A grey murk hung over the fields and dulled the sky and the air had a bitter chill that clung to her ears and cheeks and made her eyes and nose run.

As she walked through the wood her leg began to ache and she almost turned around and went back home. But thoughts of John, and his unwarranted

404

treatment of her, spurred her on. Snuggling deeper into the thickness of her jacket she continued through the wood, until the cottage came into view.

She had expected the new occupant to be away for Christmas and was surprised to see a twirl of grey smoke coming from the chimney. She gave a sigh. Nothing was going right for her today. The last thing she needed was to be seen and accused of snooping again, so she carried on walking through the wood at the back of the cottage. It would add another half-mile to her walk, something her aching leg could now have done without. But she was taking no chances of being spied by the cottage's owner and having to explain why she was out alone on Christmas Day.

Unfortunately, she had not gone far before she realized she had made the wrong decision. The ache in her leg turned to a steady throb and when she looked down at her thigh a dark red patch was growing on her jeans.

'Oh no!' she grumbled, as she put her hand to the stain and lifted blood-smeared fingers away. The gash was bleeding more now than it had done in the first place. She couldn't go on like this. She had two choices. She could go back the way she had come, or take the shorter route, which meant round the side of the cottage and down the field. She looked at the rapidly increasing stain on her jeans. It had to be the shorter route!

It was Christmas Day, she reminded herself, as she limped quietly past the cottage, finding security in the thought. If he had not gone to friends or family then he would most likely have someone here with him. He would be too busy to notice anyone walking past.

But as she tried to convince herself, she heard the cottage door opening. Her heart sank.

'Hello!' he called.

She stopped and turned, and hoped her face did not display all the displeasure she was feeling. Her leg was now on fire and felt as if an army of ants was gnawing away at it, and she really did want to get home.

'Are you all right?' he called, coming out of the door and down the path to the gate.

'Yes, thank you,' she returned, then found herself staring at him and not knowing what to say. He was still wearing black jeans, but now with a high roll-necked black sweater. It made his shoulder length hair appear very pale and very soft.

For heaven's sake stop it, she ordered herself. She was annoyed that she could find anything attractive in his appearance and her voice was sharper than intended, as she said, 'I really must be going. I'm in a bit of a hurry.' To emphasize her point she turned away. But her eagerness to be gone from him made her forget her leg and she spun round far too quickly. For a split second it felt as if the muscle was being torn in two. She cried out in pain and grabbed for her thigh and only just managed to stop herself sinking to the floor.

In seconds he was through the gate and by her side. 'You're not all right!' he insisted, in the manner of a father speaking to a naughty child. 'Good grief!' he said, as he frowned down at the bloodstain on her leg.

'I am all right,' she replied. 'I am. I am all right. I really am.' She was repeating herself, without much conviction, but it was all she could say as the events of the day welled up inside her. He was being nice to her and it was a long time since any man, other than Nicky, had been genuinely concerned for her. Suddenly it was all too much and tears rushed to her eyes and it was only the greatest will that held them back.

But though they did not fall, their glitter could not be hidden from him. 'You must come inside and get that cleaned up.' Without waiting for her agreement he wound her arm around his neck and his arm around her waist and supported her while she limped back to the cottage. 'I'll drive you home,' he said, as he steered

406

her carefully through the narrow gate, and she was thankful he seemed to think it was only her leg that was causing her concern.

'Drink that!' He pressed a glass of brandy and hot milk at her.

Rosy hesitated.

'It will help calm you down,' he said.

'I don't need calming down!' she protested, with annoyance born of embarrassment and the certain knowledge that she was lying – and that he knew it as well as she did. Since entering his home she had been made to suffer the indignity of having him administer first aid to her leg. She had drawn the line at letting him remove her jeans for her, which he had tried to do, and only her own quick action of getting them unfastened and getting them off her stopped him forcing her out of them. Now she was sitting in the one fireside chair by his blazing fire, wrapped in a blanket to protect her modesty, while at the other side of the fire her trousers were hung over the back of a chair: he had washed them for her.

'Well, it is Christmas Day and I don't like drinking alone,' he said, shoving the glass at her in a manner that made it clear she either took hold of it or had it spilt down her. She took it.

'I didn't think you would be here,' she said, holding the glass against her bottom lip but not drinking. 'It being Christmas.'

'I was working.' He sat down on the floor by her side and crossed his long legs so his knees provided a resting place for his elbows. He glanced over his shoulder and briefly flapped a hand out behind him.

She turned to the table and typewriter over by the wall, with sheets of paper everywhere: some in neat piles, others seeming to have been tossed where they lay.

'Don't writers get time off for Christmas?' she asked,

and turned back to the fire and gazed into the dancing flames.

'Only for good behaviour,' he joked.

She glanced a frown at him.

'Work to your deadline and you can have all the time off you like,' he explained. 'Miss it and you haven't got time to breathe.'

'And you've missed your deadline?'

He shook his head. 'No . . . not yet. But I haven't got much time to spare.'

'So I shouldn't be holding you up.' Just like the first time she had found the perfect excuse to get up and walk out, yet even as she spoke she felt a sinking in her chest. It was strange and not like her at all, but at that moment she wished for a Christmas fairy to suddenly appear and tell her she did not have to go back home, that she could stay there, for ever.

'You're not holding me up.' He put his drink down and leaned forward and took the brass poker and poked the fire. The flames leaped up the chimney and sent out a shower of sparks that reminded Rosy of the fairy lights on the tree at home.

She glanced around the tiny, cluttered room. There were books everywhere . . . and dirty cups, glasses and plates. 'You haven't got any decorations,' she said, thinking the place definitely did not have a woman's touch. The thought pleased her, even though she told herself it should not.

'Yes I have.' He sounded greatly offended. 'I've got a tree. There it is.' He looked over to the corner and Rosy followed his gaze.

She burst out laughing. 'That's a tree!' In the corner was a yellow plastic bucket with a large pine branch standing in it, obviously taken from one of the trees in the wood. It had several large pine cones hanging from it, not belonging to it and tied on by string, three empty lager cans were poked onto the branches, and at the top was a large bow of aluminium cooking foil.

'Well, it's the best I could do,' he said, laughing with her, then suddenly falling silent. 'You should do that more often. Laugh,' he explained, when she looked puzzled. 'You don't do it enough.'

'I wouldn't have thought you knew me well enough to know that much about me,' she replied. She had let her guard down and was immediately on the defensive. Clutching her glass tightly in both hands, she fixed her gaze on the leaping flames of the fire and hoped he thought the colouring of her cheeks was caused by the heat.

He reached over and hooked his finger beneath her chin and turned her face towards him. 'The eyes are the windows of the soul. They give away all your secrets.' He continued to hold her and stare right into her eyes and she felt the warm glow on her face turning to crimson, and knew she could no longer hide behind the excuse of the fire.

He smiled, as if he really was reading her thoughts. 'But they don't tell me what your name is,' he said. 'Or should I just call you my angel of the buttercups?' One golden eyebrow arched in question.

Her lips tightened knowingly, as she recalled the words he had first spoken to her: his little poem. *Probably brought out at regular intervals*, she thought suspiciously. *With, of course, the odd small alteration to make it fit the occasion.* 'I think it would be best if you called me Rosy . . . the same as everyone else!' she added meaningfully, and took hold of his hand and removed it from her chin.

'Rosy!' he repeated thoughtfully, and picked up his glass and took a long swallow. 'Well, Rosy . . .' he said, '. . . are you going to continue cuddling that drink, or are you going to get it inside you? Where it will do most good!'

She glanced at him, then stared down into the glass. She really should go home, she told herself, and wondered briefly if she was deliberately holding onto the drink, so she could stay there longer. Unconsciously giving a little sigh, she lifted the glass to her lips. The milk left a warm trail down her throat. When it hit her stomach the brandy came to life, turning the warmth to a deeply satisfying glow that reached right to the ends of her fingers and toes. She gave another sigh. 'Did you really make that verse up?' she asked. 'Or was it poached from . . .' she gave a shrug, '. . . Shakespeare, or someone,' she added, and had to laugh. Even she knew it had not been from Shakespeare's pen, but at that moment her mind could not come up with another name.

He laughed with her. 'Shame on you, Rosy. It was my original. Brought on by the inspiration of seeing a beautiful woman.' He took a significant pause, his eyes watching her steadily. 'Does it bother you to know you inspire me?'

She did not reply. She felt heat rushing to her cheeks again and turned her face to the fire and lifted the glass and took several quick swallows.

It was several moments before he spoke. 'Tell me what is so bad that it makes you run from your family on Christmas Day, Rosy?' he finally said.

'I haven't run from them.' She spoke too quickly, then took another long, gulping swallow of her drink. 'I like walking. I often come up here.' The last was said before thought, and even before he pointed out it was four months since he had seen her up there, she knew her mistake.

Draining his glass he put it on the hearth. Then he took hold of her hand and held it between both of his own. 'I think you need a friend, Rosy.'

Her gaze remained riveted to the fire. She could not look at him, dare not look at him. The combined heat of the flames and the brandy was doing strange things to her. She felt she was sinking into a great cocoon of warmth and safety. It was a nice feeling, yet it was also odd because it was alien to her. She had never felt anything like it in her life.

'I really should be going,' she said, making a half-hearted attempt at wriggling her hand free of his. 'They will be wondering where I have got to.'

'So there is someone waiting for you?'

She gave a nod. 'My mum will be worrying.'

'Your *mum*!' he emphasized meaningfully.

'And my sister . . . and my husband,' she quickly added, realizing she should have put John first. She did take her hand from his then, tugging it away with a force that would not be defeated.

'Why will your mum be worrying?'

She grimaced inwardly, seeing he was not going to let her slip go by unnoticed. '*They* . . .' she began pointedly, ' . . . thought I was mad to come out walking with an injured leg.' She considered she had handled that quite nicely and was giving herself a mental pat on the back, when his next words proved her congratulations to be premature.

'I thought you had fallen and cut your leg in the wood,' he said, concern crinkling his eyes.

Out of the frying-pan into the fire, she thought.

'So how did you damage your leg?' He would not let the matter drop.

'I fell over a chair. Its leg broke and stabbed into my leg.' Her voice was short and stiff, and she instantly regretted it. It was a half-truth, but she knew her manner would make him see it as all lie.

'But how . . .'

'I was acting the goat and fell over,' she retorted hotly, not giving him time to finish speaking. '*If* it is any of your business!' She put her half-finished drink down on the hearth by the side of his empty glass, clutched the blanket tightly to her and jumped out of the chair. She reached out and put her hand against her still damp trousers. 'There really wasn't any need for you to get them this wet,' she said irritably.

'Yes there was,' he replied confidently, and uncoiled his long legs and stretched his body up to stand right in front of her. 'I was lonely and you were lonely, and I wanted you to stay with me.' Bringing his head down he laid a gentle kiss, first at once corner of her mouth, then the other, then fully on the lips.

In all of Rosy's body only her eyes moved, widening in shock as they stared into his, so close and carefully watching her reaction. But her shock was not because he was kissing her, it was because she was letting him.

Coming to her senses she pressed her hands to his chest and pushed him away. 'Stop it,' she demanded, before all her determination dissolved and humiliation took its place. But her need to stop him had made her careless and she had forgotten the blanket. In lifting her hands she had let it fall. Now she was standing before him in a cream blouse that, thankfully, reached down to her thighs, but left her long, slender legs bare.

For a moment she just stood there, glaring angrily into his amused smile, which seemed to be increasing by the moment. Then she gave a groan, swung despairing hands in the air, and grabbed her trousers off the back of the chair. Wet or dry, with him watching or not, she was putting them on.

The first leg went in without any trouble, the second was the injured one. As she bent and lifted it the pain tore through her thigh and with a gasp she grabbed for the first thing available – him!

'Sorry . . . I didn't mean . . .' she mumbled, trying to push him away again and regain her balance.

He held onto her, looking down into her troubled face. 'You can't walk back with that.' His voice echoed the concern of his expression.

'I'm not stopping here!' she insisted, shocked by the suggestion she read into his statement.

But he only laughed. 'I would not ask you to,' he assured, making her feel all of ten years old and very stupid. 'I said I would drive you home . . . and I will!'

'Oh!' She gave him a crooked grimace. Then suddenly remembered her trousers were lying round her ankle and made another attempt at getting them on. This time she put the foot of her injured leg into them while they were still on the floor, with the intention of then bending down to pull them up without having to bend that leg.

He beat her to it, taking hold of the trousers and pulling them up to her waist before she had a chance to stop him. Then he brushed her hands away and fastened the button and pulled the zip up with a slowness that sent a shiver running through her.

No! No! No! she repeated inwardly, steeling her body against the feelings that were running rife through it. *You are a married woman*, she reminded herself, but as she looked up into eyes that seemed to be filled with a magic light that twinkled right back at her, she wished she was not. She wished she was free to stay there with him; to give him a proper Christmas tree and tidy his cluttered room; to return the kiss he had given her . . . and so much more!

Snapping herself back to reality she hurriedly limped across the room and pulled on her boots before he could do it for her, and picked up her sheepskin jacket. 'I really should be getting back,' she said. She glanced at the window. The light was fading fast and it would soon be dark. 'Mum will be sending Maggie out to search for me,' she added, as she slipped the jacket on.

'Maggie?' he questioned once more.

'My sister,' she replied, knowing that was not the reply he had been seeking. After their previous conversation his common sense would tell him who Maggie was. The enquiry had been aimed at why it would be her sister and not her husband. But she felt it safest not to let him know too much concerning John.

As she put the jacket on he watched her intently. Then he went to the stairfoot door and took down a similar sheepskin jacket to her own and put it on. He was usually good at weighing people up, it was all part of his art of creating his characters. But for some reason she was even better at closing herself up. She let you get so far, but no further. If she thought you were over-stepping the mark and getting too nosy a barrier came up with a very distinctive 'Keep Off!' sign nailed to it.

'I can walk,' she protested, feeling embarrassed at causing him trouble, but even more concerned for the reaction if she was brought home by him. If John was at the window . . . !

'You cannot!' he stressed meaningfully, and refusing to take no for an answer took her arm and lead her out of the door and round to the pick-up truck.

It was even dirtier than previously and Rosy's heart fell, and so did her face.

'There's room for two,' he said, and grinning mis-chieviously, added, 'Unless you have an aversion to being picked up by lorry drivers.' Then without waiting for her reply he opened the door and lifted her bodily into the cab.

'I have an aversion to being picked up by anyone without forewarning.' She flashed him a glare as he closed the door for her.

'I'll remember that next time,' he replied, and hurried round to the driver's side.

They had driven down the bumpy field and were out on the lane, when something suddenly occurred to Rosy. She looked round at him. 'You didn't tell me your name,' she said.

'Tom,' he replied simply. 'You didn't ask.'

Tom, she thought approvingly. It suited him. 'Didn't you say your uncle was Tom?' She recalled him telling her the previous owner had been Tom Bridges.

'I was named after him – the recluse of the family,' he added drily.

She laughed, then suddenly stopped. 'You're not Tom Bridges the thriller writer!' she gasped.

'You've heard of me.'

414

'I've read nearly all your books,' she said excitedly.

He looked impressed. 'For a woman that's going some. They're aimed mainly at the male market.'

'Oh my husband . . .' she began, then brought herself up short. She had almost told him she had only read them because she had to read them to John. 'My husband reads them, as well,' she amended, then fell silent. Thinking of John had brought on a surge of guilt. She had been happy that afternoon, only briefly, but she had been happier than she had been in a long time and, despite everything, that seemed very unfair to John. It was only the frustration of his condition that had made him hit her, she told herself, feeling very guilty for leaving him alone.

'Actually it's Tom Smith.'

She had been miles away and a frown creased her brow. 'What?' she said, uncertainly.

'My name,' he explained, laughing at her. 'My real name is Tom Smith. Bridges is my mother's maiden name. It sounds better than Smith.'

Rosy laughed then. Tom Smith. 'My dad would not have approved,' she said, and explained how she had once been Rosetta Smith.

They were still laughing at the coincidence, when the truck reached the grand front door of Derwent House.

Tom turned to her. 'Well, Rosy, thank you for making my Christmas Day special.'

'Thank you for the drink,' she replied. She had wanted to say more, to repeat the compliment, yet held back, telling herself it would not be right. Then with the sudden need to get this over and done with, she opened the door and let herself carefully over the high step and down to the ground without saying anything more.

As she limped round the front of the truck he pulled the window down and stuck his head out. 'Will you come and visit me again?' he asked.

She hesitated. She should say no, she told herself, yet found her head nodding and agreement slipping from her lips. 'Well, perhaps sometime,' she quickly added, and knowing the front door would be locked, turned and hurried stiffly along the drive to the courtyard.

The truck also had to come to the entrance in order to turn round, but she kept her head down. Not until she was at the back door did she look up, just in time to catch the rear lights and the tailgate vanishing round the corner of the wall.

He was gone, she thought, and felt relief, and at the same time a dull sinking deep inside her chest.

CHAPTER TWENTY-THREE

The warmth of the large fire wrapped round Rosy as she stepped into the kitchen. She stopped and looked around. The table was laid ready for tea but there was no sign of anyone. *Oh dear!* she thought, hoping they were not upstairs, having to attend to an irate John.

Slipping out of her jacket she hurried across the room, an excess of guilt filling her with the need to see if he was all right for herself. But she got no further than the kitchen door. Then she careered into Maggie coming in the opposite direction.

'What's wrong?' Rosy gasped. 'Is it John?'

Maggie took hold of her arms and pushed her back into the kitchen. 'Nothing's wrong,' she said. 'He went bananas on the ceiling for half an hour. Then mum went up and told him you'd gone out and he needn't expect her to run round after him like a scalded cat. We haven't heard a peep out of him since.'

'So where's mum now?' Rosy asked.

'In the drawing-room. She was supposed to be having a five minute sit down before getting tea and she fell asleep. So I've done it.' She pulled a chair out and pushed Rosy onto it. 'Now . . .' she said, a grin washing over her face like the tide up a sandy beach, '. . . tell me why *he* brought you home?' She had seen him often enough in the pub to know who he was.

Rosy looked confused, then annoyed. 'Where were you?' she demanded, the irritation in her voice sharpened by the addition of embarrassment at being caught out.

Maggie grinned. 'Nosebagging,' she asserted, without any sign of remorse. 'Charlie's playing in the conservatory but I'd just popped in to see mum was all right. Just at the right time!' she added meaningfully. 'Did you really expect me not to look when I heard a strange engine coming up the drive?'

Rosy glowered at her. 'When you saw it was me you could have come away,' she said, knowing she was asking the impossible.

'Anyway . . . why *did* he bring you home?' Maggie repeated, taking no notice of her sister's mood. 'What were you doing up at his cottage?' Maggie looked very interested. She had seen the way they had been looking at each other and she had the feeling her sister's life might be taking a turn for the better. But, knowing Rosy, she would need that bit of a shove, or she would give in to that little voice that told her she was being naughty.

For a moment Rosy considered lying and saying she hadn't been up there. But explaining why he should stop somewhere on the road and give her a lift would have led to greater difficulties. So she plunged in with the truth. 'My leg was playing up. It started bleeding again and he saw me limping past his place. He invited me in, saw to my leg, we had a drink.'

'And . . . ?'

Rosy's eyes rolled in despair. *Don't judge everybody by yourself*, she thought, recalling the use her sister had made of the cottage. 'And he gave me a lift home to save me walking on my leg!' she stressed pointedly.

Maggie gave an inward sigh. Rosy definitely needed a shove, and not just a little one. 'Why didn't you invite him in?' She shook her head in the manner their mother would have done, and began slicing up a chocolate yule log for tea as if what she was saying was worth only half her attention; again in the same way their mother would have done; though it was not a subject their mother would have chosen. 'He must be lonely up there all on his own,' she added, almost as if speaking to herself. 'I bet he didn't even have a proper dinner.'

418

Rosy had had the very same thoughts herself, but had pushed them out of reach. She had been so determined he should not find out about John that she had not stopped to consider him. But he was lonely, he had told her so, and it was only her own stupid pride that had not wanted him to know what kind of life she led, and how lonely she really was.

She gave an inward snort of derision. He had already known that, she told herself. He had called them both lonely people. He had seen right through her.

Fortunately John chose that moment to begin the persistent hammering on the bedroom floor again.

'Someone else heard the truck,' Maggie said drily, and lifted her eyes to the ceiling.

Rosy immediately stood up, but for once was not acting only out of duty. On this occasion her eagerness was a need to do anything to take her mind off Tom Bridges . . . Smith, or whatever he was called.

Unfortunately, being summoned by John in his present mood did more to turn her mind to the man than take it off him.

The moment she walked into the bedroom she knew he was in no better mood than when she had walked out, and that he had seen her being brought home.

'Who was that?' he demanded angrily, before she had got right into the room.

'You managed to find the strength to get out of bed then?' she replied pointedly. He was back in bed now but if he had seen her he had been standing at the window.

'Who was it?' he repeated.

'A friend of Nicky's. He saw me limping down the lane and stopped to give me a lift.' She felt a lie was safer than the truth.

'Why did you go out anywhere if your leg was hurting?' he demanded.

She gave an inward sigh. *Because I wanted to get away from the person who hurt it*, she thought. 'I wanted some

fresh air. It wasn't hurting that much when I went out.'
She kept her voice calm and steady, even though she
had the feeling she would have gained much relief from
yelling at him.

'Anyway . . . what did you want?' she asked, ignoring
the furious scowl.

'Tea! I'm hungry.'

Well whose fault is that? she thought, looking down
at the carpet where the tray and dinner had been
dropped. It was gone now and she realized guiltily her
mother must have cleaned it up. 'Maggie's got it all
ready,' she said. 'I'll go and fetch it.'

'No!' he insisted. 'Shout down for it. You stay here!'

She glared at him steadily for a long moment. 'No!'
she replied, with the same determination. 'I will go
down and get it!' And she turned and walked out before
his surprise had cleared enough for him to speak.

As she limped down the stairs fast as her leg would
allow, she reminded herself that it was Christmas Day,
and she could only feel sorry for him. He would be
remembering all the Christmases when he had been fit
and well and able to enjoy himself, she told herself.
Her guilt was still too potent to let herself think it was
all his own fault – he could still have enjoyed Christmas
if only he let himself. It was his choice to stay locked
away in his bedroom, rather than join in with everybody
else.

But by the time she had reached the kitchen the
impatient beat of the walking stick on the bedroom
floor had begun again. Any compassion she had been
feeling suddenly left her and all she could think was
how rude she had been to Tom Bridges, by not
returning his hospitality and inviting him in.

For five days Rosy deliberated about taking another
walk up the bank and through the woods. Deep inside
she wanted to go. But she had always believed in her
marriage vows: for better for worse, in sickness and in

health, and she knew visiting Tom would put those vows in peril. She couldn't explain how she knew. There was just something about him, about the way he looked at her, the way he seemed to understand her. When she thought about him in that way she had to quickly remind herself it wasn't John's fault he was ill. It could just as easily have been herself. She could have had an accident that left her infirm and she was sure under those circumstances John would have looked after her.

On the sixth day, New Year's Eve, Maggie provided the catalyst needed to make Rosy's mind up.

In the morning Maggie had gone round to the village. 'I've just seen your friend,' she announced, as she came through the door to find Rosy sitting alone in the kitchen. She might have returned to feeling sorry for John and making excuses for his behaviour, but she had not returned to spending her entire day in the bedroom with him. She now came downstairs more regularly and stayed down longer, as well.

'My friend?' Rosy looked round with a frown.

'Yes,' Maggie said, and dumped a bag of Christmas decorations on the table.

Rosy's frown increased. 'What are those for?' she asked.

'Next year.' Maggie looked like the cat that got the cream. 'The Co-op was selling them off half-price. So I had the lot!'

'Oh Maggie!' Rosy had to laugh. Maggie, like their mother, always had an eye for a bargain. She did not point out they had boxes and boxes of decorations from years gone by; too many to use all at the same time.

'That was where I bumped into Tom,' Maggie continued, taking a box of shiny balls out and inspecting them one by one.

'Tom!' Rosy repeated, feeling her stomach lurch. Oh dear, she thought, wondering just what Maggie had been saying to him.

'He was stocking up,' Maggie continued, oblivious to Rosy's distress. 'And you should have seen what with. *Tins!* Nothing but bloody tins! I told him to come down here and get himself a proper meal every now and then.'

'What did he say?' Rosy's heart began to race and she felt a weight was pressing on her chest.

'He said he thought he should wait until the invitation came from you.'

'Oh.' Rosy put her hand across her mouth, and hoped it covered enough of her cheeks to hide the warmth that had come to them. But at least the weight lifted from her chest and she could breathe again.

'So you'd better go and invite him!' Maggie stressed pointedly.

Rosy dropped her hand and for a long moment stared thoughtfully at her sister. 'I'll think about it,' she said, dismissing the subject. She could imagine her mother's reaction if she brought him to the house.

But despite contemplating Nell's disgust, Rosy did think about Tom. Over the following hours she fed John and fed herself; played two games of snap with Charlie; put fresh sheets on John's bed and changed him into clean pyjamas and then sat and read to him. But whatever she was doing, Tom and considering what his life must be like, alone in that poky little cottage, was not far from her thoughts. If he was not cooking for himself he was not eating properly. And he was working all the time.

Every so often she stopped and told herself Tom Bridges was no concern of hers – then immediately returned to worrying about his well-being.

She read the last line of Tom Clancy, closed the book, and looked up to find John had fallen asleep. Despite the low snoring sounds he was making she had been so inattentive she had not noticed. She didn't even know what she had been reading, herself. She had been speaking the words automatically and their meaning had not reached her brain.

'John,' she said, in little more than a whisper. She repeated it several times, each one a bit louder.

The gentle snoring continued and there was no response from him. Rosy put the book down on the table and stood up and pulled the blankets up around his neck. then she gazed down at him. He was her husband. Fate had been unkind to him and she felt pity for him. But, unless compassion was love, she felt no love for him. No matter how hard she tried, how deep she delved, she could not find any emotion for him that she would have named love. He, with his 'awkwardness', had killed all that long before now.

Reaching out she placed a hand against his shoulder. She did not understand why she did it. If it had been an unconscious gesture to wake him up so he would stop her doing what was in her mind, it did not work. He remained fast asleep.

'I'm sorry, John,' she whispered, then turned and hurried from the room.

In the kitchen Charlie was sitting at the table, struggling to push a needle in and out of an embroidery card: one of a set found in her Christmas stocking. Maggie was sitting in front of the fire, puffing on a cigarette and reading a magazine.

Unfortunately, Nell was at the other end of the table, kneading dough.

'Look . . . I've nearly done this,' Charlie announced excitedly, and held the card up for Rosy to inspect a green pig with purple spots.

'That's very good,' she said admiringly, taking the time to consider her best plan of action. 'What are you going to do next?'

'I don't know. I haven't decided.' Charlie put the pig down and began rifling through the cards in the box to find one suitable.

Rosy watched her intently, and tried to work out how

she was going to get the meat and potato pie out of the pantry without her mother seeing her. Of course, if she took it Nell would find out later. But that didn't worry her. She just didn't want her mother finding out first, and stopping her by making her feel she was committing a cardinal sin.

Fortunately, the empty glass and plate standing by Charlie provided the answer. 'I fancy a biscuit,' she suddenly said. 'Do you want one?'

'Yes, please!' Charlie replied eagerly.

'She's just had two,' Nell put in.

'Then one more won't hurt her.' Not waiting to see if her mother had anything else to say, Rosy vanished into the pantry. She took a plastic carrier bag from the corner of the shelf where her mother kept a supply neatly folded, and slipped the pie into it. Then she left it on the shelf while she took the biscuit tin back to Charlie. Charlie took one and so did Rosy. She was popping it into her mouth as she returned to the pantry. Then she picked up the pie and held it carefully concealed in front of her as she sidestepped her mother to get into the washroom, where the coats were kept. Once in the washroom she was home and dry. She slipped on her sheepskin jacket, hid the pie inside it and held it safe with one arm, leaving the other arm free to open the door with. 'I'm going for a walk,' she said, as she appeared again in the kitchen.

'Will you be long?' Nell asked.

'I don't know. I'll see how I feel,' she replied, not stopping as she opened the back door and slipped quickly out.

The day was even greyer than Christmas Day had been and though it was only just past three o'clock, ominous clouds were gathering and the light was beginning to fade. Speed was the priority, Rosy realized, and did not go up the bank and through the wood but took the shortest route along the lane. She was halfway up the field when the first drops of rain began to fall. By the time she reached the cottage gate the heavens had opened. As she reached the door she knew her appearance could only resemble one thing – a drowned rat!

When the door opened in answer to her frantic knocking, his expression of open-mouthed shock proved her last thought correct.

'Come in. Come in,' he finally invited, his senses returning and leaping out of the way so she could get through the door. He had been so involved in work he had not seen anyone coming up the field and she had been the last person he had expected to find standing there. Not that he hadn't wanted to see her. He had wanted nothing else and had wished it could have been her, instead of her sister, he had bumped into that morning at the shop.

'What's brought you up here on a day like this?'

She stopped just inside the door, embarrassedly aware she was dripping all over his floor. The pie, fortunately, wrapped tightly in the plastic carrier bag had come to no harm. She held it out to him. 'Maggie was worried you weren't feeding yourself properly.' She put the onus for her being there on her sister, and smiled nervously. 'She's better than radar. She can pick up every item in a shopping bag at one glance.'

He broke into a smile then, in response to her own, but also from the fact that she had come up there specially to see him. He had imagined she had got caught by the storm while walking and been forced, against her better judgement, to throw herself on his mercy. 'Thank you,' he said, taking the plastic bag and peering inside.

'It's cooked. It will only need warming up.'

'Thank you,' he repeated, then suddenly remembered his manners. 'Don't stand there.' He chided himself for his lack of thought, but he had been stunned to find her there. Pleased, but stunned. 'Get your coat off and come round to the fire.' He flapped a hand towards the small black iron fireplace. 'I'll get a towel for your hair,' he added, and vanished through the door that led to the cottage's tiny kitchen.

Rosy looked down at her sheepskin jacket, the woolly collar and cuffs were so wet they could have been wrung out and she was standing in a puddle of her own making. She thought perhaps it would be best if she just turned round and went home again. She'd given him the pie, there was no need to hang around.

But he came out of the kitchen then, a towel in his hands. 'Come on!' he urged. 'Give me your coat and use this.'

She hesitated uncertainly. 'I can't stay long and it seems silly to leave you with a mess for just a few minutes. Besides . . .' she glanced across at the typewriter with a half-finished sheet of paper sticking out of the top, '. . . you were working. I'm disturbing you.'

'I'm almost finished. Another page should do it and I can rattle that off after you've gone.' He began unfastening the buttons of the sheepskin jacket for her. He was determined not to let her get away so easily.

She stared down at his hands as they worked and he had undone the second button before she came to life. She flapped his hands away. 'I can do that,' she insisted, and forgetting she was not supposed to be staying, unfastened the other buttons for herself. Then she slipped out of the jacket before he had time to come and take it off her; which he looked about to do.

Taking the coat he handed her the towel. Then he gave her a shove in the direction of the fire, before vanishing into the kitchen again.

As well as the one fireside chair there was a small settee beneath the window. But Rosy ignored both and sat down on the rug in front of the hearth, so the fire would help dry her dripping hair while she rubbed at it. When it was reasonably dry she turned to the legs of her jeans, which were also saturated, and gave them a rub with the towel. She was still rubbing at them when Tom came back, carrying what appeared to be a glass of warm milk in each hand.

'What is the alcoholic content of that?' she questioned, guessing the milk would be heavily laced with brandy, the same as before.

He grinned knowingly. 'Enough to warm the cockles of your heart.'

He handed one to her and, as he sat down on the floor by her side, she took a careful sip. The milk was hot, but not enough to burn. The burn came from the brandy as it slipped down her throat and hit her stomach. It was far stronger than before. He was trying to get her drunk, she told herself, and suddenly wondered what she was doing there.

But just as she was about to leap up and race away he turned to her, and the look in his eyes stilled her. 'Tell me about yourself?' he asked. He wasn't sure if she was ready to give up all her secrets. But he felt he had a better chance than before, because she had come to him. She had searched him out for some reason, and he didn't believe it was anything to do with pies.

She lifted her glass and took a swallow. Then she gave a shrug. 'There isn't much to tell, really. You know where I live. I am married and my mother, sister and her daughter live with us. Well not exactly with us. They have a cottage close by, but spend a lot of time at the house.'

'No children of your own?'

'A stepson . . . Nicky.'

'Is he still small . . . or is he grown?'

'Nineteen,' she replied, wishing she could have said nine, eight, seven. Anything under sixteen, when she first began to realize he was turning into a man.

For a time he matched her. Then, in a quiet voice, as if he knew it was a subject he should not broach, he said, 'And your husband?'

She took another swallow, holding the warming

427

liquid in her mouth for several seconds, before letting it slide down her throat and feeling the burst of heat spread out inside her like molten gold. She stared into the fire, then glanced at him. He was watching her, waiting expectantly for her reply.

'John is in property,' she began, fencing the real issue. 'He has a small business of his own. Nicky is being primed to take control.' She fell silent again, her description of her husband over and done with in three short sentences.

Again there was a significant pause, before he said, 'And?'

She looked round at him. There was that look in his eyes, of compassion and caring and something else, something that went much deeper and which she could not explain because she had never seen it, never experienced it before. She had only met this man three times, yet he looked at her in a way no-one had ever looked at her before, not even John in the first flush of their relationship.

She dropped her head, stared at the liquid in her glass with a mixture of regret, confusion and guilt: regret that life could not be simple like it used to be; confusion because she didn't really know what she was doing; guilt for the husband she had left behind.

I'm sorry, John, she said inwardly. *But I'm not robbing you of anything because it had gone long before now. I'll still look after you just the same.*

She lifted her head sharply and looked him straight in the eyes, in a manner that said if she did not say what she was going to say now then she would never say it. 'My husband is twenty-five years older than me,' she began, rushing the words out before she changed her mind. 'Six years ago he had a stroke, which left him dependent on sticks or a wheelchair. Four months ago he suffered a . . .' she searched for the right words, not knowing exactly how to explain what had happened to John, '. . . a bout of depression,' she finally completed. It was how Larry had explained away the drinking binge. 'Now he doesn't do much at all. His mind seems to have been affected and he won't do things for himself. He wants me there all the time,' she concluded sadly.

Reaching over he took her drink from out of her hands and placed it, along with his own, down on the hearth. Then he wrapped his arms around her and pulled her to him. 'Oh, Rosy.' For the moment it was all he could say. He had known there was something, some secret which put the sadness in her eyes. He had imagined it to be some bastard of a husband who treated her badly; which hadn't particularly worried him because he considered that would be in his favour. But even in his wildest fantasies he could never have imagined this. He looked down at her bent head and ran his fingers through the damp blond hair. Married to an old man! The thought made him angry.

'I'm sorry.' She suddenly looked up and pushed away from him. 'I shouldn't be pouring my problems out on you. I don't know what you must think of me.' She looked embarrassed, regretting that she had confessed to him. The last thing she wanted was his pity.

Taking her face in both of his hands he brought his down close to it. 'I think you are a very strong, a very brave, and a very beautiful woman,' he said with feeling. 'I also think you are very lonely, and have every right to be.'

She tried to shake her head then. He held it tighter, preventing the movement. But she could still speak. 'I don't have any right to be,' she insisted. 'He's my husband and he's given me a lovely home and every-thing I own.'

It pained him to hear her speak this way, but he knew if he allowed his true feelings and his anger to show through he would lose her. It was obvious that what she was doing now was weighing heavily on her

429

shoulders. 'He's my husband,' she had stated, with enough feeling to tell him everything he didn't want to know: he was her husband, she was his wife; and he would bet any amount she firmly believed in 'Till death us do part'.

'But sometimes we have to take what life offers and . . .'

She did not give him time to finish. '*Not consider the consequences!*' she put in hotly, wrenching her head free of his grasp and turning from him.

Her harsh reaction proved his previous thoughts to be correct and he felt a moment's despair. 'No . . . that was not what I was meaning,' he said, and took hold of her shoulders and forced her to look at him. He peered deep into her troubled eyes and hesitated, choosing his words very carefully. 'Sometimes life doesn't turn out how we expect,' he finally began. 'Sometimes it throws things at us that are hard to take. When that happens we have to find a release, no matter how small. We need something just for ourselves, that gives us a respite from the rest of life.'

'So what you're saying is I should turn my back on John and go off and do my own thing!' she snapped bitterly.

'No!' he replied. 'What I'm saying is you are allowed to take a break from him. You need to take a break from him every now and then, for your own sake. There's nothing wrong in that. So long as what you do does not affect the way you look after him.'

Her head dropped forward onto her chest and she closed her eyes tightly. Hadn't that been what she had been telling herself all the way along the lane and up the field and into the cottage? She would still look after John, still care for him. 'But he's still my husband,' she said bleakly, lifting her head to look into his eyes and wanting to melt into his concern. 'Oh . . . I'm sorry. I shouldn't be doing any of this.' She pushed away from him and jumped to her feet, and wished she could have been more like Maggie. Maggie wouldn't have thought twice about what she wanted to do. She would have just gone out and done it, and to hell with feeling guilty.

But Rosy was not her sister and feelings of wrongness and dishonesty filled her. 'I'm taking you from your work,' she said, her guilt showing through in the uncertainty of her voice. 'And all I'm doing is moaning about my life.' She gave a grim smile.

'I've already told you my work is no longer urgent,' he said. 'And you're not moaning, you need to get things off your chest. Besides, I want to know everything about you.' Picking up their drinks he stood up and pressed her glass into her hand. 'Everything, Rosy. The good and the bad.' Placing a finger beneath her glass he lifted it upward, until it reached her lips. 'If you'd get that down you you'd be able to relax a bit, and tell me it all.' He had the sound of a teacher rebuking a naughty child.

All – she scoffed inwardly, and took a swallow, but a very small one. What 'all'? 'My life consists of washing, feeding, sitting with, and reading to my husband.'

'Ahhh!' he said, dragging the sound out victoriously. 'Now I know why you've read my books.'

She laughed then, her cheeks reddening in embarrassment of being found out. 'I did enjoy them,' she assured.

'I'm glad,' he said meaningfully. 'I shall give you a copy of the next one and you can tell me if it's up to standard.'

'I'm sure it will be.' She took a long swallow of warm milk and paused as the brandy reached her stomach. Then she glanced at the window. It was still raining and with the onset of dusk the light had almost completely gone. 'I should be getting back,' she said, and wondered if her mother had found her pie had been stolen yet.

Tom gave a reluctant nod of acceptance, knowing

he had to allow her the freedom to come and go as she pleased. 'You will come again?' he asked.

She saw the uncertainty in his eyes and smiled tightly. 'Yes,' she said simply. 'But I don't know when.' Her voice clouded. Suddenly she was not sure if she was being fair to him, either.

But the warmth of his smile was quick to assure her. He put his drink aside and took hold of her arms and, bringing his face down to the same level as hers, peered deep into her eyes. 'You're welcome here whenever you can get here,' he said, without any hesitation. 'I'll always be waiting.' Then he pulled her against him, so that the glass in her hand was trapped between their bodies and the contents in peril of spilling, as his lips came down on hers in a kiss that took her breath away.

When finally he released her she was shaking from the force of emotions the embrace had unleashed. She put the drink aside. 'Is my jacket in the kitchen?' she asked, realizing she had better go – and quickly.

CHAPTER TWENTY-FOUR

The following week Charlie went down with the flu
and Maggie, Nell and John quickly followed. Rosy
became nursemaid to all four and was far too busy to
go visiting the cottage. The situation did not entirely
displease her. She had once again been overcome by
guilt after her last visit. Knowing she had gone out
purposely to see Tom filled her with shame and she
was relieved to find she had no time to consider doing
it again, at least for the present. There were still
moments when, no matter what she was doing, he filled
her mind. Some little thing would spark off a memory
and she would find herself recalling his kiss, the way
he looked at her, how it felt to be held in his arms. At
times like that she had the desire to drop everything
and race out of the house and up to the cottage.

'Are you feeling all right?' Rosy studied Nicky's face as
she put his breakfast down on the table in front of him.
He had dark shadows under his eyes and his face
looked grey against his white shirt.

'Yes,' he confirmed half-heartedly, scraping his
fingers through his hair and making it stand on end.
He gave a big yawn. 'I'm just tired. We went over to
Nottingham last night. It was gone three before I got
home.'

'We!' Rosy repeated pointedly. 'You didn't keep
Cassie out till that time? I should imagine her father
had plenty to say about that.' Cassie's father was very
protective, especially when he knew she was out on
what he called 'that motor bike' which he did not
approve of.

Nicky grimaced bleakly. 'You could say.'

'Oh dear!' Rosy looked concerned. 'What has he said now?' In return for allowing Nicky to become engaged to his daughter, Colin Upton had given him several ultimatums: he was not to go above fifty miles an hour when she was on the back of the motor bike; if he and his motor bike ever got involved with the police the engagement was off, and a string of minor things that were too silly to repeat.

'He said it was about time I got myself a car.'

For once Rosy agreed with the man. 'Perhaps he's got a point there,' she said.

Nicky gave a sigh. 'Yes . . . but . . .'

'But what?'

'I was thinking more that it was time we got married and I got her away from him altogether.'

The breath caught in Rosy's throat and she was unable to reply. They were engaged, she reminded herself. She had known they would marry. But not so soon. She had thought she was going to be allowed to keep him a bit longer. 'Don't let him hurry you up before you're ready,' she said, and turned back to the stove, where a second slice of bread was sizzling in the frying-pan for him.

'I won't,' he promised. But she did not believe him.

After Nicky had gone to work Rosy went upstairs to check on everybody. She had moved her mother, Maggie and Charlie into the spare bedrooms, so she had them under her nose and was not having to keep running over to the cottage and back again. She found Charlie and Maggie were much improved and planning on getting up, but Nell was still feeling very poorly and had only drunk the tea on her breakfast tray. John hadn't touched anything on his tray, either. But that was because she had not been there to pander to him and spoon feed him as she had done when he was feeling very ill. He had been on the mend for the last couple of days and was now almost back to normal, and she had too much to do with everybody else to give him too much time.

She had just reached the bottom of the stairs on her way back to the kitchen, when there was a knock at the back door. She thought it must be Ivan, because anyone visiting the house came to the front door and would not have considered going all the way round the back and through the courtyard.

But when she opened the door it was to find Roy Parker, the landlord of The Derwent, standing there with a large bunch of red roses in his hand. Rosy had only seen him from a distance before and she had always thought his short stocky form gave him the appearance of a toby jug. She thought so even more, now she could see his pink cheeks, swollen with a nervous smile.

'Hello,' she said, not knowing what to call him. All she knew of him was what Maggie relayed to her.

'I've been banging on the cottage door,' he said. 'I'm trying to find Maggie. Do you know if she's all right?'

'She's here,' she said, and smiled at the look of relief that came to his face. 'Come in.' She stood back to let him in and as he passed her, she said, 'She's had the flu so I brought her over here to keep my eye on her.'

'I know she's had flu. That's why I was worried when no-one answered.' He turned to her, looking even more nervous and uncertain. 'I hope you don't mind.'

'Of course I don't.' She was about to invite him to sit down, then thought better of it. 'Come through,' she said, and led him into the drawing-room and sat him down in there.

She met Maggie and Charlie coming down the stairs. 'But you'll have to go back to school as soon as you stop snuffling,' Maggie was saying, and Charlie grimaced with disapproval, then gave several loud snuffles, to prove she was still ill.

'You've got a visitor.' Rosy inclined her head in the direction of the drawing-room. 'Mr Parker,' she mouthed silently, lifting her eyebrows in amusement.

'Roy?' Maggie questioned, but didn't wait for an answer. In a moment she was pushing past Rosy and leaving her and Charlie standing there.

'Come on.' Rosy took Charlie by the hand and took her into the kitchen.

'Why can't I go and see Roy?' the little girl asked, frowning puzzledly.

'You can see him when he comes out,' Rosy said, just as Maggie came flying through the door dragging a very pink Roy with her.

'We're getting married,' she announced, her flu seeming to be completely forgotten. 'Roy's just asked me.'

Rosy's mouth dropped open. It seemed marriage was in the air this morning, she thought, being reminded of Nicky earlier on. 'Congratulations!' she said.

'Can I be a bridesmaid?' Charlie put in, as excited by the prospect as her mother. 'Oh please! Please!' she begged.

'Of course you can.' It was Roy who spoke and Rosy felt warmed towards him. There had been affection in his voice for the little girl, who could have been a stumbling block for their relationship.

'Well!' she said. 'I think this calls for a cup of tea.' She laughed at the humble offer, but after John downing the bottle of whisky she had removed every drop of alcohol from the house; including her mother's bottle of cooking sherry, much to her annoyance.

'A cup of tea would be lovely,' Roy agreed. 'We can have something stronger one evening, when you come down to the pub.'

Rosy smiled her thanks, but did not reply. She would not be able to get down to Roy's pub, or any pub, on any evening. Leaving John during the day was one thing, but if she did it in the evening he really would have gone berserk. But now was a happy occasion and not one to go blighting by pointing that out.

When Roy had gone back to the pub, Maggie and Charlie talked of nothing but the wedding. First Charlie wanted a pink bridesmaid dress, followed by yellow. Blue, Maggie said, then asked if Rosy thought she should marry in the church? At which point Charlie asked if the reception was at the pub would she be allowed to go in there.

It was all too much for Rosy. She poured two more cups of tea and took them upstairs to get away from the subject. All she could think was that it would be the first of two weddings. From Nicky's mood over breakfast she was sure it wouldn't be long before he took the plunge. Cassie's father would lead him to it.

Her mother was dozing and Rosy left the cup of tea on the bedside table and did not disturb her. John was still in bed.

'Are you getting up?' she asked, keeping her voice even, so it did not sound as if she was bothered one way or the other. Some days he did, some days he didn't. There was no telling with him.

He decided he would get up and sit in the chair. Rosy had him dressed and was helping him into the wheelchair, when she said, 'We've got some good news. Maggie is getting married.' She didn't expect him to be concerned whether Maggie was getting married or going to the moon. But she had thought the fact that Maggie would be leaving the cottage and no longer working in the house would please him. She had never been able to get to the bottom of his dislike for her sister, but it was still as potent as the day she had insisted Maggie come home with them.

But the expected reaction did not come. The moment he was sitting in the chair he pushed her hands roughly away from him. 'What?' he demanded.

Rosy stood back, too stunned to speak and not able to reply immediately, but not stunned enough to realize his next move might be to hit her. 'Maggie . . .' she finally began, uncertainly, '. . . she is getting married.

437

To Roy Parker. He took over The Derwent when Franny retired.'

For several long moments he did not reply. He sat back in the chair, his fingers tapping out an erratic message on the wheelchair's arms, his face blank and unfathomable. Then, slowly, a bitter smile crept onto his features. 'Does he know about Charlie?' he asked.

Rosy was stunned. It was the first time she had heard him speak Charlie's name. He never spoke about her that much, but when he did she was usually 'that brat', or 'your sister's brat'.

'Of course he knows about her.'

'Does he want her?'

'Of course he does!' She was getting more and more astonished, wondering where his questioning was leading.

'Well, he's not having her!' he said bluntly. Rosy's mouth dropped open but she remained dumb. All she could think was that he had gone completely mad. 'I won't allow it,' he continued. 'Maggie can go to him if she wishes. But Charlie stays here.' He flapped his hand at her, as if dismissing a servant. 'You can go and tell Maggie that.'

'I'll tell Maggie nothing of the sort,' she gasped, finally finding her voice. 'Maggie is Charlie's mother and you have no right to order her about.'

'Oh yes I do,' he returned baldly. 'Charlie will stay here because I say so. And I have every right to say so.' He paused, fixing her with a steady gaze that at first was unreadable, then turned victorious, as he added, 'You see . . . I am Charlie's father!'

For a moment she wanted to laugh. Then something very cold ran over her flesh. She began to shake her head, then stopped herself, not wanting to give him the pleasure of proving her wrong. Without speaking a word to him she turned and walked out of the bedroom. As if in a dream her feet carried her down the stairs. She did not really know where she was going,

438

or why she was going there, until she got to the kitchen and saw Maggie and Charlie both sitting there.

Maggie looked up with a smile that slowly slipped from her face when she saw her sister's expression.

'Charlie,' Rosy said, without taking her eyes off her sister. 'Go and play in the drawing-room. Now!' she insisted, when the little girl hesitated.

'Go on, love,' Maggie urged. 'And stay in there until I fetch you,' she added. She could tell there was something very wrong.

Rosy watched Charlie go through the hall to the drawing-room, before closing the kitchen door behind her. Then she turned back to her sister with a glare as chilling as the ice that frosted the walls and painted the riverbank and fields with white lace. 'Tell me who Charlie's father is?' she said, her voice honed with steel.

Maggie's dark eyes clouded with regret and remorse and she dropped her gaze, unable to look her sister in the eye. It was obvious Rosy had found the truth.

'Come on!' Rosy ground furiously, as her mind filled with the image of her naked sister and a pair of hairy legs at the cottage. Tom's cottage! That they had debased Tom's home fed her rage. 'Come on!' she repeated. 'Spit it out.' She had not known whether to believe John, even though she could not understand what he had to gain by lying about such a thing. But now she knew the truth, from the fear that had come to Maggie's eyes – still she was going to make her say it. She was going to hear the words come from her lips!

Maggie's lip trembled and her head went lower. 'John,' she said, her voice a barely discernible whisper.

Rosy's hand came up and slammed down on the table. '*Say it!*' she screeched.

'John,' Maggie repeated frightenedly. 'John! John! John!' Each time her voice became louder, until on the last it came out loud and clear.

Rosy's gaze condemned Maggie, but she did not speak. There were no words in the English language that could have described what she felt for her, or for the man lying upstairs who was her husband. They had both deceived her. How they had deceived her.

Wheeling away from Maggie she rushed into the washroom, pulled on her boots and snatched up her sheepskin jacket. Then she rushed out of the house, pushing her arms into the jacket sleeves as she ran.

'What's wrong?' Tom gasped, having answered Rosy's frantic knocking to find her red-faced and breathless on the doorstep.

She shook her head. Fired by her fury, she had run all the way along the lane and up the field and the pain in her chest made speech impossible.

'Come inside,' he ordered, taking her arm and almost dragging her through the door. 'What's wrong?' he repeated, as he pushed her across the room and onto the settee by the window. But when she did not reply he did not press her again. Instead he crouched down in front of her and pushed her jacket gently down her arms; in her haste she had not thought to fasten the buttons.

By the time the jacket was lying at the other end of the settee, she could speak again, albeit breathlessly. 'Sorry,' she gasped. 'I didn't know where else to go.' It was a lie. She had not contemplated where she was going; there had just been one goal in her mind, one person she had to get to.

'Oh Tom!' Throwing herself forward she dropped her head onto his shoulder and coiled her arms around his neck. 'I feel such a fool.' All she could think of was the times she had seen Maggie at that very cottage. The time she had peeped through the window and seen Maggie with some man. Had it been John then? She tried to picture the legs, but could not be sure if her memory was serving her right or if she was putting her own husband's legs onto the picture. Then there was the time she had seen Maggie coming through the rain. She had known she was coming to meet a lover and she had met John coming through the woods, and just because he had turned round and walked back home with her she had turned her back on her first instinctive suspicions. 'I've been so stupid! So damned stupid!' She fell silent then and clung to him tightly.

For a time Tom let her. Then he gently uncoiled her arms and pressed her back against the settee. 'Right!' he said, taking command. 'Do you want to tell me all about it now? Or shall I get us a drink first?'

A shaky smile formed on her lips. 'Why are you always so nice to me?' she said. 'You should tell me to go away and stop bothering you.'

'Maybe I like being bothered by you.' He pushed himself up off his knees and shoving her jacket over the end of the settee, sat down beside her. 'Now come on. Tell me all. Have wolves suddenly been discovered in Derbyshire, and were they chasing you?'

She shook her head, but managed a smile at his attempt at humour. 'Not that I know of. Only rats.'

'Oh dear,' he said with feeling. 'I think we should have that drink first.'

He made to get up but she held him back. 'I'd rather have you stay by my side,' she said, and curling a hand round the back of his neck pulled his face to hers and kissed him with a passion that was heightened by her anger.

When finally he was free to pull back, his smile was one of pleasure, and surprise. 'What brought that on?' he asked.

'I want you, Tom Bridges,' she said. She had a lot of catching up to do and she had every intention of starting right there and then. She had wanted Tom on Christmas Day and then again on New Year's Eve. On both occasions she had held back, considering her poor sick husband. Well, no more. 'I want you,' she repeated, and pushing him back into the settee kissed him again. Before he knew what was happening she

441

was straddling his legs and her hand was on the zip of his jeans.

'Hold on!' he insisted, coming to his senses and quickly dragging the zip up again. 'Stop it, Rosy!' he repeated, when she stared down at him in a mixture of anger and dismay.

'What . . . ?' she began, then words failed her. He didn't want her, she told herself, only able to think she had been a fool again.

'Not like this, Rosy,' he said, taking her by the shoulders and holding her away. She looked hurt and felt humiliated. He gave a sad little smile. 'There is nothing I would like better than to make love to you,' he said, his voice as gentle as the hand that brushed a wisp of her hair aside. 'But I'll only make love to you.' His voice hardened, as he added, 'I will not be used by you. I will not have sex with you as a means for you getting back at someone else.'

'That wasn't . . .' she began, but her voice trailed away as she realized the truth of what he was saying. She shook her head. 'I didn't mean . . . I did want you for myself.'

The sadness in her eyes was so stark that Tom almost gathered her into his arms and finished what she had begun. But she was special. He had known it from the very first time he saw her standing in the buttercups, had known then that she would be something very special to him, and he would not let their first time be blighted by anger or hate.

Summoning up all his strength, he sat up and pushed her gently from his lap. 'Now let's talk,' he said, taking her hand and cradling it on his knee.

It took several promptings from him. But finally, clinging to his hand as if her life depended on it, she poured out the whole story about John and Maggie.

When she came to the end and fell silent, Tom released himself from her grip and finally went to get the drink he had offered her when she first arrived. It was his usual, brandy and hot milk, and it took a few minutes for the milk to heat up. While Rosy was waiting for him to return she worried that she should not have told him everything. Whenever she saw him she was either in trouble or full of woes. Then to go and leap on him!

But when he returned with the warm drinks he immediately put an end to her worries. He sat down by her side again and wrapped his arm around her shoulders, and for a time they remained in quiet companionship, sipping their drinks and gazing into the glowing embers of the fire.

'And what hurts most?' he asked, finally breaking the silence. 'Your husband's betrayal? Or your sister's?'

'Maggie's,' she replied without any doubt. 'John and I . . . well . . .' She gave a shrug. 'I don't know. He had the stroke and life has been hard for him. But perhaps the age difference does matter after all.' Her voice trailed away on the last and it was a few moments before she said, 'How could she come back and live with us knowing I had become John's wife, yet she had his baby?' She looked at him bleakly. 'Do you think she had ideas of getting him off me?'

'No I do not,' he replied, with great confidence.

Rosy frowned. 'How can you be so sure?'

'Because Maggie was having an affair with John *before* he married you. But it didn't continue once you had married, did it?'

'No . . . but . . .' Her confusion was increasing.

'Why do you think Maggie went to Bournemouth when she was pregnant and could have done with her family around to help her?'

Rosy shook her head.

'Because she didn't want to spoil things for you by letting you find out about the baby,' he continued knowledgeably. 'Even if she had kept her mouth shut about the father, there's nothing like seeing an unmarried woman walking round in a state of pregnancy to get the tongues wagging. Half of it is usually speculation, but someone could have had an idea and dropped it to you. Maggie did you the favour of making sure that didn't happen.'

Rosy's head dropped forward and she stared at their clasped hands lying in her lap. It was true, she thought. She recalled Maggie's strange behaviour before she had gone away. There had been a sadness about her all the time. She gave a sigh. She had not cared enough to wonder why her usually ebullient sister had suddenly sunk into the doldrums. Maggie must have been hurting so much. John had not only turned his back on her in favour of her sister, he had also told her to get rid of their baby. She thought of Charlie and thanked heavens Maggie had not done it, despite knowing she would get no help from anyone else. 'And it was me who insisted Maggie come home from Bournemouth with us,' she said. Maggie had been as much against the idea as John had been.

'I've done it all wrong,' she suddenly said. As usual, she thought. She looked bleakly into Tom's eyes. 'I have to go home. I have to go now.' Leaping up, she grabbed for her jacket.

As the sheepskin swung over him, Tom grabbed hold of it, stopping her in her tracks. 'What's the hurry?' he asked.

'She might go.' Her voice held fear and she tugged on the coat. 'Maggie might think she has to go and take Charlie away from me.'

'But won't she go to the pub? That's only across the road from the bottom of your drive.'

'I know. But they are planning to get married and she should wait until then. If I don't stop her it will spoil everything.' She recalled the morning's plans for dresses and churches and looked at the clock on the wall. She had been there for almost two hours, plenty of time for Maggie to pack and be gone. 'I've got to stop them. Please, Tom,' she begged. 'Help me!'

444

Her gaze, as it fell on him, was filled with agony and he could see that she really believed she would be ruining her sister's life if she did not stop her. She had not once stopped to consider that her sister could have ruined her life.

But, what the hell! he thought. If she could be charitable, so could he. 'Come on,' he said, leaping to his feet and dragging her out of the cottage and round to his truck without stopping to get his own coat.

The truck sped down the field, the tyres sending clumps of mud and grass flying out behind them. Then it skidded drunkenly out onto the lane, before hurtling down it like something out of a James Bond film. Rosy hoped there were no police cars around to witness the event, but was too anxious to suggest they slowed down. Fortunately, they turned into the drive of Derwent House without passing one car or seeing another person.

Rosy was out of the cab before the truck had stopped moving. 'Maggie!' she called, as she raced across the yard and into the kitchen. She came up short when she saw a pink-faced Maggie sitting in front of the fire, smoking a cigarette. Charlie was at the table, coughing and snuffling over another embroidery card.

'I thought . . .' Rosy began, her voice trailing away as she saw the two suitcases standing side by side, Maggie's and Charlie's coats draped over them. 'You're going?' she said stupidly.

Maggie looked round then. 'Yes,' she said simply, and got up and went to Charlie. 'Pack that away now and put it in your bag. We can go now Auntie Rosy's back.' She glanced at Rosy. 'Mum's still in bed. I only hung on so there was someone to answer, if he began banging.'

'But you're both ill.' Rosy stared bleakly at Maggie's heightened colour. She could not be sure if she was still running a temperature or if it was from sitting in front of the fire. It must be the fire, she told herself.

She hadn't been so bad that morning before Roy's visit, and after it she had been fine. But Charlie was still made-up with cold and in no fit condition to be taken out.

'We'll live,' Maggie replied dismissively.

It was then that Tom appeared in the doorway. 'Everything all right?' he asked, looking from Rosy to Maggie and back again.

'It will be in a minute,' Maggie assured. 'It'll only take us that long to get out.'

'No.' The noise came from Rosy but was more of a cry than a proper sound. 'Don't go like this,' she begged, regaining her full powers of speech. 'Please, Maggie. It can be sorted out.'

Maggie gave a dry snort. 'I doubt it,' she said. Then she lifted her head and faced her sister squarely. 'I suppose I should have told you right at the beginning, let you know what kind of man he was.'

'Who?' Charlie enquired, with the innocence of the young.

Tom stepped forward. 'Now you must be Charlie,' he said, and she looked up at him and gave a nod.

'Well, Charlie,' he continued, 'I have never been to this house before and I would like to look round the gardens. But they are pretty big and I think I might need someone to show me the way. If your mum says it's OK, will you take me and stop me getting lost?'

Charlie immediately took to the stranger. 'Of course I'll take you,' she said importantly, not waiting for Maggie's approval. 'Come on.' Grabbing hold of his hand she dragged him over to the suitcases to get her coat and hat, then out of the door;

'We've got a gardener. His name is Ivan. So we don't have to cut all the grass ourselves,' was the last thing Rosy heard Charlie saying, with great authority, before Tom flashed her a knowing glance as he closed the door behind him.

'Oh Maggie!' she began, but Maggie cut her short.

'I won't apologize for having Charlie,' she said, her chin lifting with defiance. 'She's one of the best things that has ever happened to me. I will say I'm sorry I ever came back here. I was desperate, or I wouldn't have done it. Even then it was only for Charlie.'

'I know,' Rosy said softly. 'Charlie means a lot to me and I don't want to lose her, or you. I know the truth now. I was too blind to see it for myself, but Tom opened my eyes for me.'

Maggie's dark eyebrows arched in surprise. 'Tom?' she questioned sceptically.

Rosy smiled fondly. 'He's good at seeing through things. People, as well,' she added, thankful now that he had stopped her tearing his clothes off him and making a complete fool of herself. 'He explained why you had run away to Bournemouth.' Maggie's eyebrows lifted further; and even further, when Rosy said, 'To leave the field clear for me to marry John.'

'Bloody hell!' Maggie looked disconcerted. 'He must be psychic.'

Rosy shook her head. 'No,' she said. 'But he picked up all the little hints and suggestions that I had missed. Or not bothered to look at,' she added regretfully. 'I'm sorry, Maggie. Because of me you left here, just when you needed us the most. I'll never forget that.'

Maggie had expected Rosy to want her down on her knees and begging for forgiveness. After all, she was the one who should be doing the apologizing. Yet it was Rosy who was standing there and saying she was sorry. Suddenly it was too much for her and she burst into tears.

Rosy's own emotion erupted then and she ran to Maggie and wrapped her arms round her. 'Don't,' she cried. 'It's all right. Everything's all right. You won't leave here until you're going in a big posh frock.'

'I . . . I'm . . . sorry,' Maggie stammered, between sobs, and she wrapped her arms round Rosy and they clung to each other and cried together.

447

'Are you feeling all right now?' Tom stopped at the door and looked down into Rosy's eyes with a mixture of concern and affection. She had insisted he stayed for dinner but now he was about to leave.

She gave a nod. 'Thank you . . . for everything,' she said meaningfully. 'I'm sorry to have taken you from your work again. And for freezing you half to death,' she added embarrassedly. She had been too concerned with her own problems to remember he wasn't wearing any coat when he went into the garden with Charlie. He had come back shivering, although he had tried to deny it.

'I have plenty of time to do my work now,' he assured. 'So you could interrupt me when you didn't have a problem!' On the last he peered into her eyes with a knowing smile.

She gave an embarrassed little shrug. 'Sorry,' she said, knowing she was repeating herself but not knowing what else to say.

He shook his head. 'There is nothing to say sorry for.' He lifted her chin and brought his face down close to hers, and touched his lips gently to hers.

'I'm sorry,' he said, pulling away and looking apologetic, then smiling crookedly when he realized what he had said.

'There is nothing to say sorry for.' She laughed as she mimicked his own words of only moments before.

He did not appear convinced. 'I am in your husband's house and he is upstairs and I should not have done that,' he said.

'Perhaps not. But I didn't stop you.' She did not know why John had decided to reveal Charlie's parentage. He had not gained anything by it, as far as she could see. But she did know she would no longer feel any guilt for anything she did with Tom.

Then, just as if he knew what was going on downstairs, the banging began on the ceiling.

Tom looked up in surprise, Rosy in despair.

'That is John,' she said dryly.

'I had better make myself scarce then.' He reached out and touched her cheek. 'Don't leave it too long before your next visit.'

'I won't,' she promised, as he walked out of the door.

As she stood and watched him get into the truck the noise from the bedroom increased. When he started the engine and drove away the hammering turned frantic.

'He's out of bed and looking through the window,' she said, as she turned to find Maggie standing in the doorway.

'Shall I go up to him?' Maggie asked.

Rosy shook her head. 'He'll be wanting his dinner. He'll be wondering why he's had to wait.' She got the plate of lamb stew from the oven, put it on his tray and picked the tray up. Then she hesitated and turned to Maggie. 'But thanks for offering,' she said, understanding that Maggie had been making known she was willing to take on shared responsibility for him now.

The pounding of the walking stick on the bedroom floor did not stop until she walked into the bedroom, even though from halfway up the stairs she had shouted, 'I'm coming! I'm coming!'

'You'll bring the ceiling down one day,' she said, as she pushed the bedroom door open with her bottom and backed in, the tray in her hands.

'Who was that?' he demanded, slapping the walking stick down hard on the bed.

She gave a silent sigh as she put the tray down on the bedside table. Then she turned to look at her husband; at the hard, uncaring eyes and the bitter mouth; the hair that had turned to pewter grey; the dry, wrinkled skin on his hands and face, prematurely covered in the blemishes of age. And she felt nothing. No affection. No compassion. Nothing!

449

Her voice was very matter-of-fact, as she said, 'A friend of mine.'

'Who?' he demanded, glaring at her fiercely.

'No-one you know. They haven't lived here very long.' Settling herself in the chair, she put the plate on her knee and forked up a piece of lamb. 'Here,' she said, holding the fork close to his mouth.

He looked at her stubbornly, his lips clamped tightly together.

'Don't you want any dinner?' she asked.

'I don't like having to wait for my dinner,' he said petulantly.

'Then you should have come downstairs and asked for it.'

'I can't get downstairs. You know that!'

'You managed it well enough when there was a whisky bottle waiting at the bottom.'

He fell silent, his mouth setting in a mutinous line.

She smiled grimly. 'You can't bear to see anyone else being happy, can you?' It was the only explanation for his earlier outburst. He didn't want Charlie, never had done. So the only thing he had been trying to achieve was spoiling things for Maggie. He did not disagree with her, and she said, 'Did you really think you would stop Maggie marrying?' She shook her head in disbelief. 'You don't want her, or Charlie, anywhere near you. Yet you were willing to hurt me in the hope that it would spoil her chances with Roy, even though it would have meant they both stayed here.' Her lip curled with the contempt she was feeling for him. 'It was spite, nothing but spite. Well, it got you nowhere. Maggie will still marry Roy, and Charlie will go with her.'

'She will not. She belongs to me.'

'And who is going to keep her here?' she said. He was so embroiled in his hate that he had not stopped to think whether his orders were viable. 'Are you suddenly going to get up and walk and stop her going out of the door?'

'I'll see a solicitor! The law will be on my side.'

'And who is going to push you to the solicitor's?' She did not bother to point out that when it came to the law he would have no-one on his side. He knew that well enough for himself, but at the moment he would have argued black was white.

'The telephone . . .' he began.

'But you've just told me you can't get downstairs.'

He did not reply, but he looked cornered and Rosy's heart softened. 'Oh John! Stop being so self-destructive. I can't understand why you do it.' Then she had never been able to understand why he chose to make himself twice the invalid he was. And she had given up trying to fathom it out. She looked down at the plate on her knee. 'Are you going to eat this?' she asked.

'You feed me,' he said.

She hesitated for a moment. Then she forked a piece of lamb up and held it to his lips.

He had cleared the plate before he reached out and took hold of her hand as she put the tray down on the table. 'Don't leave me,' he said, and the plea in his voice prodded at something deep inside her.

'I wouldn't leave you.' It was the truth. She was his wife and it was her duty to stand by him. He couldn't help being ill. Whatever the reasons were for his strange behaviour, it was all down to the illness affecting his mind. He would not have done such silly things if he had still been his old self.

'I didn't mean to hurt you.'

She looked at him steadily and knew, from the pain in his eyes, he was speaking the truth. He looked suddenly a very old man, and frightened.

Proving her correct, he said, 'I was angry that Maggie was going to . . . to be happy.' His chin sank onto his chest and he stared at his legs. 'I haven't made you happy. I did everything for you and yet I haven't been good to you.'

451

She thought of the two jewellery cases, both over-flowing with expensive gifts he had poured on her at the beginning, and she shook her head. 'That isn't true. But you make me unhappy now because you don't make yourself happy.' She sat down on the side of the bed and clutched his hand in both of her own. 'You could come downstairs. You know you could. I could take you for walks again in the wheelchair. Your life isn't over. There is still plenty that you could do.'

But he shook his head. 'My life is over. It's been over for a long time. I'm being punished.'

She laughed at that. 'What is there for you to be punished for?' she asked. 'You're just miserable because you never get out of this house. Anyone else would be the same. We'll go for a walk in the morning.' The last was spoken in a manner that brooked no refusal. She suddenly began to see herself responsible for his present depression. She had given in to him too easily. If he had said he wasn't getting up she had done no more than try to coax him a little, then given up: when she should have been dragging him out of bed and making him do things. If she hadn't been so busy feeling sorry for herself and thinking she had every right to go running up to the cottage in the wood, she might have been more aware of her husband's needs.

Letting go of his hand, she picked up the tray. 'I'll just go and wash these things. Mum's still in bed so I've got to do them,' she added, when he looked about to protest. 'But I'll come straight back to you. We'll start a new book. You be choosing which one,' she instructed, as she walked out.

That is what she should be doing, she told herself, as she hurried down the stairs. Reading books to her husband was a much safer occupation than consort-ing with people who wrote them. She must not go anywhere near the wood, or the cottage, or Tom Bridges.

But even as she told herself she must wipe him from her mind, all she could see was the image of a tall man dressed in black, with long blond hair hanging round his shoulders.

CHAPTER TWENTY-FIVE

For the following week Rosy dragged John out of bed every morning, made him go downstairs to spend the day in the drawing-room, and forced him into the wheelchair after breakfast to take him for a walk along the lane. He grumbled, sulked and moaned every inch of the way, but she was determined not to back down.

And it worked. On the sixth day he pointed out that they were late going for their walk because she had been helping Nell fold a pile of freshly laundered sheets. And on the seventh day, when they got to the bottom of the drive, he told her he wanted a change and to turn the other way along the lane.

It was the way that led to Tom's cottage and Rosy wasn't so sure. But she silently obeyed and turned the wheelchair up the hill.

At the beginning the hill was quite steep and Rosy had to keep stopping for a short rest before she began pushing again. When they reached the top of the slope, where the lane flattened out, she took a longer breather. She was standing gazing down the fields at the river, when John said, 'Who's that?'

'Where?' Rosy asked, turning to see where he was looking and following his gaze in the other direction: up the fields to the wood. In an instant the breath stopped in her lungs. Standing just inside the trees, one hand leaning on the trunk of a sturdy oak and staring right at them, was Tom. He was wearing his sheepskin jacket with the collar turned up against the cold and his hair was stuffed inside it and could not be seen. But even at that distance she was in no doubt that it was him.

'He's following us,' John said.

'Don't be silly,' Her voice was rapid and nervous and she turned quickly away and grabbed the wheelchair handles and set off walking again. 'He's up there and we're down here – how can be he following us?'

'He's come all the way along with us. He's stopped every time we've stopped. I've been watching him.'

'It's just coincidence. He's looking over to the village. He probably hasn't even noticed us.' But as she spoke she glanced up the hill, just as Tom began walking along again.

'There you are,' John said. 'I told you he was following us. Who is he?'

'I don't know,' she said, and was thankful he was sitting in the wheelchair with his back to her and could not see the uncertainty clouding her face. She could not be sure if he recognized Tom and was trying to catch her out in a lie. But she took the chance that he had not, and was grateful Tom's hair was not on view. If it had been hanging round his shoulders John would have immediately known him as the man he had seen bringing her home.

It began to drizzle then and Rosy thought heaven must be on her side. 'We'd better go back,' she said. 'I don't want you getting soaked.' And she quickly turned the wheelchair and hurried back along the lane, grateful that the hill was now sloping downwards, and even more grateful that the rain began to fall heavier and made her haste seem justified.

Seeing Tom for those few minutes unsettled Rosy. When they reached home she sat and read to John and even persuaded him into the kitchen to eat dinner at the table with herself and her mother, instead of having a tray in the drawing-room. But all the time the image of a man standing leaning against a tree was in her mind. At times it was only lingering on the edge of her consciousness, at other times it filled her vision and she was blind to anything else. Then she would return to reality and look at John, and feel an overwhelming guilt.

John ate the mushroom soup Rosy spoonfed to him. Then he took two bites of braised steak and clamped his mouth together. He had caught another cold and was feeling very sorry for himself. He blamed Rosy, for making him go out in the wheelchair. She also blamed herself, thinking she had been wrong to make him begin going out in the cold weather, after he hadn't been out for so long.

'Enough,' he said, his voice as stiff as his lips.

'Don't you even want the egg custard?' she asked. It was his favourite and very rarely refused.

He shook his head. 'Enough!' he repeated, shoving the bowl roughly away when she held it up to tempt him.

Rosy gave an inward sigh. Back to normal, she thought. He had been grumpy and nasty tempered for the last three days. He hadn't hit her yet, but she expected it at any moment and every time he moved she got ready to leap out of the way. And she had begun to think he was turning the corner and helping himself to make the improvement she knew he was capable of! She knew even more he was capable of it after the few days he had really tried, and showed her that he could.

'Come on, John,' she said, as if she was coaxing a child.

'I don't want it!' His arm flew out, his hand flapping at the air in front of her nose. He had not intended to hit her but all the same she ducked and almost dropped the tray.

It had been an automatic reaction, she realized, as she straightened up again and righted the tray. He had got her to the point where her nerves were so on edge she didn't know what she was doing. She gave a weary sigh, knowing that she had to get away from him.

Because she felt so wound up inside she feared if he did hit out at her she might not be able to stop herself hitting back.

Standing up she put the tray quickly down on the bedside table. 'I'll leave it there in case you change your mind,' she said.

'Why?' he demanded. 'Where are you going?'

'I need to go into the village and do some shopping.' She did not sound convincing even to herself. Besides, he knew well enough that she never went shopping, Maggie or her mother did it all.

As if reading her mind, he said, 'Maggie will do it.'

'She can't. It's . . .' she had been about to say personal, but stopped herself, realizing that even her most personal items were now bought for her, '. . . her wedding present. I want to look for something for her wedding present.'

Her gaze softened as she watched him lying there propped against the pillows, his face grey against the white linen. His mouth was still clamped in a mutinous line and his eyes glared hard and cold at her. One half of her saw the broken man who needed sympathy and understanding, the other half wondered why she was even bothering to give him a reason for leaving him lying there.

'If you want anything while I'm out mum will see to it,' she said, even though she thought she was wasting her breath. He would not bang on the floor and ask for anything from anyone. Until he knew she was back in the house he would be as quiet as a mouse. It angered her to think his irritability was reserved just for herself. But at least it meant she could leave the house without having the constant worry he was causing trouble and leading her mother a dance.

But he was to surprise her. 'Go,' he said, flapping his hand dismissively at her. 'If I want anything I'll call for Maggie.'

For a moment she was struck dumb. He always

ordered her to keep Maggie right out of the bedroom. But she was in no mood for argument, so she nodded her head and said, 'All right. Maggie or mum will see to you.'

She had thought that to be the end of it and she was turning away, when he stopped her in her tracks. 'Maggie will see to me very well,' he said nastily. 'She always did. Much better than you!'

Rosy froze. 'I'll pretend you never said that.' The words were forced through her teeth and she did not turn back to look at him.

He gave a sickening laugh. 'Maggie even has something to show for it. Which was more than you could do.'

She was only pleased she had got up and was not standing close to the bed, because she knew, had she been right by his side at that moment, she would have taken hold of him and shaken the life out of him.

'Because I never had anyone I wanted to do it for,' she returned sharply, refusing to allow him to see how much he had hurt her. That was not true, but she just wanted to wound him in return. Her lack of children had been a thorn in her flesh for the last years, made more painful by the realization that she had purposely waited, thinking it would be nice to have the first years to themselves and Nicky, before adding a fourth member to the family. Had she known what was going to happen she would have done her best to conceive on her wedding night.

But he had either forgotten they had decided to wait, or chose not to remember. He made a noise that was halfway between a snort and a laugh. 'Cold fish,' he scoffed. 'There's no hot blood in you. You're not a real woman!' were the last comments she heard, as she swept out of the room slamming the door on his insults.

As she ran down the stairs she recalled his own, particularly brutal form of passion. If that was being hot-blooded then she was glad she was short on it.

Ignoring her mother's startled expression she rushed into the kitchen, leapt into her boots, grabbed her coat and raced out of the house.

But by the time she had walked up the fields and was going through the wood she was wondering if there had been some truth to what he had said. Maybe she was cold and not capable of real love. Maybe John had only been a real man with a normal sexual appetite, which, had she been a real woman, she would have known and understood.

When the cottage came into sight through the leafless branches, she left the track and walked to the edge of the wood. There she stopped, stood and stared. A thin spiral of grey smoke rose from the single chimney into the sharp frosty air, dissecting the wintry sun into two perfect halves.

Tom was there, she thought, and felt apprehension begin to trickle coldly down her spine. All she could think was that he was a real man. He would need a real woman. Her confidence diminished and she turned around, walked back to the track. It was useless, she told herself. If she continued with her journey she would make a fool of herself. There was only one way she could go – back home – to Derwent House – to John.

Her heart so heavy it felt as if it had travelled all the way down the legs of her jeans and into her boots, she retraced her steps. Icy puddles crunched beneath her feet. She did not notice. A blackbird was too busy foraging through the carpet of frozen leaves beneath a denuded oak tree to see her coming. She almost trod on its tail. It gave an angry squawk of protest, but she did not look up. Not until a magpie swooped low over the track, its coarse cry cutting through the air like a blunted knife, did she lift her head.

One for sorrow, she recited to herself. She was thinking it was appropriate to the moment, when the magpie's mate followed. Like a cumbersome wartime

459

bomber, it swooped low over the rotting vegetation surrounding the trees. When it seemed to have run out of steam and be about to crash, it curved sharply upwards with the ease of a wind-tossed kite. Two for joy, she completed, just as she saw him, a dark shape standing in the trees, watching her.

The breath caught in her throat. 'Tom!' she gasped, the sound leaving her lips in little more than a whisper. It was clearly him. In black jeans and with his blond hair hanging loosely over the collar of his sheepskin jacket.

He came towards her, his long legs lifting him effortlessly over the trunk and clawing branches of a fallen chestnut that barred his way.

'Have you been to the cottage?' he asked, stopping right in front of her and smiling down at her.

Her stomach shivered. It felt as if a butterfly had taken wing inside. 'I didn't knock,' she replied honestly, shaking her head and hoping he could not see all the insecurities inside her. 'I . . .' she hesitated. 'I didn't want to disturb you,' she finally said, feebly.

'Rosy!' He took hold of her shoulders, held her at arms length and peered into her eyes with mild rebuke. 'I haven't been out of the place in days. I haven't dared go anywhere for fear you came up and I wasn't there. I was beginning to feel I'd been incarcerated in those stones. It was only the sun that dragged me out today, and all the way I've been worrying that I would miss you. Why?' He gave her a little shake. 'Why haven't you been up before?'

She gave a shrug. 'I didn't think it was wise. I don't think I should visit you again.' It was best said and done with, she told herself, in defence of her bluntness.

'What?' He looked both confused and angry. 'What are you talking about?'

She looked at him steadily, steeling herself against the hurt that was painfully clear in his eyes. 'It would be silly to start something that had nowhere to go.' She sounded far more confident than she was feeling. 'I'm a married woman, you are free to do what you want. You need someone in the same position.' She didn't know why she was saying these things.

His jaw tightened and a new light sparkled in his eyes: a fury she had never seen there before. 'Don't tell me what I need!' he blazed. 'I know what I need, what I want, and what I thought I was getting!' He dropped his hands, took a step backwards and fixed her with a glare that seemed to lacerate her skin and peel away her flesh. 'Now you stand there and tell me if we started something it would have nowhere to go! How the hell can you know that – without trying it first?'

'Because I'm married!' she countered hotly, hands slicing despairingly through the air. 'All we could have is an affair. Something secret, sordid, behind locked doors.' She stepped forward, lifted her hand to push him aside. 'Now, please, it's best if I go.'

He stood his ground, grasped hold of her hand and pulled her towards him. 'Sordid' he repeated, his lips curling in distaste. 'Is that what you think it would be? Sordid?'

'How could it be anything else?' She tugged at her hand but he held it tight.

'No, Rosy,' he said. 'It wouldn't be sordid. It would be like this.' In the next moment she was caught in one of his arms, being pressed to him. His free hand coiled in her hair, pulling her head back and lifting her mouth upwards to meet his kiss.

Her protest was brief. She gave a whimper and pressed her hands against his shoulders, to push him away. But instead of pushing they crept up and round his neck, and she clung to him and gave herself up to the feelings that were coming to life in her body.

'Come back to the cottage with me,' he said, finally freeing her lips and planting tiny kisses first on her cheeks and then on the tip of her nose.

She gave a nod. 'Yes,' she said, knowing, whether it was right or wrong, it was what she wanted.

When they reached the cottage he closed the door behind them and turned the key in the lock.

Rosy smiled, wondering if his intention was to keep others out, or her in.

He returned the smile knowingly, but did not speak. Taking her coat he hung it with his own. Then he gave the banked up fire a poke, until the rich orange flames licked hungrily up the chimney and warmth stretched out into the cosy little room.

'Come here,' he said, as he ledged the poker up in the corner of the fireplace and held out his hand to her.

Rosy went to him, slipping her hand into his, and as he wrapped his arm around her she coiled hers around his neck and welcomed his kiss.

He removed her clothes slowly, taking time to let his lips worship each new piece of her flesh as it was revealed to him. Then, as he had promised when she tried to force herself on him, he made love to her. In a way she had never experienced; in a way not even her wildest dreams could have conjured.

'Everything all right?' Tom rubbed his hand up and down her naked back and looked at her fondly. She was sitting staring into the fire, leaning on one arm, legs curled beneath her. He was stretched out behind her, his shoulders resting against the fireside chair.

She gave a nod and her hair, shimmering like molten gold in the firelight, fell over her shoulder.

'You look like the Little Mermaid,' he said, and dropped his hand and folded his arms across his naked chest. 'What's wrong?' he asked. She looked so serious.

She shook her head, smiling at his concern. 'There is nothing wrong,' she assured. 'It's just . . .' She lifted his hand and pressed it to her cheek. 'I didn't know,' she said. 'John told me I was cold. Not a real woman.'

She gave a sigh. It was all in the past now. She no longer had any doubts about her own abilities. The fault had been John's and all John's. There was nothing, not one tiny comparison between the gentleness she had just experienced with Tom, to the brutal way John had used her. She now knew he had been using her.

'Cold!' Tom laughed gently. He leaned forward and kissed her ear and nuzzled her neck. 'That is not what I would have called you.' She had taken him completely by surprise. Not even in his imagination had he seen her come to life in his hands the way she had done. It was as if she had been programmed specially for him and each time he touched her he set off a chain reaction that led to greater and greater pleasures.

Turning her face towards him he gazed deep into her eyes. 'I love you, my Rosy,' he said, and kissed her thoroughly, and was quite happy that her husband must have been a complete idiot. Because she might have been married, but she had been saving it all for him. What he had released today had never been released before.

A smug smile lifted the corners of his mouth, he was powerless to stop it. But he did have the good grace to bury his face in her hair so she did not notice.

CHAPTER TWENTY-SIX

All through the spring Rosy visited Tom whenever she could and her life changed completely. She went around the house singing and with a smile on her face. John's moods continued to swing up and down like a pendulum, but, even at his most irascible, she was better able to handle him, and instead of biting back at his harsh remarks, took no notice and soothed him over with a few well-chosen words. Maggie married Roy and became landlady of The Derwent, a position she slipped into with the ease of an expert. And Nicky and Cassie began to plan the second wedding of the year at Derwent House.

It had been only a week after Maggie's wedding that Nicky had first put an idea to Rosy. He had met her coming downstairs and asked her to go into the office with him.

'This house is very big for just you and dad,' he had said to her the moment the door was closed behind them.

'It is,' she replied carefully, taken aback by the speed with which he had broached the subject; as if he was afraid if he didn't get it said he might lose his nerve.

'Only I've been thinking.' He hesitated, his gaze dropping to the floor, and she knew she had been right, he was very nervous about what he was trying to say.

'Come on,' she urged gently. 'I won't bite.'

He looked up with a sheepish smile.

'It's me you're talking to,' she said. 'I think you know me well enough for whatever it is you're trying to get out.'

He gave a nod. Then he took a deep breath. 'I want

to arrange a wedding date and I don't want to wait too long.'

She gave a nod of understanding. 'Has Colin been getting at you again?'

'He's always getting at me. I've only got to be five minutes late getting Cassie home and I get a third degree. And . . .' he hesitated uncertainly, '. . . well . . . I was thinking about here and all the rooms you've got and I thought well . . .' His voice trailed away, his expression diminishing from hope to resignation.

Yes! she was shouting inside. *Of course you can come and live here.* It would be the answer to her prayers, he would have what he wanted and she would still have what she wanted. But a sudden thought put an end to her joy. 'Have you spoken to Cassie about this?' she asked. 'She might not want to. She might not like the thought of moving in with your father and me.'

For a moment he looked at her dumbly. Then he suddenly laughed. 'Oh no!' he gasped. 'No! No! I don't mean we would live here. I was thinking Nell could live here.' He looked sheepish again. 'I thought if she moved in here with you and dad, Cassie and I could have the cottage. I'm sorry. I suppose it was a bit cheeky.'

She smiled thinly and nodded her head, hoping her disappointment was not too evident. 'Yes, it was a bit cheeky,' she replied. The cottage was her mother's home. But, now the idea had been sown in her head she could see the possibilities. The first, and not least, that it would mean he was not far away. 'I don't know,' she said honestly. 'Let me think about it. Don't go saying anything to mum, though,' she added in warning. She wanted to work out the right way to go about it before she approached Nell with the suggestion.

After she had been to see Tom and talked the matter through with him, the way she talked most of her problems through with him, her doubts were laid to rest. Tom thought it was an excellent idea, and not because it would provide Nicky with a ready home. He thought it would be far better for Nell to be living with Rosy than being on her own at the cottage.

'She is at the house with us all day,' Rosy pointed out.

'But the night time is the loneliest time,' he said.

Yes, she thought. She knew all about lonely nights. Strangely, she had never before considered her mother might not relish going alone to the cottage every night.

As soon as she got back from Tom's she asked her.

'I'm all right,' Nell said.

But Rosy did not quite believe her. She could tell when her mother was saying what she thought was the right thing, she had a certain stiffness in her voice. And it was there now. 'Look, Mum,' she said, deciding the blunt truth was called for. 'I'm not throwing you out of your home, if you really want to stay there. But . . .' She explained about Nicky and Cassie.

At first Nell looked surprised. But by the time Rosy had stopped speaking she was looking relieved.

'I have been finding the cottage empty just lately,' she admitted. 'I got used to having Maggie and Charlie around.' She looked suddenly concerned. 'But I don't want to go upsetting John.'

'You won't upset him,' Rosy assured, feeling guilty that she had not considered her mother might be missing Maggie and Charlie. Small though it was, the cottage must seem very different with the two of them gone. It seemed she had been so busy worrying about how and when she would next get away to see Tom, that she had been blind to anybody else.

Nell moved into the house the very next day. Nicky and Cassie fetched all her things over for her. Then they emptied the cottage of all the unwanted furniture and began on decorating and refurnishing.

The wedding was arranged for the thirteenth of November, on Cassie's nineteenth birthday. Rosy thought they were very young, but the fact that Nicky would not be going too far away from her far over-shadowed any doubts she had, and her happiness and contentment continued.

It was late May when she was made to realize that dreams did not go on indefinitely.

Larry Hampson leaned back in his leather chair, made a pyramid with his hands and pressed it to his lips, and looked seriously thoughtful. 'You were right, Rosy,' he finally said, watching her carefully. 'You *are* pregnant. Around twelve weeks I should say.'

Rosy was pleased she was sitting down. Had she not been, she was sure she would have fallen to the floor. Her emotions were so violent, swirling round inside her like a vortex – one moment tossing her into a joy so immense she felt she might burst from it – the next moment throwing her into a maelstrom of guilt and regret that was so heavy she thought it would crush her.

She scraped her fingers nervously through her hair and chewed on her bottom lip. 'Oh what a tangled web we weave . . .' she quoted mirthlessly. She looked up at him and gave a grimace of resignation. 'John is impotent.' Realizing what she was saying she fell silent and toyed with her hair again. 'Please don't tell John I've told you that.'

Larry frowned. 'How long has he been that way?'

She gave a shrug. 'Since the stroke.'

'Why on earth didn't he say anything?'

'He's too proud to want people to know.' She gave a laugh that also lacked mirth. 'I think that has been the root cause of all his problems,' she said. 'He feels a failure. You're not trying to tell me you could have done something about it?'

'I don't know,' he answered honestly. 'It could be the stroke had some affect on him in that department. But it's more likely he failed once and lost his confidence. When that happens it's a vicious circle and it

467

takes time to get things right again. That, coupled with the uncertainty of finding he couldn't use his leg properly, probably had a more intense effect on him.' He shook his head in disbelief. It answered a lot of questions. He had never been able to size John up since the stroke. He'd never made the improvement he would have expected from someone of his age. He had often thought it was as if some vital part of him had been switched off, now he knew that was true.

'Well . . . it's all water under the bridge now,' Rosy said.

He did not smile. 'Do you want the baby?' he asked. 'If you want a termination I could . . .'

'*No!*' she replied, very definitely. It had not been planned but now it was there it was staying.

He did smile then, albeit weakly. 'It isn't really any of my business – but will this mean you'll be leaving John?'

She shook her head.

'There are private nursing homes close by. The money would be no problem to you.'

Her head shook again. 'I couldn't do that.' To dump John now would be even more evil than what she had already done.

She did not tell her mother about the baby when she got back to the house. She wanted to tell Tom before anyone else, but she wanted to think things out and make sure she knew what she was doing, before she told even him.

John did not help matters. He had refused to get up that morning and he was in a strange mood throughout dinner, taking each mouthful she offered without resistance.

When he had finished eating, he watched her every movement as she collected the dirty pots and put them back on the tray, then straightened his bed out for him. It was not his usual bitter glare that pierced her, but a careful watching that seemed to be seeing inside her.

It was as if he knew, she thought, and hurried with tidying the bed so she could get out of the room and be free of his gaze.

But before she could turn away he grasped her wrist. 'What's wrong?' he asked.

She was so taken aback that she could not reply.

'Something is wrong,' he insisted, pulling at her arm so it was impossible for her to stand up straight and she almost fell onto the bed. He looked into her eyes with a desperation that tore at her. She had never seen it there before and she did not understand what it was, until he repeated, 'Something is wrong! Tell me what it is?' And the panic in his voice told her what she was seeing was a deep fear.

'There is nothing wrong,' she assured. She tried to keep her voice as gentle as possible, but was well aware the words tumbled out much too fast.

'I won't let you go,' he said.

'Go where?' she questioned, and prised his hand from her wrist and laid his arm down on the bed by his side.

'Where you go when you go out,' he said meaningfully. 'Don't try and lie to me, Rosy. You've been happy these last months.'

For a long moment she could only stand and stare at him. It was as if he had the ability to read her mind. But no, she thought, shaking herself back to reality and turning quickly to pick up the tray. He was only guessing. He had always had a bee in his bonnet about her going out. Even before Tom he was accusing her of having an affair. He had no notion of the baby. She must be more careful to hide her feelings in future, she thought.

'Get some rest,' she said. 'I'll come up and see you later.' She walked out, not waiting to hear if he had anything more to say.

When she reached the kitchen she was confused and angry: confused that he could have sensed the change

469

in her, when he had been totally oblivious to her feelings throughout their marriage; angry that he should choose today to make it known. Now she felt pressured to let Tom know. He was the father and he had a right to be the first person she told. But the baby made no difference to her responsibility to John and she had wanted to be straight in her own mind about what she was going to do before she told Tom. Now she felt she could not leave it and risk finding herself barking it out to John in anger.

'You're not going out this afternoon, are you?' she asked, as she plonked the tray down noisily on the kitchen table by the side of her mother's baking bowl. 'I have to go out and I might be a long time.' She had no notion of how Tom was going to take the news and she didn't want to just drop it on him then have to race away.

Nell stopped working the pastry and shook her head. 'I take it he's in a mood?'

'A bit of one.' Rosy collected the dirty pots from the tray and put them in the washing-up bowl and turned on the tap. 'He should be all right. But I don't want him left on his own.'

'That's OK. I'll be here.' Nell stuck her floury hands back into the dough. She had planned to go shopping, but it could wait until tomorrow.

It was a lovely late spring day. The sun was high and the air was hot. Rosy was wearing a pale pink sleeveless cotton shift over nothing more than bra and pants, but her body still began to feel sticky as she walked along the lane, trying to fathom out what she was going to do. It wasn't until she reached the gate into the field that she realized there was nothing to work out. Circumstances had been taken out of her hands. She was twelve weeks pregnant and at the end of the year she would become a mother. She would have a baby to look after and she would have John to look after.

She paused halfway up the field and turned to gaze

across the valley to the village. She could not turn her back on either the baby or John. But she could not go on like this, either. For the baby's sake she had to make the world believe it was John's. It wouldn't be difficult to do. Only Larry knew John was not capable of fathering a child, and he would not be spreading the news about. But it would mean she had to say goodbye to Tom. She could not risk being seen going up there now.

'Hello there!' Tom's cheery call brought her round to see him standing framed in the cottage doorway.

He looked so pleased to see her, but all she could do was lift her hand and wave. Her mouth had gone dry and she could not even call to him.

'What is it?' he asked, as she came through the gate and up the path. One look at her face told him something was very wrong.

She pushed past him and into the house. When he closed the door and followed she was at the far side of the room, there was no usual welcome kiss for him.

'What is it?' he repeated, his voice as heavy as his heart.

He was wearing black jeans and black T-shirt. Just the way he looked the first time I saw him, she thought, her gaze washing silently over the long, lean length of him. For all her mother's pies she had brought up to him he had not put on one ounce of weight. She looked away from him, trying to erase the memories that were suddenly flooding her head. But it was no good. Wherever she turned, wherever she looked, there was something: the little settee where he had dipped strawberries in champagne and fed them to her on her birthday; the rug where they had made love so many times; the fire whose flames had cast shadows on their naked bodies in the quiet moments after lovemaking.

Suddenly it was all too much. She had to get it over and get away. Turning to him she faced him squarely. 'I can't come here again,' she said bluntly.

'What!' His mouth dropped open and his eyes narrowed in disbelief.

'I won't be coming here again,' she said. 'This is the last time. I'm sorry, Tom. But I can't go on like this. I'm not being fair to John. Neither am I being fair to you.' Her voice dropped on the last, as sadness overcame the confidence she had been forcing into both voice and manner.

'I think you should let me be the judge of that.' His voice hardened, as he tried desperately to think of something he had done to cause this.

She shook her head. 'No. I am married, Tom. I've conveniently forgotten that these last few months. It's about time I got round to remembering it again.'

'You can't call what you have with John a marriage. If it was you wouldn't have had any need of me.' He ran his fingers through his hair and let it fall in disarray around his shoulders. He couldn't believe he was hearing this. Not after all they had been to each other, and with no warning. He had never before known the feelings she was capable of invoking in his body, and he had been sure it had not been just a one way street. 'Has he found out? Has someone told him?'

'No-one has told him anything,' she said. 'But . . .' she gave a little shrug, '. . . he's noticed a change in me and he's asking questions.'

'And did you tell him?'

'Of course not!' she snapped angrily, offended that he thought her stupid enough to do so.

His hands made a despairing motion in the air. 'I don't understand. Rosy . . .' he came towards her, '. . . you can't mean this. You can't really expect me to believe it's all over – with no proper explanation!' There was more anger in his voice than bewilderment, although his expression was all the latter.

'Yes, I do, Tom.' He was right in front of her now and she moved to sidestep away, knowing that if he touched her all her good intentions would fly out the

472

window. 'I have to go now.' The words rushed from her lips in panic, as she saw his hands reaching out to her. 'No!' she begged. 'Please, Tom, don't make this more difficult than it already is.'

'I'll make it as bloody difficult as I want,' he stormed, grabbing her by the arms and pulling her back to him. 'I will not let you walk out of my life without a fight. You try to tell me you're thinking about John. Why should I believe you? He's never come into your mind before when you've been in this cottage.' His anger and fear at losing her had run away with him. He had not intended to say what he had said and he was crushed with remorse, even before her hand came up, her palm cracking against his cheek with the stinging force of a whip. It made him let her go with one hand and lift it to his face.

'Don't you ever speak to me that way again!' she said, matching his fury measure for measure. 'I know what I've been doing without anyone pointing it out to me. Least of all you . . .' she poked an accusing finger hard into his chest, '. . . because you share the blame! Whatever I have done you have done it with me, and that makes you equally guilty.' Before he had a chance to open his mouth she had pushed his hand from her arm and was hurrying to the door. Grabbing for the latch she swung it back and took both steps at the same time.

She was down the path, out of the gate and into the field before he caught her.

'No you don't!' he cried, grabbing her arm to stop her. But as he did his foot slipped on a stone hidden in the grass and he lost his footing. He fell forward, taking her with him and landing on top of her.

For a moment she was too winded to do anything. All she was aware of was flailing arms and legs and a sharp pain in her side. 'No! Please no,' she begged, bringing her hand up to his shoulders and trying to hold his weight off her. 'Don't press on me. Please

473

don't press on me. I'm pregnant! You'll hurt the baby.' Even as she spoke the pain shot through her again and she felt it was too late. Tears welled in her eyes and instead of pushing Tom away her arms went round his neck and she clung to him as if her life depended on it. 'I should have told you,' she sobbed. 'If I had, this wouldn't have happened. Now I've lost it. I've killed it by my stupidity.'

It took him several attempts to prise himself free of her clutches. He had to raise his voice in anger and insist she let him go, before she finally relinquished her hold on him and he could lift himself off her and get to his feet.

Crouching down, he took hold of her hand. 'Does anything hurt?' he asked, and the concern and fear in both his voice and his eyes tore at her worse than the pain in her side.

She nodded her head. 'My side,' she said, fresh tears pouring down her cheeks. Why hadn't she just told him.

He placed his hand gently on her stomach. 'Not here?' he asked.

She shook her head. 'Right side. In my hip.'

'Do you think it is the baby?' His fear increased now. He had imaginations of himself being the shortest lived father in history: hearing about the baby one minute, seeing it die the next.

'I don't know,' she replied bleakly.

'I'm getting the doctor.' Without stopping to hear if she had anything to say he raced into the house. He was back within seconds, with a cushion and a wool rug. 'I don't want to leave you.' His nervousness was evident in his voice as he crouched down again and placed the cushion under her head. 'But I daren't move you and someone's got to get help. Here . . .' he placed the rug gently over her bottom half. 'It's warm but I think you'd best keep that handy . . . just in case you go cold.' He didn't think there was much chance of that, in the present heat, but he was frantic at having to leave her and felt he had to do something. 'Now just hang on,' he said, fleetingly touching her cheek, before he was on his feet and racing for the truck.

As Rosy watched him careering down the field at break-neck speed she was reminded of the other time he had sped down in a similar fashion – she had been with him then, fearing Maggie and Charlie would be gone by the time she got home. He had been fast enough then. Please let him be fast enough again, she begged, closing her eyes as a fresh wave of pain washed through her.

Rosy's prayer was answered. Larry Hampson was just getting out of his car in front of his surgery, when Tom came hurtling to a stop right behind him. Tom's urgency was soon conveyed and he leapt back into his car and when they reached Rosy she had been alone for only seven minutes. But it seemed like days to her.

'Now what have you been doing?' Larry Hampson enquired sternly, and knelt down beside her and felt for the pulse at her wrist. He looked very serious as he gazed down at her from beneath his shock of ginger hair and she felt her fear increase, and expected him to comment that her pulse rate had speeded up just at that moment. 'Tell me exactly what happened?' he said, placing her arm down by her side and peering into her eyes with a concern that was almost fatherly.

Rosy told him she had fallen. Tom gave a blow by blow description that could have come from one of his novels, not one word or move was missed out.

'I see.' Larry Hampson began a gentle prodding and probing of Rosy's body, and recalled her sitting in his surgery and reciting, 'Oh, what a tangled web we weave.' Affairs of the heart, he thought. Over the years he had seen some strange cases, brought on by affairs of the heart. Some sad ones, as well.

He was hoping this was not going to turn out to be

475

one of the latter, when he ran his hand underneath Rosy. 'Is this where it hurts most.'

'Yes,' she said, giving a nod and trying not to look at Tom and let his anxiety rub off on her; she had enough of her own without letting his add to it. 'Am I going to lose the baby?' she asked, the fear in her eyes transmitting to her voice.

Larry gave a noncommittal shrug. 'I want to take a proper look at you before I go making any sweeping statements. Shout if this hurts.' He gently eased her up into a sitting position. 'Did you feel anything?' he asked, holding her at arms length and peering into her face, as if that alone would give him the answer.

She shook her head. 'My hip is sore. But there was nothing drastic.'

Larry gave a thin smile. 'Right.' He looked up at Tom, hovering round him like a lost puppy. 'Get round the other side. I want to lift her up and get her inside.'

'I should be getting home,' Rosy said, as Tom took up position.

'You'll do as you're told!' Larry responded sternly. 'And for the time being that is staying right where you're put and not doing anything silly. Or should I say anything else silly!' he added meaningfully, cocking one bushy orange eyebrow.

Rosy turned to Tom, the bleakness in her gaze begging him to do something. She could not stay there. It was impossible. Then a sudden thought occurred. She turned panic-striken to the doctor. 'You're not sending me to hospital?' That was all she needed. An ambulance turning up would never be missed and the bush telegraph would have it all over the village that she had been carted away from 'that writer chap's place'.

'I've already told you I'm making no decisions till I've examined you properly,' Larry replied bluntly. 'I can't do that until I've got you inside. Now!' Putting one hand under her knees and the other behind her back he looked across at Tom. 'Grab hold of my wrists and we'll carry her in,' he instructed.

Tom did as he was told and she dutifully put her arms round their necks and was carried into the cottage. The doorway was a struggle, they had to turn sideways to get through, but finally she was lowered gently onto the little settee.

'It doesn't hurt so much now,' she said, realizing that her discomfort over being caught at the cottage with Tom was far greater than any physical pain she was feeling. It must be a good sign, she told herself.

Larry Hampson did not comment. He pressed her back onto the settee and lifted her legs so they were sticking out over the end. Then he knelt on the floor and examined her again, with Tom hanging over his shoulder and watching his every move.

Rosy felt this time the doctor used a little too much zeal. On several occasions he caused her to grimace and groan and by the time he had finished she was convinced there really was something dreadfully wrong.

But then he sat back on his heels and said, 'I don't think there is anything a few days rest won't cure.'

Rosy smiled and Tom visible relaxed.

'*But* . . .' Larry added, with extreme seriousness, '. . . you have got to rest! It's no good thinking you can just take it easy. I mean you are to go to bed and stay there – until I tell you otherwise!'

'Not here!' Rosy gasped. 'You don't mean I have to stay here!'

'You'll be all right here,' Tom put in. 'I can look after you.'

'No!' Rosy wailed. 'I can't.' Her anxious gaze swept from Tom to Larry and back again, several times.

Larry stood up and gazed down at her, his lips pursing in thought. 'My concern is for you and junior,' he said meaningfully. He really would have preferred to see her put straight to bed and not have to endure a car ride home, especially down the bumpy field. But she was getting worked up about it. He could see her blood pressure rising as he stood and watched her, and that would do her and the baby as much good as throwing her about in the field had done. He gave a sigh and rubbed a hand wearily across his face. 'All right!' he reluctantly agreed. 'I'll take you home.'

'I can do it,' Tom offered. He wanted to be the one to take her. He had had enough of having to deny what he felt for her and he would not let her hide behind her stupid guilt any more. She was having his baby now and he wanted to make sure the world knew it belonged to him. She wouldn't like it. But he had as much right to the child as she did.

Larry Hampson had other ideas. 'In that lorry thing?' he said drily. 'Not likely!' Letting her be tossed around in that thing would be tantamount to murder. 'She'll go in my car.'

'Then I'll come with you,' Tom quickly asserted, refusing to be put off. 'I'll sit with her and support her. She'll be better with support.'

'Tom!' Lifting her hand Rosy reached out to him. 'You can't.'

He took her hand. 'You'll need holding in the car,' he said, speaking gently but with a determination that would not be ignored. 'Then the doctor will need my help to get you out of the car and upstairs to bed.' He brushed a stray wisp of hair from her face and smiled down at her with all the love he felt for her.

It made her feel very guilty for not wanting him to come home with her. But . . . there would be enough explaining to do to John, without having Tom carrying her through the house and putting her to bed. 'You can't,' she repeated anxiously.

'I think it would be better if Tom came,' Larry said. He could see the man was not going to be easily put off and their arguing was holding him up, and stopping Rosy being put to bed; where she needed to be. 'Let's get her in the car,' he added impatiently, and Tom was only too eager to agree.

Larry drove so slowly and carefully down the bumpy field that Rosy was once more of the opinion he was holding something back from her about her condition. Her anxiety turned to the baby inside her and she forgot to worry about Tom coming home with her and how she was going to explain everything to John.

But she remembered she should be worrying when the car pulled into the yard behind Derwent House, and her mother rushed out.

'Whatever's the matter?' she gasped, seeing a pale-faced Rosy in the back, propped up against Tom.

'We've got to get her into bed,' Larry said brusquely. He jumped out of the car and pushed Nell out of the way so he could open the back door. He did not say any more, feeling the full explanation would be better coming from Rosy herself.

Neither did Tom speak. He eased Rosy along the seat, then got out and went round to the same side as Larry, so they could lift her up in the way they had done before.

All Nell could do was look on anxiously, as an unprotesting Rosy was hoisted from the car and into the air.

Nell scurried into the house in front of them. At the top of the stairs she waited nervously while Tom and Larry had to turn sideways, taking one step at a time.

'In the spare bedroom.' Rosy found her voice for the first time since leaving Tom's cottage. But she could not have them take her to the bed she shared with John. There was a lot of explaining to do and she did not want an audience while she was doing it. If they all walked in on John now he would demand to know what was happening, **having** no care for who else might be listening.

Nell immediately hurried to the door to the first

back bedroom and held it open. But the others had only just reached it, when a voice boomed out, 'What's going off?'

Rosy craned her neck to see John standing at the bedroom door. He was still wearing his pyjamas and leaning heavily on both his walking sticks.

'It's all right,' she said. 'I've just had a fall.'

'Like hell it's all right!' he blazed. 'Why are you creeping in there and not coming in here?'

'We didn't want to disturb you,' Larry said. 'And Rosy needs to lie down.'

Tom did not speak, he could not. Neither could he take his eyes off the man: Rosy's husband! He had only seen him from a distance before, when she was taking him for walks in the wheelchair, and the reality was stunning. She had said he was twenty-five years older than her, which made him fifty-eight or nine. But with his silver grey hair without a trace of the original colour, and gaunt, wrinkled features, he looked more like seventy-eight. But worse than that was the bitterness he could see in him, which he felt was a permanent feature and nothing to do with the moment.

'What is the matter with her?' The stick in John's left hand remained steady, but the right hand one began to shake from his anger. Then it swung up in the air and stabbed through the door of the bedroom he had come from. 'If she needs to be put to bed, she'll be put in her own bed. In *here*!' He laid emphasis on the last, at the same time as the stick's jabbing became more frantic.

'She needs rest. She doesn't want disturbing,' Larry said, and indicated with his head for Tom to carry on through the door and into the spare bedroom. He had been up most of the night, called out three times, and only one of them necessary. He was in no mood to be messed about. 'Now, Nell.' After lying Rosy down on the bed he looked up at her mother, who had put herself in the doorway to stop John getting into the room. 'I'm sure Rosy could do with a cup of tea, and if she couldn't I could.'

It was obvious he was trying to get rid of her and Nell's tightening expression registered her disapproval. She didn't know what was going on but Rosy was her daughter and she had no intention of leaving before she had found out.

But Larry was not about to have his orders disobeyed. 'Come on, Nell!' he said insistently, when she did not move.

She cast a meaningful glance over her shoulder, just as John shambled up behind her, leaning heavily on his sticks.

'It's all right,' Larry assured, going to her and physically turning her round. 'I'll see to that,' he added, in a way that told her there was something that definitely needed seeing to.

'But . . .' she began.

'Please, Mum!' Rosy begged. 'I'll talk to you later.'

Nell looked from her daughter to the man standing by the bed, and wondered just what he had got to do with all this.

'Get out of my way!' John growled in her ear, and thrust her back to the moment with a heavy arm shoving her into the door jamb so he could get past.

'Calm down, John!' Larry's voice was just as insistent and he grabbed his arm to stop him coming right into the room. Keeping his hold on him he turned to Nell. 'Go on and get that tea,' he said, in a manner that brooked no refusal. 'I think we could all do with a cup.'

This time she went.

Larry turned to Tom. 'Bring me that chair,' he instructed, taking John over to the side of the bed and, when Tom brought the chair, sitting him down in it. Then he looked to Rosy. 'How are you feeling now?' he asked, standing back and giving her face one of his intense scrutinies.

'OK!' she replied. 'I think the panic is over.' She

gave him a hopeful smile. Her hip felt a bit sore where she had landed on it, but otherwise she felt fine physically. It was the mental trauma of having John there and knowing what she had to tell him that was now giving her the most concern.

Larry was not prepared to commit himself. 'We'll see,' he said. 'So you've still got to stay right there until I tell you otherwise!'

'Why?' John asked bluntly.

Larry's gaze swung from Rosy to Tom and back again. He thought they might have preferred to have him around when they enlightened John. There was no telling what the shock would do to him and he might be needed, professionally. But they obviously did not think so for neither of them spoke, so Larry began to turn away.

'No!' It was Rosy who spoke, stopping him in his tracks. 'Maybe you should be here,' she said, as if she had read his mind.

He turned back again. 'But I am on call – so make it quick.' He had no intention of standing there while they beat about the bush.

Rosy gave a nod of understanding.

'What the devil is going off?' John demanded in frustration, banging a walking stick down so hard on the floor Rosy expected her mother to come racing up to see what he was wanting.

But there was no sound of Nell coming up the stairs and so she fixed him with a steady, yet regretful gaze. 'I am pregnant,' she said, seeing no easy way to do it.

For a long, long moment the silence in the room was stunning. Rosy, Tom and Larry were all looking at John. John's gaze was pinned to Rosy, in an unfathomable way that she found more disconcerting than had he immediately raged at her. Then somewhere outside Ivan started up the engine of the lawn mower.

It was a signal that brought John back to life. His

gaze swung to Tom. 'And just where do you come into all this?' he asked, the calmness of his voice stunning Rosy.

She shook her head in disbelief, wondering what game he was playing. He knew very well Tom's part in it, even before Tom said, 'I am the father of Rosy's child.'

John's expression did not even flicker. 'And how do you know that?' he asked. 'Rosy is my wife. The child is mine.'

Rosy could not believe what she was hearing. She had never given away John's secret to Tom. She had assumed Tom realized she had no sexual relationship with her husband anymore but they had never spoken of John in that way. It would have been too unkind and made her feel even more treacherous. She felt bad enough having divulged the truth to Larry that very morning.

She shook her head. 'The baby is Tom's,' she said.

But John remained unmoved. 'How can you be sure?' he asked, his gaze fixing her with a determination that drained her resolve. 'Whether the baby is mine or his it will stay here with you and be brought up as mine. Because you are my wife and this is where you belong.'

'Is it true?' Tom asked. 'Could it be his?'

'No,' she said, lifting her distraught gaze to his. But as her eyes settled on him she saw him for what he was: a young healthy man, who had everything going for him. She closed her eyes, not wanting to look, not wanting to see, but when she opened them again she was looking at John: old, infirm, dependent on her and needing her in a way Tom never would. In that moment she understood, despite his calm exterior, John was acting out of fear. Terrified of being left alone, he was making it clear he would accept the child as his own, rather than risk losing her.

Whatever it was going to cost her, she could not have lived with herself, knowing she had deserted him, and

483

slowly her head began to nod. 'Yes,' she said. Her gaze flicked briefly to Larry, then to Tom, then dropped to the yellow blanket covering her legs, unable to look at either of them, as she said in a whisper, 'The baby could belong to John.'

'Rosy!' Tom uttered, the pain she had inflicted on him echoing through his voice. He lifted an imploring hand to her but she turned her head away, fearing he would see the same pain mirrored in her eyes.

'I think you had better go,' John said.

Tom turned on him. 'No!' he said. 'I don't believe it. That is my baby and I won't let you keep it from me.' He looked to Larry, as if seeking some divine assistance, yet was not sure why he should think the doctor could, or would, help him.

'The baby is mine!' John insisted, lifting a walking stick as if, had Tom been standing at the same side of the bed as him, he would have struck him.

'No!' Rosy cried in panic.

'I think you had better go.' It was Larry who spoke and he quickly rounded the bed and took Tom's arm and led him away.

He went quietly, and he was at the door before he turned to cast a last despairing glance at Rosy. She was looking right back at him and the sorrow in her was a tangible thing that reached out and touched him, and he begged to be given the power to take hold of it and drag it from her. But all he received was a shove from Larry to carry him on his way.

CHAPTER TWENTY-SEVEN

The fall had done Rosy no serious damage and after two days Larry allowed her to get up, so long as she took life easy. Which was not difficult with her mother fussing about her and even John lessening his demands on her.

At first she was amazed at the change in John, and could not understand it. Each morning he got himself up with the minimum of help. He refused to let her lift him from the bed and did it himself with the aid of his sticks, which previously he had only done when she had lost her temper with him and left him to it. He would not even allow her to help him down the stairs.

'Wait for mum,' she pleaded, as he positioned the sticks on a lower step and leaned dangerously forward on them, and appeared to be in danger of going headlong to the bottom of the stairs.

'You've got another one to think about now,' he said, as he refused her hand and would not let her get past him to go in front of him.

He had said the same thing to her many times during the past weeks. But it was not until she followed him into the drawing-room that she at last understood the reason for his unexpected concern for the child she was carrying, which he knew very well was not his.

It was Sunday, Nicky was not working and he was already sitting in the room reading the morning's newspaper.

'Can you bring a measuring rod home with you one day next week,' John said, as he made his way slowly across the carpet.

'I've got one in the cottage,' Nicky replied, looking up from the newspaper.

'Good! I'll borrow it before you take it back to the office.'

'What do you want a measuring rod for?' Rosy asked in bewilderment as she followed close behind him. 'There's a tape measure in the kitchen.'

'I want something rigid.' He stopped walking and glanced round at her. 'I want to measure where my hands come to when I'm in the wheelchair. So we can get a pram with a handle low enough for me to push while you are pushing me.'

Rosy's bottom jaw dropped open.

Nicky laughed openly. 'I think my little brother or sister has given him a new lease of life.' He looked at Rosy and inclined his head towards his father.

Rosy flashed him a glance of warning, then looked at John, to see his reaction. She expected him to be furious. But to her surprise he was smiling.

'At least he didn't say it had given the "old man" a new lease of life.'

Rosy was astounded. What Nicky said was perfectly true. John had been given a new lease of life, a new meaning to life, a new purpose. All because of a baby that was not his! She brought herself up short. That was it. He was going to parade the child as his own, using it to boost his own confidence by making the world think he was still capable of being a father. Oh Tom, she thought. It wasn't fair. It wasn't fair at all.

'How is everything going with the cottage?' she asked Nicky, quickly turning her mind in another direction, while she watched John out of the corner of her eye as he sat himself down, getting ready to reach out and catch him if he should fall. She knew the refurbishing of the cottage was going to plan but she needed something to clear her mind of Tom, which was not the easiest task in the world.

'Fine,' Nicky confirmed and closed the newspaper, folded it up and offered it to his father.

John shook his head and Rosy grimaced to herself. Having her read to him was one of the things he still insisted on and she wished he had taken the paper; having to concentrate on the news of the day would have helped keep her mind off other things.

'The cooker and washing-machine are being delivered on Monday and then the cottage is complete,' Nicky said, and opened up the newspaper again.

Rosy smiled. The wedding was only six weeks away and the two of them had worked really hard to get the cottage finished, as well as get the wedding plans sorted out. 'Is that everything done then?'

Nicky pulled a face at her over the top of the newspaper. 'It was . . . but Colin has put his spoke in about the flowers now!' His eyes lifted meaningfully to the ceiling.

Rosy had thought it very generous of Cassie's father to offer to pay for everything. But it hadn't been long before she realized it had been for his own ends. He had taken charge of everything – going ahead and booking the reception, the photographer and the cars without consulting either Cassie or Nicky. He had even tried to choose Cassie's wedding dress for her. Fortunately, Cassie had stood up to him on that one. But he had added to the guest list names of people who neither Cassie nor Nicky had ever heard and it had become very apparent that the grand occasion he was planning was nothing but a show for his own friends and colleagues.

'What's wrong with the flowers?'

Nicky gave a weary sigh. 'Cassie wanted to carry orchids. He only found out about it yesterday and he went and changed the order. He said orchids were too pale against a white dress. He's ordered her a big, ostentatious bouquet of two dozen red roses.' He dropped the newspaper onto his knee and stared at the marble hearth. 'I came the nearest I've ever come to thumping him, I can tell you.'

Rosy went to his side and rested her hand on his shoulder. 'Don't let him drive you to that,' she said. She couldn't understand the man. He was ruining his own daughter's wedding. 'It will all be over in a few weeks and Cassie will be yours!' she added meaningfully, hoping he would get some reassurance from it. But if he snapped now who could tell what the outcome would be.

'Just go and change the order back,' John said. 'And make it clear to the florist that no-one else has the right to change it again, only you.'

'But he's paying for them!'

It was almost a wail and Rosy's hand tightened on his shoulder. She wished she could have done something to help. But her offer that they would pay for half of everything had been rebuffed. He was quite able to pay for his daughter's wedding, Colin Upton had told her in no uncertain terms, making it clear that any interference would only be adding to the young couple's problems.

'You'll look back and laugh at it later,' she said. 'When you're settled in your new home and you know it was all worth it.' It would be worth it, she was sure. They were too much in love for it to turn out any other way. She brought herself up short. There had been times when she had compared Nicky's happiness to what she had found with Tom. She had loved him so much, and still did. He was back filling her mind and a lump closed her throat and she turned quickly and hurried from the room, managing to control her voice enough to explain herself by saying, 'I'll go and put the kettle on.'

The kitchen was empty but she could hear her mother out in the courtyard asking Ivan which cabbages she should pick first, and she was grateful for the few minutes' solitude to collect herself. She had made the choice to stand by John, but that did not ease the hurt of losing Tom and all he had been to her. And now John was talking about the baby as if it really was his. He had never spoken to her of Tom and he was acting as if he had never existed. Which he might not have done, she thought, her sadness increasing. She had not seen him since the day Larry had ordered him out of the bedroom. That both pleased and upset her. In a way it was a relief to know he had accepted her decision as something that was beyond her control and irreversible, and was not coming round to bother her. But even so, there were times when it hurt to believe he had given up on her so easily. Or had he given up on her because he thought she hadn't really cared for him?

It was a harrowing thought and she folded her arms about herself, feeling in need of the protection, and went to the window and gazed across the field and up the bank. The cottage was out of sight from there, but as she stared at the point where the wood curved away to provide the clearing where it stood, she could clearly picture it all: the grassy track, the garden wall, single chimney. And she knew she had to go up to him one more time. She had to have the chance to explain to him properly.

Without another thought she turned back to the drawing-room. 'I'm just going round to the village to pick something up for mum,' she said.

'I'll go,' Nicky offered.

'I need to keep having some exercise,' she replied. 'Larry said so,' she quickly added, when she saw John about to object. He closed his mouth again and gave a nod and Rosy silently thanked Larry for making the point in front of him. She should do some walking everyday, he had said. But not pushing John in the wheelchair. 'I shouldn't be too long.' She had no intention of staying longer than was necessary.

She was only halfway up the field when she realized

489

the cottage had an empty appearance about it. 'Please no,' she begged, and her gaze leapt to the chimney. It was a cold day, yet there was no spiral of smoke lifting up to heaven and her heart sank. The place looked dead, deserted, abandoned. Had something happened to him, she asked herself, feeling a coldness sinking slowly inside her?

Stop being melodramatic, she told herself sternly, and quickened her footsteps. But there were no more signs of life when she reached the gate, and hammering loudly on the door brought no response.

'Tom!' she called, standing back and looking up at the bedroom window. 'Tom! Oh please be here!'

Her pleading was fruitless. There was no Tom to hear her call and in desperation she went to the window and peered inside. Briefly she recalled another time she had peeped through that same window, and seen Maggie and, although she hadn't known it, John. She was convinced now it had been John her sister had been bouncing up and down on.

The next moment all thoughts of anyone except Tom had gone from her mind. 'Oh no!' she gasped, pressing her nose right up to the glass to get a better view. The little settee was just visible beneath the window, the fireside chair was still there, so was his desk. But the typewriter and all the clutter of books and papers had gone.

The place *was* empty and dead. He had gone. Tom had gone.

He must be away on holiday, she tried to assure herself. He could have gone off doing some research for his latest book. Or he might have gone to see his family. But even as she attempted to persuade herself that his not being there was quite normal, she knew it was not. If he had only gone away for a holiday why had he taken the typewriter and his work? All his papers? All his books?

He had gone and he was not coming back. It was a

feeling inside her that grew and intensified as she stared at the empty room.

'It's too late,' she said, rubbing a gentle hand over the mound of her stomach and speaking to his child inside her. 'He's gone.'

With a heavy heart she turned around and retraced her steps. There was a pain inside her that was so real she almost cried out from it. And when she reached home she had not thought she could ever feel worse than she then did. But she had been wrong.

It was only two weeks to the wedding, when Nicky came home early one evening from seeing Cassie. Her father had been ruling the roost again and the roar of the motorbike's engine had told them he was in a rage, even before he came through the door tearing his helmet off his head as if it was an opponent he was in combat with.

'He doesn't think the hotel I've booked . . .' his finger stabbed furiously at his leather covered chest, '. . . for the honeymoon is good enough. He says he can get us into a much better one. One that somebody he knows uses regularly!'

'How did he find out where you're going?' John took the words right out of Rosy's mouth. She knew the honeymoon arrangements had been a closely guarded secret kept from everyone, themselves included, just so Colin Upton would not find out.

'Cassie!' he spoke her name with bitterness, as he threw himself down into a chair and tossed his crash helmet on the floor. 'I know he's persuasive but she knew how much this meant to me. I could kill her for letting him get it out of her.'

'Weddings always cause arguments,' Nell said, and stood up and collected the magazine she had been reading. She did not like spending the evenings with Rosy and John. She felt she was intruding on their privacy and would have preferred to be in the room next to her bedroom, which had been made into her own little sitting-room. But Rosy insisted she had to begin treating the house like her home and not continue to consider herself the hired help. Nicky's arrival was a good excuse for her to vanish and leave them to it. ' 'Night everybody,' she said.

'Goodnight Mum.' Rosy was too concerned about Nicky's problems to stop her going, and before Nell was out of the door she got up and perched herself on the arm of his chair. 'What happened? What did you say to him?' She recalled his earlier declaration that he had wanted to hit Colin Upton and hoped he had only 'said' something to his future father-in-law.

'I asked him if he also wanted to come with us and share the bed so he could make sure everything else was up to standard . . . !'

Rosy's hand flew up to cover her mouth. 'Oh Nicky!' she said, biting hard on her lip to stop herself smiling. It was no laughing matter, as Nicky's dark expression well told her. But she was contemplating the reaction he would have got from Colin Upton. He was a big fat man with the unhealthy complexion of someone who delves far too deeply into a whisky bottle, and she imagined his highly coloured face would have turned purple. 'What did he say?'

'I didn't wait to find out.' He gave a sigh then leapt up out of the chair, so quickly that had Rosy's arm not been leaning along the back behind his head, her weight would have been all at one side and she would have tipped up. But he was too angry to notice. 'I'm going to bed,' he said, and stomped out of the room and up the stairs, his heavy boots stamping out his fury every step of the way.

'I'll go and talk to him,' she said, carefully getting herself off the arm of the chair.

'No you won't,' John said, in a manner that brooked no refusal. 'You'll come and sit down properly and leave him to sort himself out. He's big enough. That one isn't,' he added meaningfully, pointing at her stomach. 'That is the one we should be thinking about.'

We! No, she thought sadly, as she obeyed him without comment and returned to the chair she had previously been sitting in. It was Tom who should be thinking about the baby. She turned her attention to the television programme they had been wtching and hoped he would do the same. His constant consideration towards her was making her feel twice as guilty and there were times when she was beginning to resent the baby for turning him into this caring person that was alien to her.

Nicky was very quiet over breakfast the following morning and before he went to work he spent longer in his bedroom than usual. When he did come down he had a large holdall in his hands, which he fixed to the back of the motorbike. But Rosy had no reason to disbelieve him when he said it was just some things he wanted dry cleaning before the wedding, and she saw no reason to worry.

Her concern did not begin until six-thirty that evening, when she received a panic-filled telephone call from Cassie's mother. Cassie had not come home from work and when she had phoned around her friends from the office, it was to find she had not been in at all that day.

As Rosy stood with the telephone receiver in her hand she had the feeling cold water was being poured all over her. *No!* she thought. *Please, no!* But even as she put the telephone down and quickly dialled Bill Cowlishaw, she knew the answer she was going to get.

'He called first thing to say he'd got a tummy bug and he wouldn't be in,' Bill said. 'Why? Won't he be in tomorrow either?'

No, he wouldn't, she thought. 'I doubt it, Bill,' she said, her voice as flat as her spirits. 'I think he's run away with Cassie.'

'Oh Lord!' Bill replied meaningfully.

Oh Lord! Rosy thought, as she put the telephone down and sank onto a nearby stool. Now she had lost everything – Tom *and* Nicky! As if to prove her wrong the baby inside her moved and a tiny limb thrust against the side of her stomach. She still had part of Tom, she tried to tell herself, but the bleakness that had taken over her mind could not find any joy in owning anything less than all of him. And she didn't even have part of Nicky. Because of the pompous, overbearing Colin Upton she had lost all of him. Her anger seethed and she knew if the man had been there with her she would have done what Nicky had wanted to do, and hit him. She would have gained much pleasure just at that moment if she had had something to hit out at and pummel and thump, to work out the rage that was burning her up inside.

Half an hour later she almost got her wish. Colin Upton's car came racing up the drive and almost knocked Ivan over as he was crossing the courtyard. Then, without taking a backwards glance at Ivan, he leapt from his car, and like a raging bull came through the back door without even knocking.

Rosy had been in the kitchen with her mother and had witnessed it all.

'Where is he?' he demanded, as Nell gave a shriek of alarm. 'I want an explanation from him for what his son has gone and done.'

In an instant Rosy put herself between Upton and the doorway through to the hall, which she could see he was aiming for. 'Just a minute,' she insisted, stretching her spine, the huge bulge of her stomach thrust out at him. 'You haven't been invited in here and you don't go another step.'

'Get out of my way.' His arm came up to thrust her away. But before he could do it a walking stick came over her shoulder and jabbed at Colin Upton's throat forcing him backwards.

'She is pregnant!' John's voice bellowed close to her ear. 'Haven't you got eyes to see that?'

Colin Upton's eyes screwed up into tiny slots that made his fat face appear even more like that of a pig. 'Well I hope that isn't a condition that's catching in your family. Or can you give me some other reason for them running off in shame?'

Rosy gave a bark of scorn. 'You idiot!' she exclaimed with feeling. 'You're the reason they have run away. You and your overbearing attitude.'

'She is my daughter!'

'And the Victorian age is over. This is the seventies and times have changed!'

'Stop it, Rosy!' John's hand came down to rest on her shoulder, the walking stick stuck out before her. 'Don't get yourself worked up about it. It isn't good for the baby and he isn't worth it.'

'I know that,' she said, bringing her voice back to normal. 'But Nicky is worth it. And I won't have him coming here and making wild accusations.'

'I'll make any accusations I like,' Colin Upton insisted. 'She is my daughter and . . .'

'So you said before,' John inserted, cutting him off and jabbing the walking stick at his chest when he tried to advance his great bulk on Rosy again. 'But if you were so close perhaps you'll tell me why she didn't leave you a letter to tell you where she was going?'

It brought Colin Upton up short. For a moment he could only stare at them, his lips held in a tight line that seemed to be cutting off his breath, if the increasing redness of his face was anything to go by. 'They left no letters,' he said, then paused, eyeing John uncertainly. 'Did he leave a letter? Did he tell you where they were going?'

John did not reply, but his silence was very significant and Rosy felt a great breath of relief lift her chest. She was a little put out that Nicky could have confided in his father and not her, but knowing that he had not cut himself off from them completely far outweighed any hurt she was experiencing.

'Tell me where they are!' Colin Upton's eyes were once more reduced to tiny slits and Rosy realized he was not only overbearing, he was also a bully. His expression was deliberate, intended to put fear into his opponents, and she could understand how Cassie had been forced to divulge their honeymoon destination.

'I'm telling you nothing,' John said, with a calmness that seemed to have more effect on Colin Upton than if he had raised his voice and matched his anger.

His mouth tightened so much his cheeks looked about to explode. 'I demand you tell me!' he bellowed.

'And I demand you leave this house,' John replied, not shouting but with an authority that brooked no refusal. He looked to Nell, who had stood anxiously watching it all. 'Go and call the police,' he instructed her. 'And tell them we have been broken into and are being threatened. Tell them also my wife is heavily pregnant!'

Colin Upton's mouth worked but no words came out. Then he wheeled away. 'I'll be back,' he snarled, as he reached the door. 'Don't you think this is the last of it. I'll be back!'

He was safely in the car and had started the engine, before Rosy lifted the arm plus walking stick away from her shoulder and turned to face John. 'Where is he?' she asked. 'Where had he gone?' He could tell her where Nicky was. She would never have given his secret away.

But her excitement was short lived. As he returned the stick to the floor he shook his head. 'I don't know,' he admitted. At first his smile was apologetic, then it brightened. 'But it put his nose out of joint.' Laughing, he turned away and hobbled back to the drawing-room.

Rosy could only watch him go, a sinking disappointment filling her with a desolation that far outweighed anything she had ever experienced before.

*   *   *

Rosy was standing at the window of Nicky's bedroom. He had been gone for over a week and they had still heard nothing from him. During that time she had often come up to his room. It heightened her sadness but it also made her feel closer to him.

It was a filthy day, the sky was pewter grey and rain was lashing down and she could not see anything clearly that was beyond the garden. Would Nicky ever come back? she asked herself. Tom never had. She had lost count of the times she had been up to the cottage in the past six months, each time finding the place more desolate than the time before. He might come back, she thought, placing her hands over her stomach. But what was the use of him coming back? Nothing had changed, she was still responsible for John. She thought of him lying in the bed across the passage. He hadn't felt too good this morning and had stayed in bed. It was the first time he hadn't got up after breakfast since learning of the baby. But he seemed all right when she had looked in on him a few minutes ago, and he said he would get up shortly.

Movement down below brought her back to the moment. She looked down to see Ivan, head bent and Wellington boots splashing up the water, as he hurried across the muddy ground and dodged beneath the dripping tree branches. It had rained for the past four days and everything was sodden. Even though she could not see it from that side of the house, she knew the river was several inches above normal level, although nowhere near breaking its banks.

It was as she was about to turn away, that she saw the figure standing on the lane. He was standing very still and seemed to be staring at the house. In the rain she could not see him clearly, but she could see enough to know it was a man, and he was just standing there . . . watching. She found it odd and so she reciprocated, fixing her gaze on him.

He was wearing a grey coat with the collar turned up and had a grey cap pulled down over his eyes. Along with the blurring rain it meant she could see very little of him. Yet she had the feeling she was looking at someone she knew. She looked quickly down, searching for Ivan, and just caught him vanishing round the corner of the house. His head was still bent forward against the rain and he was going in the wrong direction to have seen the man and she returned her gaze to the solitary figure.

For a full ten minutes she stood, looking right back at him as he watched the house. He was watching the house. It was a disturbing realization, but one she was sure of. It made the hairs on the back of her neck stand on end and a shiver run down her spine, and finally sent her racing downstairs in search of her mother.

'We're being watched,' she rushed out, as she flew through the dining-room door to find her busy with duster and beeswax polish. Her panic was twice as bad after going first to the kitchen and finding it empty.

'What are you talking about?' Nell looked round at her as if she had gone mad.

'We're being watched,' Rosy repeated. 'There's a man. On the lane. He's been standing there for ages.' The words tumbled breathlessly from her lips and she rushed over to the window.

'He's probably waiting for someone,' Nell replied reasonably.

Rosy shook her head. 'Not there. He wouldn't be waiting there. I tell you he's watching us. Why else would he be standing in this rain? Oh damn! I can't see him from here.'

'So he must have gone.'

'No! No, you'll have to come upstairs to see him.'

'Oh gawd!' Nell plonked both duster and polish down in a way that showed she did not appreciate being disturbed. 'Come on,' she said. 'Let me see him.'

'Well . . . where is he?' Nell questioned drily. The

view from the bedroom window was of a very wet, but empty lane. The disturbing figure had vanished, as if into thin air. There was no-one walking in either direction for as far as could be seen.

'Come on.' She took hold of Rosy's arm and led her away. 'You've had a lot on your mind lately. Perhaps it was the rain playing tricks on you.'

Rosy shook her head, but did not raise any objection. She knew she had seen someone standing there. But she also knew her mother was not going to be convinced – not without seeing him with her own eyes.

When they reached the bottom of the stairs she turned worriedly to her mother. 'Do you think it was someone sent by Colin Upton?' Cassie's father had never made the promised second visit, but she was sure he would do, sooner or later.

'Don't be daft. He might come himself but what use would putting a spy on us be?'

Rosy gave a weak smile. None, she thought. Unless he was of the opinion they were hiding Nicky and Cassie. If that was the case she had little to worry about. The strange man would only be watching out for them and when he didn't see them he wouldn't be coming near the place. 'Perhaps I was imagining it,' she agreed, and extracted her arm from her mother's. 'Don't say anything in front of John. I don't want him worrying,' she said, and turned and went back upstairs, happy to go in to him now there was no sign of fear or panic on her face.

She found John already up and almost dressed. He was sitting on the bed fastening the buttons on his cardigan when she went through the door.

'The weather hasn't got any better,' she said, going to the window and peering out at the river. 'The water's got a bit higher. But nothing to worry about.'

'We won't be paddling yet then,' John said.

She did not reply. Her attention had been caught by something at the bottom of the drive. 'Oh dear,' she said. 'Colin Upton is back.' At least she thought it was his car that was stopped on the drive. Just then the driver got out and she knew it was him, from the huge bulk of his body. 'What's he doing?' she asked, speaking more to herself than to John, because he couldn't see anything from the bed.

'If it's him we'd better get downstairs and be ready for him. I'm not having him bursting in again and frightening Nell witless.'

'It's definitely him,' she said, but did not move away from the window. A second person had appeared, dragged from behind a bush by Colin Upton and now being pushed towards the car by him. 'What the devil is he playing at?' she said, just as she saw Colin Upton lift his hand and strike the other man round the ear as if he was punishing a naughty child.

'Come on!' John urged. 'I don't want to be stuck up here when he arrives.'

But Rosy did not turn and see that he was going out of the door. The second man had wriggled free and was racing up the drive. She could see him more clearly now. He was young. He was . . . Nicky! Her heart gave a leap. Her gaze swung rapidly from the young man to Colin Upton's car. He was now back in it and starting it up again.

'Oh no!' she shouted, in fear and panic. 'It's Nicky. He's got Nicky!' Forgetting her huge stomach she spun round, so fast that, like a ship when its ballast has shifted, she reeled and only just caught hold of the drawers to stop herself crashing to the ground. But at that moment Nicky was all that was important to her and she did not wait long enough to notice that her insides had turned to jelly. She raced for the door. John was way ahead of her now and had almost reached the top of the stairs.

'Stop, Rosy! Stop!' he insisted, but all she could think was that the crazy Colin Upton was chasing Nicky up the drive in a car.

'Nicky!' she cried, flapping her hands at John to get him out of the way so she had a clear path down the stairs. 'He's going to kill Nicky.'

In the next moment John had moved, but not in the right direction.

'No, Rosy!' he shouted, lifting one of his walking sticks horizontally and holding it in front of him to stop her getting past – putting himself as a barrier right at the top of the stairs. But with only one stick to support himself he was unsteady, and the speed with which he moved was greater than any he had used in years.

His leg gave way and his foot slipped. As he tottered over the edge Rosy screamed and her hands went out to him. But she was several inches short. One walking stick landed on the floor at her feet, the other clattered noisily down the stairs. John's descent was quieter and not so fast. His body turned and twisted as it bounced and rolled from the top to the bottom of the stairs, seeming to hit every step on the way.

CHAPTER TWENTY-EIGHT

Rosy stood at the top of the stairs, for a moment unable to move. John lay in a heap at the bottom.

'Oh God, no! Please no!' she begged, then suddenly leaped to life and raced down the stairs. 'Mum! Mum!' she screamed.

Nell was already on her way. She had heard the commotion and she reached John before Rosy did.

'Is he dead? Is he dead?' Rosy cried, as she fell to her knees by his side and grabbed up one lifeless hand.

Nell shook her head. 'I don't think so.' Her hand fumbled to find a pulse at his other wrist. She thought she felt a flutter but then it was gone again and she wasn't sure if she had imagined it. 'I'll get the doctor.' Pushing herself up she turned to the telephone that was right behind her.

'It's all Colin Upton's fault,' Rosy said. 'Everything is down to him.' It reminded her of Nicky and she looked up as her mother put the phone down and announced that Larry was on his way. 'Nicky is outside,' she said.

'What?' Nell peered at her oddly, wondering if the shock had turned her mind.

'Nicky!' Rosy's fear and panic increased. 'He's coming up the drive. Colin Upton is chasing him. Go and help him. Get Ivan.' She would have gone herself, but she could not leave John. Her gaze fell to his face once more, pale and bloodless, and perfectly still. There was not a mark on him and he could have been sleeping. 'Oh no! No! No!' Her voice was little more than a whimper and Nell lay a constraining hand on her shoulder.

'Keep yourself calm,' she ordered gently. 'Think of the baby. He would want you to think of the baby.'

Rosy's head nodded up and down as if it did not really belong to her. I know, she thought. 'Please go and find Nicky,' she begged. Nell did not know if she wanted him there for his own safety, or if she wanted him to be with his father because she thought the end was near, but she knew the need was great and so she hurried through the kitchen and out into the courtyard.

Rosy clutched harder at John's hand. It wasn't fair, she thought. Not now, when he had been so happy. For the past six months he had been more alive than in all the last six years put together. 'No!' she whispered, pressing his hand to her cheek. There had been a time when she would have been relieved if he had died, but not now. She could never have said that her feelings for him were as powerful as what she had felt for Tom, but she had cared for him; at the beginning and again now. And, even knowing it was not his, he had wanted the baby so very much.

Her tears began to fall and her head bowed forward. 'It's not fair,' she sobbed, just as his hand moved in hers. 'John!' she gasped, looking up to find his eyes were open and he was looking right back at her. At first her joy was so great she could not speak, and it was several moments before she said, 'Don't move. Larry's on his way.'

He smiled weakly and his head made a feeble shaking movement. 'No,' he said, his voice lacking strength.

'Don't try and talk,' she said, dashing her tears away with one hand but keeping a firm hold on him with the other. 'Don't try and say anything.'

Again his head moved in denial. 'Need to talk,' he said. 'Loved you, Rosy.'

'Hush!' She tried to quieten him, not liking the way he was speaking. He sounded as if he had given up.

But he ignored her. 'Everything I did was for you. But I didn't make you happy.'

'Yes you did!'

His head wagged with more strength and his voice was filled with the same, as he said, 'I didn't. It was my punishment. And now . . .' He paused and regret filled his eyes.

'Why should you be being punished?' she said, forcing herself to smile at him, even though she felt more like sobbing her heart out.

His chest lifted and fell again. She did not know if it was a great sigh, or if he was fighting for breath. Her grip on his hand tightened, as he said, 'Dorothy.'

She shook her head, wondering if his mind had gone and he thought she was his first wife. But his gaze was fixed on hers and she could not look away from him, and slowly another meaning of what he was saying dawned on her. 'Dorothy!' she repeated, her voice little more than a whisper. 'You don't mean . . . ?' She could not speak the last, it was too awful.

'I killed her,' he said.

It was as if they had both turned to stone. Rosy stared disbelievingly into his eyes, which looked right back at her. She did not know at what point he stopped seeing her. It could have been seconds, minutes, or hours, before her mother came and prised his hand from her grip and lay his arm gently down by his side.

'Come on, love,' she said. 'He's gone.' She lifted her to her feet and turned her away. And Rosy saw Nicky and Ivan were standing there and for a moment her confused mind thought her mother was speaking of Colin Upton, and she was pleased he was gone. Then Larry Hampson came rushing through the door and she knew she had been wrong, and she collapsed against her mother's shoulder and sobbed.

Rosy looked round. She could not remember how she got there but she was sitting in a chair in the drawing-room and her back ached. Her mother was in another chair, pulled up right by her side, holding her hand.

Nicky and Ivan were sitting on the settee over by the wall, looking very serious. Larry was standing in front of her.

'How's John?' she found herself asking, even though she could recall clearly what had happened.

Larry shook his head. 'He was gone when I got here.' He peered at her with concern. 'How do you feel?'

She gave a shrug and rubbed at her back. The pain seemed to be getting worse instead of better. 'I shouldn't have run downstairs,' she replied honestly. She must have pulled something, she told herself. 'How . . . ? What . . . ?' she asked, turning her mind away from herself and back to John, but unable to find the right words.

Fortunately, Larry understood. 'He had several fractures, including one on his skull. It could have been that which killed him. But I think it more likely to have been the shock and that his heart gave out.'

She gave a nod and a shiver trembled through her as she recalled his final moments, his last words. She looked up first at Nicky, then Ivan. 'Did you hear him?' she asked.

Ivan did not need to ask what he might have heard and he nodded his head. 'Yes, I heard it.' He had heard every word and not been able to think of anything else since. He had seen John Hardaker die right in front of his eyes, yet he could feel no compassion for the man. 'I killed her' he had said, admitting to killing his wife. But he was a murderer twice over. Because hiding the truth had made him responsible for the death of his brother. His silence had killed Joey just as surely as if he had put the rope round his neck, and he could never have found it in his heart to forgive him for that.

Nicky's head did not move and neither did he speak. 'Come here,' she said, holding her hand out to him, feeling guilt stab at her for only then realizing he must be in shock after witnessing his father's death.

But he hesitated, looked uncertain.

'It isn't Nicky,' Nell said, leaning towards Rosy and speaking low in her ear.

Rosy's bewildered gaze went from the young man to her mother and back again. 'Of course it is . . .' she began, then brought herself up short, recalling the grey raincoat he had been wearing when she first saw him standing in the hall. He had taken it off now and was in a cream Arran knit sweater with blue jeans. But the raincoat? When she saw him with Colin Upton she had been too concerned for his safety to think he was dressed like the man she had seen watching the house. No hat, but the coat had been the right colour.

'He says his name is Guy,' Nell added meaningfully.

'Guy!' Rosy's mouth dropped open and her astonished gaze swung back to him. 'But how . . . ? You can't be. He was drowned!' In the next moment she was beyond speech. A searing pain stabbed right through her, starting in her back and coming right round to the front of her stomach. 'Oh!' she gasped, falling so far forward in the chair she would have toppled onto the floor if Larry had not caught her.

The next two hours were a haze to Rosy. She could remember bits, but not all of anything. She was being carried up the stairs, put onto a bed, the pain came again and again. She thought her mother was there, then she changed to Maggie. She heard herself calling out for John, or was it Tom? But Larry was definitely with her. That was the strongest memory because he seemed to feature in everything.

'It's a girl,' he was suddenly saying. 'Come on, Rosy. You've got a little girl.' And she opened her eyes to see Larry, his jacket discarded and his shirt sleeves rolled up to the elbows, holding a tiny baby in his arms.

She lifted her hand, almost touched the child then drew back, afraid of hurting her. 'Is she mine?' she asked, a note of incredulity in her voice. But so much had happened and she was not sure if she was dreaming.

Larry nodded his head. 'All yours,' he said, and slipped the baby into her arms.

Rosy gazed down at the tiny face, taking in every detail: the contentedly puckered lips, button nose, wisps of blond hair on top of her head and blond lashes lying against pink cheeks. My daughter, she thought. And Tom's.

'What are you going to call her?' It was Maggie who spoke and Rosy looked round to see her standing on the other side of the bed, her mother was by her side.

She shook her head. 'I don't know. I thought I had a bit more time to decide.'

'How about "speedy",' Maggie joked. 'Because she didn't hang around making her entrance.'

Rosy's smile vanished as she turned back to her daughter. She was four weeks early, she reminded herself. And brought on by a terrible shock. 'Will she be all right?' She lifted a worried gaze to Larry.

'She looks fine to me,' he said. It was the mother he was more concerned with, junior was quite oblivious to the events that had preceded her arrival. 'Let me have her,' he said, taking her out of Rosy's arms.

'But . . .' Rosy began to protest.

'I want you to rest. Sleep if you can. Maggie or your mother will be watching over this one.' He handed the tiny bundle over to Nell, who gave her new grand-daughter a hug, then placed her down in the cot that was standing behind her.

Rosy watched as her daughter was lowered into the white cot with teddy transfers on the ends and a lump came to her throat. The cot, along with a pram, pushchair, toys and clothes, had all been picked out of a catalogue by John. He had wanted only the best for 'his' baby. But it had not been his. She was Tom's daughter and it was Tom Rosy wanted there with her, sharing the moment.

'Where is John?' she suddenly asked, thinking he could still be there with her, in the house.

'They've taken him away,' Larry was quick to assure. After hearing about his dying words he had realized she would want him out of the place as quickly as possible, even more so now her daughter had come into the world. 'Now rest will you?'

She relaxed down into the pillow, then had another thought. 'Where is . . .' she hesitated uncertainly. She still was not sure how much of what she remembered was dream and how much reality, and she wondered if that part had been nothing more than her imagination. 'Was Guy really here?' she asked.

'Yes,' her mother confirmed. 'He's downstairs.'

'Don't let him go . . . will you?' There was real fear in her voice. She was afraid if he went now they would never see him again. He must think he had walked in on a madhouse, she told herself, recalling his reception from Colin Upton. 'Did Cassie's father hurt him? Did you sent him away.'

'Don't worry about him. Ivan sent him packing. Now lie down and stop talking.'

'Yes,' Larry agreed firmly. 'Do as your mother tells you.'

Rosy did sleep. But it was full of dreams mixed up and confused. Tom was with her. Then John took over and Tom became a misty figure on the horizon. Nicky was also there, or was it Guy?

She woke up feeling worse than when she had gone to sleep and it took two days before she felt anything like her old self again.

'I'm sorry you returned to all this,' Rosy cast Guy a resigned sigh. They were sitting up one end of the kitchen table, while her mother was busy baking up the other end. It was the first time they had been able to talk to each other. Larry had left very strict instructions that she was to stay in bed and no-one be allowed to go up to her, and Nell had obeyed him to the letter. Not even Charlie had been allowed to sneak up and take a peep at her new cousin. But she had at least told Rosy that Guy had proof that he really was who he claimed. Rosy had laughed at that. No-one could have looked at his face and doubted his heredity. But she knew her mother had only been trying to assure her that he wasn't going anywhere and, no matter how long she stayed in bed, he would still be there when she did get up.

'It seems so strange you turning up like this, after all this time,' she said, looking closely at his face. She could now see the differences between him and Nicky. Although he was very like him and someone who had not known Nicky so well would have been confused, her expert eye could see tiny differences that put them apart. His hair was in an identical style but his face was slightly thinner, his nose a little longer, and when she had first walked into the kitchen he had been standing up and she noticed he was a bit taller than Nicky. But there was no doubting that he truly was his twin brother.

She shook her head. 'But how? Where have you been? What happened?' She doubted even he could answer the last, because he had been too small and would remember nothing of the house of his family. 'How have you found us now?'

'Durham,' he began.

She smiled. Now she recognized the intonation in his voice. Although not strong, he had taken on the accent of the people he had lived closely with. It was the most noticable difference between him and Nicky. She shook her head in confusion. 'How did you get there? Who were your parents? Why did you come and find us now?'

He smiled at the barrage of questions. 'They are all answered in this,' he said, taking an old and yellowed envelope out of his pocket and handing it to her.

'What is it?' She looked bewildered.

'The woman I thought of as my mother died recently. I was given that letter by the solicitor who dealt with her will. I was brought up to believe I was Guy Richardson, until I read it I thought I was. But it tells me I am really Guy Hardaker.'

Rosy's hands began to tremble as they took the sheet of paper out of the envelope. *Richardson!* she was thinking, but the name meant nothing to her, until her eyes went quickly to the signature at the bottom of the paper: *Jane Richardson!*

'Nanny!' Rosy gasped, her shocked gaze swinging round to her mother. 'It can't be.'

'That's what I said,' Nell replied, taking a pause from working her dough.

'You've read this! Why didn't you tell me?' She was annoyed her mother could read the letter and not tell her its contents.

'Larry said no excitement. Besides . . .' she added, returning to her baking, '. . . I thought you'd prefer to read it yourself.'

Rosy did not reply. She returned her gaze to the letter and began to read. It was incredible and so simple. She could not believe it had been that easy to steal a child, but it had been. It was all written down in front of her.

Jane Richardson had had it all carefully planned. The marmalade in her bag for Phoebe had been waiting especially for that day. Her brother was waiting on the bridge in his car and, when she shouted Rosy into the cottage for those few seconds, he came and took one of the twins. There had been no decision as to which one, it could just as easily have been Nicky as Guy. He had used ether to keep the boy quiet so they could not trace him from his crying.

Guy choked, she heard Nicky saying. If only she had believed him.

Jane Richardson's brother had then tossed the child's coat into the river and driven away.

While they had all been racing round the swollen river-bank like headless chickens, Rosy thought, regret bringing sadness to her eyes, as she pictured the little blue and red coat being swept away.

All that was left then was for Nanny to resign and go and get Guy from her brother.

The letter went on to tell Guy that the solicitor also had a file filled with all the details of his real family, including photographs, if he should decide he wanted to find them.

There was then a personal bit where it explained she had done it because she could never have a child of her own, and that she had always loved him as dearly as if he had been her own. It finished by saying she hoped he could find it in his heart to forgive her.

Rosy looked at him. 'Can you forgive her?' she asked.

He gave a nod. 'She was a wonderful mum to me.'

Rosy grimaced inwardly, picturing the dour Jane Richardson and wondering if they were talking about the same person. She could only picture the fleshless woman in the flapping black coat, and could not imagine her capable of being nice to anyone.

'Naturally it came as a shock,' Guy said. 'And I have to admit, at first, I didn't want to look for any other family. I only wanted to remember her. Because she was the one who did everything for me, and in my book that is what counts most.'

'Yes,' Rosy agreed, thinking how Nicky had been closer to *her* than his real mother.

'It was more than a month after her death before I finally went back to the solicitor and asked for the file. It was only when I looked at the photographs that I realized I had a twin.'

'Didn't you ever feel something was missing?' she asked. 'Everyone else was sure you had drowned but Nicky would never believe you were dead.'

511

He gave a shrug. 'In a way I did feel different. But I didn't have a dad and everyone else did, so I thought it was just that. Missing male company . . . I suppose.'

Rosy smiled tightly. 'And you found your dad when it was too late.' She could not contemplate how he must be feeling about that. After finally making the decision to come, to get here just a few minutes too late.

'And Nicky gone, as well.' His expression was bleak. 'Perhaps I should not have come back.'

'Of course you should,' Rosy was quick to assure. 'We'll get Nicky back. Don't you worry.' Her voice was filled with confidence. She wanted to get him back for herself and she also wanted to get him back to let him know of his father's death. She knew he would be very upset that he had been away when it happened. He would never forgive himself if he missed the funeral, as well. She was hoping he and Cassie had only gone off to get themselves married somewhere with less hassle, and that they would eventually come back of their own accord, after the honeymoon. But that would not be for three weeks yet and the funeral had to go ahead before then.

There was a way to get Nicky back, she reminded herself. It had come to her while she had been lying in bed, considering what to do about another problem: John's admission that he had killed Dorothy and what she should do about it.

It was not an easy decision to make. But John was dead and the truth could not hurt him any more, whereas publicly clearing Joey's name would help heal the wound a bit for Ivan and his mother. Besides, Ivan had heard John's confession just as she had. If she didn't go to the police he would do it, and it would look better for her if she did it herself. But the timing was worrying her.

It would have been better to wait until after the funeral. But if she did it now she could make sure it got into the papers, in the hope that Nicky would see it. She didn't think it was exactly the right way to let him learn of his father's death, but he could be anywhere and the only other tactic she could think of was to publicize the return of the 'prodigal son'. But she wanted Nicky and Guy to have time together before that story hit the headlines and they got bombarded by reporters and photographers.

The very next day she paid a visit to the police station.

It worked. The papers which nine years before had been full of the stories of a mental subnormal who should have been locked away for everyone's protection, suddenly changed their tune. Now Joey was the poor unfortunate who had been betrayed by the man he had worked for and trusted.

It hurt Rosy to read these things. But she knew it was the truth and that it had to be done, and once the ball had been set in motion she felt a great sense of relief that the burden had been lifted from her shoulders.

And it found Nicky.

At only ten o'clock on the first morning of the first story, the telephone rang and it was him. They were in Scotland. They had been waiting to get married on Cassie's birthday, the day they had first planned, but now they were coming straight back home.

Rosy wished they could have been married already. She was not sure what reception they would get from Colin Upton and if Cassie had been Nicky's wife the man could not have done anything about it.

When she heard the motor cycle coming up the drive she sent Guy into the drawing-room. One thing at a time, she thought. The return would be emotional enough as it was.

She had not been wrong. She did not go out to them

but waited in the kitchen with her mother and when the two leather-clad figures came through the door, both looking close to tears, she felt as if she had swallowed a tennis ball.

'I'm sorry,' Nicky finally said, and she opened her arms and he ran into them as he had done when he was little. 'How did it happen?' he asked. The newspapers had only said John was dead, they had not been given all the details.

Neither did Rosy give them to him. 'He fell down the stairs,' she said. Only her mother knew that it was because of Cassie's father that John had died, and she had every intention of keeping it that way. She would not blight Nicky and Cassie's future by revealing the truth; neither would she blight Guy's future by letting him know he was a part of it. She held none of them responsible. It was all down to Colin Upton, as far as she was concerned, and the man had already caused enough trouble for Nicky and Cassie. 'It was quick. He didn't suffer.' All his suffering had been done before, she thought sadly, wondering if he had been right after all, and for all those years he was being punished.

'I'm glad.' Nicky looked up embarrassedly then and moved out of her arms, as if he had suddenly remembered Cassie was there. He held his hand out to her and brought her across to the table and pressed her down onto a chair. Then he sat down himself and talked about his father. Cassie sat quietly listening. Rosy put in a word here and there, when she thought it was necessary. But mostly she let him do the talking, realizing it was his way of working out his grief and regret that he had not been there when it happened.

The length of an hour had almost gone, before he fell silent and Rosy thought the time was right.

'Other things have been happening, as well,' she said. 'There's someone to meet you.'

His gaze fell to her stomach. 'You've had the baby!' he gasped, stunned that he had not noticed before. She had not yet returned to her old trimness but she no longer had the huge bulge in front of her.

Rosy laughed. The baby was sleeping and she had clean forgotten about her. 'No,' she said. Then, 'Yes . . well . . . yes, she's upstairs. You can see her later. But there is someone else who would like to meet you.'

She stood up to take him through to the drawing-room.

'Who?' he asked, as he pushed his chair back and also stood up, all the while his eyes boring into her face. But something in her expression told him the answer and before she could go out of the room, he reached for her arm to stop her going, and said simply, 'Guy?'

It was no surprise to her that he had known. If only he had listened to him all those years ago and believed he really could tell his brother was still alive, perhaps they could have found him before now. 'Yes,' she replied, unnecessarily.

Guy had been left in the drawing-room for what he considered to be too long and had already come out and was standing hovering in the hall. He could hear everything that was being said through the open door and when he heard Nicky speak his name he moved, appearing in the doorway. For a long moment they stood like statues, their frozen gazes locked together. Then, at exactly the same time, they leaped forward into each other's arms and tears were pouring down their cheeks. It wasn't long before the three onlookers' cheeks were also covered in moisture, as well.

'Why don't you come and see the baby?' Rosy suggested, brushing her emotion aside to take Cassie by the arm and take her from the room, nodding to her mother to come with them and leave the brothers alone to get to know each other. Although she had the feeling they already knew each other. But they still had some catching up to do.

CHAPTER TWENTY-NINE

Rosy lifted her hand and blew a kiss to Nicky as the taxi pulled away from the reception. It had been a lovely day and a lovely wedding. Cassie had looked like a fairy princess in her lace and tulle dress, and she had just gone off to the airport in a mauve trouser suit that made her willowy form look like that of a model; exactly like the time she had borrowed Rosy's swimsuit. From the moment he had seen her walking down the aisle towards him, Nicky had looked so proud of her.

'Nicky got himself a beautiful girl,' Guy said, coming up by her side.

Yes, she thought, *and Cassie got herself a beautiful boy.* 'You'll soon find one for yourself and be the next,' she said.

He laughed. 'It's a pity Cassie doesn't have a sister.'

She laughed with him, with all the fondness she had soon learned to feel for him, and she recalled the first time Nicky had brought Cassie home. He had said then that, wherever he was, he hoped Guy had found a sister to Cassie. She shook her head in wonder. Guy had slipped into life at Derwent House as if he had always been there. He was so much like Nicky, not only in looks, but in all his little ways and in everything he did. It seemed incredible to think they had lived apart for most of their lives.

She looked up at the grey clouds now collecting in the sky that had been nothing but blue throughout the ceremony. *Whatever else life dealt you, it gave you two wonderful sons, John*, she said silently, knowing, if he could look down on them, he would be doing so right then.

516

'Come on.' Wrapping her arm through Guy's she turned towards the car park. Nell was already waiting by the car, her navy blue hat tipped at a rather more jaunty angle than it had been at the beginning and a flush to her cheeks that spoke of one sherry too many.

'He's been a surprise,' she said, the moment they reached her. She inclined her head over to the right and Rosy looked round to see Colin Upton, his arms loaded with wedding presents which his wife was taking from him to pack into the boot of the car. 'I thought he was certain to do something to put a damper on things. But he's been as quiet as a mouse.'

I wonder why? Rosy thought, smiling to herself. The day after Nicky and Cassie arrived home, Colin Upton had laid down the law in a big way. The wedding was off, he informed them. And it wasn't going to be on again. Nicky had burnt his bridges as far as Cassie was concerned.

But it had only taken five minutes for Rosy to change his mind. First, she pointed out to him that if he wasn't careful he was going to find himself charged with assault; because he had had no reason whatsoever to hit Guy. Then she explained that his unwarranted attack had been the cause of John falling down the stairs – and what that bit of information would do to Cassie, if she ever found out. She wasn't giving any secrets away, because she knew Colin Upton was never going to tell anyone.

Her smile broadened as she glanced back at the man, and saw the small bouquet of orchids hanging from his hand. She had made sure that he realized the wedding had not only got to go ahead as planned, but that he also had to check that everything was as Cassie and Nicky wanted it.

'Are you coming back with us, Grandma?' Charlie suddenly came racing up, the full skirt of her marine blue bridesmaid dress puffing out round her legs like a balloon.

'You're supposed to act like a lady when you're dressed like one,' Nell pointed out, but good-naturedly.

'Come back with us, Grandma,' Charlie pleaded. 'Dad's going to get the skittles out.' She turned to Guy. 'You're coming, aren't you. Please come. Everybody else is coming!'

Rosy smiled. Roy had soon become 'Dad' and a very good one too.

Maggie came bustling up then, holding her crimson wide-brimmed hat tight to her head, and explained that Roy had invited a crowd back to the pub.

'Go on,' Rosy said, knowing her mother was wanting to go but needed a shove. 'And you.' She turned to Guy. 'I've got to go and sort pumpkin out. I might come later,' she added, as she felt the first spots of rain beginning to fall. 'It's raining,' she said, unnecessarily she realized, as she looked down at her plum coloured silk dress, which showed each damp spot to perfection.

'Haven't you thought of a name for that child yet?' Maggie took no notice of the weather, but made her disgust evident at her sister's shortcoming.

'It will come to me.' She knew well enough Maggie's opinion of her because she could not find a suitable name for her daughter; her mother felt exactly the same, only she did not voice it so strongly. She didn't know herself why she could not settle for anything. She'd tried Lizzy, Catherine and Eleanor, but none had sounded right and so each time she had gone back to calling her pumpkin.

'Uh . . .' Maggie tossed her head and sent her black curls bouncing and almost lost her hat. 'I can see they'll have to whistle her when she gets to school.'

'I'll see you all later!' Rosy said, making it obvious the conversation was at an end, and got in the car and left them to it. Ivan's mum was babysitting for her and she knew she would be safe, but she had promised she wouldn't be late and she wanted to be on her own for a little while. So much had happened in so short a time, she seemed to have been carried along by events and had had no time to sit back and think. She wasn't sure she had even come to terms with John's death yet.

She knew it still had not sunk in that he had been a murderer, and she wondered if it ever really would. She didn't know why she couldn't accept it, after all she had heard it from his own lips. Perhaps it was difficult to believe you had been deceived by someone you were so close to and thought you knew inside out; or was it that she did not want to face up to the fact that she had pushed Tom aside for someone who had killed his wife?

She hadn't known he had killed Dorothy then, she offered in her own defence, and turned down the lane just as the rain began to come in torrents. Well, she should have known, she came back at herself. The thought was unnerving and she wondered if she really should have known. Had there been any little signs she had missed that should have given John's real character away? She couldn't think of any.

Neither could she think why he had taken her into the cottage that night. The memory sent a shudder running over her skin, just as she recalled John assuring her he would not have taken her in there if he had known. But he *had* known and he had taken her in there! Why? Would he have made love to her if she had not found Dorothy's body? It was a disturbing thought. But that was the reason he had taken her into the cottage: to make love to her. Or was it?

'I would not have taken you into the cottage if I had known Dorothy was there. You do believe that . . . don't you?' She could hear the words as if he was right there with her, speaking them with the strange intensity that had, at the time, confused her. But suddenly she was seeing it in a different light and she was wondering if, without knowing it, she had been his perfect alibi. It wasn't a pleasant thought, and it was one she could never now prove. Certainly, no-one would ever have thought he would take his girlfriend into a building where the body of his dead wife lay. No-one! Including herself. She had never, in all the years since Dorothy's death, thought for one moment that John could have had anything to do with it.

Then she had always been too trusting, she told herself, as she turned the car down the drive to Derwent House. But she hadn't gone far when her foot stamped hard on the brake and she clung to the steering-wheel and pressed her nose to the windscreen. It couldn't be! She stared at the shape that was standing in front of the house. She pressed her face closer to the windscreen to see more clearly. The rain was lashing down but her eyes were not deceiving her. It was a grubby yellow truck – Tom's grubby yellow truck!

Her foot leapt back to the accelerator and the car sped the last few yards, until it was standing side by side with the truck.

'*Oh thank you, God!*' She spoke with sincere feeling, and leapt out of the car and raced round the truck. It was empty. She spun round, just as he appeared in the gateway to the courtyard.

'Tom!' she cried, her eyes feasting on the long, lean length of him, dressed in black jeans, T-shirt and boots, blond hair hanging round his shoulders. He looked just like he had when she first saw him, except for being a whole lot wetter. She wanted to open her arms and fling herself at him, but she held back, fearing rejection. He might only be there to see his daughter, she warned herself, and could only stand staring at him not noticing that the rain was falling so fast it ran in torrents down her face.

'Rosy,' he said, coming forward.

'Have you been here long?' Despite trying to keep her voice calm she was aware there was a tremble in it.

'Not long.' Reaching her he stopped right in front

of her and looked down into her face with a strangely bland expression.

She could read nothing in his eyes and his mouth was a straight, emotionless line. His pale skin had a glow about it, as if he had been in the sun. 'Have you been on holiday?' she asked, and wanted to scream at the ridiculousness of it all. They were standing out in the pouring rain, getting soaked, making small talk – when she was on fire with all the things she wanted to say to him: real things; meaningful things.

He did not reply, but said, 'I see I have a daughter.'

'Yes,' she said simply. 'You knew she was yours then?'

There was silence. They both stared at each other with a bleakness that matched the weather, but neither spoke, as if fearing that to be the first to show their true feelings would be weakness.

It was Rosy who broke down first. 'I'm sorry,' she gasped. 'I'm so sorry. I thought I'd lost you for ever.'

His jaw tightened and his lips moved, but it was a moment before he said, 'I saw the papers. About John and his wife . . . and Joey.'

She had thought of Nicky seeing the papers, but it had not occurred to her that Tom would also. She bit her lip, a thought coming to her that she dare hardly believe. It was not easy to find the courage to voice it. 'You . . . you came back for me?' she said.

'I was in Portugal. Or I would have been here sooner.'

There was a note of apology in his voice and it was all Rosy wanted to hear. It told her he had wanted to get back to her and that he had known she would need him. 'Oh Tom!' she said emotionally. 'I never stopped loving you. I'm sorry for what I did.'

A tiny smile lifted the corners of his mouth and softened his eyes, but it had a resigned quality about it. 'And I love you, Rosy,' he said. 'But will you only love me until the next time you think you have something more pressing to do.' Bitterness filled his voice on the last.

'That isn't fair!' she retaliated, wounded by the charge. 'John was my husband and he was an invalid. How could you have expected me to turn my back on him?'

'I didn't, Rosy.' He spoke plainly, with a rawness in his voice that stabbed at something deep inside her. 'I never asked you to leave him and move in with me, though Christ knows how much I wanted you to. I knew all along I had to wait my time. All I was asking was that I could share a little bit of you during that wait. Was that so wrong?'

She shook her head. 'I'm sorry, Tom,' she said. But then she lifted her head, tilted her chin and fixed him squarely. 'I couldn't have done any other. He needed me in a way you didn't, and I could not have lived with myself if I'd left him. But it didn't mean I'd stopped loving you. I'll never love anyone the way I love you.'

'But will you love me as much as you love Nicky?'

She hesitated uncertainly. She had not known he was jealous of her feelings for Nicky. 'I will love you as much – but not in the same way!' she pointed out, her voice tightening as she was spurred into anger by the insinuation of his remark. 'Nicky is my son, nothing more. And you know that as well as I do!' she added furiously. Rain was running off her hair and dripping from the end of her nose and suddenly she had had enough of it, and him. 'Now,' she said. 'I have my daughter to attend to.' Pushing him aside she marched into the courtyard.

'And my daughter,' he said, catching her arm and swinging her round to face him. In an instant his arms were round her and she was pressed tightly to him. 'Rosy, I'm sorry. You hurt me so much I just wanted to hurt you back. Forgive me. Let's stop arguing and be friends again.'

She looked up into his eyes and could see her own

love mirrored there. 'Yes,' she said simply. It was what she wanted most in the whole world.

He smiled then, with the affection that had been locked away inside him for their long months of separation and which was now bursting to get free. 'Just keep saying that,' he said.

She frowned puzzledly.

His smile broadened and he lifted her hand and laid a kiss on the rain soaked palm. 'Rosy Hardaker . . .' he said, his voice full of meaning, '. . . please let me turn you back into Rosy Smith?'

'Yes,' she said simply, pleasure radiating from her smile.

'Then our daughter will be Angel Smith,' he said.

'Angel!' Rosy repeated in amazement. 'You can't . . .' But she brought herself up short. It was the perfect name. The one she had been searching for. 'Angel Smith,' she said, letting the name roll off her tongue. She suddenly laughed. 'My dad would have been proud of you,' she said, knowing her father would have very much approved of the name. It was different. Fancy enough to spice up plain old Smith.

'Good,' he said, his voice brimming with the emotion that spilled from his eyes as they gazed down into hers.

Feeling her own love for him expanding deep inside her, she wrapped her arms around his neck and kissed him, releasing the passion that had been lying dormant since she had foolishly turned him out of her life.

And with the rain running down their necks and soaking them through to the skin, he returned that passion in full measure.

THE END

PROUD HARVEST
by Janet Haslam

Hannah Critchlow, orphaned after a storm which carried away her beloved father and destroyed her home, was given refuge by the notorious Bunting family at their remote hilltop farm, Bunting's Tor. The three men of the family were feared and hated in the area: George, the autocratic and brutal patriarch; Jed, his profligate and much-favoured elder son; and Sam, the best and most steadfast of the three, who had to grow up believing that he was tainted because of his deformed hand – a deformity which had cruelly led the locals to rename the farm Bunting's Claw.

Sam had come to believe that no woman would ever want his love, and that no children would ever be born to inherit the great farmhouse and rolling acres. Only Hannah, proud and self-willed, could see the real Sam beneath his imperfect body, and only she could bring new love and hope to the doomed family.

0 552 14138 0

THE SHOEMAKER'S DAUGHTER
by Iris Gower

When Hari Morgan's father died, he left her nothing but an ailing mother and the tools of his shoemaking business. But what he also passed on to his daughter was a rare and unusual gift – that of designing and making shoes that were stylish and different. One of the first to realize this was Emily Grenfell, spoilt, pettish daughter of Thomas Grenfell, one of the richest men in Swansea. Emily, who resented the beauty and courage of Hari Morgan, nonetheless was delighted with the dancing slippers she made for her début at the Race Ball, one of the grandest events of the year. It was to be the beginning of a lifetime of friendship, hatred and rivalry between the two girls for, as Hari's business and fame began to grow, so Emily's fortune began to decline.

And between the two girls lay an even deeper tension, for Emily was about to be betrothed to her cousin, Craig Grenfell, a man whom Hari could not help loving and wanting for herself, a man who finally betrayed her. From then on, Hari was determined that nothing and no-one would prevent her rise to a triumphant success.

The Shoemaker's Daughter is the first book in Iris Gower's enthralling new series, *The Cordwainers*.

552 13686 7

THE BRIGHT ONE
by Elvi Rhodes

Molly O'Connor's life was not an easy one. With six children and a husband who earned what he could as a casual farmhand, fisherman, or drover, it was a constant struggle to keep her family fed and raised to be respectable. Of all her children, Breda – the Bright One – was closest to her heart. As, one by one, her other children left Kilbally, Kathleen and Kieran to the Church, Moira to marriage, the twins to war, so Breda, the youngest, was the one who stayed close to her parents. Breda never wanted to leave the West of Ireland. She thought Kilbally was the most beautiful place in the world.

Then tragedy struck the O'Connors and the structure of their family life was irrevocably changed. Reeling from unhappiness and humiliation, Breda decided to make a new life for herself – in Yorkshire with her Aunt Josie's family. There she was to discover a totally different world from the one she had left behind, with new people and new challenges for the future.

0 552 14057 0

A CROOKED MILE
by Ruth Hamilton

In the shadow of the Althorpe mills, the Mrtle Street residents endure cramped and often verminous conditions.

Joe Duffy, a Bolton tradesman, strives to lift his family out of the 'garden' streets. But as more children are born, Joe's wife Tess sinks deeper into the obsession that will be her undoing. When Tess screams her belief that the area is cursed, few people heed her ravings. She is ignored, even as the Myrtle Street tragedies become more frequent and begin to feature in local gossip.

It is left to Megan, the third Duffy child – the one who felt she was unworthy and unloved because she had been born a girl – to end the curse. When she becomes embroiled in a web of deceit, Megan needs all her strength, talents, and wit in order to survive. But it is her capacity to give love that ensures her family's stability, the future of the Althorpe cotton mills, and the safekeeping of the Hall i' the Vale.

552 14140 2

A SELECTED LIST OF FINE NOVELS
AVAILABLE FROM CORGI BOOKS

THE PRICES SHOWN BELOW WERE CORRECT AT THE TIME OF GOING TO
PRESS. HOWEVER TRANSWORLD PUBLISHERS RESERVE THE RIGHT TO
SHOW NEW RETAIL PRICES ON COVERS WHICH MAY DIFFER FROM THOSE
PREVIOUSLY ADVERTISED IN THE TEXT OR ELSEWHERE.